D1408896

# LOUISIANA BURN

# LOUISIANA BURN

A NOVEL BY

CARL T. SMITH

RIVER CITY
PUBLISHING
Montgomery, Alabama

For Geoff,
I hope you feel the
Cajun heat!
My Best,
Carl T. Smith

Published in the United States by River City Publishing
1719 Mulberry St.
Montgomery, AL 36106

Designed by Lissa Monroe

First Edition—2006
Printed in the United States of America
1 3 5 7 9 10 8 6 4 2

ISBN 10: 1-57966-066-5
ISBN 13: 978-1-57966-066-6



Library of Congress Cataloging-in-Publication Data:

Smith, Carl T.
Louisiana burn : a novel / Carl T. Smith. — 1st ed.
p. cm.
Summary: "Sam Larkin is drawn into an investigation of the judge who unjustly sent him to prison twelve years ago, propelling him on a difficult and increasingly dangerous quest for justice and personal retribution. A man with a cause wars against corruption and greed at the highest levels of politics"—Provided by publisher.
ISBN-13: 978-1-57966-066-6
1. Judges—Fiction. 2. Ex-convicts—Fiction. 3. South Carolina—Fiction. 4. Political corruption—Louisiana—Fiction. 5. Louisiana—Fiction. I. Title.
PS3569.M5127L68 2006
813'.6—dc22

2006009200

For my son,
Christopher Scott Smith,
whose wisdom, courage, and tenacity
I could never approach.
May you never change.

*Louisiana Burn* was written in 2003 and 2004, and the story takes place in February of 1980. This timing obviously predates the hurricane season of 2005, which forever altered the landscapes of southern Louisiana and coastal Mississippi and the lives of hundreds of thousands of people who lived and worked there.

Who controls the past controls the future.
Who controls the present controls the past.
—George Orwell

# PROLOGUE

## February 1980

IN THE PREDAWN darkness, Sam Larkin carried a flashlight to the end of his driveway, turned it off, and judged he could do his workout on nature's electricity. The winter moon and stars in the South Carolina lowcountry were more radiant than those of any other place he had been, and that, in itself, had made an indelible impression on him when he came to the area from Louisiana.

He put the light on the ground and began running his course down Osprey Landing Road, increasing his tempo as his muscles warmed. The longer he ran, the more he enjoyed the feel of the cool air in his lungs. Silhouettes of craggy live oaks, pecan trees, and tall pines formed a gauntlet that might have frightened someone not familiar with the lowcountry landscape. Sam always considered the treeline a genuine part of its charm. The sounds accompanying it—squirrels awakening and moving out through their dry-leaf nests to find food for the day, birds beginning their morning songs, deer soft-padding over their own trails—completed the cyclorama through which he ran.

His course was four miles long, but today, as he made the turn for home, he felt he could run it again. He needed to discharge energy, but the forces that stimulated his adrenaline as he ran were not positive ones. He had been struggling with them for weeks.

After cooling down and stretching out the muscles in his back and legs, Sam climbed the stairs to his deck and spent a few close and holy moments, as he always did, watching the light color the marsh and Jones Run Creek. The panorama before him never failed to hold him in awe, regardless of what was circulating in his mind.

In the house, he put on a pot of coffee, then showered. The water—hot then cold—was rejuvenating. He dried his body and shoulder-length hair and began to dress. The day's uniform was the same as the day before and the day before that: jeans, a sweatshirt, and huaraches. He had no responsibilities other than pulling his sandy, graying hair into a ponytail and securing it in place with a hand-tooled, silver ring he had purchased in New Orleans years before. It had been a gift to himself, a symbol of his new-found freedom.

It was a day for being outside, despite the time of year, not cold—it seldom was in the lowcountry—just crisp and clean. He went to the deck, sat, and sipped on a cup of chicory coffee, taking an occasional drag on his morning cigarette. He always felt that if he could avoid the morning smoke, he could eliminate the four or five he lit up during the remainder of the day. Though he frequently made conscious efforts to quit, it hadn't happened. The chicory coffee, a holdover from his Louisiana beginnings, was a pleasure he would never deny himself.

As he looked out over the marsh, he heard the familiar rumblings of a storm. The sound was far away, would take pauses during the day, but would eventually come to his island. Late afternoon or early evening, he predicted.

A small snowy egret was creeping along the water's edge not fifteen feet away. The bird lifted each leg in a choreographed strut, silent, creating no ripple on the glassy surface of the mirror in which it walked.

Hunting. Focused entirely upon its purpose—something Sam had found difficult these past few weeks.

Sometimes the remembrances came in dreams that awakened him in the cold wetness of his sheets. Other times they appeared out of nowhere while he was having dinner in a restaurant, driving his car, or performing some other mundane task, arriving with no recognizable stimulus, seldom complete scenarios, mostly just disjointed recollections. But rarely here on the deck; there was too much in nature to capture his attention.

He had killed a man, something he had never thought himself capable of doing. Even as an environmental law enforcement officer back in Louisiana, it had never seemed a possibility, and yet it had happened and never left him.

*The man—Sam didn't know his real name; they called him Chooch—had watched him for days in the yard, his crew standing behind him, their flat expressions devoid of any humanity or emotion, a survival mode prisoners adopted. Gain anonymity and fit in. The Golden Rule of survival. Sam had done the same on the day he entered the Louisiana State Prison at Angola. The man stared at him, winked, smiled, and nodded his head. The gesture made a date, one Sam knew he could not refuse.*

*Later, when he walked into the shower room, Chooch was waiting. "Hey, baby," the man said. He was leaning against a sink, and two of his crew held Sam's only Angola friend, a man he knew only as Sleeve, braced on an adjacent wall—bait if Sam hadn't come on his own. Another watched the door. There was a viper-like sneer on Chooch's face. Black hair, long and greasy, hung below a red bandana do-rag. A scar like a white worm split his face from his nose down through both lips. He was lean, and the skin of his sinewy, muscled arms, chest, and neck was covered with crude jailhouse art, a billboard of rage.*

*Sam stood inside the door, saying nothing, checking out the man's crew. Their eyes switched back and forth between Sam and their leader. The short-statured Mex was nervous, his eyes pinholes—a meth addict running on empty. He would get a refill after the deed was done; it was the price. The young man, solidly built, pretty—a bunkpunk—had a look of wonder on his face. The third, a muscled black man, just watched the door, taking care of himself.*

*"You scared, honey?" Chooch's eyes glistened with the shine of pruno, julep, jump, or some other contraband. He moved closer. Sam could see his teeth, dark, stained brown and green with nicotine and mouth moss. "Ain't no need. You jus' gone get a little attitude adjustment, you." Cajun, or raised in Cajun country. "I'm gone keep you protected and happy forever, you," he said. "At least, however long I let you forever be. See, I love you. I'm gone bitch you up and be you daddy. Take care of you."*

*Chooch stepped closer. Sam didn't move back. The Cajun raised his eyebrows in surprise. An odor like ether emanated from his body. He reached out to touch the skin on Sam's face, but Sam gripped the man's hand in his own, spreading the fingers and bending them backward, separating them. A knuckle popped. Chooch screamed, his agony echoing off the tile walls. Sam took in the crew as peripheral shadows. They weren't moving.*

*Sam knew he could stop and it would end it for this day, but it wouldn't be over. This was the date the man had made, his dance. He released the Cajun's mauled hand, then grabbed his neck as if to pull the larynx from his throat. The man's eyes widened, and he clawed at the hand sapping his breath. He could make no sound. Sam tightened his grip and felt the trachea fracture. His other hand grasped the man's long, black hair and pulled it down and backward with a hard, swift jerk. There was a cracking sound as solid as that of an ax hitting concrete, and Sam watched life pass from the man's eyes.*

*He let go. The man fell in a heap at his feet, blood leaking in oxygenated foam from his mouth. One final effort to breathe, and it was over. None of Chooch's crew moved in to help. It had all happened too fast. Over before they could protect and defend, though Sam was sure they didn't have it in them. They released Sleeve and stared at Sam, offering an allegiance he didn't want.*

HE WOULD NEVER feel guilty about killing the man; he had done it out of necessity. Preservation of self and of his friend. What he remembered was the adrenaline flow and exhilaration he had felt when it was over. It had been easy. His instincts were frightening, and he found it difficult to accept what he had discovered within himself. Fear of that potential kept the memory green no matter how hard he tried to remove it from his soul.

The snowy egret was gone from sight, though Sam knew it was still working the shoreline, single-minded, concentrating on a level beyond human understanding. Jumping mullet splashed in the brackish water, and dried palm fronds clicked their wake-up call with every passing breeze.

The forecast called for cool, dry weather. But it wouldn't be. The pink early-morning sky would become a landscape of blood red refracted light as the sun moved toward full day. Intermittent gray and purple ropes of cloud—flat and thin—would move in during the late afternoon and increase in number toward the vanishing point of the horizon. And then the storm would arrive.

Sam scanned the Spartina grass salt marsh spread before him. His present life was good: he owned a house in one of the most naturally beautiful areas of the country; he had time to paint, which was one of the reasons he had come here; there were no social pressures to live up to. He could think of nothing to complain about.

The life he was living was the one he had fantasized when times were not so serene. Yet on occasion he felt aimless, having to force himself to work at what he had come to the lowcountry to do. And there were the dreams against which he had no defense. The situation gave credence to the old cliché that realizing one's dream is not always what it's cracked up to be.

He sipped his coffee, stared at the marsh and the creek, and forcibly closed his mind. He had developed that skill in prison. His surroundings remained a wonderment to him, despite the lack of quietude in his soul.

# ONE

KAREN CHANEY SAT in the lobby of the Marriott Hotel in Metairie, Louisiana. She had been summoned there by Special Agent Neil Dougherty of the DEA, her supervisor and former partner in a brief marriage, as well as her oftentimes contentious best friend. She shifted uneasily in her chair. Neil had been unwilling to disclose the purpose of her reassignment from a drug case in Florida to Louisiana. That was unlike him, and Karen was wary.

At seven o'clock sharp Neil walked into the lobby. Karen had been waiting only five minutes. She knew he wouldn't be late or early; that was Neil. Tall with dark hair and wearing navy blue slacks and a white shirt, he looked very relaxed; most people would not guess he was a federal investigator. Karen noticed that he had thickened around the waist a little since she had last seen him. Desk work. She stood up and accepted his arms around her. After a moment, he held her at arm's length and looked at her.

"You're looking good, Karen. I've missed you."

"Do you say that to all your agents?" she asked.

"Only the good-looking ones." He said it with sincerity. A Florida tan accented her shoulder-length blond hair, and the black v-neck sweater and slacks complemented her well-proportioned body. "Any place special for dinner?" he asked.

"You choose," she answered as they started toward the door.

"I used to come over here to a place called Bateaux when I lived in New Orleans. It was out on Esplanade. I would guess it's still good. Been here for years."

"That's fine," she said.

"How are things in the Sunshine State? Did you get to see your father?"

"Briefly. He's doing fine. Has a lot of friends who keep tabs on him, which is comforting, though he does complain about the number of widows who knock on his door with mattresses on their backs."

"I'm glad I've got something to look forward to," he said, opening the car door for her. "What about you? Any gentlemen callers?"

Forced pleasantries, she thought. Their relationship had been strained ever since the operation in the South Carolina lowcountry six months prior.

"Five," she said as he cranked the engine, "but I'm only sleeping with three of them." Perhaps that would put an end to that line of questioning. His jealous curiosity was a constant irritation—as though he believed that because they had once been married, he had a right to probe her personal life.

"Well, at least you're keeping busy."

"Quit making nice, Neil. Tell me why I'm here. What's the assignment? Who's my SAC? I've never had you not give me a clue when you've assigned me to a case."

He was silent, looking straight ahead as he drove. This only increased Karen's anxiety. She knew Neil, and he rarely had difficulty expressing himself unless he wasn't sure how his words would be received. He could censure someone and know in advance the reaction it would stimulate. Praise for work well done, the same. Finally, she saw his face go from friend to command mode.

"Karen, I have to be very careful about this. The assignment is unusual for our unit. Basically, we will be doing an investigation and background check on a political figure."

"Doesn't sound too thrilling. Why would the DEA be doing that? He running drugs, laundering money, or something?"

"Not that I know of at this point, but I wouldn't put it beyond the reach of credibility. We're doing a favor for the director of the FBI. He doesn't want his agents involved."

"So, throw us to the wolves, huh? Who and where?" she asked.

"New Orleans, Gulfport, and Washington, DC."

"New Orleans is fine. Gulfport's okay. DC I don't like. Who will I be working with?"

"I'll be the special agent in charge."

"You don't sound too enthusiastic. Or maybe after last time, you have doubts about me."

"If I had doubts about you, you wouldn't be here." His voice was dark and unsure. "It's a testy issue, Karen. Drugs are one thing; the nation's future is another."

"The nation's future? Neil, what's going on here?"

He turned and looked at her. "We're investigating Thornton Hunnycut," he said.

The name, inseparable from Sam Larkin's, struck a painful chord in Karen. Sam had become her ally while she was investigating a drug operation six months earlier in South Carolina; he was a local connection and an integral part of the take-down. The problem was that she had become his lover during the operation, violating her personal ethics as an undercover operative.

Hunnycut, a United States senator and former Louisiana judge, had unjustly convicted and sentenced Sam to fifteen years in Angola state prison. And Hunnycut had been masterful. No one knew the circumstances surrounding Sam's release after four years served or the reason for his incarceration. Not even Sam himself. All records of the arrest, trial, and imprisonment had been expunged. Deleted. Not sealed—deleted. Even Neil, with all his resources, had not discovered that Sam had been in prison; Sam had to tell them.

"No," she said.

Neil parked at the restaurant, shut the engine down, and looked at her. "Look, Karen, I'm a drug man. I have no idea why I got put in charge of this operation, but I did. Maybe because I'm on familiar turf in Louisiana. Who the hell knows? I'm not even sure the operation is legal. But it wouldn't be the first time we've bent the rules with the good government's blessing, would it?"

"I won't do it," she said. Firmly. Looking straight ahead.

Sam was an enigma to her. She certainly had reveled in their time together, thought she might love him, but his life was not her life. She wasn't ready for the island and its serenity. She knew that she still required the adrenaline of life on the edge. Sam didn't.

There had been phone calls, a few days spent together when she returned to Carolina to give depositions, and several getaways when her work allowed. They had a strong mutual attraction, but they never discussed the subject of commitment.

"I might accept that after dinner," Neil said, "but first I want you to listen to what I have to say."

Bateaux, one of New Orleans's most popular Creole-Cajun seafood restaurants, was little changed since Neil's last visit, and thanks to the season, they faced no difficulty in being seated quickly. Karen was oblivious to the celebratory, waterfront ambience. They ordered drinks—a Jack Daniels on the rocks for her and an extra-dry vodka martini for Neil—then sat in silence. When the server came to take their dinner order, Karen was deep in thought.

"Karen? Your order?" Neil said.

"Oh, I'm sorry." She reacted as though she had just been awakened from a nap. She glanced at the menu and simply chose the first entrée on the list. "Smothered Grillades in Rusty Gravy."

"Fresh Fish and Dried Shrimp Gumbo," Neil said. Karen had already retreated again. "Traveling somewhere else?" He tried to smile, but it didn't play.

"Just taking a pause in my existence, as a good friend frequently says."

During dinner, their conversation was minimal. Karen picked at her food, moving it around her plate rather than eating it. The more she considered it, the more certain she became of what Neil was going to ask her to do. It would be another conflict of the personal and the professional, but sanctioned this time. At the moment, though, she had no idea what his reasons were or what her response would be. She felt like an explosives expert trying to determine the correct wire to cut. *The blue or the red? Refuse or rationalize?* Either way, she was likely to lose something important to her.

"You know we have to talk about this," he said.

Karen looked into her empty glass. There was Neil Dougherty; there was Thornton Hunnycut; there was Sam Larkin; there was Karen Chaney. And there was Karen Chaney and Sam Larkin. Then multiple pairings, multiple agendas, a maze of impossibilities.

"What's your angle, Neil?" she asked. "And I hope it's not what I'm thinking."

"It is. I need you. And I need Sam Larkin."

"Damn you!" Her throat was dry. She wanted to clear it but wouldn't allow herself. "I'd do most anything for you; you know that. But I can't do this. How can you ask me?"

"It's my job. You know that."

"Regardless of the consequences to yourself or others."

"If necessary," he said. "Listen—"

"No. You listen for a change. That was part of what was wrong with our marriage, remember? You seldom listen."

Neil held up his hands in surrender.

"I won't bring Sam into this. He doesn't need it, and neither do I. We messed up his life in South Carolina, and we opened up a bad part of his history that he didn't deserve and was trying to put behind him.

Now you're asking me to bring him back to the source of all that trouble."

"Through?" he asked.

"Probably not. You still haven't given me a reason for this 'background check.' And why do you need Sam? What can he do?"

"Let me clarify something to begin with. It's a full investigation, not just a simple background check. That may be the terminology in the request, but my full instructions indicate something far deeper than looking for mistresses or foreign bank accounts. Senator Harrison James of New Jersey is using his considerable influence—that's the *nice* way to put it—to get this undercover check on Hunnycut. James is considering, if you can believe this, Hunnycut as a running mate if he gets the party's nod as their presidential candidate."

"Hunnycut?" She was astounded at the prospect.

"He's a powerful man in the senate. A lot of people owe him favors. I would guess they believe he can deliver the South."

"So your job is to make sure he's clean enough not to hurt James's chance for the nomination."

"I think that's what James wants. But my instructions indicate a more covert, considerably deeper probe into the senator's activities, past and present."

"Somebody has a separate agenda going. Any idea who?"

"No."

Karen wasn't sure she believed him. "I don't know what to say, Neil. I don't want to do this."

"Sam is the key to this man's implosion. He was involved, and, more than any of us, he would know where to look and how to put the pieces in their proper place."

"Bait?" Karen asked, staring at him.

He said nothing.

"No way, Neil."

"Let me tell you what I know, where we are. Just hear me out."

She was silent.

"I have two agents in Washington investigating Hunnycut's congressional workings. I'll be working out of an office in New Orleans while we're investigating his judicial record here, which is a rat's nest of bribes, favoritism, and personal vendettas. I think there may be something bigger in that area that we haven't come upon yet. We're also looking into his business interests and those of his associates, including nursing homes, oil leases, and real estate, which have benefited by favorable judicial decisions and legislation from his committee. The man is a criminal, and, from all we can gather, he has no fear. He believes he's untouchable. He has a cadre of associates, including Arthur Valdrine, the state administrator, and a handful of business partners, although we don't suspect them—yet—of being main players. I don't think anything is out of the realm of possibility for any of these people. I believe ambition is Hunnycut's Achilles' heel and the VP possibility is enough to push him over the edge and make him careless."

Karen didn't respond.

"That's where we are."

"And where do I fit in?" she asked.

"In addition to his plantation in Baton Rouge, Hunnycut has a mansion in Gulfport, Mississippi. It's supposedly a vacation home, but he spends a lot of time there, and I believe it may be connected to his business interests in that area. That's where you'll be. We've leased a condo in Biloxi in your name." He smiled. "It faces the Gulf."

"Pretty confident I'd go along, huh?"

"With or without Sam, I want you in, Karen."

"Sam had a life, Neil. He was innocent, for God's sake, a law enforcement officer. Hunnycut took that away from him, put him in prison, and orchestrated for him to die there like the fucking Count of Monte Cristo. We weren't able to find out how his release was effected or how he was compensated, and now that he's reclaimed some sort of reasonable existence, you want to bring all of that back to the surface again?"

"Whether Sam Larkin admits it or not, I believe he has an agenda to settle. I saw the anger in the man last year when he talked about Hunnycut. It hasn't gone away; it's just hibernating. That uncontrolled violence you witnessed in Carolina," he said, referring to a physical confrontation between Sam and a suspect, "is symptomatic of that anger."

"You're a psychologist now, Neil?"

"Karen, I'm being serious. As you say, everything he had was taken away from him: his job, his wife, four years of time, and the whole life he had known before that. Whatever money the government—or whoever—gave him to settle didn't replace any of those things. There are some voids in that serene life he appears to be leading. I think there's a good chance he'd like to get rid of them."

"Sounds like a closing argument," she said.

"I guess it is. I don't know what else I can say."

"I don't know, Neil. I don't know if I can do that to him or to me. I have to think about it."

"One more thought. Why don't you leave it up to him? He can always say no. If he does, I'll back off that angle and never mention it again."

"Why don't I believe you?" she asked.

But it really was Sam's decision to accept or refuse. Maybe he wanted an opportunity for retribution, though she had never seen anything of that in him.

She suddenly felt guilty, as if she were protecting him from an option he might want.

"I need a week off before I start work."

Neil looked at her, puzzled. "Why?"

"I won't do what you're asking me to do without seeing him face to face. I'm not going to call him on the telephone and ask him to take a walk through hell. It's the only way I'll do this, Neil. And, quite frankly, I hope he refuses."

"A week?" She could see him running scenarios in his head.

"It's the only way I'll do it. I want to invite Sam to Biloxi. If he comes, I'll feel him out before I broach the subject of Hunnycut. I'm certain that, in or out, by the end of the week, he will feel used and taken advantage of and maybe even hate me. That ought to relieve you of one professional and one unprofessional concern."

Dougherty thought for a moment. "Okay. When?"

"I'll call him tonight."

"Work him, Karen."

"I won't do that," she said. She pictured Sam standing on his deck in cut-offs, or nothing. She had taken a rain shower with him, naked on the deck that looked out over the marsh. The lean, hard body, soft brown eyes, gentle voice, and long, sun-bleached, graying hair, pulled back in a ponytail that hung below his shoulders. There was no way she could *work* him.

"When was the last time you talked to him?" Dougherty asked.

"About a month ago in Savannah. He doesn't know where I am or what I'm doing, and he doesn't ask; he knows the kind of work I do." She paused. "I have a lot of black holes about doing this, Neil."

"I think he might welcome the opportunity."

"You also thought someday Jimmy Hoffa would turn up."

"Touché." He lifted his glass. "But he still might."

# TWO

"HOW MUCH LONGER are you going to take?" Masley Prather shouted up the stairs to his wife.

"Fifteen minutes. If you want to go on ahead, I can meet you there," she answered.

"No, I'll wait." Prather went into the den and turned on the six o'clock news. He sat down in his easy chair and put his feet up on the hassock. Once again they would be late. He hated being late. The meeting wasn't important—a Gulfport City Council meeting regarding a ground water surcharge on the coming year's property tax—but, as a real estate attorney on the planning commission, he was expected to make an appearance. He might have skipped the meeting if his wife were not on the council.

He was switching channels to find a Gulf Coast weather report when the doorbell rang.

"Well, well, this is a surprise," he said when he saw the familiar figure standing in the doorway. Beside him was a man he did not know. "What brings you out to Biloxi at this time of night?"

"Had some business over here today. Sorry to bother you, Masley." The man shot his cuffs and smiled. "This is Ben Walters. He's considering buying some commercial property, and we need your opinion on some of the local ordinances."

Walters, thin, wiry, with long, black hair and dressed in a wide-collared gold-sheen shirt, black slacks, and black-and-white two-toned loafers didn't look much like a real estate investor, but who knew these days? It was 1980, after all. Appearances seldom gave a clue.

"I would have waited until morning and given you a call, but Ben here is headed back to Houston tonight."

"Well, come on in. I've only got a couple of minutes though. City council meeting. I'll tell you what I can." Waving them inside, Prather stepped aside for the two men to enter the house. Now he and Mary Francis would be later than ever.

He was leading the men down the hall toward the den when he heard a muffled sound, not much more than a stifled sneeze, and felt a blow to his back. He started to turn, then fell to the floor. Walters was holding a gun with a plastic bottle taped to the barrel.

"Oh, Lord," he muttered and began dragging himself down the hall in an attempt to escape what he knew was inevitable. Then he heard the sound again, felt a second impact in the middle of his back. He started to scream, but a third shot silenced him.

"Go," Walters said, slipping on a pair of latex gloves. "I'll clean up. Go." Walters walked back to the door and opened it for the man to pass through. "You didn't touch nothin'?"

"No," the man said, and left the house.

There was no need to check the body. Masley Prather was dead. Walters could have accomplished it with one shot, but that would have been too obvious, and, besides, he liked to see the expressions on their faces. He went into the living room, sat in an arm chair facing the stairs, and waited for Mary Francis Prather to come down.

His smiling face was the last thing she saw. The first shot caught her in the center of her face; the second two went into her chest.

Walters picked up the shell casings and turned off all the lights except one on the end table and the porch light, both of which he knew the Prathers always left on when they went out. He checked to make sure the door would lock behind him and then calmly walked away from the house. It was a leisurely stroll to his car, an old Cadillac, parked a block away.

THE MAN COULD have been a model or a movie star, Marlene Cole thought, observing Senator Thornton Hunnycut glad-handing guests at a fundraiser at the Pelican Oaks Country Club in Shreveport, Louisiana, held for Howard Garrett, Hunnycut's friend and compatriot in Louisiana politics. Watching him operate, it was obvious to Marlene that Hunnycut had chosen better by moving into politics.

Although the event was in honor of Howard Garrett, the senator was the center of attention. Fifty-eight years old, six-one, well built, with a moneyed tan and dark hair that was silvering, Hunnycut was dressed in a navy blue Armani suit accented by a soft blue shirt and a regimental tie. In Marlene Cole's opinion, he was the most senatorial looking son of a bitch she had ever seen.

She had been with him since shortly after the citizens of Louisiana had sent him to Washington. Their relationship was complex, initiated by her when she recognized his unbridled ambition and realized that he was destined to become a power broker in Washington politics. She had made her presence known to him at every function he attended, called on him at his office to introduce herself, and gotten referrals to him from the initial contacts she had in the city. It hadn't taken long for him to take notice and begin to anticipate seeing her. Their relationship had developed into something far more significant than either of them had foreseen.

Five feet, seven inches tall, with short, dark hair, slim where she needed to be slim and full-bodied where that was an asset, she was a bounty for men's eyes. Marlene was well aware of her physical assets, and they served her well. Her electric blue eyes were slyly worshipful when she spoke with those she wanted to impress. It was a rare occasion when she couldn't capture the admiration, if not the blatant lust, of any man she graced with her attention.

Early on, while serving as Hunnycut's aide, she had played at lobbying for several small interests; however, both she and the senator had realized that there was a larger field to harvest. Hunnycut had suggested she end her professional association with his office and open her own firm dedicated to serving clients in the areas in which he held the most clout: health, education, and labor and pensions—the most fertile areas other than defense for maneuvering vast amounts of money and influence and for currying favor with fellow legislators. Education funds were a voter's carrot that he was in a position to dispense at will.

She also became his chief campaign fundraiser, a position that rationalized their continued close association and permitted him to keep her on salary as an independent contractor. It worked like magic. Within two years her business was earning more than two million dollars annually and bringing in several million more in perks. She traveled with Hunnycut as his fundraiser, or "funraiser," as she was frequently referred to by insiders. She had become a recognized power in the lobby community. And in Thornton Hunnycut's mind, she owed much of it to him, as he sometimes liked to remind her.

Out of the corner of her eye, she caught sight of Harold Musgrave heading toward the senator. Musgrave was a Louisiana oil man and entrepreneur who had made and lost millions in offshore drilling and owned a string of nursing homes and assisted-living facilities, as well as a construction firm. According to Thornton, who had pointed him out when they arrived and instructed her to keep him at a distance, Musgrave was currently on the downside of his financial cycle as a result of his legendary drinking and philandering and a run of bad luck.

She figured that Thornton's desire to avoid Musgrave ran deeper than the man's declining reputation. She didn't need to ask him about it; he would eventually tell her, as he always did. She reached Musgrave before he got within fifty feet of Thornton, who gave her a sidelong smile when he saw her make her move.

"Mr. Musgrave?" she asked.

He turned and grinned. "Do I know you?" He sipped his scotch as he took her in. "If I don't, I should."

His ruse was obvious; he knew exactly who she was. "Marlene Cole. I think we've been at the same functions a couple of times, but we've never spoken." She flashed him a smile intended to keep him with her.

"Marlene Cole. The name is familiar, but I'm sure I would . . ."

She almost laughed. "I work with Senator Hunnycut."

"Then I prob'ly should say, 'Oh, *that* Marlene Cole,' but I won't. I was just on my way over to speak to Thornton." He looked toward where Hunnycut had been, but the senator was no longer there. "Well, damn it all!" He turned back to Marlene. "I do believe you're better lookin' than he is anyway, but don't tell him I said so. It'd be a blow to his ego." He laughed.

She had difficulty limiting herself to a smile. The caricature Southerner, she thought. "Senator Hunnycut pointed you out as one of his earliest supporters, so I thought I should introduce myself. Can't know too many influential people in this business." She widened her smile. "And he certainly needs your continued support."

"Well, I appreciate that, and I'm glad you made yourself known. He has my support, but I do need to talk to him." Musgrave scanned the room.

Marlene followed his eyes. "He's probably hiding. Are you going to be here for a few minutes?" she asked, trying to nail him to the spot.

"I'll be around unless they run out of scotch."

"I'll find him," she said and started across the floor.

Musgrave lifted his glass and watched her walk away.

MARLENE FOUND THORNTON alone in the card room.

"What did old Harold want?" He took a drink of bourbon from the Waterford crystal glass in his hand, then held it up to the light to look through the cuts, as though he were appraising it.

"He said he needs to talk to you. He looked nervous when he saw you were gone."

"Sure he did. Don't worry your pretty head about Harold Musgrave. He's just fretting over some old oil leases, which I don't want to get involved with right now. Environmental issues are always embarrassing. We don't need that."

Marlene knew he was lying. He had built a career on convincing other people he was truthful, but she saw through him every time. "Could he cause trouble?"

"He won't," Hunnycut said, then smiled. "Now, why don't we go back to the hotel for some undercover work?"

"Sounds delicious."

Hunnycut put his arms around her waist and pulled her to him. They kissed deeply, and he raised his right hand to her breast.

"Mmm," she murmured. "Keep that up, and we won't make it back to the hotel. Don't forget; I've got an early flight back to Washington."

"I'd rather be going with you than making an appearance at the old home place. Scottie could give a damn if I never came back, except for what the neighbors would think. But knowing I'm in Louisiana . . ."

"She is still your wife," Marlene said mildly.

"Legal wife," he said. "Let's go."

THE STORM CAME to Matthew's Island just after 9 PM. Through the skylight above his head, Sam watched strobelike lightning illumine the night sky. There was more to hear than to see. Palmetto fronds, ripped from their crosshatched trunks, slapped against the side of the house. Thunder cracked incessantly, and rain swept in waves against the sliding doors leading onto the deck. He often wished he could convey the sound of the lowcountry in the paintings he produced.

This was a good storm, one he normally would have watched from under the cover of the eaves on the deck, or stood in naked. Rain showers were his cleansing process; however, the chill season and his lack of energy removed that option. This morning's sojourn through the past had left him empty. He couldn't even recall what he had done all day; he'd made weak attempts to draw and read, but time had passed without notice.

Now he lay in the dark, listening to the wind attack the marsh in a warlike offensive of the elements of nature against nature itself. He seldom acknowledged, much less cultivated, depression or boredom but was beginning to feel a little of both.

The ringing telephone and the soft, muted voice on the other end of the line brought him to full attention for the first time all day.

"Hi, Sam."

"Karen?"

"Expecting someone else?" she asked.

"No. Just surprised. It's been awhile."

"Are you okay, Sam? Did I wake you? It's only nine-thirty there."

"No. Nothing wrong. I just really don't know what to say." His energy level was still rising. "Do you know how frustrating it is to talk to you?"

She laughed. "Really? I'm never frustrated while I'm talking to you. Just afterwards. When I hang up, I start fantasizing. Run some warm bath water, think about how it will feel, and then I slip in . . ."

"Whoa!" He laughed. "Is this phone sex?"

"It's a start," she said, and waited.

"What I was referring to, before you started leading me into the Garden of Good and Plenty, was that I can never ask you any questions. Normal questions, like 'where are you?' or 'what are you working on?' It's frustrating. Do you remember that old movie, *Edge of the City*? John Cassavetes would go to a phone booth and call home. One of his parents would answer, but he never said anything, just held onto the phone to connect with their voices. His family knew who was calling, but they never knew from where or—"

"Sam, you sound nervous."

"Not really *nervous*."

"Why do you do this to me, Larkin?"

"What?"

"Put me on."

"Usually because I'm nervous."

Their relationship had been easy when she was in South Carolina. Neither of them had ever defined exactly what the relationship was. She had left while he was sleeping. He'd awakened to find a simple note: *Have to go. I will call in a few days, Love. You take care of you, and I'll take care of me. Maybe we can put it all together when the time is right. I think I "might" love you. Karen.* It was the only time the word *love* had ever entered the equation.

"Okay, let me ask this question. To what spur-of-the-moment stimulus do I owe this call? I thought I was forgotten."

"Never, Sam. You know that. I've just—"

"The job," he interrupted.

"I was missing you. I do more of that than I like." She took a deep breath. "We can correct that if you're willing to help me out and do some traveling."

"Where am I going?"

"What about . . . hmm . . . Biloxi, Mississippi?"

He didn't hesitate. "Why should I go to Biloxi, Mississippi?"

"Because I have a week off and a condo that looks out over the Gulf. And I need to see you."

"When?"

"I'll be there tomorrow."

"Biloxi. I'm not sure I can do that." His voice was flat.

"Please, Sam. Look, I know what's curdling in your mind. I just want some beach walks, good food, and a lot of time in bed. That's all. Remember Savannah last month? You seemed to enjoy that."

"I'm not sure I remember. What did we do exactly?" His words were framed by a smile.

"Most everything we could imagine and had the stamina for."

"Damn," he said.

"What?"

"I'm just a piece of meat."

"In your dreams."

"It's a long drive."

"You would drive?" she asked, sounding surprised.

"If I come, I'll drive."

"That'll take two or three days."

"One long day; it's about thirteen hours. I know that trip, remember?" He couldn't believe the words coming out of his mouth, that he was even considering it. "Tell you what. Let me think about it. It would take some doing. Call me in the morning. Early."

"How early?"

"Two-thirty," he said.

"That's only five hours from now."

"Yep. I'll either be ready to walk out the door or asleep."

"I wish I could ever know what's going on in that head of yours."

"No one ever has," he said.

"You're a bastard, Sam."

"I've been told that. Call me?"

"I will. And, Sam?"

"Call me." He guessed what she might say and didn't want to hear it.

"I will."

Sam put down the phone, went to the kitchen, got a glass from the cabinet, put some ice in it, and covered the cubes with Jack Daniels Black. Not a wise way to prepare for a thirteen-hour drive, he thought. He went out on the deck, stood under the eaves, and watched the raindrops, big and heavy, flattening on the treated wood.

The call had lifted him out of the lassitude he had been dwelling in, but the invitation to Biloxi was unexpected. Beach walks, food, and sex were appealing, but the word *Biloxi* put his warning systems on alert. When the glass was empty, he went back inside, lay on the bed, stared at the ceiling, and began ticking off reasons why he shouldn't go.

He didn't need the Gulf Coast; it was too close to the bayou country of Louisiana, where his life had been ripped apart. He would likely find himself drawn back to New Orleans, whose beauty and dark side he was far too familiar with. Or lured up to Shreveport to see if Celine were still there. In all these years, he had never tried to contact his ex-wife. He hadn't even known where she was until Neil Dougherty had discovered her during a background check on him when Karen wanted to bring him into the Carolina investigation.

He often thought of Celine, conjectured about what she was doing, what their life might have been if prison hadn't interrupted them, even fantasized in rare moments about going back and reclaiming her if she wasn't taken.

The saddest thing about making the trip, he thought, was that he required no one's permission, which magnified what had been burning in his head all day. His going or staying would matter to no one. He had no issues to settle and no responsibilities to keep him at home; not a single person depended on him for anything. If he saw a fork in the road, he could take it. He realized anew that he hadn't found reason or purpose in his life and didn't know where to look.

The ringing of the telephone brought him out of what he thought was sleep. He looked at the clock. It was two-thirty.

"I guess you're going to ask if I'm standing up or lying down," he said into the receiver.

"Suppose it wasn't me on the other end?"

"Then I guess whoever was calling me at this hour would think I was expecting an obscene phonecaller."

"Well? Are you standing up or lying down?"

"I'm on one elbow. You never told me how to find you."

She laughed. "Guess that did make it kind of a shallow invitation, didn't it?"

"Sort of. You don't usually forget the obvious details. You all right?"

"Just a lot on my mind with the condo and all. I didn't sleep much last night."

"What's all?" he asked.

"Work, you, travel, you. I'm sorry. I'm excited about your coming. Maybe that's why I couldn't sleep. I can't believe I didn't tell you how to find me. Guess I just assume Sam Larkin knows everything."

"Maybe I do."

"Then it wouldn't have mattered, would it?"

"It would be easier if you did tell me so I could get on the road."

THE RAIN HAD BIRTHED a heavy ground fog on Matthew's Island, clinging like a down-filled comforter, parting only as Sam's old Land Rover slashed through it and then closing again. It was a shallow fog. The taller trees rose above it, their crowns looming like giant mushrooms springing from a silver earth.

Sam had already hit the wall. The huge travel mug of strong, black coffee was half empty even before he crossed the Francis Marion Bridge into Covington, but it had not brought him around. He was having difficulty focusing on the road only thirty-five minutes into a thirteen-hour trip.

Savannah passed without notice. The sun was full and the temperature rising by the time the Lake City exit in north central Florida came into view. He couldn't remember crossing the Florida state line.

# THREE

"THIS IS QUITE a surprise, Thornton," said Arthur Valdrine. "Vice president of the United States. That is certainly an insider that Louisiana would like to have. Congratulations. It also explains why you got me out here before seven o'clock in the morning." Valdrine's position as the Louisiana commissioner of administration placed him in power, second only to the governor. And some people believed that second wasn't truly his position.

The two men were sitting in Thornton Hunnycut's private office in his home in Baton Rouge. "I would have told you last night if you had seen fit to attend Howard's fundraiser," Hunnycut said. "Can I get you something to drink? Coffee?"

"Nothing thanks. I am not a Garrett fan, Thornton, and I don't want him trading on my name for campaign financing."

"Getting ethical on me here, Arthur?"

"Never ethical. Ethics are the downfall of an honest man. But Howard and I agree on nothing. You know that, Thornton."

Arthur Valdrine was monied and had been from birth. He had attended the prestigious Webb School in Bell Buckle, Tennessee, and earned a bachelor's degree from the University of Pennsylvania and a law degree from the University of Virginia. Through all his travels, his love for Louisiana had never diminished. And when he'd weighed the opportunities available to him after law school, no other area had offered the possibilities that Louisiana did. Once home, it hadn't taken long for his reputation to spread statewide and put him in the position he now held, a position easier and less risky from which to wield power than the governor's.

"Well, Garrett is a shrimp. Let's talk about the big fish. I believe there is a good chance that James will pick me. If I get the help I need from the right people," Hunnycut said. "The country likes James, and he has the money and support behind him to carry the election. The only thing I have to do is make damn sure he doesn't get swayed by other arguments."

"How can I help you, Thornton?"

"You could answer that yourself more easily than I could tell you. James and his backers believe I can deliver the South. Without the South, he won't stand a chance of getting elected; however, for me to do my part, he's got to give me some assurances, and some of those will involve Louisiana."

"He could double-cross you."

"I intend to see that he can't. I've got some people working on finding out who else he's wooing. The governor of Illinois is a possibility, and Senator Clemmings from California. The good thing is, I don't believe he has anyone else from down here on his roster."

"And my question to you?" Valdrine asked.

"What can you do for me? You and I have been working together for a long time—quite profitably, I might add. Can you imagine what this could do for us?"

"I think that's obvious, Thornton, but, again I ask, how can I help?" Valdrine was getting tired of the rhetoric, but he knew Hunnycut. The man was a victim of his ego; bruise it and you made an enemy you wish you'd never met. He was a long way from the White House, but even in his present position, he was not to be taken lightly.

"Arthur, for all intents and purposes, you—with my help—run Louisiana. We both know that. Hell, everybody does. The governor's an idiot whose only concern is how many briefcases full of money are left at his doorstep. You know my history; you're culpable in a lot of it. Needless to say, that history could end any possibility of my becoming vice president, maybe even president."

Valdrine smiled. "Projecting a bit aren't you?"

"Never too early to look down the road and see what's there. So, for now, I want you to get prepared. There will be some cleaning up to do. Circling my wagons, so to speak. I may also need information from the party that is not available to me. You went to school with some of those boys, go duck hunting with them, and I can't guess what else." Hunnycut laughed. "I imagine some of those experiences give you a pry bar into what they know and hear. And you know it will be worth your while."

"Sounds very attractive."

"More attractive than you know. I have a big bargaining chip, and it's not just a matter of conjecture," Hunnycut said. "Once I'm named, you can bet your sweet ass I'll deliver, and when I deliver, you can double the bet that I'll collect, and those around me will profit from it."

"He'll do his homework, Thornton; you'd better come up strong and clean, or all of this is inconsequential."

"When have I ever not been able to handle those kinds of things, Arthur?"

"One or the other of us has. Usually me. But on this project you're not just dealing with a bunch of yats, coon-asses, and small town politicians. The whole country—every Democrat, every Republican and independent, including senators and house members—will be taking your days and nights apart. You'd better think about that."

"I'll do whatever is necessary, Arthur; you know that." Hunnycut looked at his friend. "What I want to know is, can I count on you?"

Valdrine smiled. "We begin by covering your ass before the digging starts. I do have a few areas of concern that I think you should think hard about."

"Such as?" Hunnycut asked.

"Scottie. Your personal lives will be under intense scrutiny. The American public will accept most anything from their next door neighbor, the more titillating the better. Accepting those same things from the nation's second lady is something else. I'm not sure the voting public will understand or accept Scottie's penchant for . . ."

"Women?"

"And other men, on rare occasions, I've heard."

"Arthur, Scottie is the epitome of discretion. She has never compromised me in any way. She's a lady to the nth degree, and that has been an asset to my career. I think there are other matters of greater concern."

"You know your wife better than I do, Thornton, but you'd better have a serious talk with her. What about Harold Musgrave? Some of the things you two have been involved in?"

"Harold's a drunk. I can discredit him anytime I want."

"Marlene Cole?" Valdrine disliked the woman intensely. They had met only a few times at political functions, but he saw her as a manipulator, and she had Hunnycut entranced.

"We have our bases covered. Everything we've done is within the boundaries of congressional rules. She has the influence to do me a lot of good. I'll handle the personal things and the District. You take care of the Southern interests."

"Give me a few days." Valdrine stood up, stretched his legs, and shot his cuffs. "Right now I have to get back to the office and see if the state government is still running."

"Arthur, I trust your judgment."

RAYMOND GAYNAUD WAS sitting in his second-floor office on Dumaine Street wondering what to do with the rest of his day—it was still morning, and he had no appointments, no plans, and no money coming in—when the telephone rang. He jumped.

"Raymond Gaynaud. Nothin' doin' here. How about you?" The fact that the caller could be a client didn't curb his brash attitude at all. He liked to imagine that he was Mike Hammer without the guns or Zelda.

"Raymond." It was Judge Artis Gaynaud.

"Well, this is a surprise." Gaynaud said. He had not heard from his father in seven months. The judge had never forgiven the slightest fault in his son's character, and there had been more than a few. Gaynaud was a free spirit, and the judge had never been able to understand that. Not even his long hair. He had often wondered if his father had ever had any fun or pleasure in his life, even at the time of his son's conception. If he had, there was no indication of it. "To what do I owe this honor? I know this call wouldn't be happening without a reason."

"A favor," the judge answered finally. The man never removed his judicial robes.

"An even greater surprise."

"An old friend, Masley Prather, was murdered yesterday in Gulfport. His son called me this morning and asked if I knew anyone out of state who could look into it for him."

"What's the problem with the local police, not to mention the fact that I'm not—"

"His son doesn't believe the locals will work too hard to discover what happened. Masley was always involved in some kind of political controversy—always played both sides against the middle, *played* being the operative word. The man was only liked and approved of on a need-to basis, and he had a lot of enemies. Some of 'em pretty powerful people. In any case, I would like you to look into it." There was silence. "You'll be paid."

"That's not the point. I'm not a criminal investigator."

"Depends on how you phrase the title."

"Thanks, Dad, but I paid my dues." Gaynaud knew that nothing irritated the judge more than the informal term for father. It was a protocol that had literally been beaten into young Gaynaud from the time he could speak.

"Well?"

"I don't investigate murders. I am a legal investigator. I do research and conduct interviews."

"You've done other things," the judge said.

"Rarely," Gaynaud said.

"Dammit, you've got an ad in the yellow pages. All I'm asking is that you go over to Gulfport and make sure the police are doing their jobs."

"And if they're not?"

"Don't concern yourself with that. Just let me know what you find out."

"And I suppose they're going to welcome me with open arms and give me access to whatever they've found. You're dreaming, Judge."

"Trust me. You'll get their full cooperation."

Gaynaud knew his father, knew the man's power, and knew he would get as much cooperation as anyone on the face of the planet would get. He just wasn't sure that, given this situation, anyone would get much.

"Bridey will pay whatever your rate is for such services. Plus expenses. Point is, he wants somebody to go over there now. Today, before the scene is corrupted any more."

"Did you say Bridey? The son's name is Bridey? Like wedding day Bridey?" He laughed.

"Last I heard, you're not in a position to make fun of a paying client's name. When you get there, contact Chief Boyd. He'll see to it that you get what you need."

"I haven't said I'll do it."

"You will," his father said, and hung up the telephone.

THE FURNITURE IN the Biloxi condo was seashore modern, all milky mauves and teals and whites. Everything—the wood, the paint, the carpet—smelled so new that Karen couldn't help but wonder if she was the first tenant. There was a great room with sliding glass doors that opened onto a deck, a kitchen with all the standard equipment, two baths, a powder room, and master and guest bedrooms. There was also a small office off the kitchen, housing a desk on which sat a speaker telephone, answering machine, and fax machine. The deck faced Highway 90 and the Gulf beyond.

She also wondered whose budget the unit came out of. Not Neil's section, that was certain.

After unpacking her clothes, she flopped on the couch. She couldn't move herself to do anything else. Not take a nap, not even eat lunch when noon rolled around. She felt only a deep sense of betrayal for what she was about to do to Sam Larkin.

At two o'clock she took a hot shower to try to bring herself mentally and emotionally up to speed. Sometimes that worked for her. Steam filled the bathroom, like a fog in which shadows floated without definition. Karen gritted her teeth, closed her eyes, and stepped into the near-scalding water. She adjusted slowly to the liquid heat as it massaged the back of her neck and up into the hairline. It was helping, the tightness easing, but not enough.

She thought of Sam, of the two of them in Covington, on Matthew's Island, on the deck of his house. The two of them standing naked in the rain after making love. She thought of the soft look in his eyes when he gazed out over the marsh and when he guided her by boat through the creeks and estuaries of the Lowcountry, the look of peace on his face when she awoke early and watched him sleeping, the muscled leanness of his body. She thought about her job and her feelings for Sam and felt foolish and sad.

After drying herself, she put on a pair of white shorts, a black sleeveless shirt, and a pair of leather sandals she had bought impulsively from a market vendor the last time she had been in New Orleans. She would try to convince Sam to go back to the city for a day, just for dinner. Something told her that if she could break that barrier, she might get him to cooperate in her investigation.

Maybe Neil was right. Maybe Sam had devils that he refused to recognize. Maybe if she put it to him that way, straight out, it would help him figure out what was causing the malaise that she had seen in unprotected moments in Savannah and even heard in his voice occasionally in their telephone calls. That wasn't Sam Larkin. He was one of the strongest men she had ever met, and there had been a few. She knew she was trying to convince herself she was doing the right thing and prayed she wasn't wrong.

The job. It was a constant presence. How would she hide her purpose? Sam was one of the most perceptive people she had ever encountered. Looking in his eyes was like facing a lie detector. He would know, the second he saw her.

She brushed her hair and left the condo to walk on the beach. Maybe she would get something to eat. Anything to fight the restlessness that was bedeviling her.

GAYNAUD COULDN'T IGNORE the debt he owed his father, and for this reason only did he find himself in Gulfport. The judge had come to him because of his innate ability to analyze a crime scene, which he had discovered while working for attorneys whose practices couldn't afford a full-time investigator. A murder scene, however, was not high on his list of favorite types of work. He much preferred corporate theft, robberies, drug labs, stolen vehicles, and other dry scenes. In most of these cases he was trying to establish innocence; in this case, he was being asked to assign guilt, and he felt ill prepared for the task.

The Gulfport police were cooperative. It was obvious some calls had greased the proverbial wheels. Gaynaud was given a copy of the CSI report, crime scene photos, and coroner's report and was assigned one bored, young officer named North, who told him to look around all he wanted but not to touch anything. North sat on the porch steps and smoked while Gaynaud went inside. Though the murders were hardly cold, there was no crime scene tape sealing the house, and the front door was unlocked. Gaynaud shook his head in frustration. So much for an uncorrupted scene.

According to the page-and-a-half police report, there were no useful fingerprints, and no murder weapon had been found. The Prathers had died from multiple gunshot wounds from a .22-caliber pistol. Robbery was apparently not the motive. Prather's wallet, containing several hundred dollars, was untouched, and nothing else in the house appeared to have been disturbed. No shell casings had been found.

The original investigator had deduced from the lack of forced-entry evidence that Prather knew his assailant and had been surprised. He had been moving down the hallway toward the kitchen when he was shot. The coroner's preliminary report said death had been instantaneous, but bloody drag marks in the hall, still visible, suggested to Gaynaud that, after being shot, the man had pulled himself along, probably in a futile attempt to save himself. There was no apparent reason for the killer to have moved the body ten feet. Evidence of a pathetic investigation.

Mary Frances Prather's body had been sprawled on the steps leading to the second floor. Gaynaud guessed she'd heard the shots and was coming down to investigate. She'd been hit once in the face and twice in the chest. The CSI report made no mention of a sweep for hairs, fibers, or any other foreign substance and no theory on the angle or trajectory of the bullets.

Gaynaud walked out on the porch and sat down next to North, who had extinguished one cigarette on the sidewalk and was lighting another.

"Any ideas?" Gaynaud asked.

"Not really. But I've heard a lot of talk about Prather."

"What kind of talk?"

"He did a lot of dirty work for some politicians. Environmental people didn't like him for how he greased the politicians and developers. According to what I hear, he was also a friend of Gustave Sykorus, who owns a bunch of strip joints and illegal gambling holes up on the Strip."

"Sykorus?" Gaynaud asked.

"Yeah. S'posed to be a member of the Dixie Mafia. Play with those boys, you gonna get hurt sooner or later." North sounded bored by the whole situation.

"Think they had something to do with it?"

"Prob'ly."

"Any reason?"

"They have somethin' to do with most everything that happens here. Besides, it was a pro."

Gaynaud smiled. "You sure of that?" He asked.

"An amateur would have left prints. An amateur wouldn't use an Angola silencer. Little bits of foam rubber spread all over the hall. Picked 'em up when we did the sweep."

"The report didn't mention a sweep."

"I can't tell you about that. Only thing we found in the whole place was the bits of foam rubber."

Gaynaud was quiet. Thinking. "Why are you telling me?"

"I'm not. Haven't told you a damned word." He looked Gaynaud straight in the eye.

"Gotta go. Good luck." He stood up, walked to his patrol car, and drove away, leaving Gaynaud to get back to his own car any way he could.

Gaynaud had decided it was a professional hit even before North's revelations. An Angola silencer was strictly "kill for hire." It was a deviously simple device: a soda can or plastic bottle, filled with some soft material, taped to the barrel of a gun to suppress the sound when a shot was fired. The only drawback was the residue it spread when the bullet passed through it.

There was little else for Gaynaud to learn. Prather's body and its movement raised some questions, but there was no definitive evidence to suggest the identity of the killer or a motive for the crime. The wife was collateral damage. Someone had simply been doing his job. The police were obviously not interested in who that person was. Or they already knew.

It was a clean kill and would probably never be pursued. Prather's friends, those on the inside, probably knew damned well who had done it, or had it done, and those not on the inside probably suspected the same people. To them Prather was no great loss, and fear of those behind the killings was far too great for speculation to become a matter of popular conversation. It was business as usual.

He would give the judge his report to pass on and hold the favor in his account to be repaid when needed. There would come a time.

# FOUR

JORDAN PETTIGREW'S LAW office was on the fourteenth floor of an office building in the heart of the New Orleans business district. It was a prestigious location and chosen precisely for that reason. To Pettigrew, image was everything. Despite coming from one of the foremost families in the Crescent City, he had spent much of his life seeking credibility and respect. But he had never been considered more than an average attorney who lived on his family's name.

He was sitting at his desk when Harold Musgrave burst through the office door. Musgrave, one of the few high-profile clients in Pettigrew's small, conservative practice, was the only client who never waited for the secretary to announce him.

"It's got to be a joke. You know what I heard at Howard Garrett's fundraiser? Thornton Hunnycut for vice president. Do you believe that? Talk about the inmates running the asylum. Tell me if it's true; I know you know."

"Calm down, Harold," Pettigrew said. "I really don't know. All I know is the rumors I hear at the courthouse."

The two men were opposites in every respect. Musgrave, with a shock of white hair and a round, puffy drinker's face predicting gin blossoms, wore a wrinkled coat and loose tie. Disheveled, the stereotypical promoter up from nothing and heading back in that direction. Pettigrew was old Louisiana money that had remained constant since cotton was king. He was immaculate, unruffled in the direst of circumstances, always socially and politically correct, his face all sharp angles with clear, cutting eyes and thin lips. His appearance and behavior befitted wealth and correctness.

"If it's true, and the son of a bitch won't deal, I'll bury him," Musgrave blustered. "Vice President Hunnycut. Shit. Bastard won't return my calls. Runs every time he sees me. I'm tellin' you, Jordan, I'll strip his ass naked if he dudn't cooperate."

"You could do that, but I don't think it would profit you. Why is he avoiding you?"

"Laurel Grove," Musgrave said. Laurel Grove was a string of assisted-living facilities and nursing homes he owned in partnership with Hunnycut, whose proprietorship was quiet but not silent. "Two weeks ago I was advised under the table that the General Accounting Office is looking into the inefficiency of the Health Care Financing Administration. Seems like they haven't been enforcing the law regarding a lot of things that could touch pretty heavy on our interests."

To visitors the Laurel Grove facilities looked to be well managed by caring professionals. In truth they were a financial miasma of Medicare and Medicaid fraud, overcharges, and bookkeeping that would leave the average CPA buried in a maze of circular payments, losses, and debits. Patient records were often rewritten or fabricated by the administrators. Forgery was commonplace, and a large percentage of the patients were kept in restraints "for their own safety" when visitors were not on the grounds. It was a horror and no secret to Jordan Pettigrew.

"Jordan, you're an asshole. But I pay you to be *my* asshole, and if the shit comes down, you're gonna be covered in it. You do know that whatever hits the fan is not selective in where it lands."

"I should think that would put your mind at ease."

Pettigrew could see that Musgrave was afraid, but not because of simple money. As he had heard the man say many times, anything that could be solved with money was not a problem. This was different, and Pettigrew knew it wasn't a hollow fear. Hunnycut was dangerous, as mean as a honey badger when threatened, and Musgrave posed a threat. On the other hand, the senator could be Musgrave's salvation.

Hunnycut had a lot of dark corners, and Pettigrew was aware that Musgrave knew them all, which made him vulnerable. The two men had hunted and fished together, visited Las Vegas on a regular basis, fucked the same women in the same bed at the same time, made money together, and partnered in business dealings that could put them both in jail.

"Think about it, Harold. If he should, by any wild stretch of the imagination, become a candidate for the vice presidency, you've got an ally. Anyone who survives the personal scrutiny he's going to be subjected to will be untouchable, as tough to deal with as Huey Long," he said, turning back to Musgrave.

"Huey Long got shot."

"Because it was the only way they could get him," Pettigrew said. "You're in the catbird seat, Harold; for God's sake, just think for once."

"What good's all that gonna do me now? I got an oil bidness that's virtually bankrupt. I got a construction bidness with five schools under contract to build, and the districts can't do a damn thing until they know what they're gettin' from the government. There's prob'ly fifteen million dollars in profit sittin' there waitin' for me, and I can't make a move. Hunnycut could give them assurance in a minute. And now the president is pushing the HCFA to come down hard on healthcare facilities. I got three things fallin' with no parachutes to open. I'm falling right out of your damn catbird seat. You're so fuckin' naïve, it's a wonder you've survived this long."

"There's no limit to the potential here, Harold," Pettigrew said, trying to calm Musgrave. "We can make it all work to your advantage sooner or later."

"Sooner or later? Sooner or later you'll have to explain that to me. Right now I don't have time. I need cash or at least the assurance of cash. And I mean now. Hunnycut is the key to the cash box."

"That's what I'm trying to tell you. Be patient; it might be sooner rather than later. As I said, he's going to undergo a lot of personal scrutiny—more than he can possibly imagine. That will make what you know priceless. If Hunnycut's got any sense at all, he knows that people will be coming to you for information. Get your stuff together and make it irrefutable. Have it ready when you need it. He knows what you can do to him."

"That dudn't make me feel really comfortable," Musgrave said.

"What do you mean?"

"Figure it out."

"Look, whichever way it goes works for you. He may be over before he gets started. If he doesn't make it, he'll need you sooner or later. Then the shoe's on the other foot."

"Sooner or later. I keep hearin' sooner or later. You're not sayin' anything, Jordan. You're not the one in a vise. You just sit up here lookin' out over the city, thinkin' nobody can touch you as much as you can touch them. All you lawyers are alike."

"Nobody's in a vise. Just hang in there, Harold. And let me tell you one more thing: you need to watch the drinking. You talk when you drink, and saying the wrong thing to the wrong person just now could be devastating. You don't want to let the booze take you down."

"Just take care of my bidness, Jordan; don't preach to me."

"I can't do one without the other. I'm not just your attorney; I'm your friend. Now is not the time to get careless. I'll let you know as soon as I hear something."

"Call me. And, Jordan, don't forget our lawyer/client relationship," Musgrave said, walking toward the door.

"Harold?"

"What?"

"If anyone starts asking questions about the esteemed senator, talk to me before you talk to them."

When Musgrave was gone, Pettigrew went to the window overlooking St. Charles and watched the sidewalk below until he saw Musgrave head toward the parking lot. Harold was a package, all right, but his mouth and the booze would be the end of him. Maybe before he paid his outstanding fees. He really should drop him as a client, but, one way or another, when push came to shove, he always paid his bill, and a wise lawyer never turned down a fee. Any client was innocent until proven broke.

Back at his desk, Pettigrew picked up the phone and dialed a number he didn't call often. It was very private and given only to a privileged few.

"Arthur? It's Jordan. Are you free for lunch? Good. Jean Patoot's Across the Lake, at one o'clock? Fine. I'll see you there."

Pettigrew hung up the phone and leaned back in his chair, trying to decide exactly how much of Musgrave's diatribe of threats he would make known to the smug Mr. Valdrine. At worst, it would be a good lunch.

SAM WAS SITTING on Karen's deck, facing the Gulf. His feet were up on the railing, and his eyes were closed. His shirt lay beside the chair. With each step she took as she approached, Karen expected him to hear her and open his eyes. He didn't. He appeared to be sleeping soundly. His face was more drawn than it had been in Savannah, and he looked thinner, though his muscles were better defined. His skin was burnished by the sun. Everything about him appealed to her, which was dangerous, she knew. He had to be tired, and she didn't want to wake him, but she couldn't bear to let him sleep. She wanted to hear his voice, see his lips move, watch a smile bloom from his face. She loved his smile.

"Sam?" she said softly. He didn't move. She went to the back of his chair, put her arms around his neck and her chin on his shoulder. "Sam," she whispered in his ear.

"I thought it was a setup," he said without opening his eyes. "Get called to an empty house, it's not usually a good thing."

Karen walked around the chair and straddled his lap. "I'm a good thing," she said.

Their kiss was tentative. Tense, not intense. Brief, as unfamiliar teenagers might kiss on a first date.

"Are you sure?" he asked.

"I guess that's for you to decide, but I'm glad you're here. Was it a rough drive? You must be exhausted. I'm sorry I wasn't here. I had no idea what time you'd arrive." She found her voice trying to outrun her anxiety and stopped suddenly. "Hungry?" she said with a grin.

"A primary life lesson. When you don't know what to talk about, talk about food. Always takes the mind off whatever it's on." Sam raised his hand to stop Karen from speaking. "Am I right?"

She laughed.

"I'm right, but I'll put your mind at ease. I am hungry, so why don't I clean up and we'll go out to dinner? After that maybe we'll be back to normal."

"I hope not," she said as she got up from his lap. "The alternative is much more interesting."

MARY MAHONEY'S OLD French House Restaurant had been built as a residence in 1737 by French colonist Louis Frazier. Constructed of handmade brick and featuring wooden pegged cypress columns, the building was protected by a roof made of slate brought over as ballast in the holds of French sailing ships. Karen had chosen the restaurant for its soft charm and had made the reservation hoping that Sam would arrive in time for dinner. Surrounded by ancient oaks, the property exuded warmth in the early evening light. Sam had the impression that they were coming as invited guests to a private home rather than a landmark restaurant.

Nothing inside disturbed that impression. It was unapologetically French, with the high ceilings found in New Orleans's Vieux Carre residences. The interior featured exposed brick walls, open fireplaces, and polished heart pine floors. Fine rosewood chairs and tables graced the formal dining room; a glass-enclosed porch contained white French provincial furnishings set against white walls; the brick-floored outdoor eating area had wrought-iron tables and chairs. The tables were all set with china, crystal, and silver. Sam chose the porch.

Karen had transformed herself for the evening. She wore a pale silk blouse that accented her curves, tan slacks, a gold belt, and sandals. The shaded light created a glow on her smooth, tanned face. Her hair fell to her shoulders.

Sam caught the scent of an unfamiliar perfume. She had never been big on perfume, usually wearing just a gentle hint, and it surprised him pleasantly.

"It's a beautiful place," he said. "You chose well."

"Actually I asked a stranger on the beach where I could take someone to dinner that would neutralize all his defenses."

"And he didn't volunteer to be the guinea pig?"

"He was eighty at least and said he had been using the place for the same purpose for forty years, including last night." Her smile was electric.

"Did he tell you if it worked? Last night, I mean."

"Guaranteed it did." Karen turned her head, and Sam became aware of their server standing beside the table. He had no idea how long the man had been there. After placing menus in front them and taking their drink orders—a Jack Daniels with a twist for Sam and a dirty Cajun martini for Karen—he disappeared as quickly as he had arrived.

"Sounds like a serious drink," Sam said.

"The first one's semiserious. The second one is serious, and the third one gets *really* serious."

"So explain a dirty Cajun martini to me," he said.

"Has a little spike in it. The olives are stuffed with jalapenos instead of pimento; they dirty it with jalapeno juice and salt the rim like a margarita."

"Sounds dangerous." He laughed.

A seductive smile crossed her lips. "Can be."

"That could be frightening," he said. He looked at the menu and raised his eyebrows. "Wow. I'm glad the taxpayers aren't paying for this."

"They are."

"No, I don't take a lady out on the taxpayer's tab. Even if it is only the fourteenth date."

Karen gave a deep-throated laugh. "You kept count?"

"Just a guess. I lost count after the second."

"Our second evening together in Carolina. It was rather memorable as I recall."

"Memorable," he said.

They decided to share appetizers for dinner—shrimp remoulade, broiled crab claws, and fried soft-shell crabs. Coffee and brandy substituted for dessert.

AFTER RETURNING TO the condo, they sat on the wicker couch on the deck and watched the moon paint sequins on the surface of the water. The sky was clear, with small threads of pale cloud faintly visible against the waxing moon. Although Sam had not yet felt the tension he'd anticipated on returning to the Gulf Coast, he found himself forming internal barriers.

Karen was unusually quiet. She seemed content to sit with her head resting on his shoulder, saying nothing. Throughout dinner and afterward, everything appeared fine, but he had the feeling that he wasn't seeing all of her, which cast a faint shadow of uneasiness. She, evidently, was feeling the same.

"Where are you, Sam?" she asked without moving. "One minute you're here, and the next you're gone. Someday I'd like to know where you go."

"I'm not sure I know." Sam leaned over and placed small butterfly kisses around her mouth. She responded, and they tested each other, teasing, before their lips truly joined. Sam pulled her body into him as they kissed. When they relaxed, Karen sat up and looked at him.

"You know what comes next, don't you?" she asked.

"I certainly hope I do." He stood and led her inside.

The feel of another human being's skin stretching the length of his own was warm and welcome, and that it was Karen's skin made it even better. He caressed each breast with his lips, then moved up, kissing her neck, her eyelids, holding her face next to his, feeling its smoothness against his own. He moved down to kiss her stomach, and lower. Her legs closed around his head as he felt small contractions begin in her stomach, progressing to sudden jerks throughout her body. The signals were familiar, and he lifted himself.

"I've missed you," he said. She sighed softly as they joined. Their rhythm began gently, then became more determined. Her muscles constricted as she increased her motion, greedy for what was coming. He heard a moan in tune with his own.

When it was over, she lay with her back to him, and he curled into her, moving her hair aside to kiss the hollow of her neck and her shoulders. His arms encircled her. The warmth and comfort of their bodies circulated between them, and they slept.

# FIVE

FROM THE OUTSIDE, Marlene Cole's Georgetown house appeared to be no different than thousands of others in that upscale community; the interior, however, showcased museum-quality furnishings and art: a Chistera desk lamp lit the entry hall; a 1920s-era Wassily chair, looking as fresh as yesterday, guarded the entrance to the living room; and original drawings by Picasso and Miró, as well as paintings by Roy Lichtenstein, Andy Warhol, Larry Rivers, and others graced the walls. Her house was a seat of luxury and a symbol of her success.

Thornton Hunnycut stood at the bay window in the living room, looking out and seeing nothing. The District of Columbia—the nucleus of power in America—lay within reach. The very thought of being the second most important element in that core of world influence was tantalizing, but it wouldn't be an easy road. He had a lot to clean up first.

He heard the swish of Marlene's bedroom slippers. She put her arms around him, slipped her hands beneath the lapels of his robe, and began gently stroking his chest. "Dreaming about being a major office holder?"

He answered with a smile. "I'm just a poor ol' country lawyer who was lucky enough to be elected to the senate." He felt her lips on the back of his neck.

"I know, darling, but now that we've served the needs of humility, and since I know you're not Sam Irvin, let's talk about what's going on in your head. You've been off center since you came back from Baton Rouge. Problems with Scottie?"

"No. Scottie and I talked. She thinks it would be a hoot, a bisexual second lady. Of course, she's also sure she wouldn't be the first."

"So what's bothering you? You can't hide it from me."

"I don't know. Maybe I want it too badly. The Louisiana governorship is there for the taking and is, financially, a better deal. I wouldn't have to be put under a microscope, either. Hell, being crooked is part of the job description down there. No reason to have power if you can't abuse it." He went to the couch and sat down, patting the cushion next to him as an invitation.

"Don't kid yourself, or me. You outgrew state offices a long time ago. This is a solid-gold opportunity. If James is nominated, he'll win. But only with you. He knows that," she said. "There's no way in the world I'm going to let you pass this up; we've worked too hard."

Hunnycut looked at her seriously, then with amusement. "It's your decision?" he asked, raising his eyebrows, skepticism bordering on hostility seasoning the look in his eyes.

"Our decision." She didn't smile. "We got here together, Thornton, and we will make this happen together. James is serving it up on a platter for you, and I don't think a future run for the presidency is out of reason."

"Marlene, I've gotten where I am by being private. No one really knows how I got here, and I'm not willing to tell. This offer could make me vice president, maybe someday president, or get me kicked out of the senate and thrown in jail."

"Thornton, it's ridiculous to worry about that."

"I'm not worried about it; I'm trying to use good judgment. Self-preservation has always been my prime motivator. It has guided everything I've done. I don't take foolish chances. Right now my being here in your house is a helluva risk. I don't think a censure committee would consider my living with a lobbyist whose clients have received an immeasurable amount of favorable legislation from my committee, not to mention frequent fucks by that same lobbyist as falling within the acceptable boundaries of gifts."

"You've never been afraid of risk."

"And I'm not now. I'm not going to take my hat out of the ring; I just have to play all the situations out in my head to my own satisfaction."

Marlene walked to the window and looked out, then turned back to him. "Your being in my house is totally acceptable; I'm your chief campaign fundraiser. Ask yourself how many congressmen and congresswomen have lobbyists involved in their campaigns without acknowledging it. We are aboveboard. You hired me. I spent the obligatory year adhering to the revolving-door policy of not lobbying you directly after resigning as your staff aide. And I was very discreet in lobbying your committee, which is allowed. We are legitimate. You hired me as a fundraiser. I simply do a job and get paid for it."

"By me and your clients."

She laughed. "And nobody knows about the fucking unless you've passed the pictures around."

"That would be the least of it. If you threw every politician, national or local, who's boffing an aide or intern or campaign hustler out of office, there'd be no one to run the country. And that includes lobbyists and members of congress. Hell, it's the national pastime."

"I'm not sure I've ever been boffed before. Sounds like something Joan Collins would be experienced at," she said. "Could we try that sometime?"

Hunnycut grinned and patted the cushion again.

She continued, "You know we're probably more aboveboard than we need to be. Money is where they usually look, and we've never used taxpayers' money for anything personal. Every dollar we've spent on you or your campaigns has come out of the campaign fund, which was raised honestly and has been accounted for."

Hunnycut gave her a skeptical look.

She moved away from the window, toward him. "Everything we've done since you've been in office has adhered to congressional and FEC regulations, and we've conscientiously disclosed our fundraising and spending. Don't worry about this end. I've covered you here. And you know how to handle Louisiana; you've been doing it for thirty years, and they still keep the faith."

"But you still know I appreciate your guidance."

"Speaking of guiding . . ." She reached down, parted his terrycloth robe, and kneeled in front of him.

THE NEXT MORNING, Karen was preoccupied. Her smile was hesitant, and she avoided eye contact. Sam knew her moods and mindsets; there was something going on, and she was unable to hide it.

After breakfast they wandered Biloxi's main drag aimlessly, browsed the shops and bought nothing, walked the beach, and said little of consequence. But their quips weren't as fast and spontaneous as usual. Toward noon they stopped at an outdoor food stand with large spool tables arranged under a gargantuan live oak and ordered shrimp and oyster po'boy sandwiches that came wrapped in waxed paper. They ate in near silence.

Sam found himself pondering his life in the lowcountry, its solitary nature, his reliance on self, and the modification of his needs to make that solitude manageable and comfortable. He had long thought that most problems were other people, and now the suspicion that one of those problems might be Karen saddened him.

Maybe peace and serenity were fairy tales, even if from the Brothers Grimm's point of view they were anything but. There was nothing serene or peaceful about their tales. Heroes usually wound up in the oven, poisoned, lost in the forest, or facing carnivorous giants. What was so different about that from modern-day problems?

"What's going on behind those eyes, Sam?" Karen asked.

"I could ask you the same question," he said, "only I haven't seen much of your eyes."

"What do you mean?" She still didn't look at him. Her sandwich was virtually untouched except for the lettuce and tomato slice that she had picked off.

"Just what I said. You're having a hard time looking at me. It's confusing me, worrying me." Glancing out to the street, he saw an old man pushing a grocery cart filled with aluminum cans, glass bottles, pieces of cardboard, a bundle of cloth, a broken umbrella, and a collapsed beach chair. Sam speculated it was the sum of the old gentleman's lifetime and felt some empathy with that. On the other hand, maybe it was all the man needed or wanted. And that would be a source of envy.

"It's just the work," she said when the silence became embarrassing.

"Sure."

Sam saw her chin quiver, as light as a mosquito landing on still water. Now her eyes were focused on the distance, not moving with nerves, but steady with resignation. He had seen guilt on her face before. Once. Back in Carolina when she admitted she hadn't been truthful with him, that she was a DEA agent. That had been work, too.

Mottled sun, coming through the tree under which Karen sat, highlighted her blond hair. The aquamarine eyes, in spite of what they had seen in her business, still reflected the innocence he had first found attractive in her. It hadn't taken him long to realize that was a misnomer. Her body, what they had shared, everything was there to make him want to stay, but it would be a mistake.

"Karen, something's going on behind those eyes, and I'm not sure that, whatever it is, I want to be a part of it. I think I'm making you uncomfortable, and I don't want to do that. So I'm going to leave." He wrapped the remains of his sandwich in the waxed paper and took it to a trash can swarming with green flies and yellow jackets. She didn't look up. "If you don't want to go back to the condo just now, that's okay. Maybe better. I'll pick up my stuff and head out. I'm sorry it turned out this way." He hadn't planned this speech, but he realized that something like it had been in the back of his mind since he'd agreed to come to Biloxi.

She finally looked up at him, and he saw the moisture in her eyes. "Sam? Sit down. Please?" Her voice was fragile, as though she didn't expect her request to be honored. "Please?"

Sam remained standing. Karen could see no concession in his eyes. She looked up through the gnarled limbs of the oak to the sky. It had become as milky and opaque as a blind man's eyes. No salvation to be found there. How to begin? What she had to tell him could blow her job and put an end to their tenuous relationship. She felt exposed, and she fought crying. She wondered how long it had been since she had cried and couldn't remember.

"Karen? Just tell me what it is."

"I think, Sam, I may be doing—I'm not sure how to put this in words—the most despicable, dishonest thing I have ever done in my life, and I can't ask forgiveness for it."

Sam said nothing.

"I truly wanted to see you, to be with you. When I left that note that said 'I think I might love you,' I meant it. In fact, while I was in Florida, I had pretty much made up my mind that it was true. I found it impossible to put you aside."

"What is it?" he asked.

She returned her gaze to the sky. There was no change in its color, nothing dramatic getting ready to happen up there, nothing in the heavens to punctuate what was going on at their table. Her face crumpled, and tears filled her eyes. "Sam, I've not been totally truthful with you, and I've taken advantage of whatever it is we have, but I have to be honest with you now."

"Someone once said that the truth doesn't require any thought, only lies do. I guess you've been doing a lot of thinking," Sam said.

She saw the coldness in his eyes, the transformation back to what he once had been. She had never seen that anger directed toward her, but she had seen the results. She knew that turbulent rivers, uncontrollable when called to the surface, flowed through Sam. She wasn't physically afraid; it wasn't in him to hurt her, but his eyes and the expression on his face were as painful as a beating would have been.

"I could try to plead innocence and say it wasn't my idea, but it doesn't matter whose idea it was. I went along with it. I have been assigned to a unit doing a background check on a possible vice presidential candidate. Thornton Hunnycut."

A long moment passed. Then, he gave her a last-straw smile and shook his head. "I'm not opening that bag, Karen. Whose idea was this? Dougherty's?"

She didn't look at him. "Yes."

"I hope you two will be very happy together," he said.

"Do you want Hunnycut to be vice president, maybe president?"

"I have nothing to say about that. I'm sure that's the argument Dougherty used on you. I'm sorry you fell for it." Sam stood motionless beside the trash can, the coldness in his eyes fading to disappointment and sadness.

"There is another reason, Sam. Will you at least listen?"

"It wouldn't do any good."

"It will make me feel better." She looked down at the food on the table. "And it might give you a little better opinion of me than you have at this moment."

"Go on." He remained standing.

"Okay. You might not like what I'm going to say, or you may think I'm wrong, and I might be, but I don't think so. When we were in Savannah that weekend, you said you were having a difficult time regaining your focus since the Carolina operation. I didn't think much about it then, but you've mentioned it several times since. And when I call and we talk, I sometimes feel you're not there. And that look in your eye right now. I see so much anger and frustration. I saw the violence in you come out in Carolina. Twice. You know what I do and what I've seen, but I've seldom, if ever, seen that kind of anger in a human being. And I believe you relished it. It was a release. I think there's still a lot of anger in you that comes from Angola and having to kill a man and losing your wife. That all came at the hands of Thornton Hunnycut. I know you, Sam. At least as much as anyone does. I know you're not an inherently violent man, but I think you may not be recognizing where that anger comes from. Or maybe you just don't want to acknowledge it. It's not something you can live with, Sam, and have the life you want."

She leaned forward. "Hunnycut's political career and Neil didn't convince me to bring you down here. Your anger did, and the loss of the happy man I first met on Matthew's Island. I think maybe it's time for you to exorcize those devils inside you and right the wrong that's been done to you. That might give you peace. Neil's investigation will go on without you, but even if we bring the senator down, I think you will wish you'd had a hand in it."

Sam stood motionless, his hands in his pockets. Yellow jackets buzzed around him. He looked down for a moment, then back up at her. "Goodbye, Karen," he said, and turned and walked away.

She watched him go out to the street and turn in the direction of the condo. She couldn't follow him or say any more. He was walking out of her life, making his own choice. She felt her sadness accelerating toward hopelessness. When she was alone, the tears finally spilled over.

JUST AFTER NOON, Pettigrew's telephone rang. He hesitated before picking it up. But a dollar was a dollar, ten minutes was an hour, and curiosity was too hard to put away.

"Jordan Pettigrew," he said.

"Hello, Mr. Pettigrew. My name is Harry Landers. I'm from the *New Centurion*, a Washington, DC, newspaper. Maybe you've heard of us."

"No. I haven't, and I don't—"

"We're a middle-of-the-road paper whose primary thrust is the Washington political scene. Right now I'm in New Orleans, and I wonder if I could meet you for an interview."

"Uh, excuse me—Mr. Landers, was it? I can't imagine what the Washington political scene would want with me. And if it's regarding one of my clients, I can't possibly talk to you."

"No, no, Mr. Pettigrew. Not that. As I am sure you know, Senator Thornton Hunnycut is in the picture as Harrison James's running mate. Of course, no one knows how that will play out, but we like to be ahead of the game, so we're doing background pieces on all of the potential candidates. I was hoping—"

"Let me interrupt you, Mr. Landers. I am not in a position to speak about Senator Hunnycut."

"You don't know him?"

"Of course I know who he is, but—"

"I'm sorry. I thought you had quite a bit of contact with him when he was a judge. You and Arthur Valdrine. That's what we're primarily interested in. His early judicial career. We have his Washington activities covered already."

"I'm sorry. Mr. Landers," Pettigrew said firmly. "I really have neither the time nor the inclination to discuss what little I know about Senator Hunnycut's background with you. It would be a waste of both of our times."

"Just a few—"

Pettigrew hung up. His hands were shaking. The lack of courage he had found so stifling in his early years and worked to overcome had resurfaced the instant he'd heard the words "reporter" and "Thornton Hunnycut." Hunnycut and Valdrine had provided him with his standing in the New Orleans legal community and all that came from it. They had blackmailed him into becoming part of their little triumvirate, and he'd been picking up on signals that could mean they were dismissing him. He knew they would not hesitate to take it all away in the blink of an eye if he made the wrong move.

The luncheon meeting with Valdrine the day before had been useless as far as he was concerned. Valdrine had dismissed his concerns about Musgrave and was noncommittal about everything else. He got the feeling that he was being left behind, that he was not a player in Valdrine's agenda. Driving back across Lake Pontchartrain after the meeting, he had decided to proceed on his own, making decisions based on his own judgments and best interests, and not be used as a patsy for Hunnycut's and Valdrine's machinations.

SAM HOPED THE walk back to the condo would ease his hurt and disappointment. Karen had also thrown a generous portion of confusion into the mix. Maybe she was right. Perhaps the increasingly frequent dreams and remembrances were a subconscious source of his lack of focus and general lethargy and dissatisfaction. It was something to think about. But not here in Biloxi.

He packed quickly, tossed his duffle bag into the Rover, and drove out to the highway. He turned west, with no destination in mind. Perhaps Gulfport or Bay St. Louis. Perhaps farther.

Highway 90 toward New Orleans was still familiar, despite inevitable changes over the years since he'd last driven it. The Gulf smell—fish and shrimp processing plants, the vegetation. Ponds, marshes, and untouched Delta land were interrupted by stretches of commercial development. But too much had changed inside him for him to feel that he was going home.

In summer the ditches running along the highway would be engulfed with Whitefield asters, their disc-like blossoms evidenced by flashes of green and rose and yellow, and once in awhile, in spring, the large white blossom of an American lotus would be visible. Smartweed, rose mallow, and milkweed proliferated along the roadside and into the open areas and marshlands. All in their season. Sam had seen them all, but now there were no flowers, just the winter greenery giving promise.

Great live oaks were reminders of South Carolina and his home there. The tall black willows, some reaching ninety feet above the earth, and green ashes with their primordial crowns signaled his return to an area he had doubted he would ever see again.

In Bay St. Louis, he bought a bottle of Jack Daniels and started looking for a motel. He didn't know whether he would spend the night or not, but too much was going on in his head for him to drive any further with no purpose.

CASEY LANDRIEU WAS just finishing the monthly filing when the telephone rang. "Musgrave Enterprises," she said.

"Hello, Casey. This is Jordan. Is Harold available?"

"Yes, I think he is. Just a moment."

Musgrave was in the bedroom in his skivvies, putting on a fresh shirt, when Casey handed him the phone. "Jordan Pettigrew," she whispered.

His home office was far from formal. Even the title, Musgrave Enterprises, had been instituted by the young woman—to Musgrave, young at thirty-six—who had answered the telephone. Casey Landrieu had begun working for him three years prior, when he was flush and wanted to improve his business image. At least, that was what she had convinced him he wanted to do. They had met on a flight from Atlanta to New Orleans, and he was so taken with her that he had offered her a job. Two weeks later, after she had found a place to live, she knocked on his door and announced that she was ready to begin work. Within six months she had moved his office from the dining room table to a converted guestroom, had a private entrance to that room put in, and was holding his businesses together with a positive cash flow. Within a year, she had moved in herself. He considered her his savior.

"Say what he wants?" he asked.

She raised her eyebrows. "It's the call you wanted isn't it?" She smiled and left the room.

He held onto the telephone and watched her go. Tall, with perfect skin and dark hair that cascaded to the top of her shoulders, she was a picture to be savored. Every time he looked at her, he asked himself how he could be so fortunate. She seemed to truly love him and, for the world, he could not understand why.

"Hello, Jordan," he said in a rough, mirthful voice.

"You sound like you just brought in a well, Harold."

"Hell, you know Gulf oil's a dead issue. What can I do for you?"

"Has Thornton been in touch with you?"

"No, I haven't spoken to him. Still got calls in to him, but I doubt I'll hear from him anytime soon."

"Listen, Harold, there's a reporter from some right-wing paper in Washington doing a background piece on Thornton. He's in New Orleans and asked me for an interview. I refused to speak with him, and you should too, if he contacts you."

"Wait a minute. He said he wanted to talk to me?"

"No. I don't know whether he will or not. Your name never came up, but—"

Musgrave chuckled. "Shame. I could tell him a lot."

"That's why I called. Don't talk to him, Harold. You don't need to get involved with all that."

"Naw, I guess not. Besides, eventually I'll hear from Thornton. You can bet on that."

"What do you mean?" There was concern in Pettigrew's voice.

"Just what I said, Jordan. I *will* be hearing from him. 'Til then, I'll just wait."

"Listen, Harold, don't go off the deep end now. Remember, as I said—"

"I know what you said, and sooner or later dudn't get me anywhere. I can't afford to wait until Thornton's nominated or elected or whatever to get some action out of him. Jordan, I hate to be abrupt, but I have a meeting, and I've got to finish dressing, so if you'll excuse me, I'd like to get on with it. I'll call you when I need you, which may be never."

He hung up, smiling. He liked ol' Jordan, even if he was weak. A reporter. He smiled as he finished dressing.

# SIX

KAREN STEPPED INTO the empty condo, and the door closed behind her. Despite the opulent vacation trappings and the atmospheric invitation to forget herself and her troubles, she found herself reliving the day her father had taken her out in his boat to tell her that her mother had left them. To find her own space, he had said, but it didn't mean she didn't still love Karen. She was just not suited to the life he led. Bill Chaney had given Karen a lot of reasons, but none of them seemed reasonable to the sixteen-year-old girl she had been. Her mother's abandonment had been the end of the world, leaving Karen in a state of lethargy, depression, and imbalance. But not for long. She had gathered herself together and made it to seventeen and beyond. Now it was time for her to do the same thing again. She needed a shoulder, though.

Buck Link was a troop commander in the Louisiana State Police, and he and Karen had a long history. They had met when she was working undercover in New Orleans. A dealer, high on his own crank, had surprised Karen from behind and tried to crush her skull with a short length of two-by-four. Had it been any longer, the added force would have killed her. Local deputies had found her, and, once she was identified as a federal agent, Link was called in to assist. They had bonded, and he'd sat at her hospital bedside every off-duty minute until the doctors guaranteed her survival. He had been her father-away-from-home and mentor ever since.

"Captain Link."

"I think I still owe you a dinner for the help you gave me on that case in South Carolina."

"Karen?"

"How many girls from South Carolina owe you a dinner, Buck?"

"I've lost count. Where are you?" he asked.

"Biloxi, Mississippi, capital of the Redneck Riviera."

"Vacationing or working?"

"I'm not sure. Supposed to be working, but I'm not accomplishing much, and I'm serious about dinner. I've got some problems I need to discuss with you. Maybe a little therapy, fatherly advice? How about tonight? Pascal's Manale? About seven?"

"My favorite. What's it about, Karen?"

"Well, I'm at odds with everything, mostly myself."

"Pascal's Manale. Seven o'clock. I'll get us a reservation. You staying over?"

"Probably not. It's less than two hours back here, and I sleep better in my own bed."

"I'll look forward to it," he said.

"Me, too. It's been too long."

SAM SAT ON the balcony of his room at the Dolphin Motel, sipping Jack Black on the rocks. He wondered if walking through his memories was taking him in the right direction. He had no reason to revisit prison; he had carried that with him ever since the day he'd entered its gates. The dreams had kept it green.

Celine was another matter. Hunnycut had stolen not only his life but hers as well. From the moment he'd left Matthew's Island and headed southwest to Biloxi, she had lain heavily in the background of his thoughts. Even though he hadn't seen her in more than ten years, he found it easy to bring up the sight of her tearful face as he was being led out of Hunnycut's courtroom in shackles. He had not seen her since.

The divorce had been handled via mail by attorneys who had told him it took a lot of cajoling to get her to agree. She had wanted to wait, at least for awhile, to fight the judge's decision, but his lawyer didn't think that was the responsible thing for her to do, and Sam had agreed. Only after he'd written a caustic letter telling her that he would never get out did she give in and file the petition. That had been their last communication.

They had met in Lafourche Parish, near Raceland, home of Freddie John Falgout, the first American casualty of World War II. Circumstances were not the best for romance: Sam had been issuing a ticket to Celine's teenage brother for a wildlife violation when she arrived at the dock to pick him up. Writing the ticket, he'd had a hard time keeping his eyes off the raven-haired beauty dressed in cutoffs and a blue denim work shirt tied at the waist. She'd stood, a look of disgust on her face, waiting for him to finish. He had been grinning as he wrote.

"You seem like you're enjoying this," she said with undisguised sarcasm.

"You're his mother, ma'am?" he asked.

"No. I'm his *sister*." Her voice was resonant and held a dark and sensuous pitch. "Not his mother," she added under her breath.

"Guess I'm sorry about that." He raised his eyebrows under the cover of his hat brim, fighting the urge to laugh. "Well, ma'am, I don't want to take him in; it's a minor violation, but I do have to have someone who will be responsible for his showing up in court."

"I'll do that."

"I'll need your name, address, and phone number in case we need to get in touch with you," Sam said, and she gave him the information.

"You said it was a minor violation. Don't you think you're taking this a little too seriously?"

"No, ma'am. Every violation is serious," he said, folded the ticket, and handed it to her.

She walked her brother to the pickup truck she had come in and drove away, leaving the wildlife officer grinning in her wake. She told him later that she hadn't looked at the ticket until she got home and turned her brother over to their father. Scrawled across the ticket was an apology for suggesting that she looked old enough to be his mother and for the trickery he'd used in getting her phone number. There was also an offer of dinner if she didn't hang up when he called, and no court date for her brother was written in.

They had had less than two years together when their world began ripping apart. When her brother was killed in an automobile accident in the first year of their marriage, they had believed that was the worst that could happen. Neither of them could have imagined what lay just a few months ahead. Over the years, he had questioned, more times than he could count, his decision to let her go, but there had been no hope, and his conscience wouldn't allow him to ruin her life while his rotted away.

Celine. Louisiana. They were only a few miles away, and her proximity made her more constant.

Back in his room, he poured himself a generous drink and sat propped up on the bed, listening to the two voices that were speaking to him, the practical and the impractical.

Karen was right: it *was* time to go back. Even so, he couldn't forgive her deception.

SCOTTIE HUNNYCUT AND Kristin Bealeux usually managed to meet twice a week for dinner at the Bluffs on Thompson Creek in St. Francisville, although conflicting schedules had made it difficult lately. Long periods apart were hard, and though they were both married and had similar social obligations, Scottie felt the brunt of responsibility. But Thornton made her anxious. His weekly phone calls had increased in frequency since Harrison James had approached him. At first the idea of being second lady had been exciting, but that had quickly worn off, and Thornton's paranoia about her lifestyle had become a nuisance. Kristin had become testy about the increased attention to security, and Scottie didn't want to lose her.

While she and Kristin were having their salads, Scottie became aware of a man watching her from an adjacent table. He didn't lower his gaze when she caught his eye. She had seen him before, sometime over the last couple of weeks, but she couldn't bring a time and place to mind. It might have been coincidence, but she didn't think so. His interest was too intense.

"I think we should leave," Scottie said to her friend.

"More Thornton?" Kristin asked.

"I don't know. There's a man over there who can't keep his eyes off us."

"Scottie, you're paranoid. Why shouldn't he be looking? He's a man, and you're beautiful." There was no concession in Kristin's voice. She was harder than Scottie, knew that they were both attractive, and expected attention.

"I'm not being paranoid. He's watching us." She focused on her salad but could not shake the feeling that she was under surveillance. Her background, her willingness to be what she wanted to be and act accordingly had always been her strengths. She had never backed away from her lifestyle. She reveled in it, but the game was becoming more serious, her calm disturbed, and that scared her. She didn't want to lose herself.

Kristin's voice mirrored her thoughts. "You're sure about it. Scottie, I'm not going to live like this. I can't have a relationship under the threat of double jeopardy. It's difficult enough to lead a double life; what you're bringing with you is too much baggage to handle. I love you dearly, but I won't go through this with you."

"Please . . ." Scottie felt tears in her eyes.

"I'm sorry," Kristin said. "I just can't do this anymore. The risk is too great. I've got too much to lose, and so do you."

"But—"

"I'm not saying goodbye. We just need a break to deal with this thing as it unfolds. As you said before, it may soon all be over." She paused and touched Scottie's hand, hiding the intimacy behind the flower centerpiece that graced the table. "I don't want to disassociate myself from you, Scottie. I love you. I don't have to tell you that, but let's just take a break and see what happens."

Scottie didn't say anything. She got up from her chair and walked over to the man's table. As she approached, he began concentrating on his food.

"Can I help you?" she asked.

"I'm sorry?" he questioned, looking up at her.

"You've been watching my friend and me ever since we sat down."

"I guess I'm caught," he said smiling. He started to rise.

"Don't get up." It was a command. "Just answer my question."

"My name is Harry Landers. I'm a reporter for the *New Centurion* in Washington—"

"I'm not running for office, Mr. Landers. My husband is. I don't like being stalked, stared at, or having lunch with an old friend intruded on by your curiosity or reporting or whatever you call it. You people go too far, and I will notify my husband," she said, the fury just beneath the surface apparent. "We're leaving now. Don't follow us." She started to turn but stopped at the knowing smile on the reporter's face.

"Your friend already has," he said.

Scottie turned, saw the empty table, and fought panic, demanding strength from within. She looked down at Landers, who was still smiling.

"You bastard," she said and left the room. Thornton hadn't prepared her for this.

PASCAL'S MANALE WAS uptown on Napoleon Avenue. It was casual, crowded, and noisy. The atmosphere, the people, and the food—especially the barbecued shrimp, always hot, sweet, and huge—put it at the top of Karen's list of places to eat in the city. She was pleased to find it hadn't changed. The shrimp were as good as she remembered, and her conversation with Buck was cleansing. Telling the story of her subterfuge to entice Sam back to the Gulf Coast eased her guilt. Buck was sympathetic. No one understood better how dedication to law enforcement could screw up a life. He had lost two wives before he'd learned that marriage and mayhem didn't mix, though some people considered them synonymous.

Link already knew about Sam. He listened without advising, just offering his assistance in any way she needed it. He asked questions that made her bring out answers from deep inside and allowed her to realize that what she had done was for the greater good. It was up to her to decide what to do from this point forward. It was exactly what she wanted from him.

After dinner, they walked up Napoleon Avenue to Tipitina's, the former home of Professor Longhair. Despite its renown, it was just a simple room with a wraparound balcony, a stage, and a couple of bars. They had a beer, taking just long enough to fall under the spell of the zydeco music. Buck, Pascal Manale's, and Tipitina's were the change of pace she needed before heading back to Mississippi and, more important, in the right direction.

Karen took Highway 90, a stretch of road that resurrected for her the feel of the Gulf Coast she had fallen in love with back when her father had been an environmental officer there. She enjoyed the small Mississippi towns that had for years been prime stops for travelers, con artists, hustlers, religious zealots, politicians, and the vacationing wealthy from New Orleans and Mobile.

Pearlington, Waveland, Bay St. Louis, Pass Christian, Long Beach, Gulfport, and finally Biloxi itself. The towns had changed over the years, had become revitalized and rehabilitated according to some, neutralized and ruined according to others. Pass Christian, with its elegant mansions, looked as it had for years, but in other towns the abandoned warehouses, fish factories, and decaying boat docks were mostly gone, replaced by convenience stores, minimalls, boutiques, motels, pawn shops, and chain restaurants.

But the old Gulf Coast charm could still be seen, in fact and in legend, behind the changes and the new-found respectability. The operational center of the Dixie Mafia's murder conspiracies, drug running, gambling, and prostitution was still there. On a more sophisticated level now, but still a way of life. This stretch had also been the preferred site for the weekend debaucheries of the New Orleans elite who couldn't be seen at home doing the things they did in Mississippi.

When she hit Beach Boulevard in Biloxi, she put nostalgia behind and began thinking about the present. Sam had taken himself out of the game. Even if she knew where to find him, she wouldn't go after him. The first step, as she saw it, was to call Neil and tell him she was back in.

Opening the front door of the condo, she had the feeling—cop's intuition—that she wasn't alone. Gooseflesh raised the hair on her arms as she removed her Ruger .357 magnum from its holster, straight-armed it out in front of her, and made her way through the dark apartment. Confident the interior was clear, she turned on the deck lights.

SAM FROZE. HE hadn't heard the car pull in or Karen enter. He knew if it was she who had turned on the lights, she would assume an instinctive, protective stance when she saw a man on her deck. He smiled and, without turning around, raised his hands. He heard the sliding glass doors open.

"It's Sam. Don't shoot." No response. "Yet?" he added, trying to play it light.

"Why not?"

The sound of her voice caused his muscles to relax, but only slightly. He kept his hands in the air. The clipped response indicated that she had undergone an attitude change during his absence.

"I'm not sure," he said, trying to determine how angry she was.

"You can put your hands down."

Sam heard the Ruger's safety click on and lowered his hands. Karen walked around and leaned against the railing, facing him, holding the gun down next to her leg. They stayed that way for a minute that seemed much longer.

"Why did you come back?" she asked.

"I changed my mind. Men can do that, too, you know."

"That's a rules change; I'm not sure it's allowed. You seemed pretty determined when you left."

"Are you looking for an apology?"

"No."

"I'll explain if you'll put the gun away and offer me a drink," he said. "Sitting out here for four hours can create quite a thirst."

"You've been here for four hours?"

"Seems longer, and I'm thirsty."

"Well, I guess if I'm not going to shoot you and I want to hear what you've got to say, we'd better go inside and take care of that."

"Do all your guests get this kind of welcome?"

"No, usually I shoot." She turned and went through the door. "Come on in. Sit down, and I'll get you a drink." She turned away quickly, but he suspected she was smiling.

When Karen came from the kitchen, she was carrying two glasses filled with cubed ice and Jack Daniels Black. Her look squared on his eyes.

"You gonna tell me?" she asked when she was seated on the couch. "What brought you back?"

"Cut right to it, don't you?" He took a sip of his drink.

"You didn't hesitate when you left." Her gaze was uncompromising.

"I can't apologize for that, Karen. I had to get away."

"Okay. Past is past. Back to the original question. What brought you back?"

"Because you were right. I had to find my anger."

Karen looked at him, although she didn't have to see his eyes to know the look that was hidden there. "I can't imagine you ever lost it. It's the only reason I could rationalize what I did. Despite your self-satisfied attitude, I believe it's there and you need to rid yourself of it."

She went to put more ice in her drink. He watched as she moved into the kitchen and wondered how many other deep-seated psychoses she had divined within him. He was more transparent than he had realized, but then most of us are, he thought.

"I guess I managed to put it aside through some misguided sense of nobility," he said, "operating on what I thought was a higher plane, or maybe I was just tired of trouble and afraid of where it might lead me." He drank the last bit of whiskey out of his glass.

"Another?"

He shook his head.

"We all do that with a lot of things. Rage, romance, and guilt to name a few. I still want to know what changed your mind," she said.

"Thinking about what you said. Realizing how vulnerable I was because of that cloud hanging over me, trying to be secretive, hiding what I am in favor of what I believed myself to be. Prison took more out of me than I could admit and put a lot of things in me that I didn't expect. I took a walk back to where I had once been in my life, and I realized that somewhere along the way, I decided to take the easy way out. Security, the money the government—or somebody—gave me, trying to achieve what I thought would be a less complicated life, there are probably a thousand reasons, but I don't know all of them."

"Self-honesty is always a heavy trip." She paused. "I'm glad it found the light of day. Do you understand now why I did it?"

"Yes."

"Where did you go?" she said.

"Some motel in Bay St. Louis."

"That's it? Bay St. Louis?" He thought he saw relief on her face, and they were quiet.

"So what do we do now? Or are we going to do anything?" she finally asked.

"That depends on you. Do you have any idea what Dougherty's doing? I mean until he does whatever he is going to do at noon tomorrow."

"What are you talking about?"

"It's what he said in his last phone call. It came in a couple of hours before you got here. Said he'd give you until noon tomorrow."

"You listened to my phone messages?"

"Well, it was pretty boring sitting out here by myself, and the machine was turned up loud enough for me to hear. I figured if you were expecting anything covert, you wouldn't have had the volume on. You should listen to it. He sounded pretty intense."

"Yelling?" she asked, a smile playing across her face.

"That, too." Karen went to the answering machine, hit the PLAY button and returned to her seat. There was no introduction; Dougherty jumped right into it.

"*Karen, if you're there pick up the phone, damn it!*"

There was a pause. "Get ready," Sam said.

"*Goddamn it! I've been trying to reach you for two days, as you know if you've picked up your messages, which I'd guess you have. We're in an investigation here. I need your help. Since I haven't been notified that you've resigned, I assume you're still on the team. I want to know if you've had any further contact with your friend from South Carolina.*" Karen looked at Sam, and he shrugged his shoulders. "*I'll wait until noon tomorrow. You can call any time, day or night. When I said fill out your time down there, I didn't expect you to be out of reach. Noon. Please.*"

"Take time off and work. That's Neil. I'd better call him."

"Tell him we'll meet," he said, his tone no longer playful.

"You're sure?" When he nodded, she said, "Okay. You asked for it."

"No. He did." Karen got up, then turned back to Sam.

"Other than Neil, you hear any other hot calls while I was gone?"
Sam shrugged. "Sorry."
"Damn! He said he was going to call."

# SEVEN

PETTIGREW DID NOT sleep, worried about the call from Landers. He thought long and hard before calling Valdrine, but he needed to tell him about the reporter. The call would serve several purposes: he would be covering his own ass, and he could find out if Valdrine, too, had been contacted. He might also get an idea where the man stood with all that was happening. Unlikely, but possible. The administrator was the coldest individual he had ever met.

It took almost an entire morning of constant calling to get an answer on Valdrine's direct line. The voice that answered was unconcerned.

"You were right to call, Jordan. There's going to be a lot of this going on now that Thornton's in the national spotlight. Did you tell him anything?"

"Not really. I simply said that being a part of the legal community, I know Thornton, but not well enough to discuss him with a reporter and that I had no intention of doing so. I'll probably hear from him again; he didn't sound like a man easily put off. Impressed me as persistent as a pit bull."

"Don't worry about it, and don't refuse to see him should he contact you again. If he thinks we're stonewalling anything, it could cause Thornton a world of harm. Above all, Jordan, don't lie, but be selective in what you say. Lies will come back to haunt you. I don't need to tell you that; you've been a lawyer long enough."

"I don't know what connection he thinks—"

"You were a criminal attorney at one point," Valdrine interrupted. "He'll know that, and it puts you in Thornton's ballpark."

"Oh, I did call Harold Musgrave to give him a heads up. He's mad as hell at Thornton right now, and you never can tell what he might say.

You should tell Thornton to contact him. He's been avoiding him and hasn't been subtle about it. Might take some of the heat off if he can throw him a crumb."

"The only person who believes that Harold Musgrave is a threat is Harold Musgrave. Nobody pays any attention to him; he's a lucky drunk. What could he really do?"

Pettigrew mulled over whether or not to advise the administrator just how much Musgrave could do, about the pending investigation of the Laurel Grove facilities, of the gun Hunnycut was holding to Musgrave's head over the school financing, of the shaky legislation that Musgrave and Hunnycut had paid for to allow them to get oil leases years before, and numerous other things he held to himself under the cover of attorney/client privilege. He decided to keep Valdrine in the dark. What Valdrine didn't know could hurt him, and there was a lot the smug bastard didn't know.

"Well, he's been in business with Thornton for a lot of years and might be aware of more chinks in that armor than we are. Remember, neither one of them was worth a single-sided slice of watermelon when they started, and we weren't around then. Who knows what they might've done to get where they are. I personally think he's a problem only if he wants to be, but who knows what he might concoct in that fuzzy brain of his."

"I really don't think he's anything to worry about, but I'll mention it to Thornton. We don't need any loose cannons out there, and a crumb will probably keep him happy. He'd have nothing to gain by sabotaging Thornton. Quite the opposite I'd imagine. Don't worry about the reporter. If we don't say anything, there's nothing for him to print. Preventive action is the key. Keep me informed."

"I will, Arthur. Goodbye."

Valdrine thought he was in control. If he only knew, Pettigrew thought. He was still worried, but the more he considered what he alone knew, the better he felt.

MUSGRAVE'S PLANTATION-STYLE house in Mandeville, Louisiana, across Lake Pontchartrain from New Orleans, stood on thirty-four acres of prime land graced with live oaks and pecan trees that had been there when men on horseback, wearing the gray uniforms of war, passed through. Musgrave stood on the gallery outside the master bedroom and looked down toward the bass pond, where dragonflies flew low above the water's surface, touching down intermittently to dimple the surface. Thousands of feet of white fencing outlined the visible parameters of his property.

Musgrave had coveted the place since he was a boy. Old Judge Riley Holcombe, a former state legislator, had owned it. One day, while raking the judge's lawn, Musgrave had told the old man that someday he would own it. The world was out there, and at thirteen, Harold Musgrave was resolved to make his mark in it.

For years he had gone out of his way to drive by the Holcombe place, plan its rehabilitation, and reassert his intentions. By the time he had the wherewithal to make the purchase, the house had fallen into poor repair and had to be virtually gutted and rebuilt. Musgrave had saved as much of the original structure as possible, reusing salvageable lumber and brick. That was where the value lay. The house was his now, though many of the older aristocracy resented a boy from across the tracks owning it.

Great slashes of red cloud were moving in over the horizon, advancing like an army, forewarning a disruption of the calm, quiet morning. Musgrave liked to watch changes in the weather, just as he liked change in his routine. The pond had begun to turn dark, and the leaves on the trees were turning upward as they did when a storm was on the way.

He heard footsteps behind him and turned to see Casey standing in the French doors.

"You are a vision," he said, looking her up, then down, then up again.

"And you're prejudiced," she answered. "Mr. Landers is here."

"Tell him I'll be down in five minutes."

"Are you sure you want to do this?" she asked.

"I'm sure. As sure as I am careful to keep everybody thinkin' I'm the same ol' crazy drunk I used to be, and I never was as drunk or crazy as they thought I was. What did Pettigrew say? That I was sometimes irresponsible? He's the only one of the bunch I halfway respect. And I think, in a way, he prob'ly feels the same. Wouldn't have put up with me this long if he didn't." He smiled. "Being irresponsible gives me an edge." He went to Casey and gave her a kiss.

"I've got to run into town," she said. "I'll be back about one."

"Take your time."

Landers was a larger man than Harold Musgrave expected. He imagined the man might have been an athlete in his day. Over six feet, casually dressed, with dark hair that, though not overly long, didn't seem to be cut on a regular basis.

"Mr. Landers," Musgrave said, as the man stood to shake hands. "Harold Musgrave."

That was the extent of the amenities. The man had a strong handshake. "Now what can I do for you?" he asked as he sat behind his desk.

"As I mentioned on the phone, Mr. Musgrave, I'm from the *New Centurion*, an independent, rather conservative newspaper in Washington. We're not the *Washington Post*, nor are we an ultraright-wing scandal sheet, but we do take an alternative view of what's happening in the capital."

"All right," Musgrave said. "Sounds a little rehearsed, but how can I, down here in Louisiana, help you with what's goin' on in Washington, DC? I'm kind of confused here." He gave a little wink.

"It's rumored that Senator Thornton Hunnycut is going to be Harrison James's pick for a running mate should James get nominated, which at the moment seems inevitable. Consequently, we're doing a little background piece on the senator, as we are doing on all the potential candidates. Fair is fair." Landers smiled. "And since I know you've been in business with Senator Hunnycut in the past, I thought perhaps you could help us out. I've already contacted," Landers referred to his note pad, "a Jordan Pettigrew."

"And what did Mr. Pettigrew have to say?"

"He refused to talk to me, but I will try again. I will also contact Arthur Valdrine."

"You might want to be a little careful with that one," Musgrave said.

"And why would that be?"

"No matter. Well, if you want to ask me some questions, I'll be happy to answer those that I can. Of course, you do realize that, in addition to being business partners, Thornton and I are also friends, so I will be discreet with my answers. And don't ask me any questions I'm going to have to plead the fifth on." Musgrave laughed.

"Certainly not."

"Also, I must ask you to keep my name confidential as a source."

"I can tell you've been through this before," Landers said.

"Not really. I just read the newspaper and watch a lot of TV." He laughed again. "Agree to that, and ask away."

"Of course. The first area I'm interested in is the senator's time as a judge. There are some holes in my research of that period."

"Well, I don't know how much I can tell you about that. He never put me in jail, but I heard he was pretty tough."

"I get that impression. He's certainly been tough for some people to deal with in DC. Ever hear anything about a case involving a Sam Larkin?" he asked.

"Can't say that I have. What'd he do?"

"I'm not sure. His name just came up in my investigation."

Pretty hard to lie successfully to a reformed professional, Musgrave thought. He had never heard of Sam Larkin, but he would damn sure find out.

THE MEETING WITH Dougherty was scheduled for one o'clock, but Sam suggested they go in early and have a real New Orleans lunch beforehand. They had been cautious with each other the night before. When Sam suggested he go with her to meet Dougherty, Karen had made the call without asking what he had in mind, and he hadn't asked her what was expected of him. They'd stuck to benign topics, avoiding the subject of Hunnycut. When benign topics were exhausted, they then avoided each other. Karen had slept in the master bedroom, and Sam had taken the guestroom.

The drive into the city was quiet. When Sam stepped out of the car onto the sidewalk, the smell of New Orleans was a comforting welcome. Unpleasant city odors were overshadowed by the mixed fragrances of evergreen tropical plants, the harsh perfumes of passersby, the carnival smell of fried foods, hard-brewed chicory coffee, and, of course, the river.

Karen watched Sam absorb it. "I've never seen a smile so full of happy in my life," she said.

"I didn't realize how much I missed it."

She couldn't help wondering if he would have said that a week ago. Her pulse quickened. "Anywhere in particular you want to go?" she asked.

"Just walk," he answered.

"Then lead the way."

"I'm not your boss, you know."

"I'm not so sure. You're pretty hard to deal with. Don't think I'd like to cross you." She grinned. "Again."

"You're easy. It's the tough guys I'm worried about."

"Neil?"

"He's easy, too. Let's walk. Right now I need New Orleans." He veered toward the French Quarter. Karen could see him tuning in to the sounds of the city. Sam could operate on two levels at the same time, a talent she had come to respect shortly after she met him. In the beginning it had been distracting, had made her wonder if he were even listening when she spoke. His reactions and responses, without fail, had proved that he indeed was.

He was taking in everything they saw, everything they heard. He lived on an island, isolated from all that encompassed city life. Now he had to reacquaint himself with the playing field and pick up a rhythm, unique in all the world, that had become unfamiliar to him. New Orleans was not a place to find oneself out of step.

They walked past the antique stores on Royal Street, crossed over on Dumaine to Rampart and saw the deteriorated state of Louis Armstrong Park. Sam led them back toward the river on St. Ann, turned south on Bourbon, and moved back east on Bienville to Decatur. Occasionally he uttered an insignificant comment, noted a change in the city, made a response, but little else. Karen let him have his freedom. They walked for two hours. By eleven-thirty she was hungry and suggested they go to Felix's Oyster Bar for lunch. From the time Felix's opened at 10 AM until it closed late at night, it was noisy and full of locals and tourists.

When the server came to their table, Karen looked at Sam. "Are we working?" she asked.

"I'm not. Why?"

"Then I'll have a Bloody Mary."

"I'll have a Jax," Sam told the waiter, "and you can go ahead and bring us two dozen raws, and when you see the platter getting low, bring another two dozen."

Karen looked up from the menu. "Raw? We could get oysters Rockefeller, oyster stew, Bienville style, omelets, spaghetti. You want raw?"

Sam handed his closed menu to the waiter. "Raw."

After the drinks arrived, they sat quietly until Karen broke the silence. "Got your city legs yet?"

"The walking helped, but I'm not completely comfortable with it. I did determine one thing: I don't think, even as much as I love New Orleans, that I could ever live in a city again. I guess I'm spoiled."

"I would be. Living where you live."

"But not like I live," he said.

"Not so sure about that anymore, Sam. I've given the job a lot of thought lately." She looked at him for a reaction. It was slight.

"That's surprising."

"To me, too," she said. "Do you have a plan, Sam?" He looked at her quizzically. "For the meeting, I mean."

"Just listen to what Dougherty has to say."

"This may be the first meeting I've ever looked forward to attending," she said. Sam had mentioned nothing about any strategy he might have, but she knew there was one. If anything, Sam was methodical, even though his actions might take unorthodox twists and turns. The thought of Neil as a sitting duck was amusing.

"It might not take long." Sam's expression was somewhere between mischievous and devilish. It made her wary and appealed to her at the same time.

"That's a dangerous look. I'm not sure I'd want to be in Neil's shoes."

"Probably not." His expression cleared as the first platter of oysters arrived.

The oysters did not last long. Sam and Karen ate with gusto, drenching the mollusks in lemon juice and a touch of Tabasco. No catsup or horseradish. The combination of the icy cold meat and the lemon, tangy hot sauce, and sea salt flavors melded into something close to what the ocean and all its condiments would taste like if they were palatable. They didn't talk until the first platter was gone and the waiter had set the second in front of them.

"So, with or without Neil, where do we start?" She concentrated on extracting an oyster from its shell.

"Here. Louisiana. This is where Hunnycut started. This is where his strengths and weaknesses are. Attack the strengths and find the weaknesses. I'm not the least bit concerned about all the political stuff in Washington. Let Dougherty handle that. We've got to find out if he did convenience store stickups to get through law school."

She laughed. "Pretty good analogy, Sam. I can almost imagine the Honorable Thornton Hunnycut in a ski mask holding up a convenience store."

"I need to know where and how Dougherty got the information on my case when you were in Carolina. He found no reason for my release, or so he says, but he knew about the compensation and Celine. What I don't know is exactly how and where he got it."

"The payments he got through personal contacts with banks," she said, "but he told me it wasn't easy. The government wouldn't cooperate. Said if it was done, it was in a previous administration, and they had no knowledge or responsibility. As far as I know, once we locked your history down, he never pursued the details of your release. If he did, which is possible, he didn't tell me. I know the compensation bothered him. Celine was a matter of public record; even I found that out. I told you that. Had a state police buddy of mine, Buck Link, check it out."

"Can we use him if need be?" Sam asked. "It would help to have a non-fed on our side."

"Yes. If I have a chance, I'll see what I can find out from Neil, but I doubt it will be much. If he knew anything, I think he would have told me."

"Then we start with background. Isn't that the way you professionals do it?"

"Yes, that's what we professionals do. Let's go talk to Neil."

# EIGHT

THE TELEPHONE WAS ringing when Casey walked into the house. She put her packages down in the kitchen and answered it.

"Musgrave Enterprises." She listened and smiled. "Yes, Senator. Will you please hold? He's in a meeting, but I'm sure he will interrupt it to take your call." She paused. "Thank you."

She found Musgrave at his desk writing checks.

"Senator Hunnycut for you on line one, sir," she said with exaggerated formality.

"He on hold?"

"Yes."

He had a grin on his face. "Let him wait."

"It's not the time to be petty, Harold," she said.

"Why not? He let me wait long enough."

She gave him a stern look.

"Oh, all right, but I was enjoyin' it." He punched the flashing button. "Thornton. Well, finally we're touching base. Been awhile."

"Harold, I'm sorry. You know how the political life is. I haven't had time to spit, much less make the calls I should be making."

Musgrave could hear the resentment in his voice. Thornton Hunnycut would rather do anything than talk to him.

"Spit?" Musgrave said with a laugh. "I can see you're glossing up your language for the big campaign."

"There is no campaign yet. It's the silly season up here; a lot of ridiculous things get said."

"Not too ridiculous from what I hear. Hell, they've even got reporters down here from Washington doing stories on you. You're a mighty important man, Thornton."

"They must be hard up for news," Hunnycut said. "I wouldn't take those things too seriously, Harold. Meanwhile, we need to talk about Laurel Grove."

"Not much to talk about unless you've got some connections with the HCFA and the GAO. Which I'm sure you have. If they come nosing around, we'll be in trouble. Wouldn't do much for your campaign." Musgrave looked at Casey, who was listening with undisguised interest.

"Harold, you know I have the connections to fix whatever problems there are; however, considering the outside chance—and I stress outside—that I should be asked to join the ticket, I'm going to have to divest myself of anything that might hint of a conflict of interest."

"Does that include Marlene Cole?" Musgrave enjoyed twisting Hunnycut's tail.

Hunnycut's voice was steely. "I'll ignore that. But I don't expect to ever hear anything like that again. You don't want me for an enemy."

"I thought you already were, Thornton. Certainly a friend and partner doesn't play hide and seek. You know we're in trouble on Laurel Grove, and you want me to buy you out. Get your name off of it. Am I on track here?"

"That would be one possibility."

"I guess it would, except for one thing. Because of the holdup on the school funds from your committee, I have three projects at a standstill and no money."

"I'm sure we can work something out until the funds are released, which I expect to be any day." Musgrave heard undisguised anger in Hunnycut's voice.

"Even so, Thornton, I don't know if I want those damned places with no friend in government to grease the wheels. They consistently create problems, what with certification, inspections, finding qualified and cooperative administrators, not to mention the damned state health department. You're up in Washington. You don't deal with it on a day-to-day basis like I do."

"These are minor things, Harold. If I change positions, I won't lose any power. In fact, it should make things easier. Marlene will work with the committee members to see that you get preferential treatment."

"How do I know she can do that once you're gone?"

"Goddamn it, Harold, you know me. I'll tell her to fuck every member on the committee if she has to." His voice took on a menacing tone. "And she'll do it. Don't ever doubt my ability to accomplish what I set out to do. You should know that after all these years."

Musgrave suspected Marlene Cole was not within hearing distance.

Hunnycut continued. "Listen, Harold. Laurel Grove is a good business for you. I'd hate to see you lose it; it's carried you through a lot of downs. Legislation can always take care of whatever problems arise. Hell, we can get a bill passed overnight to favor someone we want favored. All it takes is greasing those wheels you were talking about, and the government would look like fools if it turned its back on the elderly. We may not like them, but we've got to take care of them. Every politician knows that. Those homes are a license to steal."

"That's your take on them, Thornton. Never was mine. I hate everything about them."

"You never seemed to mind the money they generated. Why didn't you get out a while back?"

"You didn't give me a choice."

"Harold. I just need to divest myself of several things. Believe me, Laurel Grove is only one."

Musgrave knew better than to believe Hunnycut would have anything to do with him or Laurel Grove once he was no longer connected with them, and he saw the situation as a card up his sleeve to play when he needed it.

"Well, Thornton, all I can say is when you come up with a firm offer, and I get the school money, we can talk about it."

"You still don't have a choice, Harold."

"Didn't figure I did. That's the way you work, idn't it?"

"I'll get a proposal drawn up, and we can put it behind us. I'll be in touch."

"I'll count on it. Oh, and by the way, just to put your mind at ease, that reporter down here nosing around—he didn't ask about Laurel Grove or any of your other financial interests. Just seemed interested in your judicial record."

"And what did you say?" There was a dismissive sternness in Hunnycut's voice.

"What could I say? Told him I knew you weren't skittish about sending people to their final reward. He did ask if I knew anything about a case involving somebody named Sam Larkin, but I told him I never heard of any Larkins from around here. Well, let me know when you're ready to talk." Musgrave hung up the phone before Hunnycut could respond.

Casey sat on his lap, put her arms around his neck, and rested her head on his shoulder.

"Thornton sounds a bit perturbed," he said.

"You handled it well. Who is this Larkin person? It sounded like you were baiting him with that name."

"I don't know, and I was. That Landers fellow seemed interested in him, and since I never heard the name before, I figure there must be somethin' to it. I prob'ly should have waited for his reaction. I never paid a lot of attention to what Thornton did in court; he kept me too busy tryin' to find ways to make him money. Those damned nursing homes were the worst idea we ever came up with. Never felt right about that."

"Well, maybe we can find a way to get out of them," Casey said. It was a comfort to Musgrave every time he heard Casey say "we."

"He was right about one thing. I never refused the money they made."

"That's in the past, Harold. We'll figure something out," she said.

"I need to find out who this Larkin fellow is." Musgrave smiled. "Know any private eyes?"

"Only one," she said.

He leaned back and looked at her. "Now why in hell would you know a private investigator in New Orleans?"

"Because I had one check you out before I came knocking on your door."

"You're kidding."

"No. I was a new girl in town. Didn't know anybody. Well, except one person. This man on an airplane charms me and offers me a job without knowing what I can do? Sounds a little suspect to me," she said.

"You said you were a secretary. Administrative assistant, actually. It was your political correctness that impressed me. Besides, I was half drunk and wanted to go to bed with you."

"Everybody's a secretary. For all I knew, you might have been seducing me to sell me into the white slave trade."

"They couldn't pay the price."

"I'll take that as a compliment. Anyway, I called the one person I knew in New Orleans, a law clerk, and asked if she knew anyone who could do a background check and worked cheap. She suggested a guy who had done some work for her firm, and I offered him three hundred dollars for two days' work. I figured if he couldn't find out anything bad in two days, the worst you could be was a white-collar criminal who was too smart to get caught, or he was a lousy detective and I was out three hundred dollars."

"And?" he said.

"He found out some stuff that was a little gray, but you weren't married, hadn't been arrested for anything except a DUI, had some powerful friends, and were harmless. After getting the 'all clean' signal, I showed up at your door."

"So it wasn't because you wanted to go to bed with me?"

"That came later. I'm not easy."

"I know. It took three months. Tell me about the investigator."

"Well, he was reluctant to take the job. He said he didn't usually do background checks in such a situation and that his fee was normally three hundred dollars a day. At that point I decided to forget the whole thing, including you and your job offer, and hit the want ads."

"What changed your mind?"

"He took pity on me and said he would do it as a favor for the secretary who referred me."

"He probably wanted to go to bed with you, too," Musgrave said.

"Never met a man who didn't." She gave Musgrave a loving smile. "Actually, he never made a move. I was kind of insulted. In any case, he found out quite a bit about you in a very short time. If you don't know anyone else, he's probably worth talking to."

"So what's this Lochinvar's name?"

"Raymond Gaynaud. I've still got his card if you want me to call him."

"Let's do it. I'm really interested to find out who this Sam Larkin is. I'd like to know about any bullets Thornton's trying to dodge."

"I'll do it, but first . . ." She kissed him. "I love you, old man."

"Hell, all this stuff makes me feel like I'm a member of the FBI, affectionately known to us harmless, white-collar criminals as the Fucking Bureaucratic Imbeciles."

"Be careful. Somebody might be listening," she said.

WHEN SAM AND Karen left the restaurant, the light in the sky had changed, and clouds were moving in from the west. It would be raining by the time they drove back to Biloxi. Her father had taught her to read the light when he was working for the wildlife service. He would take her out on the water with him often—for companionship, he said, father and daughter bonding, but she had always felt it was his way of making up for all the time they didn't have together by giving her an education about the natural world.

The field office was located over a camera shop on Canal Street. The shop's windows advertised, on butcher paper signs, a "Final Going Out of Business Sale." By the look of the sign, the sale had been going on for ten years. The upper floors were accessed by a nondescript doorway that opened to a flight of poorly lit wooden steps, which appeared to be a designated dump for anything passersby wished to get rid of. Odors of urine, stale alcohol, and mildew hit Sam and Karen in the face.

"The standard for DEA field offices seems to have changed," Sam said, stepping over empty wine bottles, newspapers, discarded fliers, and take-out food containers that had begun to sprout.

"I thought we'd be at the district office, but this is the address Neil gave me."

"Interesting," Sam said.

At the top of the stairs were three identical doors with etched-glass windows. None of them identified the name of an occupant, and they appeared vacant. No lights, no shadows moving about, and no noises. Neil's office was the one farthest from the stairs, she had been told.

"You ready?" she asked.

"Why not?" he answered.

The office was nothing more than a long rectangular room, divided loosely into four stations, each consisting of a desk, a chair, a wastebasket, a filing cabinet, a computer, and a telephone. A coffee pot and styrofoam cups sat atop a small refrigerator. Two floor-to-ceiling windows, opaque with grime, looked out over Canal Street. The walls were empty beige, which Sam considered an improvement over the standard government green. Still, it looked more like an illegal sports book than a government office.

Dougherty was alone, seated at the desk in the back of the room. Sam thought he looked much worse for wear than when he'd seen him in Carolina. He had put on a little weight, and his hair was longer and unkempt. He was no longer a federal government poster boy.

Dougherty focused on Karen as he rose from his desk. "I was worried about you," he said. "I can't live with lack of communication from an agent in the field."

"I wasn't ready to talk to you," she said.

"That's it?"

"That's it."

"I'm glad you decided to join us, Larkin. Grab a couple of those desk chairs; nobody else is coming in this afternoon. Coffee?"

"We're fine," Sam said, sitting down.

"Karen?" Dougherty asked.

"As Sam said, we're fine."

Her reply obviously did not sit well. "Would you like to tell me where you two are?" Dougherty directed the question to Karen. Sam saw Dougherty trying to establish authority, pride, maybe even his own image. "The last few days happened. I can't ignore that or say I'm pleased, but I need to know what I can expect from you."

Sam felt Karen looking at him and knew her deference to him irked Dougherty. "I guess the first order of business, Neil, is to correct something you said."

"What's that?"

"I haven't joined you," Sam said.

The response seemed to catch Dougherty off guard. "I'm listening," the agent said.

"I'm here to cooperate, but I am not in the employ of the federal government, and I don't take orders from you or anyone else."

Dougherty stared at him. "I don't believe you're in a position to lay demands on me."

"I would say exactly the opposite. I'm not in any position at all. What I do is voluntary."

"Even volunteers take direction. So, what I will tell you before we go any further," Dougherty continued, "is that you will not get in the way of our investigation, and you will not say anything—I mean anything—to anyone regarding our work. At this point no one knows we are investigating Senator Hunnycut. We're not even in the area, officially, and that's the way it has to stay."

"That's a position we share. Like you, no one knows I'm here, and that's safer for me. I don't believe I'll live very long if anyone knows I'm back in Louisiana looking for answers."

"If you're important enough to get rid of, why didn't they do it in prison? Angola is not a particularly safe place to hide," Dougherty said.

"They tried. They couldn't. But in some ways, I was safer on the inside. Officially or unofficially, I'm not supposed to be in this state."

"Part of your pardon agreement?"

"Part. Not all," Sam said.

"Well, that's a big part of what we want to find out. How your release was orchestrated, who was involved, how the records were removed, where that generous compensation originated, and how it was disguised. Most of all, we want to know why."

"I do, too."

"I assume you have something in mind. Tell me what it is."

"First, that I'm not a piece of bait. You have to let me in on the playbook. Every step of the way. I have to know what you're looking for, where you're looking for it, and how. And I don't want to ever be followed or mentioned in any of your reports without my permission."

"And what do we get from you?"

"I'll keep you informed of everything I learn that pertains to your investigation, but that's all. If I have to expose my presence to achieve what I want, I will. That will be my choice. I won't compromise your investigation, so I trust you won't compromise mine."

Dougherty sat with his hands together, forefingers steepled over his lips. He got up from his chair, turned around to the windows, and gazed down toward Canal Street. After a few moments, he turned back to them.

"Right now we're pursuing information in several different areas, on several different levels. Some of it just involves research, and some covert work is also being undertaken—"

"Come on, Neil," Karen interrupted. "You sound like you're giving a press conference. Just talk to us."

Dougherty gave her a look. She knew it went against his grain for him to share information with a civilian, but in this case, he had no alternative.

When he spoke again, he spoke to Sam. "I have a team of four agents: two in the District, and Karen and I here. Again, as far as the Agency is concerned, we've been dropped behind enemy lines, and they don't know who we are."

"Why?" Sam asked, wondering if the man would be truthful.

"Because the FBI doesn't want to get caught in the shit. The director's doing a favor for a friend."

"I was told the check was for Harrison James," Sam said.

"You said you weren't interested in the politics of the operation." Dougherty smiled. "In any case, four associates is all I feel comfortable with. I'll be honest, Larkin. You make me nervous, but you are our best bet for turning over the rocks."

Sam started to speak, but Dougherty silenced him with a gesture. "You said you wanted to know everything. Let me talk. I have one agent in Washington working on the senator's congressional dealings. The clout behind a significant portion of his decision-making appears to be Marlene Cole, a former assistant, probable lover, and highly influential lobbyist. I'm not sure even Hunnycut knows how much income she has or its source, but it's huge, and she's powerful in her own right. We're trying to tie his influence to her clients, which, in itself, would eliminate him as a vice presidential possibility, but only if they've broken the rules, which it appears so far they've managed to skirt.

"Second, we're checking into his judicial record here in Louisiana. Of course, irregularities in that area are hard to prove and easy to hide. The problem is, we can't use your case as an example because, as of right now, it doesn't exist. The good news is, we can use your case because it doesn't exist. Thank God for paradoxes. And third, we are investigating his business interests and the legislation in those areas that has been of major benefit to those interests. We know Hunnycut has a cadre of associates—Arthur Valdrine, the state administrator, and a lawyer, Jordan Pettigrew, among others."

Karen saw Sam tense but said nothing.

"We're trying to lock down the details on the nature of these relationships and any other illegal activities that might have occurred over the years. There is also Harold Musgrave, a business associate of Hunnycut's, who we understand has a drinking problem and who may be the most vulnerable of the bunch. He could be our avenue. I put nothing out of the realm of possibility with these people, especially Hunnycut himself. I also believe ambition is his Achilles' heel, and the VP possibility is enough of a carrot to make him careless. That's it. I've told you everything we're doing."

"You didn't tell me how you're going about it," Sam said.

"And I won't at this juncture. That's for your protection and the protection of my field agents. That's the ballgame, Larkin, but if this investigation is compromised by you or Karen, God help you."

"Don't try to use me, Dougherty, unless I give you permission."

"Understood."

BACK ON THE street, Karen could see that Sam was not pleased with what had taken place.

"You don't like Neil, do you, Sam?"

"I don't trust him," he said without breaking stride. "There's a difference. Whether I like him or not is inconsequential. There are many people I don't like whom I would trust with my life. He's not one of them. Not yet anyway."

Karen paused. "Sam, who's Pettigrew? You reacted."

"Just a name that sounded familiar."

She knew it wasn't the truth, but now was not the time to press the issue. She trusted Sam. He would tell her what he knew when it was pertinent.

IT WAS LATE afternoon before Casey reached the private investigator.

"Raymond Gaynaud," the voice answering the telephone said. It was resonant but not intimidating, not very businesslike, one of the reasons she'd liked him the first time she called.

"Mr. Gaynaud, this is Casey Landrieu. You did some work for me several years ago."

"Casey Landrieu. Three hundred dollars. Two days' work. Checking out an oil man. Musgrave, I think. Tall. I remember you as tall. And striking. I hope you're not calling to tell me my information was wrong and you want a refund."

"Do you really remember all that, or are you cleaning out your files, and, by some serendipitous coincidence, mine happened to be on top?"

"I remember. In my profession that's a requirement. To forget can be dangerous. What can I do for you, Ms. Landrieu?"

"As you recall, I'm sure, I asked you to research Mr. Musgrave because I was considering taking a job with him."

"Yes. You met on a plane from Atlanta, and you weren't sure whether he was legitimate or not."

"Amazing," she said. "I did take the job, and it's worked out very well."

"I'm happy to hear that," Gaynaud said. "Does that qualify me for a bonus?"

She laughed. "Harold—Mr. Musgrave—needs some information on someone regarding a business transaction, and, based on how efficiently you worked for me, I suggested we contact you."

"I appreciate that. I would imagine, considering this is business, that this will be a little different than what I did for you before, and, since I'm sure he's not as attractive as you, I will warn you that the cost will be greater."

She heard the grin in his voice. "I assumed that. Your fee for something like this?"

"Let's start at three hundred dollars a day. If the assignment proves difficult or dangerous, we'll discuss an increase. Remember my work isn't limited to an eight hour day, so—"

"You don't have to convince me, Mr. Gaynaud. I called you, remember? That figure seems fair."

"Then I guess we're ready to proceed. Who are you looking for, what am I supposed to find out, and what's the time frame?"

"We would like this done as soon as possible. Several things are hanging in the balance, and Harold can't make a decision until he gets this information. A client of Harold's mentioned the name of a man with whom he's associated, and we just want to know who this man is, what he does, and where he might be located. Harold doesn't like to be in the position of not knowing who he's doing business with," she said.

"A name might be useful," Gaynaud said.

"Of course. The man's name is Sam Larkin. That's really all we know, other than he's probably from Baton Rouge or New Orleans. Certainly Louisiana."

There was silence.

"Mr. Gaynaud?"

"Yes. I was just thinking. It would help a lot if I know who this Larkin is associated with and what his business might be with Mr. Musgrave."

Gaynaud's voice had changed. Still friendly and comfortable, but confused now, Casey thought.

"Harold has a number of deals with the government. You know, construction, oil. Consequently, he has to keep everything totally confidential. He doesn't want anyone to know about this investigation. Can you work with that?" she asked.

"Give me a couple of days. If I can help you, we've got a deal. If I can't, you don't owe me anything."

That he was ready to end the conversation was obvious, and the change in his voice puzzling, but two days was not a long wait considering that Sam Larkin might just be dust some misguided reporter was blowing in the wind. "I can't ask for more than that, Mr. Gaynaud," she said.

"Raymond, if you'd like."

"I like. Thank you."

"As is always said, I'll be in touch."

When the phone was back in its cradle, Gaynaud sat back and focused on the wall in front of him. "Sam Larkin," he said to the quiet of his office. "Wow."

VALDRINE WAITED UNTIL the end of the day to call Hunnycut regarding Landers. With Sam Larkin's name having been thrown into the mix, it wasn't a call he was eager to make.

"Hello, Thornton," he said, consciously maintaining a businesslike tone.

"Arthur? Kind of late for a call, isn't it? Must be something important."

"I just want to keep you informed. There's a reporter down here researching you. He's talked to Jordan Pettigrew."

"I hope Jordan told him what a valuable asset I am to the state of Louisiana," Hunnycut said.

"I'm sure he did, but from what I gather, he's doing more than just a profile."

"How so?" The sound of impatience was prominent in the senator's voice.

"Most of his interest, Jordan said, was in your judicial career."

"Has he contacted you?"

"He called; I haven't responded, but I will. We can't hide from these things, Thornton. There is, however, one disturbing note."

"Damn it, Arthur, lay it out for me."

"He brought up the name Sam Larkin." There was silence on the other end. "Asked Jordan if he knew who he was."

Valdrine waited for an explosion, but there was none, just a serious note in the senator's voice. "Tomorrow morning, Arthur. Be at Louis Armstrong at eight o'clock. I'll have a plane waiting for you. We need to talk, and I want to do it in Washington." The line went dead.

It wasn't a request; it was an order. And that did not sit well with Arthur Valdrine.

# NINE

EARLY SUNLIGHT STOLE in through the slats of the blinds, lightening with a warm red aura the room in which Sam Larkin lay. It was time to begin. He got out of bed, made coffee, and was sitting in a rocker on the deck when he heard Karen finally moving around inside, fixing coffee for herself, and heading in his direction.

"Another perfect day in paradise," she said as she came through the door, wearing an oversized T-shirt that looked familiar, one of his she had taken possession of during a stay in Carolina. She wore nothing under the shirt, which revealed a vague suggestion of her nipples. He liked that about her; she was totally uninhibited about her body and what she did with it when they were in bed. He momentarily second-guessed his decision to sleep in the guest room, but it was where he had to be for the present.

"Nice outfit," he said. "I wondered what had become of that shirt."

"I told you: once I wear something it's mine." She gave him a no-nonsense smile, making him wonder about a possible double-entendre. She leaned against the deck railing, looking at him.

"I forgot," he said.

"Don't." She sipped her coffee and continued. "Sam, I think it's time for you to let me in on what's going on in that mind of yours. Let me know what we're doing. Where to start. What you want me to do. I need some direction."

He looked up at her. "You said professionals start with background. Consider that a starting point. You're all alone in this. Where do you start?"

"That 'all alone.' You're being hypothetical, aren't you?" she asked.

"If I'm here, you're not alone."

She left the railing and sat in the rocker next to his. "Easy stuff first. Records," she said.

"What kind?" he asked.

"We already know a lot of background stuff; forget that. Gray areas: we know he has a house in Gulfport. Any business interests he has there, and anything else that has money or influence as its basis. People: who he associates with other than the obvious, particularly people with whom there is no logical connection. Most important, anyone who knows anything about your case."

"That last one should be a short list," he said.

"In Carolina, you always had the right answer, yet I never saw you thinking. You did what needed to be done and damn the consequences. Where is that guy? I kind of liked him."

"He's still there. You said Hunnycut had a house in Gulfport. Start there." He waited for an argument, but got none.

"And while I'm tracing real estate transactions, what are you going to be doing?"

"Going to Shreveport."

Karen was silent, and for the first time since his return, he saw true uneasiness on her face.

EXITING THE PRIVATE Lear 35 at Washington National Airport, Valdrine fought to keep his displeasure disguised. He didn't like anyone, regardless of who it was or what their motives might be, to exercise control over him. But Hunnycut had left no room for compromise. Valdrine could only hope the coming meeting would give him an opportunity to vent his ire.

A gray Cadillac was waiting on the tarmac. He had expected a limo, the transport Hunnycut usually arranged for him. The change in standard was demeaning. He was put farther off balance when the car took him to Georgetown and stopped in front of a Federal-style brick home.

"This is the house," the driver said without turning around.

Valdrine sat without moving.

The driver made no move to get out and open the door for him. Valdrine got out of the car, shot his cuffs, yanked the alligator briefcase from the seat, and slammed the door. As soon as he was out, the car moved away.

Marlene Cole answered the door. Her short, dark hair and brilliant blue eyes created a perfectly balanced composition of beauty and sensuality. Although Valdrine had seen her many times before and didn't particularly care for her, he had never seen her looking quite as appealing as she did on this early morning.

"Good morning, Arthur." She stepped aside to let him enter.

"Marlene," he said, trying to conceal his surprise and discomfort at being there.

"Thornton is in the living room; you can go on back. Can I get you some coffee?"

"That would be wonderful," he said as he started down the hallway.

"Arthur." Thornton Hunnycut dropped the morning edition of the *Washington Post* to the floor and lifted himself from his chair. "I'm glad you could make it."

"I don't believe you gave me a choice, Thornton," he answered in a clipped voice. The whole idea and circumstance of this meeting were discomfiting. "I expected your office. But this is a beautiful place. I didn't know senators lived like this."

"I don't. It's Marlene's. I felt this would be more private and secure for what we have to discuss. We've got some problems, and I need your help." He didn't give the administrator an opportunity to respond. "Don't worry, Arthur, you will profit by their being solved."

"*We* have problems?"

"We. Come down off your pedestal. Don't ever think you're invulnerable."

Marlene came back into the room with a tray holding a silver carafe, three china cups, croissants, butter, and a variety of jellies. Valdrine was uneasy with her joining them.

"Thornton, I have to be right up front about this, and if it offends you or Marlene, so be it. I am not comfortable discussing any of what you seem to think is so critical with anyone other than you, and—"

Hunnycut held up his hand. "Marlene is already privy to enough to put me in jail for two hundred years. In addition to that, she is my insurance and a helluva lot harder to deal with than I am. If that doesn't sit well, then I can call the car to take you back to the airport. And you can take your own chances."

Valdrine heard the finality in Hunnycut's voice and wondered if he would make it to the airport alive if he chose to leave.

"I would think hard on it," Hunnycut said, "because if I do become vice president, you might find the Washington lifestyle to your liking."

"What are you suggesting?" Valdrine asked.

"If I deliver the South for James, I will have significant input on some of his cabinet choices. I have already established with him that I will not be a presidential shadow."

"And how did he take that?"

"He was impressed. Talking to him, you'd think he's a fucking innocent. Exactly what he wants the public and maybe even the party to perceive. *Mister Smith Goes to Washington*. But you and I know you don't get this far if you're naive. He's got someone doing his dirty work."

"And if he gets elected, that will be your job? Doing the dirty work?"

"I would imagine; it's the job of most vice presidents—that and damage control—but it also gives me leverage on who's on the team."

"Attorney general?"

"Not out of the question. You certainly have the qualifications, and if the South gets him elected, he will have to give them something in return. Hell, even a lunch date in Washington requires a payback." Hunnycut smiled.

"I'll go along with whatever you say for the moment, but, as I said, I'm not comfortable." He could feel Marlene Cole's eyes burning down on him. It was obvious that she didn't like him any better than he liked her.

"I'm not concerned with your comfort. Let's move on."

"I'm listening."

"Yesterday I spoke with Harold Musgrave. It seems the reporter who's calling you went to see him as well. Man named Landers. I checked with the paper he said he worked for, the *New Centurion*, and they did acknowledge he was one of theirs. What bothers me is why they would send him all the way to New Orleans. I mean, they're a low-circulation, right-wing rag that's hardly making it financially, and they pay a reporter to go to Louisiana when I'm right here? Seems they'd contact me first. Doesn't make sense." Hunnycut was up and looking out the window. "I wonder if it's a ruse."

"Maybe they're trying to make a name for themselves. Finding the right story first can give a paper such as that a lot of credibility. More important, I would think, is what Harold might've said to the man."

"According to him, virtually nothing. But he did say, as you did, that this Landers was more interested in my judicial career than anything else."

"Your record there is more than exemplary."

Hunnycut turned back to Valdrine. "That reporter mentioned Sam Larkin. Hell, Arthur, Harold didn't know about that mess, so how could he bring up that name on his own?"

"He couldn't."

"Well, obviously he did. What about Jordan?" Hunnycut asked.

"That would be absurd. He would be putting himself in jeopardy. Landers didn't get that name from Jordan, believe me. He knows the penalty for that."

"If that's true, we've got to find out where Landers is getting his information. If he's aware of Larkin, he may know about a lot more skeletons in the cupboard. But more importantly," Hunnycut said, "he's approached Scottie."

"Landers?"

"Literally broke up a dinner date she had with a friend. That's going over the line. Jordan, Harold, now Scottie. That's three strikes." There was no misinterpreting the look in Hunnycut's eyes and no temperature low enough to describe it.

Marlene had said nothing, but Valdrine knew she was cataloging everything being said. He didn't know whether she knew the story behind Hunnycut's concern with Sam Larkin or not. The man was a skeleton; Hunnycut was correct on that.

"Any idea where Larkin is now?" Valdrine asked.

"I put that case in the dead file a long time ago."

"Maybe we need to find him."

"If you don't, my career in Washington may be over, and yours won't ever start. These threats need to be eliminated."

"I get your point. You don't need to belabor it. Anything the present AG can do to help?"

"Couldn't, shouldn't, wouldn't. He's the most pristine candy-ass I've ever come into contact with. Add incompetent to that. There's something going on in Louisiana that I don't know anything about. I know the party will be doing background checks before the convention, but it's a little early for that, and they don't use newspaper reporters to do their work for them publicly. This guy's working out in the open. Like he wants a reaction. He's a maverick, and he must have a source."

"Maybe not. You know reporters. They create as many stories out of whole cloth as politicians do fears and conspiracies."

"But they don't make up names like Sam Larkin."

"I'll meet with him and handle that. Anything else bothering you besides Larkin?" Valdrine asked.

"Musgrave. He's not running true to form. When I spoke to him, he sounded like a man holding a full house who knows the most anyone else has is two pairs."

"Was he drinking?"

"When is he not? What he wasn't willing to discuss was buying me out of Laurel Grove without school funds from the government being released and some assurances that the HCFA and the state health department will get off his back. He says he doesn't have any money to buy Laurel Grove until the funds are released to the schools, so he can begin to fulfill his construction contracts."

"If you want out, why would you suggest he buy you out? Why not just pay him off to get your name clear of it?"

"First, it wouldn't pass scrutiny if I just gave it to him, and, second, because I hate to give that son of a bitch anything. More significantly, if it ever should come out that I had an interest in that corporation, I want to be able to say I sold out because he was pressuring me to use my influence to create favorable legislation for him."

"That sounds prudent."

"He's blackmailing me, Arthur. He's screwed up so many deals with me over the years with booze, women, and gambling that I can't count them, but the bastard knows too goddamn much for me to ignore him. He's a leech of the first degree. Laurel Grove will not be the end of it. Believe me."

"Still, a payoff is the logical step, and I'm sure you can handle the HCFA. I will have no trouble with the state."

Hunnycut turned and gave him a hard look. "Do that, and he'll come up with something else. I don't trust that bastard an inch."

"Are you asking me for an alternative solution to the problem?"

"What I'm asking you to do is whatever you have to do to guarantee that Musgrave is not a threat and Landers is off my case."

"Maybe Marlene can help with that," Valdrine said. "I'm sure she has numerous press contacts."

"I do," she said, "but we have to protect Thornton at all costs. If they get an indication—"

"I'm aware of that, Marlene." Valdrine cut her off with a note of condescending superiority then turned to Hunnycut. "Never mind, Thornton. I'll do whatever's necessary. What else?"

"I think those are the two major problems. Of course, I do expect you to exercise your influence with those political friends you mentioned before."

"Rest assured."

"That's a nice phrase, Arthur. Oh, and one other thing. Don't ever try to exclude Marlene from anything we do. If you're speaking with her, you're speaking with me, and if you're speaking with me, you're speaking with her. Keep that in mind."

Valdrine looked at Marlene. There was nothing in her eyes. He and Ms. Cole would have their day, and he was looking forward to it. "Advice taken," he said.

Hunnycut put his hand on the administrator's shoulder. "You are my right-hand man, Arthur, and my friend, and you will never regret it." He smiled. "Rest assured."

"I'm counting on that."

"Now that the business is taken care of, I've got a table reserved at the 116 Club. We could go to the Capital Grill, but that's all politics. The 116 is open to the public, a more catholic zoo. It's not too early for your face to start being seen around the Hill." Hunnycut looked at Valdrine. "Marlene's suggestion."

"Thank you," Valdrine said, and nodded in deference to the lady.

GAYNAUD LOOKED AT the papers scattered on his desk. Although he had been jolted at hearing Sam Larkin's name after so many years, even more surprising was what he had not been able to find out about the man. Ol' Sam was still a mystery. Larkin had served time, that much he knew, and why. But that he could find no record of it—no trial record, no probation hearings, and no date of release—was beyond belief. That there was no evidence of the man's existence after Angola was even more perplexing.

All the facts he could gather, along with what he knew, suggested that Larkin had performed a disappearing act and covered his tracks well. It was just the kind of problem that teased Gaynaud's curiosity and challenged his abilities.

"Well, well, well, Sam. What have you gone and gotten yourself into?" he said to the window. He'd had a lot of conversation with that window; it helped him think.

"I think it's time for a reunion," he said.

JUDGE ARTIS GAYNAUD was sitting on a stone bench in the immaculate back garden of his manse on St. Charles Street. This was a meditative ritual performed at the beginning of each day, a ritual begun years before when he was more active on the bench than he presently was and needed to prepare quietly for a day's dealing with other people's miseries.

Gaynaud startled his father when he walked through the creaky garden gate. It was the first time in ten years he had visited the house in which he had grown up. His absence had been mutually agreeable. Telephone calls were the extent of the relationship between father and son. They had not been face to face since Gaynaud's mother had been buried three years previous.

"Raymond?" the judge asked as he worked to push himself to his feet with the aid of his walking stick. "I didn't expect this."

"Judge," Gaynaud said. "No need to get up. I apologize for disturbing you during your quiet time. I just need to ask a couple of questions, and I'll be on my way." He thought of the childhood warnings against interrupting the judge's daily quiet time.

The old man sat back down slowly. "You caught me by surprise," he said.

"You're looking well."

"I'm old. First damned thing in my life I never had to make a decision about. It's not fun. Hell, it isn't even interesting."

"Wow, a joke. Be glad you've had your years; a lot of people don't get as many," Gaynaud said, settling himself cross-legged on the grass, facing his father.

"Find something else on the Prather murders?"

"No. You asked for an analysis. There wasn't much there that a rookie beat cop couldn't have picked up in a minute. It was a hit. Not much else to be said."

"Well, it doesn't seem to be going away. That Prather boy—"

"Bridey?" Gaynaud still found the name humorous.

"I get about one call every other day from him. Believes it's some kind of conspiracy and that everyone from the police to the Dixie Mafia is involved."

"Not much I can do about that."

"Well, Bridey keeps pushing."

"I need you to repay that favor, Judge."

"I don't believe I owe you any favors, Raymond."

"Okay, then I'm asking for a favor." He couldn't hide his annoyance. "I'm working on a background check for a client, and I'm running into a brick wall. The guy was in prison ten or twelve years ago, that I know; but there's no record of it. No record of the trial, no prison record, no release. And there's nothing to suggest that he's been in Louisiana since that time."

"Where'd you get your information?"

"An informant. And, before you ask, the informant is reliable."

"You have a name for this man?"

"Sam Larkin."

There was silence.

"Judge?"

"I never heard of the man. Now I've got to get to court; I'm sorry I can't help you."

The judge was lying, and Gaynaud thought he discerned fear in the old man's voice. "I know that's not true. I'm going to find out the story. I know the man was in prison. There's got to be a reason."

"Raymond, even I could not have the record of a trial expunged. You know enough to know that. Whoever told you there was a trial—this informant you say you have, hell, even if Larkin himself told you there was a trial—was lying."

"Not under normal circumstances, but there are people who can do most anything in this state. Legal people, politicians. Hell, maybe it goes beyond Louisiana. I have no idea why no records exist, but I won't stop looking." He stood. "I just wish you would make it a little easier for me."

"Why are you so interested in this Sam Larkin?"

Gaynaud searched his father's eyes. Why not, he thought. "He saved my life."

Judge Gaynaud shook his head negatively but remained silent. His son turned and moved in the direction of the garden gate. As he reached for the latch, he heard his father's voice, dry and old, like a winter-bound, brown leaf blowing in the wind.

"It does go beyond Louisiana, Raymond."

He turned to see his father walking, stooped and slow, back into the house. There was helpless resignation in the old man's posture.

PATOOT'S ACROSS THE Lake was a step up from the trendy chains such as T.G.I. Friday's or Bennigan's. Pettigrew spotted Valdrine in a booth in the back of the dining area. That was surprising; the man usually arrived a few minutes late, making a statement that he was too busy to be on time. Given Valdrine's nasty tone when he'd called to set up the meeting, Pettigrew had been careful to arrive on time. Exactly.

But he had also promised himself that Valdrine and Hunnycut would no longer control him.

"Arthur," he said, as he sat down.

"You're on time."

"Always."

Pettigrew squeezed the lemon slice into the water glass already set out for him and took a sip. "So, Arthur, what is it that you want to talk about?"

"Sam Larkin," Valdrine said.

No preliminaries. Straight to it. Pettigrew set the glass back on the table before his hand had a chance to shake. Larkin's name, especially coming from Valdrine, put his adrenaline in overdrive. "What brings him up?" he asked.

"Thornton Hunnycut, Harold Musgrave, and that reporter from Washington." He gave Pettigrew an accusing look. "Who have you discussed Larkin with, Jordan?"

"No one. Parker Hamill years ago, but he's dead, as you well know."

"Let's not get into that. No one else?"

"No." Pettigrew found the strength to look Valdrine in the eye. "Why don't you tell me what's happened."

"According to Musgrave, the reporter asked him if he was familiar with the name, and then Musgrave pointedly mentioned that to Thornton."

"Thornton finally called him?"

"He's trying to extricate himself from Laurel Grove, and Musgrave isn't being cooperative. On top of that, he's throwing Larkin's name around. Thornton flew me to Washington to discuss it. He wants to find out how Landers got that name. You came up."

"I have no idea. I've not mentioned it to anyone. I know what's at stake," Pettigrew said. His stomach was rolling, and his head had begun to throb. He worked at keeping his face expressionless. It was like trying to see how long he could hold his breath under water.

"Hamill knew the risk as well, but he tried to use it anyway. Don't make that mistake, Jordan. Did Musgrave ever mention that name to you before he spoke with the reporter?"

"No. I haven't thought of that man in years," Pettigrew said.

"That's good. I'll tell Thornton that it wasn't you, but you have to do something. See what you can get out of Musgrave. He trusts you. Ask him about the interview. What the reporter asked and what he said. We have to run this down."

"I'll do what I can."

"Any attention to that name has to be stopped before it sees the light of day," Valdrine said.

"I agree," Pettigrew said. He had buried his guilt about Sam Larkin long before, and he didn't want it resurrected. On the other hand, if it came to a matter of survival, Larkin could be an ace up his sleeve.

Valdrine looked at his watch, drained the last bit of scotch from his glass, and slid out of the booth. "I'll expect to hear from you later tonight. The latest by tomorrow morning," he said, as he stood up and shot his cuffs.

"I'll give him a call."

"Do that," Valdrine said, and left the restaurant.

Pettigrew remained seated, silently sipping his water, settling his nerves. He couldn't imagine Larkin's rising phoenixlike from the ashes of their collective past, yet he had. And that was bad news. Then again, maybe it was good news for Pettigrew. Who knew?

# TEN

KAREN DIDN'T SLEEP much. Aside from snippets of uneasy rest, for most of the night she found herself watching the clock on the night table and counting off the minutes until dawn. She tried to concentrate on the charge she had undertaken: real estate transactions, financial background, business investments. But her thoughts repeatedly refocused on Sam and Celine.

Just after six she heard Sam rummaging around, closing the back door, and leaving the parking lot in the old Rover. She had waited for a touch, a word, anything. He was gentle and thoughtful, but nothing beyond that, as though there had never been anything more between them. It hurt, but she had been patient. Now, lying in bed, knowing where he was going, she began to wonder if she would ever see him again.

She got up and went into the kitchen. Sam had already made coffee. There was a note beside the mug, sugar bowl, and spoon he had set out for her.

*I hope I didn't wake you. Have a good day. I will call and let you know where you can reach me. Sam*

She balled up the note and threw it in the trash can. Sam Larkin was incorrigible. His thoughtfulness in making coffee for her, and then his thoughtlessness in leaving a note that contained all the emotion of an office memo.

She took her mug into the office. She had never allowed emotions to get in the way of work, but now she found herself doing little else. Taking care of business at hand would help her get back on track.

She dialed Neil's number. While the phone was ringing, she visualized Sam in the Rover, wondering what was going through his mind.

"Hello?" the voice answered.

"No *Dougherty*? No *This is your DEA*?" she asked.

"I'm very unofficial these days. What's up?"

"I just thought you'd like to know where we are."

"That's a surprise. Does the Lone Ranger know you're calling?"

"No. He's gone. On his way to Thibodaux to see if he can track down Celine." Using Sam's ex-wife's name gave her an uncomfortable feeling of intimacy with the woman. "He checked with information in Shreveport yesterday, and there was no Celine Larkin or Celine Aguillard listed, so he decided the best place to start was with her father in Thibodaux."

"Sounds like a plan. What about you?"

"I'm going to the chancery clerk's office in Biloxi and research the purchase of Hunnycut's Gulfport house and any other holdings in Harrison County that have his name on them."

"I'd also like to suggest that Larkin eventually contact the attorneys who represented him at his trial. They have to know something and can't claim client privilege with him. I don't want him to do it right away; it would expose him, which neither he nor I think is wise at this point. But eventually."

"Why didn't you check out those people when I was in Carolina?"

"Think, Karen. I couldn't have found the lawyers because there was no record of a trial, not to mention they wouldn't have to tell me anything. And I didn't check out the wife because Larkin admitted he'd been in prison. After that, things happened so fast, it was over before I could get started. It was a pretty frantic three or four days."

"I recall," she said, "but it seems like a cakewalk compared to what we're doing now. We're like a boat in a fog bank."

"I've got some things going here. I think we'll see some responsive action soon, and if the Hunnycut group does respond, they'll make mistakes."

"They have to be pretty good about not making mistakes to have gotten this far. I just want this thing over. I'd like to get back to a normal life. Give me a good ol' drug peddler any day."

Dougherty laughed.

"It's not funny."

"Emotions and profession getting in each other's way?" he asked.

"Damn you."

"You're beginning to say that a lot," he said. "Karen, thank you." His voice was gentle. "I owe you."

"You certainly do," she said.

"Keep me posted."

"Same."

When she hung up, she thought about what Neil had said. Sam had never told her much about his defense attorney. He was weak, he'd said. Led him down the primrose path with "don't worrys," but there had never been a discussion of any depth. She couldn't recall Sam ever mentioning his name. There was nothing she could do on that front until he got back.

NO SENSE OF urgency bedeviled Sam as he drove Highway 90 toward Louisiana, despite his having awakened early, anxious to get on the road. "Journey proud" his parents had called it, the childlike, Christmas Eve anxiety and excitement before a trip. Not that his family had taken many. Maybe that was the reason for it. Like those infrequent trips, this was something different. Going to see an ex-wife who might not know he was still alive. What he couldn't decide was if he was being fueled by anxiety, curiosity, or excitement.

The drive was three hours by interstate. Taking Highway 90 through Waggaman and Mimosa Park to Boutte, and then south through Vallier and Des Allemands before turning west on Route 1 through Raceland and the sugar cane plantations would take more time, which was what he wanted. It was an easy choice.

When he entered the Cajun country, he didn't see as many changes as he had in other parts of the state. Cajuns were not prone to change. There were some new commercial enterprises—food stores, motel chains, and gift shops primarily—but the swamp and plantation tours, along with Cajun crafts and historic museums, still appeared to be the backbone of the meager local economies. Those and sugar cane.

He decided to get a motel room in Thibodaux before driving out to Boudreaux Aguillard's place. A shower and fresh clothes would make him more presentable. He found a Ramada Inn that, he suspected from the looks of it, had once been locally owned and more recently put under the banner of the national chain. There was nothing modern about the place, but it was inexpensive and would serve his purpose.

Unpacking, he found the same questions regarding Celine again at the forefront of his thinking. What would he say? What would she say? Did she know he was out of prison? He couldn't imagine how; there had been no newspaper or TV reports of his release. Would she welcome him with open arms? Want to start over? Rebuild their life together? Would he consider it? Would seeing her bring everything back to life? Would it be a Hollywood ending? He didn't think so.

HARRY LANDERS WAS surprised that Commissioner Arthur Valdrine had made himself available so easily. He had agreed to a meeting without hesitation. Unusual for a politician of Valdrine's generation, Landers thought, but good fortune is good fortune.

When he entered the commissioner's office at 11:30, he hadn't anticipated either the number of people waiting to see the man or the variety—every type from the expected suits to a ferret-faced guy dressed like a poverty-stricken Elvis Presley. Landers was ushered in before the others.

"Mr. Landers," Valdrine said, rising from his desk and coming forward to shake hands.

"I appreciate your seeing me, sir."

"Well, we're very proud of our senator. Have a seat." He gestured to a chair sitting to the left of his desk. "But I'm not sure I can tell you anything that you don't already know."

"As I mentioned on the phone, we are pretty sure we have what we need regarding Senator Hunnycut's political career in Washington, but to make the portrait complete we'd like to know more about his career in Louisiana. Any significant accomplishments you can tell me about that might not be a matter of public record, particularly his part in state politics and his judicial career?"

Valdrine smiled. "It would take me all day to list the things Senator Hunnycut has done for this state." He spent the next twenty minutes giving a thumbnail sketch of a politician and judge whose reputation might be rivaled only by Judge Learned Hand's. Finally he looked at the grandfather clock in the far corner of the office and signaled the end of the interview.

"I hope what I've told you helps, Mr. Landers. If you'll excuse me, I have to get back to the business of government." He rose from his chair, shot his cuffs, and came around the desk.

"I appreciate your time, Commissioner. This has been very helpful."

They shook hands, and Landers started to leave but stopped before he got to the door and turned back to Valdrine. "One other thing. Are you familiar with the name Sam Larkin?"

Valdrine's expression didn't change. "No, I can't say that I am."

"The name came up in our research," the reporter said. "No one seems to know him."

"Sorry. Can't help you."

"Well. Again, thank you."

"Happy to help," Valdrine said, smiling, as Landers left the office.

Walking through the reception area, Landers noticed that Elvis had left the building.

“THORNTON? TELL ME about Sam Larkin. Who is he?” Marlene asked. They were having a late breakfast.

“Nobody really,” he said, sipping his coffee.

“Don’t give me that. He must be somebody, or you wouldn’t have flown Valdrine all the way up here to discuss him. I don’t like being left out.”

“We didn’t discuss him. I just told him I couldn’t understand why that reporter mentioned his name. We did talk about other things if you recall. I need Arthur’s support. Simple as that.” There was rebuke in his voice. Not angry, but sharp.

“You’re holding out on me, Thornton.”

He looked at her, showing his sincere politician’s face, a sure indication that he was about to lie.

“Sam Larkin was involved in a federal case I adjudicated ten or fifteen years ago. It was nothing of significance. His name bothers me because this is not the time for some lowlife to start bringing my judgments into question. They always do, trying to get decisions overturned. It happens in every judge’s life, but it would be a distraction now.”

“Is he still in jail?”

“As far as I know. Sam Larkin is not important, just an irritation.” He smiled. “What is important is you and what I can do for you today.”

“Other than the obvious, I could use some help on the HMO legislation. The AMA is upset with some of the limits and restrictions a couple of your constituents are proposing. The good right’s strong push is getting stronger where my clients are concerned. They want to eliminate any modifications and limits, and, of course, they’re using the old socialized medicine ploy. It’s becoming a war between the doctors, the AARP, and the insurance companies, and I can't advise my clients what's going to happen."

"Wait 'til they hear what's being proposed on tort reform. Nobody will be able to sue anybody for anything. Then you'll have the doctors, hospitals, and big business celebrating and the lawyers, AARP, and general public ready to start a shooting war. I think they're both going to be big campaign issues."

"I know you have to be careful, but I need to know if this HMO thing's going to pass."

"Probably not. Certainly not the way it stands. I can handle most of the swing Democrats and probably even a few Republicans without jeopardizing my position. At least enough to keep it from coming up any time soon."

"That might keep the wolves away from my door for a little while, but we need to get something definitive I can tell them."

"Trust me," he said.

"I heard that once from a guy with his pants down," she said.

"I never get the last word."

"You never will."

Hunnycut got up from his chair, laughing. "My dear, if you'll excuse me, I've got a country to govern."

"Not yet, but that day may be closer than you think." She would be patient, but she wouldn't forget about Sam Larkin.

# ELEVEN

KAREN SAT ON the deck of the condo, going through the notes she had made at the chancery clerk's office. Like employees in most small-town governmental offices, infused with their own importance and a decided paranoia about strangers' peeking into their personal domain, those working for the chancery clerk gave help grudgingly and served what they did give her with a lot of questions. In the end, however, what she discovered opened a number of doors for inquiry.

The history of ownership of the senator's Gulfport house was murky. A number of transactions involving the property had taken place over a very short period of time, and not even fluctuations in the real estate market could explain why the property's value had moved up and down to such extremes in the lead-up to Hunnycut's ownership.

In the clerk's office, she hadn't taken the time for analysis, just hastily written down the basics of each transaction. She hadn't wanted to provoke any more curiosity than that occasioned by her simple presence, so she had hidden her interest in the variations in sale price.

The first step in the ladder of ownership was an attorney named Masley Prather. Now that she had time to think, the name jumped out at her. His murder had been headline news in the local paper the day she had arrived in Biloxi. She ripped her notes from the legal pad and began editing and outlining the facts she had into an organized chain of ownership and relationships.

Prather had been paid in cash and all of the tax bills, appraisals, assessments, and property owner's notices sent to a Biloxi address belonging to Gustave Sykorus. The house had then been sold to Parker

Hamill for more than a hundred thousand dollars below the appraised value and previous purchase price.

Within six months, Hamill had passed the property on to Arthur Valdrine for the original appraised value. A quick profit of a hundred thousand dollars. It couldn't be coincidence that the difference in both sales was exactly one hundred thousand dollars.

Valdrine had then turned around and sold the house to Hunnycut for two hundred thousand dollars less than he himself had paid. Hunnycut had come out at least two hundred thousand to the good.

The common denominator in the whole process was Masley Prather. Not only had he owned the house, he was the attorney of record in all the sales. He had known the why and wherefore of each transaction, perhaps a deadly position to be in.

Karen stared out into the sunlit waters of the Gulf. She needed more information. Questioning the locals was not an option, and Sam was out of reach. She tried calling Neil, but there was no answer at his office. Her hands were tied, a most helpless and uncomfortable situation for a law officer. All she could do at present was go to the newspaper office and check out the coverage of the murders.

SAM DIDN'T NEED to ask directions. He knew exactly where he was going. Boudreaux Aguillard's house wasn't in Thibodaux, but closer to Kraemer. The only difference he noticed in the area where Celine had grown up with her parents and her brother was that there were a few more houses along the main road. It appeared, though, that Boudreaux had managed to hold on to the six or seven acres that made up his property.

The house itself was a small white clapboard with a tin roof. A porch ran the width of it. A slough from the bayou bordered one side of the tract and a stand of hardwoods the other. The lawn was winter green and well kept. The afternoon sun was bright, and live oaks cast their shadows over half the house when Sam drove slowly past. He wanted to take it in before stopping.

A midsized car was parked in the driveway, a tire-worn dirt path hardened with years of use. There was a swing on the front porch where he and Celine had spent many evenings, talking, revealing, projecting. Looking in the rearview mirror, he spotted an old, faded yellow pickup truck parked near the rear corner of the house. He recalled the day years before that he and Boudreaux had spray-painted it with Rust-Oleum to prevent it from disintegrating. Boudreaux had chosen the color, and Sam and Celine had shared a private laugh about it.

He turned the Rover around and drove back to the house, pulled into the driveway, and sat thinking about what he would say to Boudreaux. How could he explain? He needed to find Celine, get information. And make his peace with her. He needed Boudreaux's help to find her, but he wasn't certain that Boudreaux would welcome him.

The curtain at the front room stirred, and a long, breathless moment passed. Then Celine came out on the front porch and looked toward the car. She was wearing faded jeans and a red T-shirt and was barefoot. Her shoulder-length hair was shining and dark, accentuating her olive complexion. She was still slender, well proportioned, looking lean and strong. Looking better than good.

Sam stopped breathing. He muttered something even he didn't understand, grasped the door handle, and stumbled out. Facing a loaded gun would have been easier. When he started around the car and she could see him, her hands went to her mouth. He stopped, not knowing what to say or do.

"Celine?" he managed to get out, his voice raspy and dry. She stared at him. "I don't want to disturb you," he said, realized how ridiculous that sounded, and shook his head.

"Sam?" She came down the porch steps, stopped, then took a few hesitant steps toward him. Her eyes showed disbelief.

"Guess I haven't changed that much," he said.

"Your hair is long." She laughed nervously. "Oh, my God. It's Sam," she said, trying, he thought, to convince the conscious part of her brain that he wasn't an apparition, wanting to put something concrete into the scene that was playing. "Oh, my God." In her dark eyes he saw a collage of shock, joy, relief, and fear. "You're alive."

"I was when I woke up," he said and smiled for the first time. Celine obviously didn't know what to do, how to react, what to expect, and neither did Sam.

There were a few lines around her eyes; he hoped they were laugh lines. The sun lit a few strands of gray in her hair. Experience that only deepened her beauty. He felt chagrined, seeing the years' treatment of her. They remained, standing, in awkward silence.

"I didn't know," she finally said. Her voice was subdued. "Sam, I . . ." Tears were forming in her eyes.

"I'm sorry," he said, not knowing why or for what except for everything. Everything. "Celine . . ."

"Come inside," she said. "I need to sit down." She turned and started back up the porch steps. Sam followed.

Boudreaux's house appeared unchanged. It was dark and cool, shaded by the canopy of huge live oaks. The vaguely musty smell characteristic of old houses next to bayous was homey and reassuring, easing his initial discomfort. He felt one Sam Larkin, the new one, leaving and another taking its place, the old innocent Sam Larkin. Maybe this was part of that backward step in the right direction he had decided on while sitting in the motel room in Bay St. Louis.

The couch was still adorned with thick, clear plastic covers, which had yellowed over the years. When they were dating, he and Celine had often laughed at the unpleasant sounds of plastic against bare skin. She always referred to the covers as her father's alarm system. The picture of the Virgin still hung on the wall behind the couch, a further protective measure attributed to Boudreaux. Carnival glass and knickknacks abounded on every table surface. Her mother's collection of glass and ceramic shoes—*why would anyone collect glass shoes?*—filled a set of shelves on one wall. She had died before Sam met Celine, and Boudreaux considered the collection a monument.

Boudreaux's La-Z-Boy still faced the television set. Sam could picture the old man sitting there after dinner, dressed in a plaid short-sleeved shirt, red suspenders, and jeans. Each night after dinner he sat, sipped a drink, and watched *Tic Tac Dough*. The old man loved Wink Martindale, would occasionally play the game show host's one and only hit record, "A Deck of Cards," on the record player and cry with its sadness. Sam wondered where he was. Maybe off fishing.

"Sit down," Celine said, gesturing toward the La-Z-Boy. "I'll get us some sweet tea." She went into the kitchen. Sam looked at Boudreaux's chair. He couldn't sit there. He sat on the plastic-covered easy chair.

Celine brought tall, sweating glasses of iced tea with lemon slices, handed one to Sam, and sat on the couch.

"Nothing much has changed," Sam said.

"Most everything, I'd guess," she said, lifting her eyes to his. "If you're wondering where Boudreaux is, he passed six months ago. I used to live in Shreveport, but I came back here when he got too sick to take care of himself."

The news hit Sam like a hammer; he had loved Boudreaux like a father. "I'm sorry," he said.

"Thank you."

They were silent, sipping their tea.

He picked up a framed picture on the end table next to the chair. It had been taken the first Christmas of their marriage. Boudreaux, drink in hand, was sitting in the La-Z-Boy; Celine was kneeling to the right of the chair; and Sam was kneeling on the left. All three were wearing Santa Claus hats, and Sam sported a bright smile. He realized that he hadn't felt that kind of smile on his face in years.

"It was a happy time," she said.

Sam looked up and saw the sadness deep in her eyes, a reflection of his own. There was no joy or relief in them now, only pain and resignation.

"You made a mistake, Sam."

"More than you know."

"I would have waited."

"I was a dead man, Celine. I couldn't let you do that. I was in prison and wasn't getting out."

"So was I, Sam." She looked down at her glass and ran her forefinger through the moisture that had gathered on its outside surface. "You told me to forget, to believe you never existed. Do you realize how ridiculous that was? And when I tried to talk to you, you wouldn't see me. My own husband wouldn't see me, for God's sake! How was I supposed to handle that?"

He couldn't reply. His anticipation at seeing her again had been painful, but it was nothing compared to what he felt in this moment. In this place.

Finally he said, "I did what I thought was right at the time, Celine. I didn't have much to look forward to then, and I didn't want you sitting and waiting, trying to find a shred of hope to get through each day. Like I was doing. The idea of your being free was the one thing that made my days livable."

He replaced the picture on the table. "It was selfish, not asking you what you wanted, not giving you a choice, and I had to live with that selfishness. It took a lot of lies, fabricating your world the way I wanted it to be and praying that it was. It was for me, not you, that I did that, and it hurt, but I didn't know any other way to handle it. I still don't. You know what? I hoped to find you with a husband and a couple of kids. Then I would know I did the right thing, and that might erase some of the guilt."

She put her tea on the side table and looked at him. "You left me confused. I still am. I didn't move from Lake Charles to Baton Rouge to Shreveport to find jobs or a better life; I just didn't know what else to do. I couldn't understand, despite what you said, how you could just say 'forget me; it's over.' How you could turn off two lives like that. At the time, I knew—or thought I knew, though I'm sure my perceptions were naïve—what you were facing, but I wanted to go through it with you. I knew you were innocent. I was so scared for you. And for me. And you wouldn't let me help. You don't think that dropped a lot of guilt on me?"

She stood and began to pace. "In each place I lived, after the newness wore off and I was settled, the past came back. I guess I was like the alcoholic who believes he will quit drinking if he moves. But, you know what? They sell liquor everywhere. The past travels with you just like an addiction. When Daddy got sick, I came back here to try to put it to rest. I thought this was the only place I could do that."

"And then I show up," he said. He had to say something. Respond.

"I wasn't going to say that. I'm glad you did. At least I know you're alive. That clears a lot of doubts and gives me something tangible to be angry at." She waited for a response, but there was only silence. "Why did you come?"

"First, I wanted to see you, which I could have done from a distance, but that would have felt cowardly."

"Old honest Sam," she said, and, for the first time since he had arrived, he saw the hint of a smile on her lips.

"Not as honest as I used to be. I also need to ask you some questions. I need some information, Celine. About what happened after I went to prison."

"I don't know that I can help you there," she said. She was still pacing.

"Can't or won't?" he asked when she returned with the tea.

"I don't know. I'm not sure what I remember. I finally took your advice when I was in Shreveport. I made you dead. Cleaned the slate. Tried to believe that the whole thing never happened."

"It didn't."

"What do you mean?"

"For all intents and purposes, it never happened. There are no records. The trial never occurred. I was never sent to prison."

Celine shook her head in confusion, then smiled joylessly. "And that's why you're here? The money? All of that? I can't tell you anything about it. I never understood any of it and was forbidden to ask."

"By whom?" Sam asked.

"The lawyer who deposited the money in my account. He said it was alimony in a lump sum and I was never to question it. If I did, he couldn't guarantee my safety or that of my family. He was pretty cold. For awhile it led me to believe you were alive, that the money was just a payoff you had arranged. It allowed me to hate you part of the time, and that was a relief."

"Part of the time?"

"In truthful moments, I knew you could never do that. At least, the old Sam couldn't, but I didn't know how you might have changed in prison."

"Do you remember the lawyer's name?" he asked.

"Hamill. He only contacted me twice. God, Sam, this brings it all back. Over the years I've imagined that you might have escaped and be on the run, or you had been released or were dead. It was easier than thinking about you rotting in prison. But, somehow, I never imagined that you might show up."

"I'm sorry," he said, realizing how lame that sounded. "For my coming back, intruding . . ."

She locked on his eyes. "You never left me alone. Every now and then, no matter how hard I tried to avoid it, no matter what I was doing, there you were, everything I remembered of you and us."

He saw a crack in her composure, a deeper sadness.

"Where do we go from here, Sam?"

GAYNAUD HAD GOTTEN Celine Aguillard's telephone number and address in Shreveport from long-distance information, but the number was no longer in service, adding to the frustration of his father's refusal to help him. Gaynaud knew the judge had answers, but the old man was a stone wall. He was surprised that his father had even admitted that the problems involving Larkin went outside Louisiana.

The rest of Gaynaud's morning had been spent at the courthouse and the bureau of records, digging up names, addresses, anything that would give him a start in locating Larkin. The search was nearly fruitless. Most of his findings led to dead ends, and the few promising ones would take far too long to pursue. Larkin's divorce records were the only documents that held any immediate hope. The New Orleans attorney who handled Celine's petition was Parker Hamill; however, no one with that name was on the list of licensed attorneys in Louisiana.

Another item to follow up was Celine Aguillard's address at the time of the divorce. Thibodaux, Louisiana. The Lafourche Parish courthouse might yield the names of relatives he could question. Aguillard was not a common name, as far as he knew, and for that he was thankful. Old Sam had put some distance behind him, wherever he was, or *if* he was.

Gaynaud also thought that the date of the Larkins' divorce could be helpful. Sam had probably been imprisoned within a year previous to it. At the *Times-Picayune*, he discovered that the chief prosecutor in New Orleans at that time was Arthur Valdrine, now the administrator of the state. Back then, he'd been little more than a political hotshot on the rise; he had come a long way, and Gaynaud could expect no information from him. Celine Aguillard was the only promising avenue.

Leaving the newspaper building, he looked up at the sun and blue sky overhead, highlighted with randomly scattered, cottonball clouds. "I wonder where that sun is shining on you, Sam. Wherever it is, I'm gonna find you." He had found that talking to himself kept him going forward in the face of obstacles. And he never argued with himself.

Back in his office, he dialed Casey Landrieu's phone number. That she wasn't being totally forthcoming was obvious, and that was forcing him to work in a closet with the door closed. If it were any other case, he would sign off, but he was working for his own reasons now. He had thought of Sam many times over the years but had never tried to find him.

"Harold Musgrave Enterprises," Casey answered.

"Raymond Gaynaud here. I just wanted to check in with you."

"I appreciate that," she said.

"Basically, the progress report is that I'm not making any progress. I need a little more to go on. Unless I know what I'm looking for, you're wasting your money."

"I really don't have anything else I can give you, Mr. Gaynaud."

"I thought we decided on Raymond."

"Raymond. As I told you, the name came up in a project Harold is working on. It seems to be unrelated, and he wants to know why Larkin was mentioned. Beyond that we know nothing."

"Can you tell me about the project? I mean—"

"It's too sensitive right now," she interrupted. "Harold doesn't want any of the principals to know he's investigating. I'm sorry I can't be of more help."

"You do know that the same confidentiality exists between an investigator and client as a doctor or lawyer, don't you?"

"No disrespect to you, Raymond, but I've heard too much in my life to put faith in any unwritten confidentiality promise."

"Let me ask you one other question. Arthur Valdrine. What's his relationship with Mr. Musgrave?"

Casey cleared her throat. "The state administrator?"

"Yes." Leave her out in the boat alone.

"I would say Harold knows him, but I don't know to what extent. He knows most of the political figures in the state. Mr. Valdrine has never been invited to dinner, if that helps."

He was gaining respect for the lady. She knew how to skate.

"I didn't mean to be presumptuous. His name appeared down one of the avenues I was pursuing. Probably doesn't mean anything, but I'm really at a dead end here. Like I said, I don't know what I'm looking for or why. I'll give it another day, but if I don't come up with something pretty strong, I'll have to throw in the towel. I don't take money under false pretenses."

"Throwing in the towel surprises me. I wouldn't think that of you. And don't concern yourself with the money. Just do what you can," she said.

"I'll be in touch."

PETTIGREW LET THE telephone ring. The office was closed for the day, and the only reason he was still there was distress over the concern Arthur Valdrine had expressed at their meeting. He didn't want to talk to anyone, but on the fifth ring he relented and picked it up.

"Jordan Pettigrew."

"Jordan, I've got some work for you," Harold Musgrave said.

Pettigrew was caught off guard. The mountain had come to him. "Harold, I was planning to call you. Guess it's just good fortune that I decided to work late and picked up the phone. I'm glad you called."

"I doubt that you're glad," Musgrave said with a chuckle. "Thornton called, but the sumbitch didn't say what I wanted to hear. He thinks nobody can pierce that senatorial armor. I don't think that's so smart, all things considered, 'specially where he wants to go."

"I'd be careful there, Harold. Now, do you want to tell me what you have in mind, or are we going to play twenty questions?"

"Old TV show. I remember that. You know, Jordan, as I've said many times, you're an asshole. One of these days that fact is going to come crashing down on you, and you're going to need every friend you can get to either help you or bury you. You should be a little more concerned about how you treat people. The toes you step on today might be attached to the ass you're kissing tomorrow. You ought to keep that in mind."

Pettigrew was losing his patience. "Harold, I don't need a lecture at this hour of the day. I'm not going to—"

"I know what you're not going to do; you tell me that all the time. So, without wasting your time or mine, I'm gonna tell you what I want you to do. Thornton wants me to buy him out of Laurel Grove. I told him I don't have the capital to do that until the school money is released, which he assured me he would take care of. Now we both know that takes time, but he wants the buyout immediately. He suggested that we remove him from all the ownership documents and he, being the benevolent soul that he is, will let me pay him later. At that point, it will be considered a personal loan. And he thinks stupid ol' drunk Harold is gonna buy into that little scheme."

"He said that?" Pettigrew wasn't surprised by the proposed deal but by the fact that Musgrave had seen through it.

"I said he did, didn't I? The next step, I figure, is he'll let the state and the federal government come in and close the facility down for improprieties, most of which he'll tip 'em off to, claiming he was merely an investor and had no active part in the operation. In fact he'll say that when he saw what was going on, he was appalled, withdrew his investment, and then blew the whistle. That leaves ol' Harold to burn. And that ain't gonna happen."

"I think you're being paranoid."

"I want you to draw up a bill of sale for Thornton's interest in Laurel Grove."

"But if you don't have the funding . . ." Pettigrew objected.

"I believe I can scrape together a hundred dollars, Jordan."

"But—"

"That's the price I'm offering. One hundred dollars. Thornton's like a man in a covered wagon, and there's a thousand Indians shootin' arrows at him. In addition to drawing up the agreement of sale, I want you to present it to him. I don't even want to talk to the man."

"Afraid?"

"Not in this life."

"You're insane, Harold. His interest has to be worth a couple of million dollars."

"His interest is the vice presidency. Plain and simple, as you would say."

"He won't accept it, and beyond that, he'll think you're nuts."

"Most everybody thinks that anyway. You just do what I ask. It's the only way he's gonna get his name off the property."

"I can do it, but I won't take responsibility for it if he asks whose idea it was."

"That's fine. You just do it. By the way, Jordan, you ever hear of someone named Sam Larkin around here?"

Pettigrew almost dropped the telephone. "No—no, I don't believe I have," he stammered.

"Well, that reporter from Washington who interviewed me seemed awfully interested in him. I got the idea it had somethin' to do with Thornton's tenure as a judge."

"I doubt it. You know reporters. What else did he ask?"

"Not much. Just background stuff. How long was he a judge. Who his supporters are. Asked a couple of questions about Scottie, but nothing pertinent, if you know what I mean."

"And you didn't say anything?"

"Nothing you couldn't read in the papers," Musgrave said.

"A piece of advice, Harold . . ."

"Am I gonna have to pay for it?"

"No, this is free of charge. If I were you, I wouldn't talk to any more reporters, and I wouldn't ask people about Thornton or anything that has to do with him right now, especially if you have any idea of this harebrained proposition of yours being taken seriously."

"Oh, I want it to be taken seriously. But it's curious why that reporter seemed so interested in this Larkin fellow."

"To be trite, Harold, curiosity killed the cat."

"And satisfaction brought him back. Always remember, Jordan: satisfaction brought him back. Let me know when you have the documents ready for me to sign. You know where to find me."

The line went dead.

As he often did when he was feeling insecure, Pettigrew locked his office door, went to the safe in the back wall, and removed two large accordion files. He took them to his desk, opened one, and took out a handful of folders. When he was seated at his desk, he opened them one by one and glanced at the first few pages of each. The action was for reassurance rather than knowledge. Just to know that the papers were still in his possession. Some folders were thicker than others, but he knew all of the information each one contained. Word for word.

AS HE HUNG up the phone, Musgrave looked across his desk to Casey.

"He knows damned well who Sam Larkin is. Sure's hell, he does. Soon as I mentioned that name, he started pumpin' me. He was afraid all right." He walked around the desk and put his arms around Casey. "Darlin', this is gonna be fun to watch."

"Be careful, Harold. I can't afford to lose you."

"Me either," he said, and laughed.

# TWELVE

W*HERE DO WE go from here?* Celine's question continued to roll around in Sam's head. It was an open-ended question, and he didn't know the answer. *Where do we go from here?*

"Got any ideas?" she asked when he didn't answer the first time.

"How about dinner," he asked. She agreed, which surprised him as much as the natural way the question had come out of his mouth. He suspected she accepted more out of curiosity than anything else.

While Celine went to get ready, he called Karen from the kitchen phone, but her line was busy. Trying again a few minutes later, he got the answering machine.

"Karen, I'm in Thibodaux. I haven't found out anything useful yet. I'll give it one more day and try to reach you tomorrow. Take care." You talked to machines the way they talked to you.

Anticipation made the clock move slowly. In the kitchen, Sam tried to rub the wrinkles out of his cotton shirt, tucking and retucking it into his jeans. He combed his hair, pulled it back tightly, and secured it with the silver ring.

He heard Celine move through the house and out onto the front porch. He followed her and, seeing her sitting in the rocker, was struck again by the past. During their courtship, he had always arrived early, and she had always been waiting on the porch. He felt a strong surge in his chest and the air drain from his lungs. Her hair, her eyes, her high Cajun cheekbones and full lips. She was exotic without trying to be. She, too, was wearing jeans, along with a pale yellow shirt and light tan sandals.

"Anxious?" she asked.

They knew they were thinking the same thing.

"Seems familiar, doesn't it?" Sam said.

They laughed and were free to stop taking themselves too seriously. The past was left behind, and they moved into the present.

"Can I say you're beautiful?" he asked.

"Anytime you feel like it," she answered. "Are you up to driving back to Thibodaux?"

"I don't have a schedule. Got some place in mind?"

"Bubba's Yard."

"S'go," he said from out of the past, and they headed to the Rover.

ON THE WAY to Thibodaux, the conversation centered on what they were seeing, the changes that had taken place, but they did not single out sites that had been significant in their courtship and marriage. For brief moments, Sam could believe they were still a couple, but that wasn't an idea he thought wise to get comfortable with.

Bubba's Yard was pure rural Louisiana. The parking lot was small, filled with pickup trucks and people leaning against them drinking beer and talking. Inside, the restaurant was sectioned into two dining rooms and a sports bar, from which they were assaulted with loud Cajun-accented conversation and cheers for whatever was happening on the many television screens surrounding the bar. Sam and Celine sat away from the noise in the back dining room, which overlooked water and marsh.

In the beginning, being together was easy. They ordered drinks, discussed the menu—both chose the crawfish etouffeé—and laughed at the logic of anyone's coming to Bubba's Yard in Thibodaux, Louisiana, to order steak. Once the drinks were served and the orders taken, conversation became more difficult, dwindling finally to an uneasy silence.

"I guess the cat got two tongues tonight," Celine said.

"I'm happy being here. It's good to be with you, and I don't have a clue what to say."

"Then I'll start," she said. "What's it been like for you? I've spent so many years wondering, imagining, guessing, and never really knowing anything except that one day you were there, and the next day you weren't. Suddenly I didn't seem to matter to anyone. Tell me about the time you've been gone, Sam. All of it."

He paused, not knowing where to begin. He had never tried to think about *all of it*. Prison made living a day-to-day project. If you survived yesterday, you put it in the past, hoping that any lessons learned would remain in your mind to be used to survive another day. You never presumed on tomorrow. The time prior to prison became an enemy, all memories did, things that could drive you insane with grief for their loss if you dwelt on them or allowed yourself to miss them. There wasn't any future, so it deserved no time. After prison you worked at erasing *all of it*. Sometimes with such concentration and focus that you missed the present. He had never thought about *all of it* objectively, and he knew now he never would until Thornton Hunnycut was also behind him.

"Sam?" Celine was looking at him.

He had been somewhere else. He gave her a chagrined smile. "I'm sorry," he said, embarrassed.

"Taking a pause in your existence?"

He smiled. "You remember that?"

"You used to say it all the time when your mind was in those faraway places. I always envied your ability to escape and lose yourself."

"Escape," he said. "Prison was worse than I could have imagined. I did things, found someone I didn't know lived inside my skin. I learned what survival was, what dignity was not, the value of privacy, the glory of freedom, and the horror that goes with losing it. I learned I could kill a man I didn't know and risk my life for another because I didn't care much about living the way I was living and saw no chance of it changing."

"You killed a man?" she asked softly, looking at him, but not staring.

"Not now," he said.

"What about after prison? Did you ever think about . . ."

"Looking for you? Yes."

"Why didn't you?"

"I was afraid I'd find you. I knew I wasn't who I used to be and that I'd never be that person again, and I didn't know who you would be. I didn't want to interrupt your life. I was filled with guilt, but—no—I didn't want to find someone I wanted and couldn't have. So, I put you behind me. Or so I thought. You visited me a lot over the years. Angola performed an emotional lobotomy on me, Celine, and I didn't have anything to offer anyone, particularly you. I'm not sure I do even now." He drank from his water glass. "Most of me was gone when I was released, and despite my anger and bitterness and desire for retribution, when they told me that a condition of my release was that I leave Louisiana and never come back, I accepted it. I was tired, and I left. And that cost what little bit of me that might have been left."

"It's hard to believe," she said.

"What?"

"That you could do that. I can't imagine you going down without a fight."

"There was no fight left. I went to South Carolina and took two years building a house. I learned a lot doing that. Taught school for a few years."

Celine stared hard at her drink, a skeptical look on her face—suppressing a smile, he imagined. "You taught school?" She looked up and laughed.

Here and now, it seemed unrealistic to Sam too, but it had been good at the time, had given him some sense of worth where he'd thought there was none. "High school biology."

"An ex-con? With a ponytail?"

"The hair was no problem, and the prison record doesn't exist." He paused, took a breath. "Celine, I need to know anything you know about what happened back then. Any names. Anything."

They were interrupted by the arrival of the food. They began eating, and Celine answered his question.

"I don't really know much, Sam. A lawyer, Parker Hamill, contacted me. He said you had retained him to handle the divorce. There would be no lawyer's fees for me. It didn't matter that I didn't want a divorce. He said there would be some money if I went along with your wishes and suggested that it would be nasty if I didn't. When I signed the papers, he gave me a bank check for twenty thousand dollars, which he claimed was from you. It made me hate you. The final payoff, I guessed. I felt cheap taking it, but I needed the money. Most of our savings had gone for your defense. And I had no idea where you'd get that kind of money."

She put her fork down and leaned in toward Sam. "Then out of the blue, four years later, I received a call from Mr. Hamill telling me that sixty-eight thousand dollars would be deposited in my account the following week. The deal was that I never question it and that I send him our tax returns for the three previous years. As a bonus, he said, his firm would do my taxes free of charge for five years. All I had to do was keep careful records and see that he got them by the first of March each year."

"And you did?"

"Yes."

"Ever hear from him after that?" Sam asked.

"No. Not even a question about my records. You'd think something would have needed explaining. And he wouldn't tell me anything about you."

"I don't know him. I didn't hire him." The name was vaguely familiar to Sam, but that was all.

Celine looked at him, seeing the questions behind his eyes. "Can we put all this away now and just enjoy our date?" she asked.

Sam almost choked on the food in his mouth. He coughed and took a sip of water. "Date?" he said. "This is a date?"

Celine looked at him. "Doesn't it feel like one?" she asked, the corners of her mouth curling upward.

THE DRIVE BACK to the house was quiet. Celine was right; it was like a first date, filled with all the chagrin and embarrassment of not quite knowing what to do next. Through all of their time together in the last few hours, they had not touched. He wondered if she had noticed. Surely she had, but too much time had passed, too much damage had been inflicted, and neither of them needed the complications.

When he pulled into the driveway, the house was dark save for the lone front porch light, which cast a soft halo in the gathering mist created by the cooling night air. After he cut the engine, they sat listening to the hot-dry bugs and tree frogs, nature's instrumentalists. There was heat lightning in the distance, and the muted rumble of thunder. It would build to a crescendo before morning, bringing another Louisiana frog-strangling rain.

"Come in?" she asked.

"Do you think . . ."

"I want you to." She opened the car door and stepped out.

Sam had no sooner stepped inside the house when Celine turned and put her arms around him, resting her head on his chest. He was shaken. His arms encircled her, and he held her so tightly he was afraid of crushing her. She pulled back and looked up into his face.

"I've been waiting all day, Sam," she said. "I had to do that."

"Knew I wouldn't?"

"I know you, Sam."

"Yes. Yes, you do. You always have."

He pulled her to him and kissed her. Everything about it was familiar, her lips, the movement of her tongue, the taste and fragrance of her. They held that one kiss for a long time, then separated to brush tears from their eyes.

"Will you stay?" she asked.

He didn't answer. Couldn't.

"Just tonight. No more than that. I need you tonight, Sam, so I can move forward tomorrow. Does that make any sense?"

"More than you know."

She turned out the porch light, took his hand, and led him through the dark house.

In Celine's bedroom, the room she had grown up in and where they had slept together on visits to Boudreaux, Sam felt awkward and clumsy and profoundly at home. Celine again put her arms around him and rested her head on his chest. The feel of her, the lemony smell of her hair were like a waking dream. His hesitation was erased when she turned her head up to be kissed.

They undressed in the dark and slipped into bed. She began kissing his chest and his neck. She was leading, and he was following. She positioned herself astride him, her hair hanging down and feathering his face. Her hand found him, guided him. "Sam," she said, repeating his name in whispers quiet as butterfly wings, and began a slow, rhythmic motion.

It was a gentle night, the love-making soft and languorous, more tender than passionate.

Outside, rain fell heavily without lightning or thunder. They moved together in darkness as black as an underground cave's, listening to the rain play its cadence on the tin roof. They held each other, feeling the joy of skin and warmth and safety and saying nothing.

BUCK LINK WAS beginning to feel more than his age. Thirty-one years as a member of the Louisiana State Police doubled the average mileage on a man's body. His knees were beginning to go, and his back was a constant reminder of altercations, Samaritan-like helpfulness to motorists in trouble, and pushing the human anatomy in and out of situations for which it was not intended. Now that he was a troop commander, most of those physical demands were a thing of the past, but the pain was a constant reminder.

A call had come in to the district barracks about a torched car in the marshlands between Barataria and Lafitte. It wasn't something he would normally concern himself with, but Link liked to show up unannounced occasionally, to observe his officers at work.

He headed out of New Orleans to Route 45—Barataria Boulevard—and turned onto Route 301 toward Lafitte. He loved the wide-open marshlands bordering the Lafitte-LaRose Highway. From just across the Intracoastal Canal Bridge, they stretched to the horizon. The subtle, verdant colors of the grasses and the chromelike snakes of waterways were unusually visible in the early sunlight; morning fog and haze typically painted everything in monochromatic shades of gray.

Then, the glow of flashing blue lights in the distance. As he slowed, the shapes of men moving around the skeleton of a burned-out vehicle gained definition. Raleigh DuBose's Jefferson Parish sheriff's car was parked on the opposite side of the road, along with two deputies' cars and a fire truck. Two state police cars were parked some distance in front and in back of the fire-blackened automobile. The convention of law enforcement vehicles appeared to be overkill, but it would be DuBose's party once the preliminaries were complete.

Link parked his car and opened the door, feeling the familiar stiff pain in his lower back as he got out. He walked over to DuBose, who was overseeing the operation.

"What you doin' out here, Buck?" DuBose asked.

"Just passing through the neighborhood," he answered. Link was an imposing figure—six feet, seven inches tall, tanned, with graying hair and a disarming smile that gentled the sharp intensity of his eaglelike features. "What have we got here?"

"More'n we expected. Thought it was just an abandoned car somebody torched for amusement or 'cause they got angry when it died on 'em. But we got a body in the back seat."

"Any ID yet?" Link asked.

"No. Hardly anything left. Body was on the floor, which is why we didn't see it right off. Car was too hot to get close to. Whoever done it used a high-powered accelerant. Body damn near melted into the carpet."

"No amateur then."

"Wouldn't think this was his first time, unless he did a lot of research. Course I'm just assumin' based on the evidence," he said with mild sarcasm. "Obviously the fire took away all the physical identification, but whoever did it also took a hammer to the victim's teeth. We're gonna sift the rubble, but I doubt we'll find any of 'em. Looks like a long-term John Doe. Prob'ly somebody we'd have eventually put out of circulation anyway. Some lowlife gettin' rid of some other lowlife. We'll give it a whirl, see what we come up with."

Link gave him a confident smile. "You'll come up with something, Raleigh."

"We usually do. These dudes ain't too smart. Burnin' a car draws attention in itself. Woulda been better to throw the guy in the bayou and let the gators feed on him. Wouldn'a known about that for a year."

"If ever. Get me a report, okay?"

Link started to cross the road back to his car but paused to allow a car to pass. It was old and beat up. It slowed as it passed, and the driver, thin-faced, with long, black, greasy hair and a flowered shirt, looked out and perused the activity. He had a smile on his face that could have been a greeting or an acknowledgment, were it not so creepily simplistic. Damned rubberneckers. The car eased past, and Link continued across the road, doubting anything positive would come out of the investigation. The pros didn't make many mistakes, and he agreed with the sheriff: it surely looked like a professional job.

SAM OPENED HIS eyes to a gray cast of morning light tinged with a deep rose color that bespoke more rough weather. Celine lay next to him, her legs stretched full length and her breasts against his chest. He kissed her shoulders, and she opened her eyes. She rolled onto her back and he moved above her, taking the lead, as she had done the night before; she followed. Afterwards, she closed her eyes and curled into him.

It was difficult for him to take his gaze from her and his mind away from their reunion. It would be easy to fall back, he thought. And wrong. As beautiful as the night had been, he was sure she knew that as well. They had both been given a gift of freedom. He drifted back to sleep.

HUNNYCUT WAS IN his office early. The sun was just beginning to show against the skyline. He had slipped out of bed without waking Marlene; she had kept him up later than usual with her insistence on explaining, in detail, how her clients' interests in the HMO legislation should be manipulated. He assured her time and again that he couldn't foresee any problems, that it required only a few swing votes to lock in, which he had never failed to capture when the stakes were important.

Education funding was the head of his hammer, and his committee, the handle. He had firm control of both. There was never enough in any state's coffers to fund the damned educators and the do-good programs they promoted. As far as Hunnycut was concerned, education was drowning in a sea of warm fuzzies, radicals, and idealistic bullshit; however, with elections coming up, education was also the most malleable and nonpartisan issue for gaining or losing votes. The idealists put the children's welfare first, and the pragmatists wanted to insure a generation that was capable of supporting them in their old age. They both needed Thornton Hunnycut.

Looking over the day's agenda, he saw nothing pressing enough to relegate Marlene's interests to second place. The bill that contained the HMO limitations would pass the House, that was a certainty. But if it could be amended with a couple of less palatable items that would overwhelmingly favor one party over another, house passage might not be quite as simple, and senate swing votes would kill it. Make it distasteful enough, and even the president would be in a bind. Hunnycut's greatest talent was orchestrating long-term committee holdups, eventually resulting in little or no legislation at all. And his name was never even brought into the fray.

As he was calling his list of the swing voters, ranking those he could easily control over those who would require a larger carrot, his office phone rang. It was too early for anyone other than Marlene, so he ignored it. He didn't need another prep session.

The phone continued to ring. Finally, he reached over and answered impatiently.

"Thornton, it's Arthur. I called the townhouse, and Marlene said you had probably gone to the office early. She sounded quite irritated."

"I doubt that was because you woke her up. She's got other things on her mind." He looked at the gold clock on his desk. "Hell, must not even be first light there in the Pelican State. What prompts a call at this hour? Something doing down there that I should know about?"

"The Pelican State is fine as far as we're concerned; however, the Magnolia State might have some problems."

Although the words sounded like idle banter, Hunnycut could read the urgency in Valdrine's tone. It was not just a "checking in" call.

"I'm in the middle of something right now, Arthur. Let me call you back in thirty minutes."

"Certainly."

It was a three-block walk to Union Station, Hunnycut's comfort zone for calls that required caution. In Washington, one never knew. He could only wonder what problems might have surfaced in Mississippi. Valdrine always handled Hunnycut's interests there, business and otherwise, and had always done it efficiently.

The morning rush had already begun, and there were probably enough legislators in the station to create a caucus. The senior senator from Louisiana was hardly noticeable in the hustling mass of government and business types, all in expensive dark suits, regimental ties, and highly polished black shoes. Only a tattoo or an identifiable scar might have differentiated one from the majority, and the majority had neither.

Hunnycut chose a pay phone located in a shadowy recess near a stairwell. Valdrine answered on the first ring.

"Tell me about Mississippi," Hunnycut said in a tone reflecting neither patience nor camaraderie.

"I received a call from Biloxi late yesterday, an ex-secretary for a law associate of mine who works in the chancery clerk's office there and keeps an eye on whatever's happening for me. Someone—a woman, blond hair, independent and with, I was told, an 'official' attitude—was researching your house," Valdrine said.

"She asked for information on my house?" Hunnycut asked.

"Among several others. But yours was the only one that seemed to get special scrutiny. The other properties appeared to be diversions."

"No idea who it was?"

"No. My source didn't know why she was looking, but I imagine she's another reporter. Or it could have been comparables for a sale. No way to know. I just wanted you to be aware of it."

"Find out. Any other good news?" Hunnycut asked. He heard Valdrine take a deep breath.

"Unfortunately yes. I was also notified that the FBI has taken a role in the Prather murders."

"The FBI? You told me the police ascribed it to a disgruntled client or random killings. What brought the FBI in?"

"Masley's son, Bridey. Evidently he was raising all kinds of hell, blaming anyone he could come up with as being responsible. Because of Masley's position in the community, they said they'd look into it. It's only perfunctory, I'm told, just to shut him up."

"When did you learn about this?" Hunnycut asked.

"A couple of days ago. My informant called."

"And you didn't think it necessary to call me then?"

The subdued rage in Hunnycut's voice was palpable even through the telephone line. Valdrine figured the only thing preventing a total meltdown was the fact that Hunnycut was in a public place. "You're in Washington," he said. "What could you do? You're out of touch with what goes on down here, especially in Mississippi, and, pardon my telling you what to do, but that's the way it should stay. You don't need to be associated with this any more than necessary."

"There's a woman checking out my house and the FBI looking into the murder of a friend and business associate in Gulfport, and you think my name won't be associated with any of it? Don't be a fucking idiot. Does the FBI have any leads?"

"No. The son even called in Artis Gaynaud's boy to look around. He's beginning to get a reputation as an independent crime scene analyst. He didn't find anything either. Said it was clean."

"I don't like it."

"Nobody likes it, Thornton, but don't worry about it. Everything will be handled. Take my word on it."

"Why should I?"

"Because you can. I'm more interested in the girl than I am in Masley Prather. That's an old headline at this point," Valdrine said.

"Sounds like you're rationalizing, but I'll take your word on it—for now. What about Pettigrew?"

"I talked to him. He's clear on what to say and what not to say. He knows where he stands. I even brought up Hamill's name as a warning. He flatly denied saying anything about Larkin to that reporter. He also said he has never heard from Larkin over the years and has no idea where he might be. Let me monitor these things. You do what you have to do to get James's nod. I just wanted you to be aware."

"You better damned well be sure I'm aware of everything that goes on down there when it happens. And not days after the fact. Don't let that happen again. You don't want to become a liability, Arthur."

"I won't, Thornton. I just thought it was better to—"

"It wasn't. I can't talk anymore. I have to get back to the office."

"I understand," Valdrine said.

"I hope you do."

# THIRTEEN

WITH HIS EYES closed, Sam listened to the early morning sounds of Thibodaux. They were familiar: egrets leaving their nighttime roosting places for a day of foraging; the breeze whistling, flute-like, through the leaves of the live oaks; a set of wind chimes anchored in the eaves of the front of the house, tinkling out the music they had played for years. In the midst of all this, he felt her presence.

"How long have you been there?" he asked without opening his eyes.

"A few minutes. I watched you smiling."

He opened his eyes to look at her, sitting on the side of the bed. She wore a red silk robe tied loosely so that one side hung open revealing her left breast. Sam lifted his hand and traced the delicate curve of its underside. Her nipple hardened; she smiled. "You said I could say it any time. You're beautiful."

"Thank you."

Despite her smile, he could see the question in her eyes, whether or not to abandon herself and fold back into him. Finally, she shook her head, almost imperceptibly, answering her own question, then leaned forward and kissed him on the forehead. "Coffee's ready," she said. "I'll see you in the kitchen." She pulled her robe together as she left the room.

Sam lifted himself from the bed and put on his jeans and shirt. Then he sat back down. His head was spinning. The promise of another life was before him, and he wasn't sure what to do about it, didn't know how to react to what had happened or what was going on in his head. He went into the bathroom, splashed his face with cold water, pulled his hair back, slipped the silver ring over it, and went into the kitchen.

Bright sunlight filled the room. Celine had put on white shorts, which contrasted strongly with the brown skin of her legs and midriff. She wore a faded blue work shirt, probably Boudreaux's, pulled snug and tied below her breasts.

"Good morning," he said as he sat at the table.

"You back," she answered. It was exactly what he expected her response to be. A lot of little things, almost forgotten, were returning to him. She poured the coffee, put sugar and milk on the table, and sat down across from him. "Thank you for last night, Sam."

"I think I should be thanking you, but I don't know what to say. I woke up early and watched you sleep."

"I slept well. I needed what we had. Not so much physically as emotionally. I feel free, but don't ask me to explain exactly how. I've been hurting for a long time, a lot of it because we never said goodbye. But now I'm free."

"I'm glad," he said.

"I wanted to stay in there with you this morning."

"I wanted you to, but you were right. You were always ahead of me when it came to . . ."

"No, not ahead, but I think I know where we can go and where we can't. At least right now. I've had more time to think about it than you have. For all my pain, I didn't have to survive day by day, as you did. In that respect, I had it easy."

"I wouldn't say that."

"Last night was better than I thought it would be." She smiled and put her hand on top of his, caressing the place where his wedding band would have been. "I've got to go to town this morning."

There was no easy way to say what was necessary, and he knew she was trying to make it easy for both of them. "And I've got to get back to New Orleans," he said.

They stood up. Celine took the cups to the sink, then came back to him. She put her arms around him and closed her eyes, as they held each other back through a lifetime. Finally they lowered their arms, and their eyes locked for a long moment.

"I want to keep you out of what's coming, and I'd feel better if you got away from here for awhile, but I'm sure you won't," Sam said.

"I can take care of me. Will I hear from you?"

"Let's see how things turn out. For both of us. Today is tomorrow. Now you can look forward." He pulled her tighter to him. "There's still the part of me that will always love you, Celine."

"You back."

She looked up into his eyes and without a word asked him to leave first. He let go of her and turned for the door. He wondered if she would stop him. She didn't. He closed the door behind himself.

RAYMOND WAS PARKED in a pull-off on the opposite side of the bayou from the house. He had been there since before dawn. The door of the house opened, and a slender, muscled figure with a ponytail stepped out on the porch and walked toward an old, green Land Rover parked next to an even older truck.

"Sam Larkin," Raymond said to the emptiness of his car and smiled. "Not much of a vehicle, Sam," he said. "But better than that old truck, I guess."

THE MESSAGE FROM Sam on the answering machine was brief, to the point, and not what she wanted to hear. Karen was relieved that he had called, but the call didn't lessen her anxiety.

Throughout the day the Larkin-Aguillard reunion had been no less than an obsession for her. Her sleep had been fretful. The scene played in her mind with as many variations as she could come up with, a soap opera. Surprises, happy endings for them, happy endings for her, misery, and acceptance.

She talked to herself, developing logical sequences of events, imagining the first postreunion conversation with Sam, playing it out in her mind—questions, answers, and reactions—word for word. Sometimes the dialogue was loving, sometimes friendly, sometimes heated. And at times, there was no conversation at all.

Lying in bed, she watched the light brighten through the window and determined that she would not spend another day like the one she had just been through. In times of stress, action was her tranquilizer.

SAM WENT BACK to the Ramada, grabbed his duffle bag, and checked out. The skies were deceptively bright, but he could smell more rain coming, a fresh, green fragrance that no perfume could imitate. He rolled down the windows of the Rover to let it in.

He didn't know what he would have said or done had Celine allowed him to orchestrate their reunion. In mere hours she had purged the negative feelings and associations and regenerated the good parts of their history. In that regard, she was far wiser than he. He hoped he could hold his own memories of their few hours together, take them for what they were, and not intrude on her life again. She didn't deserve that.

He concentrated on the two-lane blacktop road, the simple geometrics of the painted parallel lines—a center line changing, with reason and logic, from solid to broken, constant and predictable. Sam wished the course of his life were that uncomplicated. With all that lay in front of him in exposing Hunnycut, he now had to factor in Celine's safety and the peace that she was due.

He was not looking forward to the prospect facing him in Biloxi. Karen would be full of questions that he wouldn't answer, couldn't answer. Not yet, maybe not ever. He would share the information about Parker Hamill and find out what the lawyer's role had been. Exactly who he had been working for. That was all he would tell Karen. He had, in truth, learned nothing else that she and Dougherty needed to know. The rest—his time with Celine—was theirs, a time out, and that is what it would remain.

He realized that he was being followed, and not very well, by a white Crown Victoria that looked like a recycled police vehicle. It had been parked at the gas station across the street from the Ramada when he left. Just another car in another gas station.

He had not thought about it again until he saw it pass when he stopped for gas near Des Allemands. After he filled the tank, paid, and left, it had appeared behind him again. To his knowledge, Dougherty, Karen, and Celine were the only people who knew he was in Louisiana, and Dougherty had been warned not to put him under surveillance. If this was a federal agent, Dougherty would get no further cooperation from him. The possibility that it wasn't Dougherty's agent was more unsettling.

He considered his options and decided that losing the tail was most practical. He pulled into a sprawling, two-story motel outside Kenner, parked, and went inside. He watched the Crown Vic park at the other end of the building.

"How are you today?" the clerk asked when Sam walked through the inner door. "How may I help you?"

"I'd like a room, but I'd like to take a look at it first, if that's possible."

"No problem at all," the clerk said. "Any preferences?"

"Second floor. Back of the building. I'm a light sleeper, and sometimes the traffic keeps me awake if I'm in front."

The young man pulled a key from the rack behind the desk and handed it to him. "Just drive around back, and you'll see a stairway and vending machines. Take a right at the top of the stairs, and it's the third room in."

"Thanks." Sam took the key, went back to the Rover, and drove around to the rear of the building. He climbed to the second floor, walked through the alcove, and stood where he had a clear view of the Crown Vic. The driver got out of the car and walked the length of the building to the office. He was tall and muscular and had dark hair almost as long as Sam's own. Not a federal agent. As soon as the man was in the office, Sam went back down the stairs.

The Crown Vic was still in its space when he exited onto a residential street that ran along the side of the motel. He headed back west in case the tail had caught him leaving. He drove fifteen miles with no sign of the old white car before he turned back east toward Highway 90. The tail would expect him to hit the interstate.

Thunderheads were beginning to form over the Gulf as Sam crossed into Mississippi. Passing a gauntlet of fast food restaurants, the smell of deep-fat fried foods reminded him he had not eaten anything all day, but he wasn't hungry. His adrenaline was flowing—he felt an urgency to get back to Biloxi.

CELINE SAT ON the porch and watched the scarlet sun slowly put the day to rest beneath the darkening landscape of sugar cane fields, the few houses that were within sight, and the bayou that bordered the property. The house was her only anchor. She looked up at the porch ceiling, wood-slatted and capped with green-painted tin. Dirt cylinders created by mud daubers crowded tightly against the ceiling's beams. The house's white paint was peeling, something Boudreaux would never have allowed had he been healthy enough to do anything about it. Sam had painted the entire house the summer of the year before he'd gone to prison. When he took breaks from the heat, she had brought him sweet tea, and they had sat on the glider talking, laughing, and sipping the cool drinks.

They had often spent evenings sitting on the porch at twilight, chewing on fibrous sticks of sugar cane and laughing when strings of the tough material got caught between their teeth, or at the backyard picnic table, eating mounds of crimson crawfish Sam had caught, colored lamps strung in a square around them and Boudreaux playing his accordion renditions of "Belizaire's Waltz" and "Evangeline." Nights in front of the television set, seeing who could answer the quiz show questions first. She had moved from one end of Louisiana to the other, trying to evade these memories.

The telephone rang. She walked into the house, the sound of the screen door's slapping shut behind her echoing as she picked up the receiver. "Hello?"

"Hi." The voice. For the second time in two days Sam had blurred her parameters of reality and memory.

"Sam?"

"I seem to be."

"Where are you?" she asked.

"Near Biloxi. What are you doing?"

"I was on the porch thinking about sugar cane, colored lights, and boiled crawfish." It was the easiest way to tell him where her mind had been.

He was silent for a moment. "It would be hard to go back," he said.

"I know. I'd be afraid to try."

"Celine, someone followed me when I left Thibodaux. I don't know if whoever it was followed me to your house or not, but they might have. It's me they're interested in, not you, but I wanted you to know. Keep an eye out. If you see anything—and I mean anything—call one of the two numbers I'm going to give you. One is my number in Biloxi, and the other is a man named Neil Dougherty. He's a federal agent in New Orleans."

"A federal agent? What's going on, Sam?"

"I'll explain it when I can." He gave her the numbers. "Celine. Be careful. I don't ever want to drop anything on you again. I couldn't live with that," he said.

"Neither could I. Maybe I should have told you to leave when you pulled in the driveway."

"I would have understood."

"I shouldn't have cared whether you did or not." Anger rose, anger at Sam, at memories, at her weakness, at everything life had done to her, and then she softened. "Will you call me again? Just to check?"

"If you want."

"I want." She paused. "Do what you have to do. I'll be okay."

"I wish you would leave for a few days."

"I can't do that, Sam. I've run enough. I'll be okay. I still have Boudreaux's shotgun."

"Take care of yourself. I mean that."

"You back."

KAREN HAD GONE back to the chancery clerk's office, but it was obvious that her presence had been registered from the time she walked through the door. The look on the desk clerk's face was one of nervous suspicion. She adjusted her plan and asked if she had left some papers there the day before. After a curt "no," she left. If there were further work to be done in that building, Sam or Neil would have to do it.

She went to the library and copied all the newspaper articles regarding the Prather murders and returned to the condo. She would like to have talked to the reporter who covered the story, but, judging from the reaction in the clerk's office, she couldn't imagine the newspaper office's being secure.

The newspaper coverage indicated a perfunctory investigation at best. There were no clues and no suspects, and, in what she suspected was politically sensitive law enforcement, the case, for all intents and purposes, was closed.

The facts looping through her head were leading nowhere. It was time to turn her thoughts to something else. But when she tried, honestly concentrated, the only subject left was Sam, and there was no consolation to be found there. The Prathers, Hunnycuts, and Valdrines of the world were not personal; Sam was. She couldn't turn him off.

It had been a busy day, and she was emotionally drained. Sitting in the comfort of the couch, sipping a Jack Black, she knew she could close her eyes and be asleep in moments, but she wanted to be awake if Sam returned. Still, it all caught up to her. She felt herself start to fade, her eyes involuntarily closing, when she heard footsteps coming up the front steps. She automatically slid her hand down between the pillows of the couch to feel the Ruger .357 she had secreted there out of habit. When she heard the key in the lock, she felt a momentary relaxation followed by exhilaration—he was home—and then panic about how she would react when he walked through the door. Two days of no communication, save one unsatisfying telephone message, and burning questions about what had transpired between Celine and him put her at a loss as to what to say.

"Don't shoot," he said as he stepped into the room. It had been a standing joke since he first walked into her condo in Carolina unannounced and had seen her hand slip out of sight.

"Why not?" she asked. The same old script. But this time he didn't hear any humor in her voice. She didn't change her position on the couch.

"I'm not sure."

"If you're not sure, how can I be?" she asked.

"Guess you'll just have to make a decision. Shoot me, or welcome me with open arms," he said.

"Open arms are not negotiable." She pulled herself up and looked at him. Shit, she thought, he's unhateable. She wasn't certain there was such a word, but she thought it anyway as she hurled the glass she held in his direction. It didn't come close.

RENÉ GROSJEAN DIDN'T recognize the man who appeared out of nowhere and mounted the steps into the woman's apartment. He had not seen a car enter the parking lot. The man didn't look formidable. But whoever he was, he had a key.

Grosjean hated this kind of work. It took too much time. He liked his jobs short, highly profitable, and sweet. This one qualified only as profitable, though it would keep him out of prison for the rest of his life. The thing he liked least was not knowing why he was doing it. The caller just told him to be at the chancery clerk's office in Biloxi when it opened. The person at the desk would signal him if the subject female came in. He was to get her license tag number, stay with her for twenty-four hours, and report in.

He had followed her to the library, where she copied some newspaper articles, and then back to the condo complex. No one had come or gone until the man with the ponytail appeared. Nothing unusual seemed to be happening. Eventually the lights went on in one bedroom and then in the other. Shortly after, the house went dark.

Grosjean swallowed two amphetamines, leaned his head back against the grease-stained headrest, and closed his eyes. He would not sleep. All of his concentration went to his hearing, separating and blocking out the sounds of Highway 90, focusing on the building and doorway in front of him. Any sound coming from that direction would get his attention. It was a learned skill that never failed him.

THE SCOTCH DIDN'T taste very good. Metallic. Hunnycut picked up the bottle from the table next to his chair. The label—Ardbeg Provenance, 1974—assured him he was drinking very fine single malt scotch, a case of which had been a gift from a pharmaceutical company. There shouldn't be anything wrong with the whiskey; he had just opened the bottle. Maybe it was just the taste of his dream dying.

Marlene, sitting on the couch, surrounded by files and papers, was watching him. He had come home unusually early. When she asked him why, he had been succinct: "I'm pretty sure I just lost the nomination."

The statement caught her off guard. "What do you mean? You heard from James?"

"No. I was told today that the opposition is looking into our relationship, how you might influence my decisions, adultery, money I may have made through you, any fucking thing they can find. The whole ball of wax."

She was smiling. "I've heard those rumors for weeks. I can't imagine you weren't aware of them before now, or didn't expect it," she said.

"No, I didn't know, goddamn it! Why didn't you say anything?"

"Number one, I was sure you knew and didn't consider it any more significant than I do. Number two, don't you think we're doing the same thing to their candidates? No one, and I mean no one, is clean in this town. I could bury half the politicians in Washington. So could any other lobbyist. They have nothing." She got up, went to the chair, and sat in his lap. "And they won't have. You're making a mountain out of a molehill."

"If they bring it to the floor, it would be enough for James. I'd be out in a minute."

"Has he called yet?"

"I told you no."

"And you think he doesn't know what's going on? Come on, Thornton; he knew it was happening before we did, and I knew it within hours. There is one simple fact that is inescapable, and James is as aware of it as is his campaign manager, his strategist, and everyone else involved: Your candidacy does not guarantee him a victory, but he sure as hell can't win without you. He's not going to take a chance on losing."

"You may be correct, but he can't win with a tainted partner on the ticket either."

"You won't be tainted," she said.

"And how do you plan to manage that?"

"Thornton, neither the senate nor the house nor the president has any power. The lobbyists do. We are in control. You, of all people, know that. It's not the way the system was designed to work, but it's a fact.

You've said it many times: the country should vote for their favorite lobbyist instead of a politician. Key point: own the corrupters, not the corrupted."

She went to the bar and poured herself a drink, the same scotch that Hunnycut was drinking. "That watchdog group, the Government Guard, is the real push behind this investigation, if you want to call it that. I know how to get to them. They're powerless. Lobbyists stick together in times of stress; everyone's vulnerable, but I'm less so than most."

"You know who to get to?" He paused. "How, might I ask?"

"To put it in a very unladylike manner, I can be fucked, Thornton, but I'll never get screwed."

He found himself smiling. "What's the difference?"

"You have to have my permission to fuck me; I never allow anyone to screw me. Trust me. It will be taken care of."

"I hope you're right."

"I am. Now, let's go to dinner somewhere. Out of the District. In fact, why don't we go somewhere overnight?"

"I can't just—"

"Of course you can. I'll have the arrangements made in thirty minutes. This'll be fun."

"I have no doubt of that," he said taking another sip of scotch. It tasted better.

IT WAS LATE when Gaynaud returned to his small office. He was exhausted, but he still had one more thing to do.

"Well, let's see what we've got, Sam," he said out loud. He looked at his notepad. The license tag on the green Land Rover was from South Carolina. Armed with the tag number, it had taken him only three calls to get the home address, telephone number, and an answering machine greeting. It was the first time he had heard Sam Larkin's voice in years. It sounded older and less intense. Calm.

The information, however, was no help in locating Sam here in Louisiana. If he *was* in Louisiana. Gaynaud was still angry at himself for having been suckered at the motel in Kenner. He should have given Sam more credit.

"You were only carrying an overnight bag when you left Thibodaux, not enough clothes for a trip from the East. You've got a base somewhere, my friend, or else you're spending a lot of time in laundromats." Larkin had registered as Sam Harrelson. On the run, which he doubted, or hiding, which he suspected. Sam had led him to Kenner, then lost him. In his experience, most objects of a tail who had any street smarts at all would double back the way they had come and, when secure, resume the direction toward their destination. If he was covering himself in Louisiana, his base probably wasn't there. First law: remove yourself from where the action takes place. Always have a place to run to.

"Mississippi," he said, scribbling the possibilities on the notepad. "I'd bet on it. I'd also bet you didn't come all this way just to see your ex-wife and then leave. Nope. You've got unfinished business in Louisiana, and you'll be back. You got me once, Sam, but not twice."

Gaynaud flipped through his rolodex, found the number he was looking for, and dialed. A gruff voice answered.

"I don't care what you got goin'. Send out a rookie. It's the middle of the night, and I'm sleepin'. Who the hell is this anyway?"

"Raymond Gaynaud, Bill. I'm glad you're having such a good evening."

"Raymond!" The voice was suddenly infused with enthusiasm. "What the hell causes you to ring my phone at this hour? I was beginning to think you was dead. What's it been since I heard from you? Three months? Four?"

"I have no idea, but it's been awhile. I need to hit you up for a favor."

"It might require a beer or somethin'. Whatcha got that needs doin'? And I hope it doesn't have anything to do with a woman."

"Nothing specific, and I don't want it to get out in the department, okay? I'm looking for an old friend of mine. He's driving a green Land Rover, probably eight or ten years old, pretty beat up, with a South Carolina tag on it. It's a true tag; I checked it. I think he might be staying in your neck of the woods, maybe Gulfport or Biloxi, somewhere just outside Louisiana, and wondered if you could keep an eye out."

"That's a lot of territory. Gimme the tag number. And if I see this luxury automobile?"

Gaynaud gave him the tag number. "See if you can pin down an address where he's staying. Nothing else."

"You don't want him to know you're looking for him." It was a statement.

"Not yet."

"He wanted?"

"No."

"I'll keep my eyes open in Biloxi, Raymond, but I don't get over to Gulfport much. That's about the best I can do without letting anyone else in on it."

"You're a true friend, Bill."

"I'm an asshole. Ask anybody that knows me."

It was a long shot built on conjecture, but it was better than no shot at all. And it was time to put Ms. Landrieu against the wall about her interest in Sam Larkin.

It had been a long time since Gaynaud's body had touched a bed, and he could feel it beginning to shut down. He got up from his desk, turned out the lights, closed the door, and headed for the parking lot. He was already dreaming.

# FOURTEEN

BUCK LINK WAS curious. He'd had no word from Raleigh DuBose. He had been unable to stop thinking about the burned-out car—mainly due to the grinning rubbernecker, whose face kept lingering in Link's mind. He knew it was unlikely they would come up with much, but if the car was stolen, which was a reasonable conjecture, DuBose would have a starting place. He should have heard something by now. If the car didn't come from Jefferson Parish, the sheriff would probably need the state police. He had decided before he reached his office that DuBose would be his first call of the day.

"Good mornin', Buck. Kind of early, isn't it? What can I do for you?"

"That burned-out car on 3257. You ever come up with anything on it?"

"I was gonna call you on that."

Link read it as a lie.

"We were able to read the VIN—surprising considering the condition of the car. Turned out to be a rental from the airport in New Orleans. Been out for several weeks. Guy by the name of Harry Crowell rented it, but he's not from anywhere in Louisiana, even though the address says he is. The clerk who rented him the car didn't remember him. Course he might not have been the one in the car. Might have been the hitter rented it. That would explain the phony address."

"You still believe it was professional."

"No doubt. Somebody that's just pissed don't bother to break out somebody's teeth, and the fire was hot enough to destroy any other identification. Used a lot more than gasoline. Hell, there wasn't much more than a grease spot left."

"I assume you checked missing persons."

"We put out all the necessary signals, shot the name through the FBI, but haven't gotten an answer yet."

"I understand," Link said, though he could never understand people not doing what they agreed to do. "Raleigh, I'd appreciate it if you'd fax me all the reports and anything else you've found. I'll see if I can assist you from here."

"All right, Buck. I always take all the help I can get."

A rental car, a bogus address, probably a phony name, an unidentifiable body. *Another day in the world of questions*, Link thought when he hung up the phone. He yearned for a day, just one day, when there were more answers than questions. He had pretty much a whole career under his belt, and he hadn't had one yet. Living with things he didn't know was like going through life illiterate.

CELINE'S VOICE SOUNDED tired. Sam guessed she'd had no more sleep than he. "You all right?" he asked.

"I'm not awake enough to know," she said. He could picture her head on the pillow, the phone held to her ear. "You?"

"Probably as tired as you. Nothing happened out there overnight?"

"No."

"I lost whoever was following me in Kenner, so I don't think he's interested in you."

"That's a helluva statement to hear first thing in the morning."

Sam laughed. Celine had not lost her sense of humor, one of the things that had seduced him in the beginning. "I don't think the guy meant to do me harm. He had plenty of chances," Sam said, trying to convince himself. "Somebody just wants information."

"I'm glad. I didn't sleep very well."

"Me either. Call me if you suspect anything, but I think you're in the clear."

"I hope so."

"Go back to sleep, Celine."

"I will," she said and hung up the phone.

A breath of disappointment went out of him. How could anyone not be interested in her?

THE COFFEE WAS ready, and Sam was getting breakfast together when Karen came into the kitchen, shielding her eyes from the light pouring in through the windows.

"Still determined to reside in the guestroom?" she asked.

"Better than being having glasses thrown at me."

"Sorry about that. I think I visited Jack Daniels a few too many times while I was waiting for you. Now he's visiting me."

Sam poured a cup of coffee, added sugar and cream, and sat it on the counter in front of her.

"Thank you," she said. She was wearing one of his T-shirts and looked more exhausted than he felt.

Sam went through the domestic routine of breakfast—frying bacon, flipping eggs, toasting wheat bread—while Karen sipped her coffee and said nothing.

"This'll help," he said as he put her plate in front of her. "Are we ready to work?" he asked, seating himself at the counter with his own plate.

"You first," she answered, looking at the food before her with obvious distaste.

"Not until you eat." He watched her lift a small forkful of egg to her mouth and take a bite out of a piece of toast.

"Now?" she mumbled, overchewing her food to put off trying to swallow it.

"Not a lot to report, really. Celine doesn't know much more than we do. A lawyer named Hamill handled it all. Divorce, original payment, bank deposit, and confidentiality agreement, in addition to a not-so-subtle warning. Since the deposit, she's heard nothing."

"Hamill? That name came up on Hunnycut's house." Coming suddenly alive, she detailed the transfers of property, the escalations and deflations in value, and the fact that Prather had been the attorney of record in all of the transactions. Then she told him about the Prather murders.

"What does Dougherty have to say about all this?"

"I've tried to call him several times and only got the answering machine. He hasn't responded, which is strange, but you never know about Neil. I wouldn't have given him everything I found in any case, because I was waiting for you." Karen's face looked grim. "There are a lot of connections showing up, and a couple of murders. I'm not sure where to go with it. I need your input, and, by the way, your telephone messages were not particularly revealing."

Sam took a deep breath. "I was followed when I left Thibodaux."

Karen's jaw tightened. "Followed? Here? Someone knows you're here?"

"Not here. I dumped him in Kenner. I don't think it's anyone who wants to get rid of me; he had plenty of chances."

"It's time to tell Neil what we've got and find out where he is on this." Karen went to the phone and dialed. "He's still not answering. I hate to leave another goddamn—Neil, we need to talk to you. Don't know where you are or what you're doing, but get back to me as soon as you get this message. Please." She slammed the phone down, her face worried. "You think all of this goes back to Hunnycut?"

"I don't know," Sam said, "but I don't believe in coincidence. I think it's him or someone acting on his behalf. When we do talk to Neil, I think we should leave Hamill's connection to Celine between us for the time being."

"Okay." Karen looked at Sam, drumming her fingers on the phone. "How'd she look?"

"Not now, Karen." He started collecting the breakfast dishes, piling them in the sink. "I think it's time to go to the city and start the ball rolling."

"I shudder to ask," she said.

"Then don't. Not yet."

"What if Neil's not there?"

"Leave him a note. We need to meet with him, Karen."

"SO," MUSGRAVE BLUSTERED, as he entered his home office with a broad smile, "You're Rockford."

"No. Gaynaud. Raymond Gaynaud," he said, a little confused. He was undecided on how to approach Harold Musgrave; he knew little about the man. He was confident, though, that he would leave Mandeville knowing why he'd been hired or leave unemployed.

"I know who the hell you are." Musgrave laughed. "You must believe all those tales you've heard about me. I am not drunk or addlebrained, and you don't even vaguely resemble James Garner."

Gaynaud grinned at his faux pas. "Ah."

"Casey says you've got some information for me. Let's hear it." Musgrave sat down behind his desk, Casey in a club chair to his right.

Casey looked stunning. Three years earlier, when she had hired him, her physical beauty had been obvious but not polished by confidence or self-assurance. The missing parts were now in place. Gaynaud cleared his throat and began. "Before I begin with what I have, which is very little, I want to make something clear. I'm pretty much stymied because I don't know why I'm looking for information about Sam Larkin. You could be looking up an old high school classmate for all I know. If that were the case, knowing the high school and its location would be a help. I haven't found much on any Sam Larkin, and I doubt the one I have managed to come up with could be involved with corporate transactions of any kind. What I'm essentially saying, Mr. Musgrave, is that the ball's in your court. If you can't give me more to go on, I'm going to have to let you turn the job over to someone else. I have a couple of people I could recommend if that's your wish."

Musgrave pulled a cigar from a humidor on his desk. "I believe you told Casey that the confidential relationship between someone such as yourself and your clients is as sacrosanct as that between a lawyer and client, doctor and patient. That correct?"

"Yes."

"You willin' to go to jail to protect that? If it should become necessary, that is?"

The idea of going to jail was something Gaynaud didn't want to contemplate. But he said yes and meant it. The job was the job, and he'd chosen it.

"All right. You tell me exactly what you've got, and I'll decide if we should proceed."

Gaynaud told them about a Sam Larkin who had been a Louisiana environmental officer ten or so years before; had married in Lake Charles, Louisiana; divorced a couple of years later; and evidently left the state. He had found nothing to indicate this Larkin had ever been involved in oil or any other type of big business operation. He did not mention the fact that he knew a Sam Larkin who had served time in Angola. "That's it," he said. "Without more information, I have no other paths to pursue."

Musgrave sat quietly for a moment, contemplating the cigar as if he might take a bite out of it. "Any idea who handled the divorce?"

This was a good question, one that surprised Gaynaud. He pretended to look at the small spiral notepad that he had referred to when he was giving his report. All of the pages were blank, but a notepad was expected, especially by people who watched television, and Harold

Musgrave obviously did. "An attorney by the name of Parker Hamill," he said.

"The one who committed suicide?" Musgrave sounded surprised. Casey didn't react. Either it was all new to her, or she was one hell of an actress.

"I don't know anything about that. He's not listed in the Martindale-Hubbell directory. Guess that may be why. When did this happen?"

"Hell, time dudn't mean much to me. Six or seven years ago, I'd guess. There was quite a bit of controversy about it. Lotta people didn't think it was suicide, thought he mighta been helped along."

"Why's that?"

"Who knows. Lotta bullshit was put out."

"How might your Sam Larkin connect with a six-year-old suicide?"

"Dudn't, as far as I know," Musgrave answered, but Gaynaud could see his mind working.

"Well, I guess that's it for me," the investigator said and started to get up from his chair.

"Dammit, son, sit back down! I'm not finished yet. I've just got to figure out how to put this. Confidential, correct?"

"Perfectly."

Musgrave told his story, and once he began, it flowed. His problems with Hunnycut, Pettigrew's and Valdrine's association with the senator, the senator's possible place on the presidential ticket, and the reporter Harry Landers's mention of Sam Larkin in connection with the senator's judicial record.

Gaynaud kept silent. He had guessed that Larkin was in some kind of legal bind, but nothing this big. He had apparently become a very important person and maybe didn't even know it. Perhaps Gaynaud could return the favor he had carried for years.

"Parker Hamill used to do grunt work for my attorney," Musgrave continued. "Never was a partner or member of the firm far as I know, but I think Jordan's office was his only source of income."

"This is all very interesting," Gaynaud said, "but I'm still not sure why you have an interest in Larkin."

"He's an ace, son. When you play with these bastards, you know they're gonna cheat, so you better have an ace up your sleeve to trump the king they've got up theirs."

"Suppose they have an ace, too?"

"If they did, they wouldn't be worried about Larkin. I'd figure he's the ace, and I do believe they're worried. Hell, maybe even panicked. You should hear the way these ol' boys react when I say his name. What I want to know is why. That's why you're here. You're supposed to be the detective."

"Well, at least that gives me some direction," Gaynaud said, rising from his chair. "You'll hear from me the minute I come up with something. And, by the way, if you hear from that reporter again, let me know. Find out where I can reach him, or give him my number."

"Will do. Keep us posted, Jim," Musgrave said and winked.

Gaynaud looked sideways at him.

"Rockford," Casey reminded him. "Jim Rockford."

Gaynaud smiled, shook his head, and left.

SAM DROPPED KAREN at the camera shop and searched for a parking place. He found one a block from Pettigrew's office. He thought about Valdrine, Pettigrew, Prather, and Hamill. The latter two were unknown factors, mystery men. Valdrine and Pettigrew, on the other hand, were not mysteries. He thought for a moment and decided he could take a few minutes to scratch an itch he could reach.

At the intersection of Canal and St. Charles, he turned south toward the central business district. Amongst the high rise office buildings, the winter warmth was more apparent. It felt good. He couldn't avoid wondering, though, if it was his own internal temperature rising in reaction to his plan. He found the building he was looking for, entered the lobby, and scanned the register. The elevator took him to the fourteenth floor. He walked to a solid mahogany door marked with an engraved gold plaque: *Jordan Pettigrew, Attorney-at-Law*. No partners. Sam found that interesting.

As he was staring at the door, ready to walk away, it opened and Jordan Pettigrew stood before him.

"Can I help you?" the attorney asked.

"No," Sam said, smiling. "I think I'm on the wrong floor. Is this the sixteenth?"

"Fourteenth," Pettigrew said and moved past him toward the elevators. Sam followed him. Pettigrew went down. Sam went up.

ATTORNEY GENERAL. A presidential appointment. The chief law enforcer in the land. A lofty position. Right up there with Bobby Kennedy, and all done without a brother to name him. Really, better than the vice president, whose only job was to sweep out the president's closets and attend fundraisers and funerals. The only question in Valdrine's mind was whether or not Hunnycut could pull off his part, get the nomination, and get James elected. A lot of pieces had to fall into place, and Valdrine intended to see they did.

His home was in the Garden District, a neighborhood replete with Mansard roofs, Ionic and Doric columns, cast-iron grillwork, etched glass doors, ornate weathervanes, and immaculate gardens and lawns. He loved the place. Leaving it would be the only drawback to being attorney general. It was difficult to imagine trading it for the capital, Georgetown, or somewhere across the river in Virginia. As far as he was concerned, there was nothing civilized about Washington, DC, or its suburbs, including the people.

He was drinking his morning coffee on the patio when the telephone rang. He wasn't surprised; he was expecting several calls.

"I jus' drop de girl, me," the heavily accented Cajun voice on the other end of the line said. "She come to N'awlins. She not alone. She wit some guy stayin' wit' her in Biloxi. He drop her off at some camera shop on Canal. Don' follow de guy since you tell me to stay wit de girl. He be back, yeah."

"What did he look like?"

"Six foot. Maybe mo'. Built okay. Not dangerous. Long hair pulled togedder in back. He come las' night. Won't no car, no. Mus' live close by."

"Stay on the girl."

"At's my job," Grosjean said, and hung up.

Dealing with René Grosjean one on one was like walking a tightrope. His greasy hair, the fifties clothes, and the simple-minded smile that hinted he knew more than you would ever know made Valdrine uneasy. The man was a sociopath. Everyone feared psychopaths, but they were easier to deal with. They had feelings, hatred if nothing else, maybe even a conscience. The sociopath had neither. You were never sure just how crazy sociopaths were, and they feared nothing because they didn't care. But for precisely these reasons, Grosjean had been his handyman for years and did his jobs well.

AS THE ELEVATOR descended, Pettigrew thought about the encounter outside his office. The man had not looked lost, and his question about the sixteenth floor didn't add up. Surely he could count. Of course in this day and age, who could tell. The man had smiled and sounded pleasant, but the smile had not reached his eyes, and he had affected a familiarity that Pettigrew couldn't understand.

Ridiculous, he thought, leaving the elevator and proceeding through the lobby of Place St. Charles. He had been on edge ever since the Hunnycut thing began, and he couldn't stop the paranoid thinking that the situation engendered. "Forget it," he muttered to himself. "Stay out of it."

Stepping outside, onto St. Charles, he realized that he had no idea why he had left his office. His thinking was becoming distorted. He looked at his watch. *What the hell*, he thought, *I'll have lunch.*

SAM WALKED QUICKLY back toward Dougherty's office. Karen was standing on the sidewalk in front of the going-out-of-business camera shop. She started moving toward him as soon as he came into sight.

"Dougherty?" he asked.

"Not there. I left him a note. Where have you been? What's that Cheshire cat grin for?"

"I'll tell you later."

"You're a real bastard sometimes, you know that?"

"So I've been told. Car's a couple of blocks this way," he said. "Hungry?"

"A lot more than I was at breakfast. You choose."

"Frankie and Johnny's. It's been a long time."

In his other life, the restaurant had always deserved a stop when he was in the city. The tables were covered with plastic tablecloths, the bar more than well used, and the waiters had more personality than manners. It was a down-and-dirty eatery in a city famous for them. Karen had heard about it but had never made it there.

"I can see it's your kind of place," she said after they had picked their way through to one of the few empty tables and ordered. Their drinks, a Jax for Sam and a sweet tea for Karen, came only minutes before their soft-shell crab po'boys. The sandwiches were enormous, with fried crab legs hanging over the edges of the bread.

"How am I supposed to eat this?" she asked, staring wide-eyed at the sandwich.

"Anyway you can," he said.

She took the sandwich in both hands, examined it for the best angle, and put it to her mouth. As she bit into it, pieces of crab fell to the plate and table, and the juices and sauce ran down her chin. Sam laughed.

"What?" she mumbled, her mouth too full to say any more.

"I'm picturing the headline: *Crime-fighter Loses Battle With Po'boy. Ends Up With Saucy Chin*."

They lingered over lunch—no way could the po'boys be eaten quickly—compiling a list of names. They agreed that Hamill, Prather, and Musgrave were the paths to pursue next. Over time, Sam had learned that the belly was usually the most vulnerable spot, after the groin, to attack, and it was his guess that Hamill, Prather, and Musgrave were deep in the belly of Thornton Hunnycut's organization.

"So what do you plan to do?" Karen asked.

"Have a cigarette and then pay the bill."

"You could stop, you know," she said as he lit up.

"Some things once begun cannot be stopped. For me, one of them is the occasional cigarette."

"Okay, I've been patient, Sam. About that grin you were wearing earlier. And what took you so long to park?"

He grinned again. "I said we had to get the ball rolling."

"And?" she asked.

"He didn't recognize me. I can't believe he didn't even recognize me."

"Who?" she asked. "Who didn't recognize you?"

His grin got even wider. "Jordan Pettigrew."

"You saw Pettigrew? Where?"

"Outside his office."

"What were you doing there? How'd you know where his office is? And why he should he recognize you?"

"He was my lawyer."

Karen stared with her mouth open.

"If you want to call him that. Sent me away to die and didn't even recognize me."

"You seem awfully pleased about that."

"Makes him accessible," Sam said. "He won't see me coming."

Karen was still shocked. It would take a long time to know all of Sam Larkin, if anyone ever could. But then, that had been apparent from their first meeting. "Your lawyer. Jordan Pettigrew. Maybe he didn't see you."

"He saw me. I talked to him."

"You what?"

"You know, lips moving, sounds coming out."

"What did you say? I can't believe this."

"He asked if I was lost. I asked if I was on the sixteenth floor, and he told me I was on the fourteenth. Then he went down and I went up. I probably could have killed him right there and gotten away with it."

"How?"

"By telling him who I was."

"God, Sam. I can't believe you didn't tell me this before. You've been holding all of this . . ."

He shrugged.

"Do you want to let me in on the next move?" she asked.

"Find out who Musgrave is."

"I can do that," she said. "If he's anybody, Buck will know."

A call to Link from the pay phone in the back of the restaurant, and Karen learned that Musgrave was listed as CEO of a complex of nursing homes and assisted-living facilities that he co-owned with Hunnycut. There were also other businesses, including Gulf oil drilling ventures, that had passed through the two men's hands over the years. Link had been told that although Musgrave was the operator of the healthcare facilities, Hunnycut called all the shots and collected most of the revenue. There were also rumors that the facilities were in trouble over financial records and treatment of patients. A brief article had been in the paper a few months before, but the inquiry had died a silent and sudden death.

Sam got the address for one of the nursing homes out of the phone book. On the way back to Biloxi they drove around the perimeter of the campus of brick buildings. It appeared to be a pleasant, well-maintained place where seniors in their golden years would be happy to reside. *But only if they didn't know where they were*, Sam thought.

It was fully dark when they pulled into the parking lot of Karen's complex. Sam had paid for three days' parking for the Rover at an Exxon station about a mile away when he returned from Louisiana. If whoever was following him on the trip from Thibodaux was looking, he didn't want the Rover anywhere near the condo. But he didn't see the old car that pulled into the lot as they entered the building.

Karen flopped on the couch while Sam fixed himself a drink. An offer to make one for her was met with a gag.

"Aren't you tired?" she asked.

"Not yet. I'm going to stay up for awhile. I've got some more thinking to do."

"I can't think. I'm practically in a coma. Forget this couch, comfy as it is." She forced herself up and into the bedroom. "Don't stay up too late," she said.

"I won't."

Karen left the bedroom door open.

AT THREE AM Karen reached over to touch Sam, but he wasn't there. She got up to see if he was still awake, but the lights were out and the guestroom door was closed.

"Celine," she whispered as she went back to her own empty bed, a hollow space aching in the middle of her chest.

# FIFTEEN

THE SUN HAD broken the horizon, bright and sharp, for a beautiful morning. Celine was tired. Sleep hadn't come easily since Sam's visit. Her emotions were in turmoil, running in waves from elation to fear. She was getting ready to go to the grocery store when she saw an old Ford Crown Victoria pass slowly in front of her house. Too slowly.

She watched from the window as it passed out of sight and then came back from the opposite direction. She thought about calling Sam, then decided that would be foolish. Perhaps the driver was simply lost. She stood at the window and watched, her heart rate accelerating.

The third drive-by was no coincidence. She went to the bedroom and removed a Remington twelve-gauge, twenty-six-inch modified-choke shotgun from the cabinet Boudreaux had built into the back of the closet. The gun was designed for birds on the wing, which made it difficult to miss any target at close range. Celine was no stranger to guns. She had spent many a fall and winter day hunting duck and quail with her father. She checked the chamber. Empty. She loaded three number-two shells from a box stored in the cabinet drawer and then went back to the living room window.

The car was parked in the driveway. She couldn't see the driver's face through the glare on the windshield, but she could tell he wasn't moving. She knew where he was; he didn't know where she was. Her pulse racing, she waited and watched while he sat there for five endless minutes. She wanted to call Sam, but she didn't know if it would be to scream at him for bringing all of this into her life or to ask for help. Help was probably the smartest choice, she thought.

Finally, the car door opened. The driver was tall and well built, with olive skin, much like her own. His hair was shoulder length, well groomed, and jet black. He stood without moving, looking straight at the window behind which she stood. She was standing to the side, and the curtains shielded her, but she sensed that he knew she was there. If that was the case, he was giving her time to shoot him, his way of saying *I'm not here to harm you*.

She leaned the shotgun against the doorjamb and opened the front door, leaving the screen door latched and locked. Ready. If the man made an aggressive move, he was dead. And then she'd call Sam to come rescreen the door.

"My name is Raymond Gaynaud," he called from where he stood. "I know your name is Celine Aguillard Larkin. I'm an old friend of Sam's. I'm trying to help him. I'd like to talk to you if you have the time and inclination and have decided not to shoot me."

*How could he know that*, she wondered. She said nothing.

"Tell me to get lost and I will."

"How do you know Sam?" she asked.

"We were in prison together. Angola. He saved my life."

The frankness of the statement caught her by surprise. He didn't necessarily look like someone who had spent time in prison, but, then, neither did Sam. Gaynaud was handsome, but not soft looking in any way, his voice quiet yet deep. Looking at his size, well in excess of six feet, she wondered if the lifesaving hadn't been the other way around.

"Stay right there," Celine said. "I'll be out in a moment." She carried the shotgun to the phone and dialed the first number Sam had given her, but the line was busy. Talking to Gaynaud was a risk, but the man seemed okay. Probably a stupid decision, she thought, but she had done crazier things in her life.

She opened the screen door and stood, still halfway inside. The shotgun was within easy reach. Gaynaud had moved onto the porch. He stood up from the rocking chair and held out his hand. The man certainly wasn't afraid.

"Raymond Gaynaud," he said.

Celine did not take his hand and did not move from her position. "I'd prefer you remain seated," she said. He returned to the rocking chair and sat. "You said you were trying to help Sam. Can you explain that to me?"

"I'm a private investigator, strange as that may sound coming from an ex-con."

"How does an ex-con get to be licensed as a private investigator?"

"My father's a judge in New Orleans."

"I guess that makes sense," Celine said.

"A client hired me to find out whatever I could about Sam. The client doesn't even know who Sam is, so his motive is simply to get information. My personal concern is not based on my client's request, but on who he is associated with, and not in a positive way, I might add."

"Who are we talking about?" Celine asked. "Would I know them?"

"Thornton Hunnycut, among others."

"It's all opening up again." Celine looked straight at the man. "Did you follow Sam out here the other day?" she asked.

"No. I got your name from the divorce filing and traced you here. Sam just happened to be here when I arrived. I didn't know it was his car in the drive. We haven't kept in contact, and I haven't seen him in years. Innocent cons seldom do."

"You were innocent?"

"He was; I wasn't. I got caught with a certain amount of marijuana." His forthrightness was again surprising.

"And it was you who followed him when he left?"

"Yes, I did, but he lost me around Kenner. I hope someday we'll laugh about that."

"If you're looking to help him, why didn't you stop him when he left?" Celine asked.

"You learn something in prison, Celine—may I call you Celine?"

She nodded.

"You learn to be very careful about invading another person's space or intruding on his life unless specifically invited. It can get you killed." Gaynaud sat forward. "So far I've just been bothered that someone was interested in Sam. If I knew he had become a bad guy, I would have forgotten it, but from what little I've been able to learn, he hasn't. It was only yesterday that I found out exactly what my client's motive is—basically using Sam as protection against the people I mentioned, and they make me nervous. That's my only explanation."

Celine saw no reason to doubt Gaynaud's story. He seemed believable. She stepped out on the porch but stayed close to the door. "So why are you here, Mr. Gaynaud? Why not go directly to Sam?"

"Raymond, please. I have no idea where he is or how to reach him. I thought you might be able to help me. I also wanted to ask you about Parker Hamill. He seems, at some point, to have been a key player in whatever was going on. I know he handled your divorce. I don't know what else."

"That's all I know. I never heard from him again. Maybe you ought to look him up."

"He's dead."

"What? What happened?" she asked.

"Suicide. Or so it was ruled. Some have their doubts, but I haven't had time to pursue that yet."

"I didn't know—no, I don't know anything. Some phone calls about the divorce, and then I never heard anything more."

"What about Sam? He's a threat to them, Celine. Hunnycut won't allow him to get in the way of his political ambitions. I need to know what to do."

Celine went into the house, returning with the phone number for the condo. "He didn't give me an address. Do you have a card?" she asked. "I'll give Sam your number if he calls."

"You don't expect to see him again?"

"I don't think so," she answered.

Gaynaud tore a corner off the paper and wrote down his number. "My card," he said with a broad grin, and stood up to leave. "Thank you for talking to me." Gaynaud paused for a moment, scanning her face. "Sam Larkin was a lucky man. More than years were taken away from him."

Celine watched him drive away, wondering just how much trouble Sam was in.

KAREN TRIED CALLING Neil at eight o'clock in the morning, approximately thirty minutes after he usually arrived at the office. His answering machine was full and would accept no new messages. She tried again every half hour until noon with the same result. With each call, her panic increased. Between calls she and Sam, once again, went over each piece of information they had collected, graphing the timeline and relationships of each of the components. Despite the repetition, Karen's mind was not on the work.

At twelve-thirty she fixed a cup of tea and went back to the kitchen table, where they were working. Her complexion was pale, and her body was sagging.

"Something's wrong, Sam," she said.

"Why don't you call Regan in Washington?" Michael Regan was heading up the investigation in the capital, the only other participant in the operation whose name and contact number Dougherty had given her.

"I did, yesterday. He doesn't know anything and hasn't been able to make contact either. He did say that even after years of working with the man, which I know myself, there was no way to predict Neil's actions."

But that statement had not eased her mind. Neil always kept her informed even when he kept everyone else in the dark. Karen was his confidant, confessor, and shoulder. In spite of their having been married and divorced, their trust in each other on both the professional and personal level had never wavered.

Sam looked at her. "Call Buck," he said. "You can't operate in denial, Karen. Maybe he'll know nothing, which would be a relief. There could be any number of reasons you can't reach Neil, and they're not all bad."

"I'm not sure I—"

"You don't have a choice," he said firmly. "And you know it."

Karen lowered her head, trying to hide the tears that were forming in her eyes, the look of fear in her face, and the quivering chin that seemed to have a mind of its own.

"Maybe I'll—"

Sam did not let her finish. "Now, Karen. Do it now. Good news or bad news, there's no way to move on. None of us can function with a question that dominates ninety percent of our thinking."

Without another word she went to the phone and punched in the number to Buck's direct line, one part of her mind hoping he wasn't in, the other hoping he was.

"Commander Link," the voice answered.

"Buck. It's Karen." Her voice was subdued.

"You don't think I know you well enough to recognize your voice? Or to recognize by your voice that something's wrong? What can I do for you, sweetheart?"

"I need you to check on something."

"Just ask."

There was a moment of silence and a deep sigh. "I haven't been able to contact Neil for several days. Now his answering machine is full. I went by his office yesterday and left a note asking him to contact me immediately, but so far nothing. I know he could be undercover to the extent that it's difficult for him to make contact, but it's not like him, Buck. He'd find a way. I'm scared."

Link said nothing. Then he cleared his throat.

The pit of her stomach began churning, and dread began descending upon her. "Buck, you might recognize my voice, but I recognize your silence. Talk to me."

"First, don't jump to any conclusions," he said, a note of warning in his voice.

She pictured him somber, holding the phone to his ear, his eyes searching the room for the correct words.

"I do have one case that we don't know much about at the moment. I'm reluctant to mention it because I don't have enough information."

Karen braced herself. "Tell me what you have."

"We got a call on a burned-out car out on State Route 3257 in Jefferson Parish a couple of days ago. At first it was just the car, then a body was discovered on the back floorboard. It was pretty bad. Unidentifiable. Powerful accelerant, no ID, and virtually nothing to go on."

"Professional?" she asked.

"I'd guess." Buck's manner changed from friendly to businesslike, which Karen knew was the easiest way to handle those things you did not want to say. "That's not too unusual around there. Lot of the city boys dump their garbage out there, and they don't leave us much to work with. The sheriff is working on it, and I will be, too. We did find out through the VIN that the car was a rental out of Louis Armstrong. The renter's name was . . . hold on a minute." Karen heard him shuffling papers. "Here it is. Harry Crowell, but the address—"

Karen felt herself crumbling, her knees going weak, a cold sweat breaking out on her arms and forehead. "Buck, let me try him again, and I'll call you later today. I've got to go right now."

"Wait, Karen, I—"

"I'll call you back, Buck." She hung up the phone.

She went back to the table and sat down. Sam was reading their notes and had not been listening. He looked up and found a stone-cold face staring out at the Gulf.

"Karen?"

She heard the words coming out of her mouth, a truth she could not avoid or deny: "Neil's dead."

Sam stared at her in silence. Finally, he reached for her hand. "Did Buck tell you? Why didn't he call earlier?"

"Buck doesn't know. I didn't tell him." Karen spoke haltingly, swallowing after every few words, speaking like an automaton, with no expression. "Buck has a case. A burned-out car in Jefferson Parish. There was a body in the back. No ID. They traced the VIN to a rental at Louis Armstrong. The renter's name was Harry Crowell. That's the name Neil always uses as his first line of cover. He's gone, Sam."

Karen had been steeling herself, imagining she was out of her surroundings, assuming a professional identity only. She retreated into her brain instead of her heart to protect her heart from things too painful to process. It wasn't normal, but her job wasn't normal, her life wasn't normal. She couldn't allow emotion to overtake her, and she felt guilty about that, but it was what she was trained to do. Regardless, though, her tears began to flow.

Sam got up and put his arms around her. She buried her head on his shoulder and sobbed.

BY FOUR-THIRTY in the afternoon, Karen had pulled herself together enough to make the calls she knew she had to make. Ignoring the hollowness in her body and the pain in her heart, her mind reasserted its authority. It wasn't a time to collapse. The real fall would come later, she knew. When she was back inside herself. When she had time to feel. When she was alone with all the thoughts and memories that she and Neil Dougherty had shared.

Buck Link would be the first. She faced the conversation with apprehension. She should have told Buck right away. Holding back information was not good law enforcement. It wasn't even adequate law enforcement. It could be called obstruction of justice if somebody really wanted to make the argument, and it certainly wasn't something to do to a friend, but she hadn't been able to bring herself to verbalize what she knew. The words wouldn't form before now.

His first reaction was silence, then anger, followed by disappointment. It took only a few words from Karen to change the color of what she had done from a lack of trust to shock and pain. They made an appointment to meet at the Bluebird Café on St. Charles the following day at eleven.

The second conversation was with Michael Regan in Washington. She had never met the man, but Neil had laid high praise upon him as an agent and as a friend. Her only previous contact with him had been the brief phone call inquiring if he'd had had any contact with Neil in the last few days.

"I'm glad to hear from you, Karen. Were you able to get with Neil? I still haven't been able to reach him, and I have several things I need direction on. It's not like him."

"Michael, Neil is dead." Karen could hear the beat of her own heart in the silence.

"Dead?" Agent Regan broke the word into two slow syllables, suggesting disbelief.

Karen explained.

"Goddammit!" she heard him whisper. After a few moments he spoke again. "I'm sorry, Karen. I know—"

"I'm okay, but I'm going to need some help down here. Things are getting out of hand, Michael."

"Neil is now the first priority, and finding the son of a bitch that did this. I could care less about Thornton Hunnycut at this point," he said.

"They're tied together, Michael. I have no doubt about that, and you won't either, once you think about it. I need a SAC down here and maybe more. I can't operate by myself."

"No. Don't even try. I'll be down tomorrow to take the field office. I probably won't get in until late, so plan to be at Neil's—the office—at nine the following morning. I've got the address. I understand it's over a . . ."

"Camera shop," Karen said.

"We'll assume we're working two parallel cases now, and you're going to have to bring me up to speed on your end. I understand you have a civilian who's involved in the investigation." She heard discomfort in his voice.

"Sam Larkin. Neil approved him. Asked him in, as a matter of fact," she said, not leaving an opening.

"I want him there, too. It's unusual, Karen, but I'll listen to what everyone has to say."

"Without him, you don't have me, Michael."

A pause on his end. "We'll talk day after tomorrow. And, Karen, I don't want any name for the body, beyond Harry Crowell, released."

"You don't have to explain. I'll see you at nine o'clock."

"Karen, I'm sorry."

"So am I," she said. She hung up the phone and turned back to Sam, who was sitting on the couch watching her. "We're meeting him at the office day after tomorrow at nine AM."

"I heard my name come up."

"Yes. He's not thrilled, I'm sure, but he doesn't have a choice. He doesn't know the situation. Neil was operating two separate units; there was no need for Regan to know everything going on down here. Neil never gives information to anyone, even me, unless there's a need. It's an easy way to keep an inventory on who knows what, and his philosophy is that the fewer people who know a piece of information, the more secure that information is."

"I'd agree with that," Sam said.

"I'm tired, Sam, and hungry. Could we just eat something here and go to bed? Today's been tough, and I think the next few days are going to be tougher."

# SIXTEEN

VALDRINE SCANNED THE *Times-Picayune.* His particular interest was mention of a death in Jefferson Parish. Until today, he had found nothing; however, in this morning's edition, buried in "Parish News" was a small article concerning a body found in a burned car on Route 3257. According to Sheriff Raleigh DuBose, the incident was classified as a probable homicide, with the investigation ongoing. The victim was identified as Harry Crowell, address unknown, who had rented the car from an agency at Louis Armstrong International Airport.

Valdrine closed his eyes and tried to clear his mind. Then he read the article again. Grosjean didn't make mistakes; he was a machine. Yet, the name didn't fit. Harry was right, but the Crowell part was wrong. There had to be an explanation, though he couldn't imagine what it would be. Getting the wrong man was not necessarily damaging, but finding out the present whereabouts of the *New Centurion* reporter and what he might be doing was critical.

Grosjean had not contacted him the day before, Valdrine assumed, because he had nothing to report. He had instructed the Cajun to keep communication at a minimum unless something significant occurred. Grosjean checked his answering machine regularly and was conscientious about answering messages.

He dialed the phone. The machine picked up. There was no greeting, just a beep. "Call me," he said into the receiver.

An hour later, the phone rang.

"I don' know nothin' 'bout no name, me. I got de right man. I don' make no mistake. He dead."

"Then why in hell does the paper say it was Harry Crowell that was found, not Harry Landers?" Valdrine barked into the mouthpiece.

"Don' know. Maybe he got two names, him."

Why would he use two names? The man hadn't tried to hide the fact that he was a reporter; the paper had verified his employment. But Grosjean had never failed him. Not yet. Valdrine would have to see how it played out.

"What about the girl?"

"Ain' done nothin'. Stay wit dat man at de house all day yesterday. Day befo' drove aroun' N'awlins after dat meetin'. Eat at Frankie and Johnny's down on Arabella and Tchopitoulas. Den drove out by some nursin' home place out—"

"Was it Laurel Grove?"

"Might be," Grosjean said. He sounded bored.

"Why didn't you call me?"

"Didn' t'ink dere was no need."

"There was."

First Hunnycut's house in Gulfport, now maybe Laurel Grove. Too coincidental. A reporter. He had to think the woman was another reporter. Valdrine realized he was faced with consideration for his own skin. Everyone couldn't be "handled."

"Boss? I got to get some res', me. T'ree days wit no sleep. I got a cousin—"

"No. Just you. Nobody else. Take six hours; you can pick her up again. I don't like it, but there's no choice."

"My cousin—"

"No cousin, René. Just you."

"Don' say my name on the phone. Ain' good. Six hours." Grosjean hung up.

Valdrine was sweating. He had lost control of the situation somewhere. A second-rate reporter and an ex-con were threatening him, not just by their presence, but by their very existence, and he wasn't handling it.

THE UNDEVELOPED, OPEN areas on Route 9 provided a catalogue of Mississippi vegetation. Water-filled roadside ditches were abundant with small water plants, scrub bushes, and marsh grasses. Sweet gum trees, along with swamp chestnuts, bald cypresses, mayhaws, and black gums sported a variety of shapes and colors that exemplified nature's penchant for majestic abstraction. Karen watched the scenery vacantly as she and Sam drove into the city.

Over morning coffee they had discussed at length the approach they would take with Buck. Karen was still chagrined about her delay in telling him what she knew, but she would do her best to keep the emotion surrounding Neil's death to a minimum. That event had created an urgency that the upcoming presidential election could not supercede, and urgency would be relieved only by action and results.

The Bluebird Café was one of Buck's favorite places. He had met Karen there several times over the years, always at eleven o'clock in order to beat the heavy lunchtime traffic. The buckwheat pecan waffles, homemade sausage, and *huevos rancheros*, served at any time, allowed diners to miss the next meal of the day without a single hunger pang.

Link was already there when Sam and Karen walked in. Sam noted surprise in the man's eyes when he saw the ponytail, jeans, and sweatshirt. A character evaluation was already taking place. Perhaps he should have told Karen to warn Buck. There was enough to accomplish without having to overcome preconceptions. Link rose when they approached his table.

Karen did the introductions. The two men shook hands, and Karen and Sam sat down across the table from Buck. Link locked in on Karen.

"Karen, I'm sorry about Dougherty. I will use every resource I have to find whoever did this. There's not much else I can say, I know."

"I appreciate that. Right now I just want to take it one step at a time and deal with the rest later, but we need your help."

"Anything I can provide. You know that." Sam watched Buck relax as they put the emotional aspect of Dougherty's death aside and moved into dealing with solving the murder. He was impressed with the man. Link didn't ask for respect; his demeanor demanded it without being officious.

Buck turned to Sam. "It's good to finally meet you, Sam. I've heard a lot about you, though most of what I've heard takes the form of questions from the lady here."

Sam could understand why Karen felt the way she did about Buck. He had no doubt that in any kind of conflict, he would want Buck on his side. "I could say the same, only without the questions," Sam said, still feeling a bit awkward. Link was a law officer; Sam had been in prison. No matter how innocent he was when convicted, the fact remained that he had served hard time. It made him different in everyone's eyes.

They ordered coffee, opting talk over food.

"I've gone over everything Sheriff DuBose has sent me," Link said, "and whoever did this is as good as or better than anyone I've come across in a while. He made no mistakes, left nothing behind."

Sam stepped in. He didn't want to appear presumptuous, but he did want Link to know that, apart from what the feds were doing, this was his and Karen's investigation.

"Commander, I'm sure you know my background and, perhaps, some of what we're doing from Karen, but I'd like to run through the short version of where we are."

"Of course. Saves a lot of questions. Karen brought you here, and I trust her. She has a stake in this, and you're part of that."

Sam explained why he was operating independently and that though he was cooperating with the agency, what he did was according to his own plan. He detailed what Karen had found about the real estate transactions and Prather murders and mentioned that he had been followed when he'd left Celine's house.

"One person I think could be a key to a lot of what's gone on, and thought you might be able to help us with, is Parker Hamill."

Link's eyebrows rose. "The attorney? How might he be involved?"

"Based on what Celine told me, he was employed by my trial attorney and handled the divorce I requested. I never met the man, and he wasn't my attorney of record—Jordan Pettigrew was. Hamill also appears to have arranged the payments to Celine when I was incarcerated and, I assume, the payments to both of us when I was released."

"He was involved in Hunnycut's house, as well," Karen added.

"We'd like some background on the man before I look him up. Anything, legal or illegal, that you may be familiar with."

Link lifted his coffee cup and took a swallow. "Parker Hamill," he said, putting the cup back on the table. "Somehow I knew that can of worms would reopen itself some day."

"I beg your pardon?" Sam said.

"Well, first of all, he's dead, so you won't be looking him up."

Sam leaned back in his chair. "This is a bigger closet than I thought. Skeletons keep falling out."

"When did he die?" Karen asked.

"Offhand, I'm not sure of the exact date, but I would say about six years ago would be pretty close. He was declared a suicide. Body was found in Hudson Park, near the lake, as I recall. There was quite a bit of controversy about it."

"What kind of controversy?" Sam asked.

"The coroner who ruled it a suicide said there was one bullet wound through the roof of the mouth and out the top of the head, that Hamill had obviously driven there and done the deed himself. A few days later, when that hit the papers, a witness who'd been jogging in the park that day just before daylight came forward and said he had seen two men in the car that Hamill drove into the park and was subsequently found in.

That started the ball rolling. A lot of questions were asked, and suddenly a number of other people came out of the woodwork with supposed facts that cast a lot of doubt on the coroner's report."

"Such as?" Karen asked.

"Some of the stories appeared to have merit, some didn't. The park maintenance man who discovered the body said there was no gun in Hamill's hand when he looked though the car window. It was obvious the man was dead, so the worker didn't try to help, just called 911. The crime scene reports by the NOPD said a gun was found in Hamill's right hand. That brought to light the fact that Hamill was left-handed. The gun itself, according to a reporter with an undisclosed source, was made from the parts of two different guns, typical of a drop gun used by some cops to avoid departmental inquiry when they are involved in a questionable use of force."

"And none of this was ever followed up?" Sam asked.

"What I've told you so far isn't all of it. This same reporter came up with a number of other things. There were no crime scene photographs, or if there were, none you could find now, anyway. The body had carpet fibers on it, suggesting it might have been moved. The most damning thing, however, was the fact that there was little blood in the car, and none on the headliner, or any damage to the fabric, which sure as hell is impossible if the death occurred inside that automobile."

"I can't believe none of this was ever pursued," Karen said.

"Not to any significant degree. The press got pretty excited about it for a few days, and there were some letters to the editor screaming cover-up, but nothing else happened. Hamill was an asterisk, not very important in the legal community, wasn't married, no scandal, no ex-lovers or wives, and there didn't seem to be any motive for killing him. Even less reason to come up with such an elaborate scheme to hide it."

"What else did this reporter with the undisclosed source find?" Sam asked.

"According to him, a lot of documents either did not exist or were destroyed."

"What about the car? Was there any investigation regarding the lack of blood or damage to the headliner?" Sam asked.

"Not that I know of. We were pretty much held out of it. The NOPD kept it close and handled everything."

"Is the reporter still around?" Karen asked.

"His byline stopped appearing in the paper about two weeks after the original article. I have to believe that if what he wrote was bogus, he would have been exposed and fired, but no such revelation from the paper ever appeared in print. He just disappeared without ever disclosing his sources."

"Unbelievable," Sam said.

"Not really. Look at your case," Link said. "Son, there is more invisible power in Louisiana politics than those who make the jokes about it and laugh at the corruption in this state could ever imagine. With some of the stuff I've learned over the years, I could be a rich man today if I wanted to be, and when I say rich, I mean with a capital R."

"I don't doubt that," Karen said.

"So Hamill worked for Jordan Pettigrew, but he didn't appear as second chair at your trial? Any other attorneys who took statements or anything?" Link asked.

"Wasn't needed, according to Pettigrew. The arrest was a mistake, 'plain and simple' I think was the way he put it, and I would be out of court free and clear in a matter of minutes following a preliminary hearing."

"I'd say they set you up pretty good. Why did they change their minds and let you go?"

"Not a clue. That's what I'm looking for."

"No other lawyers. Hard to imagine Pettigrew not having someone else there to blame if it went badly for you."

"He was a one-man show." Sam thought for a moment. "Of course I guess that's not really true; he had a lot of help from the prosecutor and the judge."

"Hunnycut was the judge, I know," Link said. "Who was the prosecutor?" Sam looked at Karen and then at Link.

"Arthur Valdrine," he said.

Karen stared at Sam and then lowered her head in frustration.

"And all the records disappeared. Makes sense, and Hunnycut could probably do that," Link said, and turned to Karen. "What official action are the feds going to take?"

"I spoke with Neil's chief agent in Washington right after I called you. His name is Michael Regan, and he's flying in tonight. We're to meet with him tomorrow morning at nine o'clock. He will be taking over Neil's position and will probably bring a couple of other agents with him."

"I would have thought they'd bring in the whole agency," Link said.

"I don't think Regan is going to advertise what has happened."

"You mean keep it secret from the agency?" Link said with disbelief.

"Possibly for a few days anyway. What I'm saying is presumptuous. I'm just trying to react like I know Neil would react. I don't know what Regan's thinking is at the moment. He did say he wanted it kept quiet. No disclosure on Neil's ID beyond Harry Crowell. I would guess that his motivation is that if the perp knows he killed a federal agent, he will rabbit."

"It was in the paper this morning, and the only name they gave was Harry Crowell; however, I do know that the sheriff assumes that it's a phony. Is there any way that the two could be put together?"

Karen shook her head. "Neil was too meticulous. I don't even know exactly what he was doing. I'm hoping Regan can shed some light on that." For the first time, she was aware of referring to Neil in the past tense. She coughed to hide the catch in her throat.

"Right now, as I said, we have nothing," Link said, "but I'll keep you posted on anything I come up with."

"And we'll do the same. Anything else you can think of?" Sam asked.

"Nothing except the fact that right now I need a pecan waffle. Care to join me?"

"Don't mind if I do," he said. It was the first smile on anyone's face Sam had seen since he'd left Thibodaux.

MARLENE COLE WAS working the phone, mining Capitol Hill for information. She followed the rules: secure lines, no names, prearranged call times to avoid administrative assistants, and, with some contacts, code words to designate times and places for meetings. She and Thornton often laughed that lobbyists, congressmen, and industry reps had a far more sophisticated network than the FBI, CIA, and NSA combined.

"What are we looking at?" she asked. It was the seventh call of the morning, this one to a contact who monitored the Government Guard, the watchdog group that was raising questions about the Hunnycut-Cole connection.

"Nothing new. The group is working the ethics committee with the usual—campaign contributions, gifts, living arrangements, associates, and records of coincidental legislation. I do know that some things involving nursing homes are high on their agenda, probably because the GAO is looking into the practices of the Health Care Financing Administration. You know the routine. Throw a dog a bone, and he'll pounce all over it. The group is pushing for an independent counsel to be appointed, but I don't think there's much chance of that happening. Congress likes to keep these kinds of things in-house. Too much damage if the wrong person gets swept in."

"They're on a fool's errand," Marlene said. "We're covered."

"I'm sure you are, and I wouldn't be overly concerned. We both know there is no ironclad consensus on what part money plays in American politics. The drug cartels would love to be able to launder money the way the politicians do. Every once in awhile there's a scream about something, and some minor changes are made, or a lesser dog is thrown under the wheels, but nothing significant ever happens. Can you tell me anyone in this system who is immune to money? When the bottom line is approached, it's always business as usual."

"Do you know the names of the congressmen who are being pushed about the independent counsel?" she asked.

"I do."

"Can we get to them and to someone in the group who's approachable?"

"Not a problem. Two of the group members have personal proclivities which make them extremely vulnerable, and one of the congressmen has a piece of legislation involving your power base," the voice said, referring to Hunnycut, "that I have no doubt you can help with."

"I don't want any trouble before the nomination. Once that's in, we can spin the accusations as political muckraking before the voters have a chance to form an opinion."

"I wouldn't worry. I know of very few members of the congress—and I might be wrong about those few—who don't have somebody going after them. All it takes is money or pleasure to keep the ball in their end of the field."

"I need the names," she said.

"Dockside three."

Marlene cut the connection. "Dockside" was the designation for a small restaurant near the aquarium in Baltimore Harbor. Three was the meeting time less two hours. One o'clock. It was only nine-thirty; in four hours she would have the names of the people whom she would, as she liked to say, jellify.

She had just one more call to make. Her curiosity about the man Valdrine and Thornton had discussed had not lessened, but Thornton had never mentioned him again. When she asked, he avoided the subject.

She picked up the phone and dialed Ed Briggs, an ex-FBI friend who debugged her townhouse once a month.

"Hello?" a sour voice said. She knew immediately that he was suffering through a massive hangover. It was his standard morning persona.

"I need you to do something for me. Do you have a pencil and paper?"

"Hold on." She could hear him shuffling around. "Okay."

"I need information on someone. Male. Probably from Louisiana. No idea of occupation or age."

"Just any male from Louisiana, or do you have a name?" he asked sarcastically.

"Sam Larkin. I would guess Samuel, but I don't know that. I need anything you can find."

"Nothing like a challenge," the man said. "This might take a few days."

"As soon as you can. It's important."

"You got it," he said and hung up.

Marlene leaned back in her desk chair and began mentally cataloging all of the elements she had any control over that were necessary to assure Thornton's nomination.

The next call was to her contact in the Secret Service. It was time to check out the man himself. Harrison James.

WITH THE TELEPHONE number Celine had provided him, it took Gaynaud almost no time to nail down Sam's physical location. Calling on the telephone was not the approach he wanted to take in reconnecting with Sam. He wasn't sure what the man had become and could only guess from what Celine had said that he was still honorable, the same Sam Larkin who had saved his life in the shower room at

Angola. He would surely have been dead if Sam hadn't knowingly taken the bait and interfered. The first meeting in their new lives had to be face to face.

On the drive to Biloxi, Gaynaud kept one eye on the Gulf. The water, reflecting the morning sun like an open cask of pirate's treasure, was a view he never got enough of. The sight of an occasional shrimp boat, dragging its nets between the shore and the horizon, made him wonder why he had ever chosen the profession he had. The men working the boats had a freedom he had not experienced since his early teens. They didn't make a lot of money, but the course of their job wasn't limited, in most cases, to delivering bad news.

When he got to the condo complex, the green Land Rover was nowhere to be seen. He parked at the far end of the lot under a spreading live oak and settled into the seat. Waiting might be a waste of time, but it was a large part of his job, and he had, after all, found what he was looking for.

The sun had raised the temperature, but the Gulf breeze, with its sharp salt-sea odor, was refreshing. He picked up his notepad. It contained a scant list, primarily names. Relaxing now after the drive, he found his eyes wanting to close.

His attention was diverted when an old car pulled into the lot and parked several spaces down. It didn't look like a car that would belong to someone who lived in one of these condos. They weren't elaborate, but with a Gulf view, he couldn't imagine that they were cheap.

He leaned his head back and closed his eyes, mulling over the names of those who had come under his scrutiny. Arthur Valdrine: likely the prosecutor in Sam's trial. Hunnycut: definitely the judge, possible vice presidential nominee. Parker Hamill: handled the divorce, possible suicide, possible murder. Jordan Pettigrew: role unknown. Harold Musgrave: Hunnycut's business associate, in conflict with the senator on nursing homes. Casey Landrieu: hired him, beautiful. Celine Aguillard: ex-wife, also beautiful. His job had some benefits that outweighed the appeal of the shrimp boats. He turned these names over in his mind, trying to fit them together in various configurations.

But something was bothering him, a shadow in his subconscious forming a roadblock to his thinking, something he couldn't put his finger on. He opened his eyes to check the townhouse, and it hit him. The old car. It had pulled in and parked—Gaynaud looked at his watch—thirty minutes or more ago. The driver was still in the car. He tried to construct a visual line, but given the angles and the other cars, it was impossible without getting out and exposing himself. Not a good idea. Wait, he told himself. Just wait. At least watching two objectives was a little more interesting than observing only one.

Two and a half hours passed, and the other driver made no move to leave his automobile. It didn't take a detective to determine that he was also staking out something. Or perhaps he—or she—had simply lost the house key and was waiting for a spouse to come home and unlock the door. Or maybe someone who lived in one of the units was having a wife or husband checked out to see if there was any hanky-panky going on.

While he was playing this game of possibilities, getting more bizarre the longer he went, a thin, wiry man with shanks of greasy, black hair appeared from between the cars and headed for the condos. Gaynaud grinned at the way the man was dressed: black pants, pink shirt, and black loafers with a white yoke. He looked like a bad Elvis impersonator.

What he did when he walked up the steps to Sam's unit got Gaynaud's full attention. Pretty good himself, he had never seen anyone approach a door, pick a lock, and enter a building as smoothly and efficiently as Pink Shirt did. He might as well have had a key, and the open disregard the man had for the possibility that someone might see him was something to behold.

Gaynaud opened his glove compartment and removed a Glock 9mm that he had never used, slipped it in the waistband of the back of his pants, and stepped out of the car. Maybe Pink Shirt was just going to toss the place for reasons of his own or steal something and leave. If the man remained inside, Gaynaud would have to stop Sam from walking through the front door.

It was a moment, and Gaynaud recognized it. People were traveling up and down Highway 90, only a few feet away, going grocery shopping, to the drugstore to pick up a prescription, to a movie, people totally unaware of what was going on around them. Maybe in the units someone was ironing, nursing a sick kid, having sex, not knowing that a petty crime, possibly with ties to a potential vice presidential candidate, was taking place in their own parking lot.

The door to the unit opened, and, without looking in either direction, Pink Shirt closed it and walked back down the steps as casually as if he were leaving for work. He put the handkerchief he was carrying into his pocket, smiled, nodded to Gaynaud as he would to a slight acquaintance, and went to his car. Gaynaud watched as the car pulled out of its space and headed toward the exit. He followed it. He could come back to Sam. It was more important to know who this aberration was.

The man went to a public phone at a convenience store on Highway 90, made a brief call, got back in his car, and headed west. Gaynaud was right behind him. He had a gut feeling that Pink Shirt was a piece of the puzzle. He was good at what he did. His picking the lock was sufficient to prove that, but he surely didn't have any taste in clothes.

They merged onto I-10 West toward New Orleans. There was no indication the man knew he was being followed. Gaynaud tried to get the tag number, but it was mudded over, which meant it was probably stolen.

Not too many travelers were headed into the city, so Gaynaud found it easy to keep the car in sight while maintaining a good distance. Pink Shirt stayed in the right lane unless forced to move over and pass a slower car. He never exceeded sixty miles an hour, taking no chances on breaking the law, but an innocent driver never obeys the speed limit on an interstate. He assumed the man wasn't drunk, but he had to be guilty of something other than bad taste to drive that slowly. Gaynaud almost missed the man's brief turn signal.

"Thank you for being considerate," he said out loud as he took the Paris Road exit and headed toward Chalmette. Pink Shirt then took a right onto West St. Bernard Highway, went a couple of miles, and turned left on Aycock. They were in Arabi, in a neighborhood Gaynaud would not feel safe walking in. He caught a stoplight, stuck behind another car. All he could do was watch as two hours of surveillance went down the toilet.

When the light changed, he turned right and drove a few blocks at more than legal speed, trying to head the other car off, but when he got back to the street where he had lost him, Pink Shirt was nowhere in sight. Gaynaud had blown it. For the second time, he had lost his quarry. He needed a class in mobile surveillance.

# SEVENTEEN

MUSGRAVE KNEW THAT Pettigrew wouldn't be happy to see him. He never was, really, but Pettigrew hadn't called about having the buyout papers ready for his signature, and Musgrave was getting anxious. Hunnycut's reaction was one he couldn't wait to hear. Pettigrew's secretary saw him coming but had learned years before never to try to stop him; he hardly ever acknowledged her. She hardly ever acknowledged him either, although she was a bulldog when it came to heading off anyone else trying to see Pettigrew. Today though, Musgrave took a different approach; he stopped at her desk and gave her a big smile.

"Mornin', Theresa. Is his honor in?"

Theresa, caught off-balance, could only say yes.

Pettigrew, busy—or trying to appear busy—looked up when Musgrave walked through the door.

"Mornin', Jordan," Musgrave said, and took a chair without being asked.

"Harold. I wish you'd called. I've got a pretty busy morning, and I have a board meeting this afternoon for one of the charities I'm involved in. I really wish—"

"Oh, I'm not gonna take up much of your time. Was just in the neighborhood. That is what people always say when they drop in unexpected, idn't it? I just wanted to see how you were comin' along with those papers you were gonna draw up for me."

Pettigrew looked down at his desk and then up to Harold Musgrave. "Harold, I've been meaning to call you. I'm not sure what you proposed is a bona fide and realistic enough offer to present to Thornton. I mean—"

"I thought the law was that any offer had to be presented."

"Well, in real estate, yes, but—"

"So I need to get a real estate person to present my offer? It is real estate, I guess. I don't see that as a problem." He started to get up.

"Sit down, Harold. You know you're going to irritate the hell out of Thornton with this offer. I thought you needed money. He's willing to sign it over to you with a note, and you'll get all the income, which we both know is substantial. I don't see your problem with that." Pettigrew looked as though he had just brought peace to the world.

"And when it all comes tumbling down, as I explained to you before, I go into bankruptcy or, more likely, to jail all by myself. Idn't that part of the deal, Jordan? Wouldn't you think so?"

"It's not important what I think. Do you really believe that's what's going to happen?"

"Indeed I do. That or worse. I know what's goin' on out there, and you and I both know who the deciding vote is on how those places are run. Now, I don't need to remind you that I can—"

"I know, bring the whole thing down on Thornton's shoulders. You've told me that a hundred times, but do you know what that would do?"

Musgrave laughed. "Prob'ly get me killed."

Pettigrew's face sobered. "I find it hard to believe you said that."

"Don't try to bullshit a bullshitter; you know more about that than I do. Okay, you've got another week, but if nothin's done by then, I'm gonna find me a real estate person that'll do what I ask him to."

"I'll do it, Harold, but I won't be responsible for—"

"You've never been responsible for anything, Jordan." Musgrave got out of his chair. "By the way, you ever hear from that reporter again?"

"No. No, I didn't."

"Funny. He told me he was going to talk to you again. Was gonna call me, too. Sure would like to know who that Larkin fellow was he was askin' about." Musgrave turned and threw a hand up in a goodbye wave as he walked through the door.

"Have a good day, Theresa," Musgrave said on his way out.

For all Harold Musgrave's bluster, Pettigrew thought, at least you knew where you stood with the man, which was more than he could attribute to any of his other associates. Of all the people Pettigrew did business with, Musgrave was probably the only one who never seriously disappointed him. The criticisms Musgrave leveled at him were meant to be taken with a grain of salt, and that's the way Pettigrew took them. It was the reason their association had lasted so long.

In the quartet that he, Valdrine, Hunnycut, and Musgrave comprised, Musgrave was, without doubt, the most trustworthy. If Pettigrew ever needed to trust anyone.

"IT'S AN EARLY spring sky," Sam said, as he and Karen walked down toward her car after their lunch with Buck Link. He had never had waffles for lunch, but Buck had been absolutely on target. They had been delicious, and he was replete.

"How can you tell?" she asked.

"It's starting to clear up. Humidity's falling. Humidity holds dust, soot, and all manner of other things."

"Did you teach that to all your biology students in South Carolina?"

"That's actually General Science One, but it's not taught as a rule, and I didn't learn it in college. Got it from an old fishing and hunting guide, a bootlegger, when I was working the outdoors. And, yes, I taught it. That was one of my problems with teaching; I didn't stick to the curriculum."

"Don't like to be told what to do, do you, Sam?"

"Not much," he said as they reached the car.

"Now what?" she asked when he was behind the wheel.

"I'm not sure." He wondered how to tell her what he was going to do or whether to wait and tell her after the fact. "Any ideas?"

"Well, we've got three murders and a questionable suicide, with no connections between them except that they're connected. Connected in my mind anyway. I can't believe that the murders of Masley Prather, who was involved with Hunnycut; and Neil, who was investigating Hunnycut; and Hamill, who may or may not have committed suicide and was also involved with Hunnycut, are not related."

Sam was suprised at the objectivity Karen had mustered regarding Dougherty's death. He could only believe it was temporary and that after the case was over and her mind no longer focused on the job at hand, it would fade and her grief would manifest. It was part of the professional in her. "And you've got a police force in Biloxi who has closed the first case and isn't interested in reopening it. An agent dead in a burned-out car with no clue as to who did it. A suicide-slash-murder that was swept under the rug and covered up. I think it's time we stopped spinning our wheels."

"How?"

"Maybe they need to know I'm here."

She looked at him. "But you said you wouldn't be—"

"I said I wouldn't let Dougherty use me to bait his trap. I didn't say I wouldn't use me to bait my own trap."

"Do you want to explain that to me?"

"It's called a Louisiana burn, having someone chase you until you catch them."

"Learn that in Angola?" she asked.

"From an expert. Only problem was, he didn't circle around fast enough and got caught before he could clear himself."

"How long was he in for?"

"Life. Another rare case of the injustice of justice."

"An expert who got caught. You'll have to tell me that story some time. So what do you plan to do? How are you going to bait your trap with you?"

Sam looked at her, the serious but mischievous grin she had seen so many times on his face, mischievous but dangerous. She did not find it comforting, but it did make her feel that Sam was being Sam again, and she welcomed that.

"You sure you want to know?"

"Tell me."

"Here we go," he said.

"Oh, shit."

MARLENE COLE ARRIVED at the Best Western in Fredericksburg early, a tactic she always employed for such events. The hotel was a traveler's stop, not the kind of place a casual observer would suspect for this kind of meeting. She registered as Carol Rich from Dalton, Georgia, an alias she had used for years. In her room, she dialed the number she had been given. When the answering machine on the other end picked up, she spoke the numbers, "Two, one, four," then hung up, left the door to the room ajar, and went to her car to wait.

It had not been a simple matter to arrange this little *tête-à-tête*, but her contact had found a man too vulnerable in his private life to refuse her request. He was made to order, a significant member of the Government Guard. This meeting, in the Government Guard's eyes, would be tantamount to treason on the man's part if it were exposed.

She waited thirty-five minutes—the driving time from his home near Dumfries—and spotted him immediately when he arrived. She shook her head at his naiveté. He was dressed in the government uniform: navy blue suit, white shirt, tie, and highly polished black shoes. Marlene was wearing jeans, a College of William and Mary sweatshirt, and a light jacket. She couldn't help wondering, as she watched the man climb the stairs to the second floor, how people reputed to be so intelligent could be so dumb. She waited ten minutes after he entered the room, then followed him up.

The man was sitting on the edge of the second bed, near the bathroom. He stood when she entered the room. "I want you to know—" he began.

Marlene cut him off with a finger to her lips. Make him more insecure. She pulled a small transmitter detector from her pocket and ran the device up and down his body. There was no indication that he was wearing any sort of wire. She turned the detector off and put it back in her pocket.

"I have your word that you are not wired, am I correct?" she asked.

"You do. What about you?" His face was pasty, his jowls sagging.

"You can use this," she said, retrieving the detector from her pocket, "or I can take off all of my clothes. You wouldn't be interested in that though, would you?"

The man sat back down on the bed, red-faced. "I trust you," he said.

"You have no choice."

The man was bald, overweight, and defeated; his clothes didn't hide that. He barely resembled the personage whose picture she'd seen in the *Washington Post* and in the news magazines. Sad that a man with power and influence, a positive public persona, and the general respect of the unknowing public could be brought to this point. Marlene sat at the desk and pulled a legal pad and pen from the drawer, where she had placed them earlier. The man said nothing. He just stared at her, wishing she were dead, she was sure, or at least wishing immeasurable pain upon her.

"I need to know what your organization has and where they are putting their emphasis in this ridiculous quest. I want everything. I want to know what I have to do to call off the dogs and send them in another direction. I can give you a dozen senators or reps with a lot more to hide than Thornton Hunnycut."

"Well, I can't—"

"Stop," she interrupted. "I don't want to hear what you can't do."

He began with campaign fundraising, illegal payments before her departure from Hunnycut's staff; Hunnycut's stay at her townhouse; packages Hunnycut had pushed through that benefited her clients; the fact that the senator's campaign had spent several hundred thousand dollars a year on hotels, meals, alcoholic beverages, limousine services, private charters—the list went on. Occasionally Marlene smiled as he went through what he referred to as "the damning evidence."

"Let me ask you a question: how many other congressmen are they looking at?"

"None as seriously as Hunnycut. There has been an indication that the organization will petition for a grand jury in several states, in addition to the committee hearings."

"What can be done—and think carefully before you answer—to divert this interest?"

"I don't think it's possible."

"Who got this inquiry going?" she asked.

He was silent, but his face sagged even more as the color left it. She wondered if he were going to melt like Silly Putty, jellify. "Look, I'm leaving here in ten minutes, and you're either off the hook or you're not. It's up to you. This could be the first minute of the rest of your life, one way or the other."

"Senator Clemmings."

"From California? A member of Senator Hunnycut's own party?"

"And a potential vice presidential candidate himself," the man said.

"And you know this to be a fact."

"He has great influence with the organization."

"Cash?" she asked.

The man nodded affirmatively.

"I'm sorry." She asked looked at her watch. "Seven minutes."

"One hundred fifty thousand dollars and the usual promises."

"What promises?"

"Some Interior legislation support," he said.

"And you know this for a fact."

"I was there. Look I—"

"I guess that's it then," Marlene said and stood up.

"That's all? What are you going to do?"

She had never seen such a palpable look of fear on a human being's face. "Destroy the credibility of the Government Guard."

"Even you don't have that kind of power. How would you do that?"

"Tell them about this conversation."

"You assured me—" He stopped. For the first time that afternoon, he looked confident. "You can't prove this meeting ever occurred, nothing I said. No one will believe you."

Marlene put her hand into her jacket and retrieved a microrecorder. "You should have asked me to take my clothes off. Most men would have. It's kind of an insult, but then, I was pretty sure you wouldn't." She picked up the pad of paper and pen and looked at the man, who now looked as though he were going to cry. "I may not have to play this for them; I'll just tell them about it. If it's true, and they respond as they should, I'll keep your name out of it. I'm not totally cold." She left the room and walked to her car. The drive back to Georgetown would be pleasant.

THOUGH IT WAS only midafternoon, the sky had begun to take on a gauzelike haze, the first signal that the day was moving toward its conclusion. Sam and Karen were sitting in her car in the central business district, four blocks off St. Charles.

"Well?" she asked, looking at him.

"Well what?"

"Do you know how you're going to do it?"

"Just walk in and introduce myself to Jordan Pettigrew."

"I like your plan, Sam. Big move, no strategy. Want my gun? You could walk in and shoot him. People do it all the time. That would draw attention."

"You don't think much of this idea, do you?"

"I'm just not sure where it's going."

"What can I tell you? It's not a just matter of me coming out; I've got to put them on notice, get them nervous. That's when people make mistakes." He opened the door. "Don't worry about me."

"Should I worry about them?"

"Maybe," he said with a grin.

"If you're not back in an hour, I'm calling the cops," she yelled as he walked away, then to the empty driver's seat. "You're hell to deal with, Sam Larkin, damn you."

KAREN WAS ON target: Sam didn't have a plan other than to get into Pettigrew's office. Beyond that, as he had done so many times in his life, he would let the situation develop on its own. He tried to clear his mind of expectations, made an effort not to think about who he was, who he was going to see and why. Forget the history, hide the anger, be a cipher. He felt the comfortable discomfort of a boxer loosening up for a fight. Pettigrew might know who he was facing, but not what.

Walking toward the attorney's door, Sam wondered what he would do if Pettigrew wasn't in. Leaving his name might be more frightening to the man than actually seeing him in the flesh. Might not be a bad idea.

Pettigrew's secretary was seated behind a large desk centered squarely in front of the inner office door. The first line of defense. When Sam closed the door behind him, she looked up. From the disinterested look on her face, he could tell that his appearance didn't create the impression that he was anyone of consequence.

"May I help you?" She asked it as if she thought he were lost and had come in looking for directions.

"I hope so," he said with what he thought was a disarming, humble expression. "I was referred to Mr. Pettigrew by a friend of Arthur Valdrine's. My name is Samuels."

"Just a moment," she said, picked up the phone and punched a number.

"Mr. Pettigrew, a Mr. Samuels is out here. He said he was referred to you by someone in Mr. Valdrine's office."

Sam smiled. He hadn't said it was anyone from the administrator's office, but, what the hell, it worked. The secretary got up and opened the door for him.

When Sam entered the office, Pettigrew stood and came around the desk to greet him. His face held a perturbed look, as though there were something he should know but didn't. He extended his hand.

"Mr. Samuels?" Recognition flashed in Pettigrew's eyes. "I saw you in the hall yesterday."

"I guess I was not only on the wrong floor, I wasn't even right about which floor I was supposed to be on," he said.

"Mr. Valdrine referred you? In that case, have a seat and let's see what I can do for you." The referral had taken another step up. Friend, staff member, and now the man himself. And people ask what's in a name. Sam was enjoying himself.

The attorney folded his hands on his desk and looked at him. "How can I help you, Mr. Samuels?"

"Do you handle many criminal cases in your practice, Mr. Pettigrew?" Sam asked.

"Criminal cases." He sat back in his chair and clasped his hands behind his head. Posturing, Sam thought, posing with a confidence he didn't yet possess. "Not for a long time. I'm surprised Arthur would refer me in a criminal case, but I guess I could still do it if he asked me to. We've been friends for many years. It must be important to him."

"I would think it is."

"What kind of charge are we talking about?"

Sam could see "No" waiting on the man's lips. "Before we get into that, what's 'a long time'? Since you worked a criminal case, I mean."

Pettigrew thought for a moment. “Probably eight or ten years, but depending on the nature of the crime, most statutes don’t change that much. I’m sure—”

“I don’t mean to sound impertinent, Mr. Pettigrew, but was your record good in those cases? Get most of your clients off?”

“Most,” Pettigrew said, obviously perturbed by his questioner’s arrogance. “You know, Mr. Samuels, I’m not sure I want this to go any further until I speak with Mr. Valdrine. Regardless of what you say he said—”

“I never said I spoke with Mr. Valdrine. I said a friend of Mr. Valdrine’s recommended me, but,” Sam shook his head shamefully, “that’s really a lie. I’ve never spoken with anyone in Mr. Valdrine’s office, and I haven’t seen the man himself in probably eleven years.” He stood up, not knowing what kind of reaction to expect out of the attorney, but wanting to be able to duck in a worst-case scenario.

Pettigrew also stood. “What the hell is going on here?”

“I figured the only way I could get into your office—which is very nice, by the way—would be to lie my way in.”

“Well, Mr. Samuels, you can leave in a more straightforward manner. Get out of here. You’re a reporter, aren’t you? The *New Centurion*? They knew I’d recognize Landers, so they sent you in his place. You people are scum.”

“Landers?” Sam shook his head. “I’ve never heard of a Mr. Landers. I’m not a reporter, Mr. Pettigrew.”

“I’m calling security.” Pettigrew reached for the telephone, but Sam reached it first and held the receiver down.

“Don’t,” he said. “I haven’t touched you, so there’s no assault charge. Unless the telephone complains. And you can relax; I won’t touch you. I just wanted to see you face to face again.”

Pettigrew missed a beat. “Again? Since yesterday? What—”

Sam turned to leave, stopped, and turned back toward the shaken attorney. "I'm surprised you didn't recognize me, though it has been eleven years, and I do look a little different."

Pettigrew looked angry as well as confused. "What are you talking about?"

"I lied about my name as well. Samuel is the first name. Samuel Larkin."

He walked through the office door, closing it behind him as the color drained from Pettigrew's face and the man sank heavily into his chair.

"THERESA, PLEASE HOLD all calls," Pettigrew said into the intercom. "I have some critical work to get accomplished in a very short time, and I don't want to be disturbed."

"What if—"

"No one. Nothing," he said. "In fact, take the rest of the day off. I'm closing the office for the day."

After he heard her leave, Pettigrew went to the office's outer door to make sure she had locked it. He didn't know why he was checking; Theresa would never leave the reception area unlocked if she was out of the office. Satisfied that his space was secure, he went back to his inner sanctum and opened his safe. He withdrew the files he had always known would protect him against Valdrine and Hunnycut should circumstances demand it; however, he knew they would not shelter him from Sam Larkin.

He laid the files on his desk and stared at them. No need to open them and reread the information he had pored over so many times before. Nothing would have changed. Instead, he sat back to analyze what had happened this afternoon and what could happen in very short order if he weren't careful. He was shaking.

Sam Larkin. The phoenix he had never expected to rise had burst forth in full flame, walking boldly into his office. He believed the man was legitimate even though he hadn't recognized him. The long hair, the clothes—he had only seen him in his prison garb and that had been years ago—and he was thinner than Pettigrew remembered, but obviously in better physical condition. Notwithstanding his youth at the time of his arrest and imprisonment, the man he remembered appeared softer. There was nothing soft about the man who had entered his office this afternoon.

He could not remember having been struck by a person's eyes before. Yet when he had seen Larkin in the hall the day before, it had been the eyes that impressed him most, hard and deliberate despite the smile. Sam Larkin would not go away. He had made Pettigrew his hostage.

Larkin had chosen him, Jordan Pettigrew, to witness the act of his resurfacing—a logical choice on his part. He had been, after all, Larkin's defense attorney and was easily accessible. Valdrine would be hard to get to, and Hunnycut, impossible. Did Larkin intend to see each of them on his own terms? Pettigrew dismissed the idea. He felt certain he would be the only one. It was he whom Larkin would feel the most animosity toward.

Perhaps Larkin expected him to break down under the pressure of his return. The question was, why at this particular time? And why was the reporter bringing up Larkin's name at every turn? Where had Landers even come up with the name? Hunnycut's political career was threatening to bring them all down.

Pettigrew sat, his hands together, forefingers templed in front of his lips, and focused on what his life would have been like, would be like, if he had never aligned himself with Valdrine and Hunnycut and all the rest. He was not cut from the same cloth as they were. Power had never been his drug of choice, and he never thought of himself as bulletproof. They had seduced him, *seduced* being as good a word as any other he could come up with.

Having gone to law school later in life than most attorneys, he was not a kid when he had begun his practice, and he had struggled. Money had not been a problem—he was born with that—but gaining respect from the legal community and maintaining the family's reputation in New Orleans society were. He well remembered the day Valdrine, an assistant district attorney, invited him to lunch for the first time. It had taken only a few of these meet-and-eats for the assistant DA to make his motive apparent.

Valdrine had called early one morning and asked to meet at Patoot's Across the Lake. In the ensuing years, Pettigrew often thought Valdrine used the place as a reminder of that first meeting, a warning. In that first meeting, what the assistant DA suggested was so far below Pettigrew's level of integrity and such a perversion of his sense of justice that he had almost laughed in the man's face. And that was the last time he had ever considered doing that.

"Let me ask you something, Jordan," Valdrine had said. "Where are you? What state? What city?"

"You're joking."

"No, I'm not. What state? What city?"

"Louisiana. New Orleans. Why?"

"Do you think what I suggested is unique in New Orleans, Louisiana?" Valdrine asked, his eyes burning into Pettigrew's.

"I would hope it doesn't occur anywhere."

"Don't be naive, Jordan. It's done all the time. I'm not asking you to go in the tank; just let me control the trial. I need to make the DA's office look good and the judge look good. The defendant will not get convicted of anything serious. He'll get a slap on the wrist, and in a few months or maybe even weeks, his record will be expunged. It's his first offense."

"I don't understand why—" Pettigrew began.

Valdrine shook his head. "I'm sure you don't. I'm sorry I brought it up. I guess I was out of line. Let's just eat lunch and forget about it. This conversation never happened."

They ate in silence, though Pettigrew suddenly didn't have much of an appetite. After they finished and Valdrine had ordered his second scotch, Pettigrew finally spoke.

"Why?" he asked. "Why me? Why this particular case?"

"How's your practice going?"

"Okay. I guess." It wasn't going well at all. "Nothing to shake a stick at."

"What's the family think about that? Okay? Nothing to shake a stick at?"

"I'm not sure they think at all," Pettigrew said.

"Oh, they think. I can guarantee that. They're Pettigrews. Your grandfather was quite a force in this city. Your father lived on that his whole life, and what was his contribution to the Pettigrew name? Drinking? Making moves on anything in a skirt? In legal circles, Jordan, and, pardon me for being harsh and blunt, you're a joke. Your practice is nowhere, and, as far as I and the others can tell, there's no improvement in sight. You're one step above, or maybe below, an ambulance chaser, and I truly believe that's not where you want to be or should be. You're a Pettigrew."

Valdrine's last line had sounded as though it might have come from a forties movie, but it struck home. Everything Valdrine said was true. Pettigrew felt it every time he went into the courthouse, any municipal building, even the watering holes where members of the legal community gathered. All the family's money and history had not bleached that away.

"And doing this will change all that?"

"It will. Yes. The DEA made a mistake. It happens in law enforcement, and it needs to be rectified."

"Why don't they just admit it? Release the guy. Who would know it ever happened?"

"If you'd be kind enough to let me finish, I'll explain. The man they arrested is a law enforcement officer. If they try to sweep it under the carpet, a number of things could happen. A lawsuit is a possibility, but beyond that, the publicity he would stimulate is not anything the state or the DEA needs. As you know, a false arrest would only amplify that. Whether you go along with this or not, it will happen. People with self-perpetuating jobs know a thousand ways to protect their own asses."

"So you know he's innocent, but you're going to try him anyway."

"First, we don't know he's innocent. He says he is, and maybe he's right. He says the local sheriff will back him up, which he won't."

"You're sure of that."

"Yes. Jordan, he doesn't have a choice; we're dealing with the federal government here. The trial will be handled by a judge who is going to run for the Senate—"

"Hunnycut?"

"I didn't say that. The judge needs all the help he can get in Washington, and he doesn't need to put a bug up the DEA's ass. Think about it. You're going to try a case. Simple as that. There are just some issues you won't press on."

"Like discovery." Pettigrew said. He wasn't hearing the whole story, and he knew it. A small drug bust would not gain Hunnycut any favors in the capital.

"If you want a guilt-free practice, I don't know what kind of law you should make your specialty."

"And if I don't do what you ask?"

"Become a court stenographer. Or a novelist. Some attorneys are doing pretty well at that." There it was. Valdrine had come out of the shadows and given him no room to move.

"And this guy's going to get off light?" He couldn't believe he was considering the proposition.

"Maybe nothing at all."

It had taken Pettigrew two days to call Valdrine and say yes. The assistant DA had not sounded surprised. When the trial was over, the sentence passed, and Sam Larkin taken away to spend the next fifteen years in Angola, it had taken Valdrine five seconds to shrug his shoulders and dismiss the whole event. What Pettigrew had learned was that Valdrine and Hunnycut now owned him, lock, stock, and life.

He got up from his desk and went across the room to an antique sideboard converted into a liquor cabinet. He removed a bottle of Laphroaig from the cabinet and filled a Waterford crystal lowball glass halfway to the top. He drank what was in the glass and poured it half full again. He carried it to his desk and dialed Valdrine's secure line.

"Arthur Valdrine," the voice said.

"Sam Larkin just left my office," Pettigrew said, and hung up.

During the next hour the phone rang and rang and rang. Pettigrew imagined he could hear urgency in the ring. It was a pleasant sound.

His gaze returned to the files that lay before him. His insurance, a guarantee of safety. If such a thing existed. The tab at the top of each folder was labeled: *Client/Attorney Interview*, *Client/Attorney Conferences*, *Initial Client Statement/Charges*, *Attorney/D.A. Conference*, *Attorney/Judge Conference*, *Bail Hearing*, *Official Trial Transcript*, *Sentencing Hearing*, *Parker Hamill*, *Notes*. It was, perhaps, that final folder that was the most valuable. That and the trial transcript. Below every heading was the case number and the client name: *Samuel T. Larkin*.

Only Pettigrew knew this information existed, and that was his trump card. He had been instructed to destroy everything, but he hadn't. Ironic that the one time he hadn't followed orders might turn out to be his saving grace.

# EIGHTEEN

AT THREE O'CLOCK in the afternoon, Buck Link sat at his desk, rolling a Franklin half-dollar between his fingers, first one way and then the other, in ceaseless motion. He had learned the skill in fifth grade from a friend whose father had worked in traveling carnivals throughout the South, fleecing the unsuspecting with shell games. The coin trick had provided Link with a lifetime of therapy. He had also used it as a ploy during interrogations to distract a subject, getting answers he never would have gotten otherwise. Today it was therapy.

Since the day he had seen the burned-out car, a picture had remained in his memory. A face in a passing vehicle. The driver, bone-faced with black, greasy hair and a flowered shirt, had grinned at him as he drove by. At the time, he'd seen it as an expression of passing acknowledgement, but the more he thought about it, the more he suspected it had been something else: pride.

He let the Franklin half-dollar rest and called a friend at the NOPD, Lieutenant Jim Fraley.

Link had met Fraley several years before during a death-by-auto investigation, and they had become casual friends, meeting a few times for a beer after work. He could have asked for the captain, with whom he also had a good relationship, but there was no reason to attract more attention than necessary.

"Buck Link, Jim. Hope all is going well with you and yours."

"Fine with me and as well as can be expected with the rest of the family when the breadwinner's a cop. Glad to hear from you, old buddy. A beer or a favor?"

"Last first and first later."

"You're quick. What can I do for you?"

"I'd like to borrow a forensic sketch artist and an Identi-Kit. We've got a kit, but I know the sketch guys like to work with their own."

"Anything I ought to know about? My jurisdiction?"

"Not really," Link said. "An incident in Jefferson Parish. I saw somebody drive by the crime scene, and I'd like to try to get a likeness of him, just on the happenstance."

"Let me guess. This the burned-out car with the body in it?"

"That's the one. Looks professional, so I thought I'd give every shot an opportunity. Oh, and, Jim, I'd appreciate your keeping this between you and me until I see what we come up with. If I think it's worth following up, I may want you to let a couple of officers you're secure with see what we've got. I don't want general disclosure on this."

"You got it," Fraley said.

The forensic artist arrived at state police headquarters just after four o'clock. He began with the Identi-Kit, allowing Link to choose a combination of overlays depicting various facial features: hairlines, eyes, mouths, ears, noses, chins, lips, and eyebrows, as well as head shapes.

Once Link chose the basics—more difficult than expected because the subject had been seated in a car, and Link's view had been more three-quarter than full face—the artist began asking a series of questions to bring the subtleties into focus. It was then, using the foils as a guide, that he began to draw.

It was not a simple task. Any one thing, a mere tightening of the skin here or a sag of the skin there, could change the entire aspect of the creation. When the artist completed all he could with what he had, Link was elated with what he saw. The man might not be guilty of anything more than driving by the scene of a crime, but Link had a good likeness of him.

He faxed copies to Fraley to circulate among a few choice, trustworthy members of the NOPD, to Raleigh DuBose in Jefferson Parish, and to other parish sheriffs with whom he had good relationships. Given the little he knew and the DEA's desire to keep the identity of its agent confidential, he wasn't ready to begin a full-scale manhunt; however, the longer he looked at the picture, the more his confidence grew that the man in the sketch was involved.

ARTHUR VALDRINE COULDN'T remember when his confidence had last been challenged, but Pettigrew's telephone call had left him swinging in the wind.

Sam Larkin. *The ghosts always come back to haunt you*, he thought, *especially when they aren't ghosts*. Larkin should have been taken care of in Angola, but it hadn't worked out that way. Valdrine had suggested eliminating the problem when Larkin was released, but Hunnycut, in a strange fit of morality, wouldn't allow it. It was paradoxical that Hunnycut had sent Larkin to prison and then saved his life, a move he might soon regret.

Reestablishing contact with Pettigrew was essential. The attorney was weak and, no doubt at this juncture, scared. Too scared even to discuss what Larkin had said, what the bastard wanted, why he had suddenly appeared. Merely "Sam Larkin just left my office." The perversely blunt nature of the message enraged Valdrine. But attempts to call Pettigrew back at his office were unsuccessful, and a call to the building's security desk confirmed that he was no longer there.

There was no reason to call Hunnycut. What could he do from Washington? Why make him aware of something he was helpless to resolve? As always, it was left to Valdrine to take care of problems. He performed willingly, he admitted. He preferred handling chores himself. It was his role: the engineer. The situation had been so since the beginning of his association with Hunnycut.

Hunnycut talked tough, but it was Valdrine who got moving when the situation demanded it. He never doubted that a move upward was worth any price he had to pay. Larkin, too, would be handled.

He dialed Grosjean's number and left a message telling him to call anytime after the next hour.

He drove to Pettigrew's home. There were no lights on. He walked through the formal garden and around to the back of the garage. The faint aroma of roses and tea olives floated in the air. There were windows in the back wall of the garage; Valdrine could see that Pettigrew's car was not inside.

He didn't think that Pettigrew was capable of suicide, but the man was a guilt freak, and Valdrine believed strongly that guilt took people beyond the parameters of reason. And if he was capable, his suicide would simplify the situation—unless he left a note exposing them.

Grosjean returned his call at eight-fifteen, minutes after Valdrine had arrived back at his Garden District house. "We have some problems," Valdrine told him.

"Yeah. I figured dat, me. You callin'."

"What about the woman in Biloxi?"

"I don' t'ink it's nothin'. She gone when I got dere this mornin'. Shoulda let my cousin watch her, you want twenty-four. I was dere most of the day, but she din't come home, no, so I gone in. Nothin' dere 'cept clothes. Coupla writin' tablets. Nothin' on 'em. A fax machine. Nothin' in the trash neither. Look like she jus' shackin' up wit dat boyfrien'," Grosjean said.

"Describe the boyfriend for me again."

" 'Bout six foot one maybe. Long hair, kinda light, maybe some gray. Pull it back in a ponytail tight to his head. Hang down between his shoulders. Maybe a hundred and seventy-five pounds, maybe eighty. Dat 'bout it."

"You still in Biloxi?"

"No."

"Why did you leave?" Valdrine was getting irritated.

"No need to stay, no."

"I decide that," Valdrine said.

"You won' get somebody else to do de work?"

"No. Nobody else." He could visualize the matter-of-fact smile on the Cajun's face. "But I need you to find another person for me." Valdrine told him where Pettigrew lived, the location of his office, and the kind of car he drove. "The best bet will be his house. Go there now. If he doesn't come in tonight, call me in the morning, and then go to his office. He usually gets in before nine. Stay there at least until noon and check in. If you locate him, let me know immediately."

"My cousin could—"

"No cousins. Not yet. Just do it."

"You payin'," Grosjean said, matter-of-factly.

"You're damned right I am. Remember that."

IT WOULD BE a late dinner. Sam stood at the counter cutting up onions, bell peppers, and celery—the Cajun trinity—in addition to mushrooms and broccoli. A heaping bowl of jumbo shrimp, fresh from a seafood shack next to the docks, was waiting to be deveined. He'd volunteered to cook dinner because he couldn't think of anything else to occupy his time. His brain worked better when his hands were busy with rote tasks; pure thinking seldom produced anything of value for him.

He put on a pot of water for the pasta and poured olive oil in a large Teflon fry pan, which in no way compared to the cast iron skillet he used back on Matthew's Island. He put the vegetables, with some bruised garlic, into the pan to sauté and seasoned them with a generous sprinkling of LaDon's BBQ Shrimp Mix. He preferred a combination of his own spices, but circumstances required compromise. The pasta went in the water at the same time the shrimp was added to the vegetables, and in three minutes the meal was ready.

Karen had gone out to sit on the deck and await whatever he was fixing. She had been there only a few minutes when he called.

"What was it you called this back in Carolina? Orgasmic Pasta?" she asked as he set the plates of food on the table.

"Something like that."

"Good food, poor substitute."

Sam ignored the barb, but he was surprised by her levity. He guessed it was another attempt to assuage Dougherty's death, for the moment anyway. It had been her tack all day.

"I need some input," he said. "Facing Pettigrew was fun, but I can only hope it accomplished what we intended."

"I'm sure Hunnycut and Valdrine knew you were back in the area before we got home. Maybe I shouldn't be sitting so close to you."

"I may have to be a little more aggressive if the burn is going to work."

"Give it a couple of days. I think they'll find you."

"How? I'm in Biloxi."

"I don't have a criminal mind," she said with undisguised sarcasm, "but I do know that you're not naïve. You know they'll find you, but it might take a little while. You just can't wait."

Karen had him nailed. A couple of days, a little while. Patience was not one of his virtues. He liked to face whatever was coming and get it behind him.

After cleaning the kitchen, they sat at the table drinking coffee sweetened with Jack Daniels. It was likely that, if he were found, an attempt would be made on his life. Karen asked him about Mr. Smith and Mr. Wesson, and Sam assured her that the stainless-steel, K-frame .357 magnum had indeed accompanied him on his trip south.

It was well after midnight when they gave up trying to conjecture what would happen next. Neither of them was relaxed, but both were exhausted. Sam let Karen go to bed first and then went to the guestroom.

AN EASTERLY WIND blew sheets of rain against the glass doors on the beach side of the condo, creating a syncopated, percussive sound. Wearing an over-sized T-shirt and holding a cup of hot coffee with both hands, Karen stood at the sliding glass doors looking out. Even though the Gulf temperatures remained warm in the daytime, the weather confirmed that winter still held sway.

When she tried to see beyond Highway 90 to the Gulf, a shroud of rain and fog hid the landscape. It was early, and the change from night to morning was barely discernable. Cars were operating with their lights on, neon signs from the business places in view were nothing more than watercolor washes spreading blurred reds, greens, yellows, and blues with no definition, as on a wet sheet of gray paper. The interior of the condo was still dark.

Sam was not yet awake, or at any rate hadn't emerged from the guestroom. That was unusual, but they'd had a late night, and the emotional temper of the last forty-eight hours had been intense. His not joining her in bed continued to trouble her. It had to be his decision, she reasoned as she gazed out into the nothingness beyond the doors. She had to give him time, though she didn't know why or for what, and she couldn't really accept what she was telling herself anyway. She was not going to be put on hold. His time would run out tonight.

In fact, she decided, it just had. She put the coffee cup down and pulled the T-shirt over her head, letting it fall to the floor behind her. She had taken one step toward the guestroom when the doorbell rang.

Karen froze in her tracks. Her mind went blank. She was standing naked in the middle of the room, and someone was on the other side of the door ringing the bell. No one except Sam and Regan knew she was here. Knew *they* were here, she corrected herself. Unless they had been followed the day before. It was too early for the Welcome Wagon or a vacuum cleaner salesman. She lifted the T-shirt from the floor and pulled it back over her head.

She moved quickly to the bedroom, grabbed the Ruger from the night table, and eased a shell into the chamber. The bell rang again. "Persistent son of a bitch," she muttered as she rejected the impulse to take the time to wake Sam. If he were still asleep or groggy, he would be of no help. If he were awake, he'd already be on the way. Besides, she could take care of herself, had done it in situations tougher than this.

She went to the windows facing the parking lot. The bell rang yet again. It wasn't even fully light, for God's sake. She held back the curtain farthest from the door and peered out to the porch. The rain, half-light, and fog allowed her to determine only that whoever was punching the bell was wearing a black, hooded poncho. Looked like a hulking version of the kid on a box of Morton's salt. Without the umbrella. Not good. She crossed to the door, listened, changed her mind, and went to the guestroom.

Sam was not asleep; he had awakened on the first ring of the bell and opened the door just as Karen put her hand on the door knob. He was giving whoever it was five rings to leave before making a move.

She crossed to him and whispered, "The front porch. I can't see who."

Without saying a word, Sam, K-frame S&W in hand and wearing only his jeans, moved to the great room and quietly opened the sliding glass door onto the deck. The rain was still coming in sheets. One step beyond the overhang, and he was drenched. His long, wet hair hung in shanks around his face. The rain was cold on his bare skin.

At the corner of the house, he leaned against the building and looked around to the front door. His grip tightened on the gun, and he was about to step out when the hooded figure leaned in close to the door and spoke.

"I know somebody's in there. I saw your shadow moving across the curtain. I'm drowning out here." The figure, whose concentration was focused in the other direction, was unaware of Sam's approach from behind.

"Who are you?" Sam heard Karen's voice ask from the other side of the door.

Before the man could answer, Sam placed the barrel of his gun behind his right ear. "Don't move." The man stood perfectly still as Sam patted him down. "Turn around."

The hooded figure obeyed. There was a grin on the face. "Sam," he said.

Sam stared. "Sleeve?" he asked. He had not thought of the jailhouse name in years.

"That's me," Raymond Gaynaud said as Sam lowered the gun. "Had me worried there for a minute. Can we go inside? I'd really like to get out of this rain." His smile had broadened.

It took Sam a moment to recover. "It's okay, Karen. Let us in," he yelled at the door. The deadbolt clicked, but the door didn't open. After a second, Sam pushed it open, just in time to see Karen darting into the bedroom, the T-shirt doing little to hide her bare behind.

"Sleeve! Good Lord!" The sudden appearance of this man from his past was beyond serendipitous. The thought crossed his mind that someone had sent him. "Drop your rain gear by the door while I put on dry clothes."

Sam tossed Gaynaud a towel, then went to the guestroom to change. When he came back into the kitchen, Gaynaud was sitting at the table, smiling.

"Coffee?" Sam asked, going toward the pot on the counter.

"I'd pay for it," Raymond said. Sam filled two cups and brought them to the table.

The two men stared at each other. They had leaned on each other in prison, comrades in a hostile environment. Provided therapy for each other, and hope when it was needed. Raymond had been released two years before Sam, and the two had been out of contact since then.

Sam was about to take the lead and start asking questions when Karen came out of the bedroom. She had put on jeans and a sweatshirt and combed her hair. More presentable, but less eye-catching than she had been in the T-shirt. The men stood up as she entered the room.

She raised her eyebrows. "Gentlemen. Wow!"

"Reflex," Gaynaud said and put out his hand. "I'm Raymond Gaynaud."

"And I'm confused," Karen said, taking his hand. "You two have a lot of explaining to do."

The two men gave her a brief history, then Sam asked the first question. "Don't misinterpret what I'm about to ask, Raymond, but why are you here? And even more important, how in hell did you know where to find me?"

"I was hired to find out who you were." He explained the call from Casey Landrieu, his talks with his father, the fruitless research on Sam's case, Musgrave's explanation of his reasons for interest in Sam, his going to Celine's and following Sam as far as Kenner.

"The only thing to do when you're lost is go back and start over. So I went back and spoke with Celine. She gave me a phone number, and I had a cop friend do a reverse search to get this address. I was here yesterday and waited several hours, but nobody showed up." His face darkened. "I shouldn't say nobody showed up."

"What do you mean?" Sam asked.

"Someone else was also here, waiting. Whoever it was got impatient, picked the lock, and came in. Didn't stay long and didn't appear to take anything that I could see. He wasn't an amateur. When he left, I followed him to Arabi in the city, caught a stoplight, and lost him."

"What did he look like?" Karen asked.

Raymond described the man. "I call him Pink Shirt."

"You're a private investigator?" Sam asked. "I thought your father was going to help you get reinstated into law."

"He did."

"After prison?" Karen looked at him questioningly.

"Good-ol'-boy state, and the judge was pretty powerful at the time. In Louisiana and a lot of other states, unless your conviction involves a perversion of the law, like jury tampering, you can apply for reinstatement, and, with a little juice on your side, you usually get it."

"What happened?" Sam asked. "You always said you were going to bring some sanity to the system."

"I didn't really have a taste for the law once I found out how it works. And I guess the conditions of my reinstatement had a lot to do with it. I was allowed to work only for my father's firm, would be carefully watched—something I'm sure the judge used to pull all of this off—basically being a slave on the massa's legal plantation. I figured it wouldn't be much different than prison, so I didn't show up for the final hearing."

"The best part," Gaynaud continued, "is that they announced my disbarment in the paper. Only in Louisiana would they announce the redisbarment of a disbarred lawyer." He was laughing. Sam saw no regret in his friend's face. "What about you? What are you doing here?"

Sam gave a brief history of his life in the lowcountry, then looked to Karen. She looked back, leaving it up to him to decide how much to tell Gaynaud. It was a brave step, going against every principle she had been taught as a federal agent. Sam explained the situation, including making his presence known to Pettigrew. "We can use your help, Raymond. I'm not sure what move to make next."

"They're going to come after you. That's a given. The thing that confuses me is ol' Pink Shirt breaking into this place before Pettigrew knew you were here."

"Maybe it was random," Karen said, "just a burglary."

"He watched the place too long. He sat there for several hours. And he didn't take anything I could see; he had a purpose."

Karen smiled. "Maybe it was me."

"Maybe it was," Raymond said, but he wasn't smiling. "Now all we have to do is figure out why."

They moved from the kitchen table to the living area. "I was doing some background work on Hunnycut's home in Gulfport," Karen said.

"That's why you think Pink Shirt might be scoping you?" Raymond asked.

"Possibly. It would explain how he knew about this place. Something had to lead him in my direction, and the clerks at the chancery's office gave me some serious looks when I was there. I wouldn't be surprised if someone there had me followed back here."

Karen got her notes and laid them in front of Raymond to look at as she explained the labyrinth of transactions involving the house. Before she began talking, Sam noticed his friend's eyes widen at the notes he was holding. Raymond sat quietly and stared at her while she talked. Before she was finished, Sam interrupted.

"What did you see, Raymond? You did everything but turn blue when you looked at Karen's notes."

"Masley Prather," he said.

"They were murdered. He and his wife." Karen said. "I hadn't gotten to that yet."

"I investigated it. Went to the crime scene, such as it was."

"Why?" she asked.

"A favor for the judge. He knew Masley, and Prather's son asked him to have me do it. I've got the police report in the car, but it doesn't say much that the papers didn't print. It was a professional hit. Nothing taken. Angola silencer. Clean. The cops attributed it to environmental politics, if anything. With what you're saying, I guess they're wrong. Especially considering your agent. I also saw Parker Hamill's name in your notes."

"Questionable suicide," Sam said.

Raymond explained that both Celine and Musgrave had mentioned him. "It's getting heavy, Sam."

Raymond suggested they let him take the lead and find a legal way to get to Valdrine and Pettigrew and, thus, to Hunnycut. Maybe by going public, they could put them on the defensive. He had a friend at the *Times-Picayune* who might be able to help.

"That would take too long," Sam said. "It's me they want out of the way. I need to become more visible, more accessible, give them something to shoot at if I'm going to catch them."

Raymond laughed. "A burn?"

"We had the same teacher," Sam said. "Tell me about Musgrave."

"I got a strong impression that he's after Hunnycut as much as you are. The senator's playing games with him on the Laurel Grove health-care facilities. Hunnycut needs to get his name off of them, but he's not willing to compromise or give anything to do it. He's holding up everything else Musgrave has going. Musgrave thinks Hunnycut's trying to finesse him and hang him out to dry, and he wants to beat him to the punch."

"Will he talk to us?" Sam asked.

"Without a doubt."

"Let's do it. We have a meeting in New Orleans this morning. See if you can set it up for this afternoon. Maybe one or two. We shouldn't be too long. Karen and I will go in my car, and, if we're lucky, at some point during the day, someone will tag us."

"I'm ready." Raymond said. "Looks like we're gonna have some fun."

"Yep. Just as soon as you take me to pick up my Rover."

THE RAIN WAS still coming down hard enough to justify a sprint to Raymond's car. "Lose ten minutes when you drop me off, Raymond."

His friend looked at him. "You going to call Celine?"

"Why?"

"Because if you're not, I am." Raymond's face was serious. "I see a problem in your eyes, Sam. And, my friend, I saw the same look in the lady's eyes. Is there a problem?"

"No." The answer was succinct. Too much so, Sam thought when he heard himself say it. "It's not a problem, Raymond. We both know where we are on that score, but I need to let her know what's going on. I don't think they'd have anything to gain by going after her, but . . ."

"They might not know that," Raymond said. "I don't think we've scratched the surface on this deal, Sam. 'Pears to me you're just a part of something that's been going on a long time, and now you've got a guy with political stars in his eyes, and everyone else is trying to hold on to the wagon. Pardon my grammar, but it ain't Thornton Hunnycut that's doing the dirty work, and that's who we have to find. Whoever it is seems to have no limits to what he'll do to protect the man, and that puts your ass and everyone around you in trouble."

"I agree. It's not Hunnycut himself, but he's behind it."

"Any ideas?"

"Valdrine," Sam said. "Pettigrew isn't strong enough for that kind of action."

"So what do you tell Celine?"

Sam was quiet. "I'll try again to talk her into leaving the area for awhile."

"Think she'll do that?

"All I can do is ask."

"Confident, huh?" Raymond said and laughed.

The rain's intensity had increased again, and Sam was wet by the time he entered the small building.

"I'M AT AN Exxon station in Biloxi," Sam said in answer to Celine Aguillard's question. "Picking up my car."

"Why are you calling? Am I in danger again?" Her voice was cool, which bothered him.

"No. I don't think so. Raymond Gaynaud found me this morning. He said he'd been to see you."

"Sam, I . . ." Her voice was apologetic.

"No. No, that's okay. I'm glad you told him. I need his help."

"I'm sorry," she said.

"There's no need to be. I just want to make sure you're safe. Pettigrew knows I'm in the area, thinks I'm in Louisiana, and I'm sure by now Valdrine and Hunnycut know as well. I don't think they'd bother you, but I'd feel better if you weren't around." Celine didn't answer. Sam expected a stubborn refusal and waited for it. It didn't come.

"I have a friend in Des Allemands. I can visit her. Dee Corbin. She's listed," she said.

"D? As in the letter?"

"D-E-E. I think it's Diane, but the listing is Dee."

"Got it," he said. "How soon can you leave?"

"A couple of hours. If for any reason you can't get me there, call here and leave a message. I'll check in."

"I'll feel better knowing you're not at the house. Take care, Celine."

"Back at you, Sam."

HER FATHER'S SHOTGUN was resting against the front door jamb, not a very safe place. Someone could break down the door and grab it before she could react. She had relaxed her guard after the first day. She picked up the gun and, satisfied that no one could get close to her without regretting it, carried it into the kitchen. She wondered at the feeling inside her chest—a strange brand of anticipation, almost hope that someone would come.

"You're going crazy," she said to herself. "You really don't want anyone to come. But you sure as hell aren't going to run either. Sorry, Sam." She thought about Sam standing in the rain at the gas station. It reminded her of past times when he had come in from work wet to the bone. She leaned her head back and momentarily closed her eyes. "Sam. Sam Larkin."

# NINETEEN

RENÉ GROSJEAN CALLED at seven o'clock to tell Valdrine that Pettigrew had not returned to his house, so he was on his way to the lawyer's office on St. Charles Street. He didn't mention that he had, out of boredom, gone into the house and looked around. Nor did he mention that he had noted Pettigrew's house as a good mark for his cousin, whose primary occupation was burglary.

At eight forty-five Valdrine called Pettigrew's office only to be told by Theresa that Pettigrew would not be in. She had been left a note saying that he was ill, and she didn't know anything else. A call to the house was again unanswered. Grasping at straws, he dialed Musgrave on the off chance he'd heard from Pettigrew. Of all the people he knew, he liked Harold Musgrave the least, on general principles. He was amazed the man had made fortunes. He wasn't amazed he had lost almost every one he'd made.

"Now this is an early-morning shock, Arthur. Must be important for you to call me."

Musgrave's voice was so boisterous, it momentarily startled the administrator. "Good morning, Harold. I'm trying to get in touch with Jordan. He's not in the office today. I tried his home, but he's not there either. I thought you might have some idea where I could reach him. I know you two do a lot of business and thought he might have mentioned where he'd be."

"No, he doesn't keep me apprised of his schedule. In fact, I was going to call him myself today. He was supposed to have some papers ready for me to sign and send to Thornton. He's taken too damned long with them as it is."

"I'll be speaking with Thornton later today if you want me to pass something along."

"Not really. It's just the buyout papers for Laurel Grove. He's anxious to get out of that venture before all the political stuff starts."

"I'd say it's already started," Valdrine said. "Did you two come to an agreement?" This news was a relief. Laurel Grove was a problem he didn't want Hunnycut dropping in his lap.

"*We* haven't," Musgrave said. "I have." Valdrine heard a chuckle in Musgrave's voice and knew he was being set up for a punch line; it was one of the most irritating things about the man. "I'm offering him a hundred dollars."

Valdrine laughed. "You are kidding, of course."

"Not in the least. Those things are a pain in the ass. He wants out, and that's all I'm willing to pay. I'm not sure he has a lot of choice," Musgrave said.

"Oh, I'm sure he has other alternatives, Harold."

"Well, don't be surprised. By the way, you ever hear any more from that reporter? He said he was going to get back to me, and Jordan as well, but neither of us has heard from him."

Valdrine braced in his chair. "No, I haven't. He must have gotten what he needed and gone back to the capital."

"Shame. He was overly curious about some guy I never heard of. Seemed right important to him. You ever hear of anyone named Sam Larkin?"

"No, the name is not familiar."

"Peculiar. This Landers said it had something to do with Thornton's judicial record. Guess I can ask him when I talk to him."

Valdrine cleared his throat. "I don't think Thornton needs to be bothered with any more reporters than he's already got in Washington, Harold. I'd leave that alone if I were you."

"You may be right. Well, listen, I've got a boatload of stuff to get done this morning. If you find Jordan, tell him to call me. I'd really like to get this Laurel Grove thing taken care of before I have to negotiate with the vice president. But, then again, if he doesn't dump 'em, he might not be vice president. They're a mess."

"Then I'd try to get them cleaned up, Harold. We need Thornton in that position. He can do us all good."

"That'll be the day," Musgrave said. "Hope you find Jordan."

"Thank you, Harold."

IT WAS ALMOST ten o'clock when Sam and Karen walked into the office above the camera shop. Two men were seated there. The one whom Sam assumed to be Michael Regan rose when they entered. He did not have a pleasant look on his face.

"I've heard the South was slow, but I didn't know it applied to federal agents in the middle of an investigation into the death of one of its own," he said.

Sam stopped just inside the door and looked at the man. He was not imposing. Short, thick, balding, with a desk-job middle and glasses. An accountant, Sam thought.

"I'm Sam Larkin," he said calmly. "This is agent Karen Chaney."

"The meeting was scheduled for nine o'clock." Regan was trying to establish his authority, which didn't play. Sam surmised that establishing authority was basic DEA training. Dougherty had tried the same thing.

"Traffic," Sam said. "We're here."

It was obvious Regan didn't appreciate being confronted by a civilian. "Have a seat." He gestured to the other man in the room. "This is Phil Grimsley. He'll be working with us." He turned to Karen, speaking a little more softly but without losing his authoritative tone. "Karen, I hated to call you in on this."

"I'm okay," she said, taking a seat. She knew what was going on in both agents' heads. She had been to contingency meetings like this one. Everyone always played the "what if" game, putting themselves, in this case, in Neil's shoes—imagining all of the possibilities of what he might have been subjected to, wondering if he had known what hit him, how their own families would react if the same thing happened to them, things they had not done in their lives, things they had done—most of all, why they had chosen a career that required putting themselves in harm's way on a daily basis.

"As usual in such circumstances, there is nothing to say that will make any of us feel any better. We're all angry and hurt, but that has to be put aside. We can't hate whoever did this because, as our old nemesis, James Hoffa, once said in reference to his battles with Bobby Kennedy, 'When you begin to hate, you forget to think.' A fighter who gets angry in the ring will lose. I want us to think. I won't accept failure. So, I'll begin by telling you what we have."

Regan began a rundown he had undoubtedly rehearsed. "Neil Dougherty has been killed. How? By whom? For what purpose? It could have been robbery or a random killing. At this point there's no way to know, but he was an agent and he is dead. He was working undercover as a newspaper reporter representing a DC newspaper, the *New Centurion*."

"Do you know what name he was using?" Karen asked.

"Harry Landers."

"Pettigrew mentioned him," Sam said.

"Neil told me he had spoken with him. I'll get to that later."

Everything in its place, Sam thought.

"As far as we know," Regan continued, "Senator Hunnycut and his associates, Arthur Valdrine, Jordan Pettigrew, Harold Musgrave, and Marlene Cole are not cognizant of our operation; however, we are not closing our minds to anything. I would have to believe that if Neil's death has anything at all to do with any of these people—and I repeat that at the moment I have no evidence to support that theory—he was probably considered no more than an irritating paparazzi trying to make a name for himself. If that is the case and any of those people are involved, I want them to continue to consider him no more than that."

Regan turned to Karen. "I will be working with the state police and the Jefferson Parish sheriff's office to learn what we can about the murder. Meanwhile, the investigation into Hunnycut is ongoing. The greatest honor we can do Neil at this moment is to continue the work he set in motion."

Karen met his gaze but said nothing.

"There are a number of rumors on the Hill. According to those rumors, the Senate Ethics Committee is considering an investigation of Senator Hunnycut, based on allegations of influence peddling and gift rules violations, the latter a result of his long-standing and close personal ties to Marlene Cole. It also appears that he spends a lot of time at her townhouse. Everyone on the Hill knows that to get to the senator, you have to go through Cole. Dollars are always involved, and it is not unusual for those interests to get legislation passed, stalled, or defeated. The problem is, as always, when dealing with the congressional cult, proving those allegations. To that end, we're doing our own research into this and feeding it through an anonymous conduit to the committee. The investigation is being pushed by the Government Guard."

Regan picked up his coffee cup, looked into it, and replaced it. "If the senator is not already aware of what's coming down from his peers, he will be within days. Maybe hours. I choose to believe he already knows. Although, based on our observation of Ms. Cole, he may not have informed her. One thing that is unusual is that a few days ago Hunnycut sent a plane to New Orleans to pick up Arthur Valdrine. Valdrine was only there for half a day. We did not have surveillance equipment in place; consequently, we do not know the content of their meeting. But, Valdrine did not appear happy when he left Washington. In my last conversation with Neil, he did tell me that, as Landers, he had interviewed Pettigrew, Valdrine, and Musgrave but had managed to obtain little information and planned to see them again."

He picked up his coffee cup and drained it. "That's what I have. I haven't had time to check Neil's living quarters; that's next on my agenda, but I really don't expect to find anything. I am sure, Karen, that you are familiar with Neil's work habits." He paused and stretched his neck muscles. "Now, you two bring me up to speed on where you are and where you plan to go."

Karen outlined the chain of real estate transactions, providing thumbnail sketches of Prather, Valdrine, and Sykorus. "There are a couple of things that are even more suspect. When Masley Prather owned the property, all tax billings, assessments, and property owner's notices were sent to Gustave Sykorus. He owns a string of bars and strip joints that are known for gambling, prostitution, probably drugs. Sykorus himself reportedly has ties to the Dixie Mafia, but he's never been convicted of anything serious. The rest of the transactions appear to be nothing more than real estate sales. Except for the price differential. The one common thread in all of these transactions is Masley Prather, the original owner of the property. He and his wife were murdered recently. It was a professional hit, according to our source."

"And who would that be?" Regan asked.

"For the moment, that's confidential to protect the source."

Reagan sighed in frustration, and Karen continued. "In addition to originally owning the house, he was the attorney of record in each of the transactions. Now, the murders may not have any bearing on what we're doing, but I believe those two killings, along with Neil's, and the connections to the Hunnycut group, are too coincidental."

"And what's your plan of attack from this point on?" Regan turned to Sam. "You haven't said anything, Mr. Larkin. Neil told me you were cooperating with him, but that you and Karen are operating pretty much on your own. I'm not sure I'm comfortable with that."

"Neil wasn't either, but I didn't work for him. His strategy was to have me where he could keep an eye on me and get my reports. I presume he told you what my only interest in this case is and will continue to be."

"He did."

"What he was looking for and what he thought was critical was the exact circumstances of my arrest, conviction, release, and payoff. I'm working on that through my own sources."

"And would you care to disclose who your sources are?"

"If I did, you would learn nothing, and neither would I. They are personal, and I'm operating on a bond of trust with each of them. Neil understood that, which was why he was willing to allow me my own investigation as long as I shared what I found at the appropriate time and did not hinder his operation in any way." Regan did not respond. "I suppose he told you that is the only way I'll take part," Sam said, looking straight at the man. Regan tried to hold his eyes, then looked away. "I'll tell you what I told him: I'll help you, but I'm not going to take orders."

Regan looked back at Sam. "Then I don't suppose you think I have any choice."

"No, sir, you don't," Sam said.

"But I do. I don't like this, even if Neil did. If I discern any lack of faith on your part, or I feel you are in any way not being candid about what you find, then we will have a problem. I would like both of you to stay in contact with me. Daily. Keep me apprised of what you are doing."

"We will," Karen said, trying to defuse the pissing contest. "I might also add that I have been working with a state police commander, Buck Link, who is a personal friend. He's trustworthy, and our investigation hasn't been compromised by his involvement. I'll pass on your information about Neil to him."

"I appreciate that." He stood. "Now, I've got to go to Neil's quarters and see if there is anything there that will be helpful. Thank you for coming in."

"YOU DIDN'T HAVE much to say," Karen said when they were back on the street.

"I said everything he needed to know." Sam looked at her. "I wouldn't want him to hinder *our* investigation."

"By the way—personal sources? A bond of trust? Where did that come from?"

"Who the hell knows," Sam said, and shrugged.

"Amazing," Karen said, laughing.

It was good to hear her laugh.

THE TELEVISION WAS on, and Pettigrew, sitting up on a king-sized bed, his back against the headboard, was staring at it, but he wasn't watching it. Zephyrlike moments slipped from the set to his brain—a commercial for a mortgage company, a tort lawyer advertising for clients—but little registered. Fear was the only thing on his mind. Sam Larkin was a reality, and he could not let the man go.

After leaving his office the day before, he had driven across Lake Pontchartrain to Hammond and checked into this motel. It was independent, anonymous. As he filled out the registration form, he noticed the desk clerk checking out his Ermenegildo Zegna suit, crisp white shirt, and tie. Apparently not the wardrobe of their usual guests. After being given his key, he moved his car to the back of the building, away from the road, and went to his room.

At two o'clock in the morning, thinking he should be hungry, he went to the vending machines and purchased some cheese crackers and a Coke. It was the only time he had left his room. The crackers remained unopened, and the Coke was only a third gone.

At nine o'clock he called his office and told Theresa that he was still sick. At nine-thirty the phone rang, giving him a chill. He hadn't left a wake-up call. He picked it up and said nothing.

"Mr. Daniels?"

He couldn't remember what name he had put on the registration.

"This is the front desk. Will you be staying another night? You didn't say when you checked in."

"Yes."

"What time would you like housekeeping—"

"It won't be necessary," Pettigrew said. "I'm resting, and I don't wish to be disturbed."

"Of course, sir. Thank you."

The bed was still made. He had not tried to sleep, just sat on it with his legs stretched out in front of him. He was holding the TV remote, had been all night. Every so often, when he thought about it, he would randomly flip the channels; the slightest hint of control over something gave him comfort. He had no idea what else to do.

HUNNYCUT HELD THE receiver of a public telephone in Union Station to his ear and waited for an answer. He was livid. Evidently Arthur Valdrine thought the senator had nothing better to do than run from his office to the train station to return his calls. The man was a self-important, pompous ass who needed to understand that there were higher priorities than whatever was going on in Louisiana at the moment.

Things had turned cold for him on the Hill since rumors of an investigation had surfaced. The committee had not addressed him, but the Government Guard's allegations had created a lot of talk. Marlene told him there was nothing to worry about, and he scoffed when colleagues brought it up, but the chill was hard to ignore. Other politicians had lived through investigation and scandal and survived, but few of them had had the vice presidency as a prize.

"This better be good, Arthur," he said when Valdrine answered.

"There are some developments down here, Thornton, that I'm going to have to take care of."

"Tell me."

"Sam Larkin is back."

"Back? What the fuck do you mean, he's back?"

"He walked into Pettigrew's office and announced himself."

"What? Why now? What did he want? He was never supposed to come back to Louisiana."

"Pettigrew told me nothing. Just that Larkin had been to his office. Then he hung up on me. I told you that Larkin should have been taken care of a long time ago, but I was overruled. And now Pettigrew's disappeared."

"What do you mean disappeared?"

"Not at home, not in his office, disappeared. Didn't go home all night. I've got someone watching the office. He can't stay away forever. I also have someone checking the surrounding area for his car."

"Could Larkin have something to do with his disappearance?"

"I have no idea, but I doubt it. Sam Larkin wasn't a criminal, remember?"

"Revenge can make people exhibit criminal behavior. I wouldn't lose that thought; it might come in helpful. He was a fall guy before; you might have to use him as a fall guy again."

"I don't think you'd want him in police custody, Thornton."

"I never suggested that, Arthur." The implication in his voice was clear. "Sounds like you've got a mess on your hands."

"He won't be a threat. I'll take care of Larkin."

"See that you do." He had heard enough. "Arthur, I may not be available for the next few days, but I want you to know I'm not pleased with what's going on down there. I'm wondering if you can handle national politics. It's a rough game. You've got a lot riding on how you handle this. As long as Larkin's around, he's a threat." Hunnycut's voice went from steely quiet to harsh. "Goddamn it, Arthur, I don't need this. I've got a committee on my ass, and now this is falling on me. We paid good hush money, and now he's back. That part is on your shoulders, and I expect it to be cleared up. I've come too far to let you fail me."

"Rest as—"

"Damn it! Don't you dare say 'rest assured.' You told me that about Landers, and nobody even knows where the hell he is."

"Dead," Valdrine said.

"What?"

"He's dead, Thornton. He left nothing behind. Nothing. René ran his apartment."

"Why didn't I read about it? He's a capital reporter. I don't care how insignificant he or his paper is, the papers would have—"

"He was using a phony name. But rest—" He stopped himself. "He is dead."

"Arthur, you're the most powerful man in the state, and I put you there. My God, you've got the whole fucking state at your disposal. Thanks to me. The next time you call, I expect good news." Hunnycut slammed the receiver back in its cradle.

TO VALDRINE'S WAY of thinking, Hunnycut had just given him carte blanche. Not that he needed the senator's permission. Everything he'd done in the past and everything he would orchestrate in the future only gave him more power. The good senator had no idea that their telephone conversations were being recorded. Valdrine wasn't worried that they implicated himself as well; power was all he ever worked for, and he left nothing to chance on that front. It was his calling.

There were a number of things working and several options that would solidify his position while removing threats to Hunnycut and himself. Finding Larkin was foremost on that agenda. He had engaged two NOPD freelancers to scour the area for Pettigrew's car. Valdrine didn't know their names, but the intermediary—another officer in the department he had worked with over the years—gave them credit for being outstanding at what they did. Bill and Joe, as the intermediary referred to them, would do anything for the right price. Finding a car was child's play.

Larkin, Pettigrew, and Musgrave. Musgrave was a question mark. At present he didn't appear to be much of a risk, but time would tell. And the woman in Gulfport was another question mark. He needed to stay calm. Nothing successful in politics was ever done on impulse; it was a matter of staying calm and operating three moves ahead.

# TWENTY

MUSGRAVE WAS SITTING on the gallery, eating breakfast, reading the newspaper, and listening to the rain. He had gotten a late start, an increasingly common occurrence. Five-thirty had been his wake-up time his whole life, but now he couldn't remember the last time he had risen at that hour. Perhaps it was age, he thought. Or Casey. Or peace of mind. Maybe a combination of all three. Whatever it was, he didn't feel guilty about the new schedule; he enjoyed it.

He didn't hear the French doors open, but he felt Casey's presence even before she came up behind him and put her arms around him, her hands on his chest. She leaned her head down against his. He lowered the paper and covered her hands with his own.

"You're the only thing that makes me sad about getting older," he said.

"Why should I make you sad?" Casey asked.

"Because I'll only have you for a short while."

"I'm not going anywhere."

"But I am. Can't last forever, and I'll be damned if I'll hang myself around your neck, some drooling old codger who can't remember your name. 'Course, no matter how bad it gets, I'll remember the rest of you."

She kissed him. "You're not going anywhere, Harold. We've got a long time together. Hey, we might drool on each other." Her smile was electric.

"We've already done that a few times." He laughed.

"More than a few, and I look forward to more."

The telephone rang, and Casey went inside to answer it.

Musgrave wondered if they were still in a courting stage, or if they had been able to keep that initial thrill alive. If so, they were the only couple he knew who had managed it. Most of the people he knew celebrated going in opposite directions. Even the ones who were faithful, happy, and, so far as he knew, loved each other. He had never for a moment not missed Casey when she was not in his sight.

"You look like the cat that swallowed the canary," he said when she came back onto the gallery.

"That was Raymond Gaynaud," she said. "He's on his way out here. Says he has a surprise for us. He also said one of us had better get the checkbook out. Harold, if we find out who this Sam Larkin is, what do you intend to do?"

"Depends on who he is." He lost his smile. "When Arthur called this morning, he asked if I knew where Jordan was, said he'd tried his house and office, no luck. Now, that's strange and peculiar. I've never worried about Jordan, but he's a creature of habit, and none of that sounds right. I don't trust Valdrine."

"You don't think . . ."

"At the moment, I don't think anything."

Casey's eyes met Musgrave's, and she saw something in him she'd not seen before, and knew unequivocally how he had survived.

He continued, "But what I do know is, if they try to fuck with my life or with you, they will wish their mamas had flushed them down a toilet on the day they were born."

Casey said nothing. Musgrave smiled at her and then laughed.

MARLENE COLE SAT in Senator William Clemmings's outer office. Getting the appointment had been difficult, but she had indicated that she might be willing to switch sides and help him secure the nomination for "considerations." He was not an easy man to convince, but Cole was a long-time master at manipulating men.

When Marlene was thirteen, a bawdy aunt who had been married four times and made money on each one had given her a life lesson about men: feed 'em and fuck 'em, and they'll walk up Mt. Everest backwards for you. She'd learned early on that it was true—and that there were many different ways to fuck men.

Clemmings was smart and cautious; she had picked that up on the telephone. He was also good looking. Tall and slim, with dark hair and a California tan. He wouldn't call off the dogs easily, but she had faith in her skills and had done her homework.

He gave her a practiced politician's smile and shook his head when she was ushered into his office. "How in Heaven's name did Thornton Hunnycut ever corral a lady like you?"

"I'm sure I could come up with a number of reasons, some you could guess. And some you couldn't. However, no one has ever 'corralled' me, Senator." She seated herself in a chair across from him.

"Point taken. I don't have a lot of time, Ms. Cole, but your proposition interests me. No pun intended. You caught me without warning, or I could have allotted more space in my calendar. Let me start with what I know to be fact. I know James needs the South, but he also needs California, so, in that respect, Hunnycut and I are in a standoff. As you know, the problem with Hunnycut is, shall we say, his behavior."

"Are you referring to me?"

"Only partly. His record, his financial dealings. You know what I'm talking about, Ms. Cole." He leaned back. His expression lost its charm and bordered on a sneer. "Let's quit bullshitting each other. He's one of the most corrupt politicians on the Hill, and you of all people know it."

"Are you suggesting that you are without sin, Senator?"

Clemmings gave her a condescending smile. "Ms. Cole, I don't know anyone on the Hill or elsewhere who is without sin, but I'm certainly not in Hunnycut's class."

"Let me ask you a question: have you ever heard the senator deride his constituency?"

He laughed. "I'm not sure I would have noticed if he did."

"He hasn't. He's a professional politician. You on the other hand—"

"Wait a minute; I thought you came here to—"

"To what? Give up Thornton? Not on your life, Senator. Not yet anyway."

"Then I think you'd better leave. I don't like liars, Ms. Cole."

"Lying is the basis of success in Washington. I think you'd better listen, Senator." She took several sheets of paper from the thin leather folio she held in her lap. "I have a list of fellow senators who have said that, on numerous occasions, you have referred to San Francisco as, and I quote, 'the faggot farm.' Can you recall ever saying that? I don't think you can deliver California with that kind of rhetoric. You might not even get re-elected to the Senate. I'm sure the homosexual vote is substantial in your district."

"Prove it," he said. He got a look in return that left no doubt that she could.

Marlene continued, "There is also the matter of one hundred and fifty thousand dollars in cash paid to the Government Guard to push for an investigation of Thornton Hunnycut."

"That's ludicrous," he said. "Now I want you out of here. I—" Before he could finish, he heard voices coming from a microcassette recorder Marlene had taken from her pocket and clicked on.

*"Who got this inquiry going?"*

*"Senator Clemmings."*

*"From California? A member of Senator Hunnycut's own party?"*

*"And a potential vice presidential candidate himself."*

*"And you know this to be a fact."*

*"He has great influence with the organization."*

*"Cash?"*

*"One hundred and fifty thousand dollars and the usual promises."*

She switched the recorder off.

"That doesn't prove anything, and you know it. Tapes, editing. Means nothing," Clemmings blustered, but his face had grayed.

"The man will testify to it. You willing to take a chance on that? Call them off, Senator, even if it costs you another hundred and fifty grand, or I will make this public. If I do, the vice presidency is gone and your political career will be a thing of the past." She stood up.

Clemmings stared at her. "I guess I'm caught between the cunt and the current."

"The current is going out to sea, Senator Clemmings, but the cunt will be around for a long time. Take heed. I'll expect to hear in the next forty-eight hours that the Government Guard didn't come up with enough to push their probe. Are we clear on that?"

She turned and left his office.

MUSGRAVE WAS SITTING behind his desk when Casey ushered Gaynaud in, along with another man and a woman. He stood up. "Well, I didn't know this was goin' to be a party. And with pretty girls, too." He held out his hand, and Gaynaud took it. "You do good work, Rockford."

"Harold, Casey," Raymond began, "This is Karen Chaney. And this is Sam Larkin."

Musgrave broke into a wide grin. "Pleased to meet you, Ms. Chaney. And you, Mr. Larkin. Y'all pull up some chairs. I got a feelin' this is goin' to be interestin'. Come on, come on, make yourself at home."

Casey brought in a tray with a large pitcher of sweet tea and ice-filled glasses. After serving the tea, she sat down next to Musgrave.

"Sam Larkin," Harold said. "You've caused a lot of concern among some people around here. Even had a reporter from Washington askin' about you. I guessed all along that Raymond here knew more than he was tellin' us, but I figured, in time . . . damn, I like bein' right. Now, y'all want to get started tellin' me what you have to tell me?"

Gaynaud told him about Sam's involvement with Pettigrew, Valdrine, and Hunnycut. Musgrave listened carefully. When Gaynaud was finished, he sat silently for a few moments. Finally, he spoke. "Dudn't surprise me a bit. I knew that bunch was scared of somethin'. You comin' back would surely put their jeans in a wad. You could put quite a kink in Hunnycut's plans, Sam."

"That's not the entire reason I came back, but it is an added benefit," Sam said. "What I would like to know is if you have ever heard anything that might have related in any way to my case."

"Nothin'. Didn't even know you existed until that reporter let your name drop. I had an idea he might have done that with more than just curiosity in mind. When I asked Jordan if he knew who you were, he panicked, so I knew it wudn't somethin' he wanted to discuss. And, I figured Arthur and Thornton prob'ly had somethin' to do with that."

"Raymond said Pettigrew is your attorney," Sam said.

"If you can call him that. Actually Jordan's not a bad man, certainly not in Arthur or Thornton's category. In fact, he's even opened up to me once in awhile. Beneath it all, I think he likes me. Problem is, I think they've got him over the barrel on somethin'. Prob'ly you. I've been tryin' to get him to do some papers on Laurel Grove to send to Thornton, but now I understand why he dudn't seem to want to do it."

Musgrave explained his proposal for the nursing homes. Sam smiled at the kick the old wildcatter got out of trying to outwit the senator.

"I did get a strange call from Arthur this morning. He was lookin' for Jordan and couldn't locate him. Not at home or in the office," Musgrave said.

"*He* called *you*?" Raymond asked.

"And that's unusual," Musgrave said. "Jordan's a creature of habit, as they say—whoever *they* is—and for him to not be in the office on a work day dudn't make sense."

"We'll see what we can find out."

"If I can interrupt," Karen said.

"I never met a woman I wouldn't let interrupt me. You all are smarter and more interestin' than us," Musgrave said.

"Do you know anything about Hunnycut's house in Gulfport?"

"Been down there a couple of times on business. Right pretty place, though I don't know why he'd want it. Hell, he's got a beautiful home in Baton Rouge and spends most of his time in Washington, anyway."

"What about his wife?" Sam asked.

"She stays there some, but that's another story. They don't have a real marriage, from what I can tell. Scottie's a lovely woman, but she has some unusual tastes. I'll leave it at that."

"I was wondering how Hunnycut got the place?" Karen asked.

"I don't know all the details, but through gossip in the inner circle, you might say, and a couple of nights when Arthur had too much to drink, and a couple of trips with Thornton, I gather it was a payoff. Some sort of deal Thornton put together for a mob guy, Sykorus, I think it was, down in Biloxi. Anyway, this Sykorus was supposed to go to trial in Mississippi for something pretty serious and hadn't gotten all his ducks in a row to beat it. Couldn't get a postponement, so he worked a scam with Arthur and Thornton to get arrested over here on some minor charge and be held past the trial date over there. Is this making any sense?"

"So far," Sam said.

"Is all that possible?" Casey asked.

"Darlin', in Louisiana and Mississippi anything's possible. So anyway, Sykorus misses the trial date. Nothin' the court could do 'cause he was in jail in Louisiana. I guess they could have extradited him, but they decided to wait until he was released and came back to the state, which they knew he would. Consequently, with the crowded court schedule and all, by the time he did go to trial in Mississippi months later, he had greased the proper wheels and got off. Pretty smart deal, if you ask me."

"What about the house?" Karen asked again.

"As I remember, Sykorus owned it, sold it to somebody, and Valdrine bought it from whoever that somebody was, and then Thornton bought it from him at some ridiculous price. Everybody who needed to be paid off made money through the sales, but the financial advantages all came out of Sykorus's pocket."

"Pretty clever," Raymond said.

"They're a clever bunch."

"Why were you so interested in me?" Sam asked.

"Protection. If they were as scared of you as Jordan sounded, knowin' about you gave me two possibilities: gettin' what I needed to get or gettin' me killed. In which case, I wouldn't need anything, but they'd have a helluva time accomplishin' that."

"You think they've killed people?" Sam asked.

Musgrave looked at him from under hooded eyes. "You think they haven't?"

"Masley Prather and his wife?" Karen suggested.

"I read about that. Didn't know 'em. Might have met 'em down at Thornton's house, but I can't be sure. The name was familiar."

"Hamill?" Sam asked.

"I wouldn't be a bit surprised. He was givin' 'em fits about somethin'. I do remember that. I was livin' pretty hard back then. Lotta drinkin', so some things aren't as clear as others, but I do remember he was givin' 'em trouble."

"I think it would be wise not to mention that I was here," Sam said. "For your own safety, if not for any other reason."

"You're prob'ly right. If it was just me, I wouldn't care, but I sure as hell don't want anything to happen to my lady."

"I don't want anything to happen to anyone," Sam said.

REGAN STOOD AT the windows of the makeshift office, watching the sun settle toward the concrete and steel horizon, his eyes occasionally drifting along the streets below. New Orleans was as far removed from the buttoned-down capital of the United States as one could get. It wasn't his kind of city; the people he was working with were not his kind of people; the case was not his kind of case. He felt like the proverbial fish out of water and marveled at the way Dougherty had managed to handle both sides of the see-saw so well.

The telephone's ring interrupted his thoughts.

"Agent Regan, this is Commander Buck Link. Karen Chaney gave me your number and asked me, as a personal friend, to cooperate in any way I could with your investigation."

"Yes. She said I might be hearing from you. What can I do for you, Commander?"

"I've got something I think will interest you. I do have to tell you, I'm not sure how long you're going to be able to keep your presence here low profile or a lid on Dougherty's murder. Karen did mention that. What about the Bluebird Café on Prytania about ten tomorrow morning?"

"I'll find it." Regan felt the first excitement he had experienced since getting involved in this investigation. All that anyone in both Washington and New Orleans had been able to come up with was a list of suspicions, even with Dougherty's undercover work as a reporter. But they had not been able to make a true case for any of it. Maybe Buck Link was the answer.

MARLENE COLE WAS mixing a drink at the bar in her house, congratulating herself on a good day's work when Hunnycut walked through the door.

"Well, good evening, darl—" As she turned to greet him, his large hand, wide open, caught her full on the side of her face. She fell backwards, tripping over the hassock that sat in front of an easy chair. "What in God's name—"

"Don't ever try to run my life without consulting me!" he shouted.

"What are you talking about?"

"Senator Clemmings. You saw him?"

"Of course I did, but—"

"What else have you done, Marlene? I think you just cost me the vice presidency."

She sat sprawled on the floor, holding her cheek. It burned. She tried to think, but she was dazed, and she was angry. Only one man had ever hit her before, her father, and he had lived to regret it.

What had she done? Looked into the mysterious Sam Larkin, set two researchers onto trying to find chinks in Harrison James's armor, met with Clemmings, gotten background on the Government Guard and its members.

Thornton had not turned away. From the look on his face—one she had never seen before—he might hit her again if she tried to get up. "Clemmings told me today about your attempt to blackmail him."

"He's trying to derail you, Thornton. He's vulnerable. I've got him. He's not going to do anything except what I told him to do. His calling you was a panic move." She was beginning to regroup. She would turn Thornton around.

"Not according to him. He's going directly to the organization with your little proposal. They accepted the money; they're as guilty as he is, but he believes your little tape recording is useless. He said there wasn't any proof that it was from a Government Guard member." He turned away from her, toward the bar.

"He's bluffing," she said, getting to her feet. "That tape scared the hell out of him. He turned white. Actually gray. He'll get thrown out of Congress if that becomes public, not just lose a one-in-five chance of getting on a ticket that has a fifty-fifty chance of being elected."

He turned back to her. "So what's your plan now? Just sit and wait to see what he does? And if he does what he says, what then? Let the committee bow to the pressure and investigate? Get me thrown out of the Senate and maybe both of us put in jail? Helluva plan." He turned away in disgust.

Her open-handed blow to the back of his head was hard and on target. It stung him and knocked him off balance. He grabbed the edge of the bar, righted himself, and turned toward her, his arm cocked back and his fist clenched.

"Don't you dare," she said with quiet force. "If you ever so much as touch me in anger again and don't finish the job, I will be the last person you ever touch on this earth. And don't say you're sorry. Sorry is a character evaluation, not an apology."

Hunnycut's arm dropped to his side, the fire fading from his eyes. "I was wrong to—"

"You're damned right you were. Thornton, remember what I said, but forget what you did. We don't have time to beat each other up, physically or mentally. Clemmings is not going to push, and neither will the Government Guard. He's just trying to get you to make me back off."

"You have the Guard locked, in addition to Clemmings?" Hunnycut poured himself four fingers of single-malt Scotch and added two ice cubes.

"Three of them, and that's enough. There's not a closet big enough to hold the bones from all their skeletons."

He sat down on the couch, the wind taken out of him. "Let's get drunk," he said.

"To begin with," she answered and sat down next to him.

He leaned over and kissed her lightly, and she smiled. Thornton Hunnycut had made the biggest mistake of his life.

IT WAS LATE, a clear night—stars, moon, the whole heavenly light show. Sam fixed a drink and went out on the deck. He watched the cars on the highway pass by, and, as so many times before, wondered where they were all going, what they went home to.

Karen had gone to bed. Emotional fatigue generated by the case, Dougherty's death, and perhaps their own relationship appeared to be taking their toll on her. The first might be solved with research and tenacity; the second might eventually be relieved by acceptance and time. There was no simple way to resolve the third condition.

His own feelings toward Celine and, he believed, hers for him, were still there and always would be, to some degree. He had seen how easy it would be to try to pick up what had been, had nearly let himself be carried away by those feelings when he sat in Boudreaux's living room, reliving memories, when she kissed him, and when they made love. It would have been easy to try, but Celine had recognized that she and Sam were in the past, and not enough of that could ever be wiped out to make a future.

Earlier in the day, Karen had expressed concern about Celine's safety and asked if he had called her. It was a straightforward question, as far as he could tell, but it had made him think. He had already made up his mind to tell her about Celine, but too much had happened in the last few days to broach that subject. Still, the fact that Karen was anxious about her safety told him something.

He finished his drink and went back into the house.

KAREN WAS NOT asleep when the door to her room opened and Sam slipped into bed beside her. He nestled into her back and brought his hand around her waist to her breast. He held it as he would something fragile. It was the first genuine, loving movement he had made toward her in days. She covered his hand with her own.

"What brings you back, Sam?"

"You did," he answered.

Karen turned over on her back and looked up at him. His hair framed his face, softening the dangerous look he had when it was pulled back tightly against his head. She had never been impressed with long hair on a man before Sam. He leaned down and kissed her with feather-light brushes of his tongue on her lips. He kissed her neck, her eyelids, her mouth. It was a deep kiss that reminded her of South Carolina and all they had had there.

She pulled him on top of her, sucked in her breath, closed her eyes, and guided him with gentle, slow movements toward reunion.

PETTIGREW HAD NEVER fallen victim to malaria; however, he thought he was experiencing all its symptoms: sweats, chills, diarrhea, flashes of delusion, hallucinations. He didn't know whether his temperature was elevated or not, but his heart had not stopped racing since he had heard the words "Sam Larkin" come from the mouth of the man in his office, and he guessed his blood pressure was off the scale. In lucid moments, he knew he was having a panic attack, and it paled anything he had known before to insignificance.

He had been in the motel room for more than two days. The drapes were pulled, and it was dark except for the flickering of the muted TV. The only trips outside had been to the vending machines three doors away to get soft drinks and crackers. He had no way of knowing what was going on in his world without revealing himself. He couldn't sit still, and he had nowhere to go.

He still sat in the middle of the king-sized bed, with his back against the headboard. He had to decide where to go from here, but he didn't know where that might be, only that he couldn't stay here forever. Maybe if he started with results and worked backwards, some logical revelation would come to him.

The results he came up with were grim. Death or prison, which were most likely synonymous. His knowledge of Sam Larkin, the fact that Larkin had chosen him to contact first, was a death sentence. Even if Valdrine got to Larkin, he would still have to clean up everything that was connected, which included himself. Turning himself in to the authorities was useless; he wouldn't survive a week in prison.

There was also the possibility that Larkin himself would kill him. Pettigrew knew he was capable of it. According to Valdrine, Larkin had killed a man with his bare hands in Angola. It was that brutal act of survival that had moved Hunnycut to suggest the plan they had put into action. It had been bizarre and risky, but Hunnycut had believed in it. It fit his concept that every person on the face of the earth could be bought, that money and freedom were fair exchanges for revenge and silence. He had underestimated Larkin.

Pettigrew turned his head away from the silent television screen and caught his reflection in the mirror next to it. The sight was pitiful. Tears began to run down his face. His tongue captured one in the corner of his mouth, and he tasted its salt. There was no honor in what he saw. Everything in his life had been thin, without any useful or virtuous purpose. He realized that he had known it all along. All of the important qualities—integrity, honesty, sincerity, morality, principle, sacrifice, and love—were nothing but a house of cards in Jordan Pettigrew, and Sam Larkin had brought about its collapse. Perhaps he should be grateful.

He made a decision. He left the bed, went into the bathroom, turned on the shower, and undressed. By the time he stepped in, the water was hot, and he focused on the sensations it created as it hit his skin. He wanted to feel everything: the ripping of the paper around the small bar of soap, how the soap fit in his hand, the slickness of it when it got wet; the opening and closing of his eyes in the face of the shower head; the soapy washcloth scrubbing his arms and legs. He had never felt so fully and intentionally. He could even imagine a loss of weight as two days' worth of grime sloughed off his body. The focus was exhilarating, something he had missed in his life, never been conscious of, something he wanted to remember.

His quest for tactile sensitivity continued as he dried himself as roughly as possible, grateful that the harsh detergents used by the cheap motel left the towels coarse. When he dressed, he was conscious of touching each button, each piece of cloth. He had done these things every day, yet never experienced them. He ran his fingers through his hair, no longer worrying about whether it was thinning, not caring if it was in place, just being involved with the feel of it. The texture of it.

He had no razor, but he brushed his fingertips upward on his face, enjoying the rough stubble. He vowed to become just as meticulous in his sensitivities and awareness as he had been about his manners and his dress. For the rest of his life, however brief that might be.

# TWENTY-ONE

BUCK LINK CAUGHT a slight break in the crowd at the Bluebird Café between nine forty-five and ten. Not that it really mattered. In uniform, Link could get priority seating at any restaurant, but he never used that perk and resented the hell out of those who did.

He needed Regan's cooperation; on the other hand, he didn't want him in the way. Federal agents, in his opinion, were given an extra measure of piss and vinegar, pride and ego, to go along with their badges.

Regan arrived, and after opening pleasantries and a beverage order, jumped right to the purpose of the meeting. "What have you got, Commander?" The anticipation in his face was obvious.

Link doubted that the agent's brain had rested since his call the day before. He opened the manila folder sitting on the table in front of him and slid the sketch artist's rendering across the table.

Regan looked at it carefully and then raised his eyes to Link's. "Who's this?"

"Could be our man."

"Neil's guy?"

"Maybe." Link described the events that had taken place at the crime scene, his nagging memory of the grinning man, and his decision to call in a sketch artist. "This could be nothing, but somehow I don't think so. That look was filled with—what do I want to say—disdain, close to dismissal. Superiority. A you-guys-don't-have-a-clue look."

"We're basing this on a look?" Disappointment shrouded Regan's face.

"All of our indications are that it was a professional. We've got some wannabes down here, as well as some real pros. Whoever did this is close to being real, but if this man did it, I think his roots are showing. He hasn't quite made it over the emotional line. I saw pride in this guy's face." He stabbed at the picture with his forefinger. "He drove by slower than a gawker, taking care to meet my eyes. And the look—this guy was bragging."

Regan picked up the picture and studied it. The face looked like something out of a Fellini movie; all it needed was exaggerated makeup.

"I can't help you with the ID unless we get something physical, prints or something." He analyzed the face. He couldn't decide if it looked pleasant, demonic, and caustic.

"I'm not asking for that. I just wanted you to know what we're doing. I've sent copies of this to a couple sheriffs and a guy I can trust at NOPD who are going to quietly check around. I think once we find this guy, if he's involved, and we identify the victim as federal, and if this is indeed a conspiracy, then someone is going to panic."

"That's a lot of ifs." Regan changed direction, telling Link about the Prather murders and Prather's connection to the real estate transactions. "I doubt this is connected, but it's very tempting to think so. I understand the police over there wrote it off as a hit and then stopped looking."

"Might be something there. Certainly worth checking out. Of course, if this guy's from Mississippi, that broadens the search, but we'll find him, and when we do, he sure as hell won't be smiling."

"Can I keep this?" Regan asked, holding the picture.

"Of course. You going to eat? The pancakes here are great."

"I don't think so," Regan said as he stood up to leave.

JORDAN PETTIGREW HAD formulated a scheme for his escape. For the first time in memory, he didn't feel tethered to New Orleans and the cast of characters who surrounded him. For the first time in years, he could look at himself and not see caution lurking beneath the shadows of his face. The plan had come to him in the early morning hours. He had arrangements to make, and every move would have to be carefully orchestrated, but he believed he could pull it off.

It was not only escape he sought; it was also retribution. His descent into panicked sloth had given birth to anger, something that for him had always been compromised by fear. Valdrine and Hunnycut had known about and fed that fear. He knew that to survive, he would have to take the other two members of the triumvirate down. It was the only way to assure his safety; there was no doubt in his mind they had their dogs out looking for him.

But he couldn't do it alone, which was a problem. The escape he could coordinate. The airports would be covered, but Valdrine would never imagine Pettigrew's getting on a Greyhound. The bus station was within walking distance. Once there, he would go to the first destination available. He had cash, which he had been smart enough to pick up on the day he'd closed up his office and fallen out of sight. He would leave no credit card trail.

The second part of his plan was more complicated. He needed an ally he could trust, who would do what he asked without too many questions. The problem was that he didn't have any friends like that and had never thought he'd need one. The only name who even came close was Harold Musgrave's.

Despite their contentiousness over legal matters, they had shared some small moments of camaraderie, and Musgrave held as much contempt for Valdrine and Hunnycut as he did. Also, Pettigrew was the only one intuitive enough to see through Musgrave's pose as a soft-brained drunk. He had seen Musgrave work it. The man was his only choice, if such a choice existed for him.

He knew that waiting would be the most difficult part. He was anxious to get on with it, but he didn't want to do anything during daylight hours. He went to the bathroom to put some cold water on his face. In the mirror, he perceived a change in the countenance looking back at him. It didn't appear to be sagging as much. Self-respect might be as effective as a facelift for recapturing some vestige of youth, he thought.

It was only ten-thirty. It would be a long day. He opened the curtains enough to let in some light, leaving the sheers closed, retrieved a box from the closet, and sat at the desk to read his files on Sam Larkin for the last time.

KAREN AND SAM picked up Raymond, as decided the day before. The bits and pieces they had gathered from Musgrave were helpful to the overall picture but, excepting Pettigrew's sudden disappearance, gave them nothing to act upon. Karen suspected that he would be found in the same condition as Neil: dead.

"I think we should go by Pettigrew's office," Sam said. "I've got a feeling that if he's not already dead, he's a sitting duck, and I put him in that position."

"They might be waiting for you to show up again," Raymond said, then grinned. "This may be your opportunity to burn them."

Sam grinned back. "Let's do it."

As they circled the block looking for a parking space, Raymond suddenly sat up in his seat, locking in on an old car parked across the street from Pettigrew's building. "That's him," he said.

Karen turned around.

"That's who?" Sam asked, glancing in the rearview mirror. Raymond had his back to him, looking out the back window.

"The guy who was in the parking lot in Biloxi. Pink Shirt. The guy who went into your place. Parked at the end of the block. Other side."

Karen and Sam looked and saw the old car. "You're sure?" Karen asked.

"Ninety-five percent."

"I need to talk to him," Sam said.

"Doesn't look like he's going anywhere. Park, and I'll do a walk-by to make it a hundred percent."

Another turn around the area, and Sam found a spot a block away. They passed the car again; the driver was slouched down, almost out of sight.

When they got out of the car, Sam and Karen hung back while Raymond proceeded down the street. He assumed a new walk, as if he had turned on a jukebox in his head and was bouncing along to its rhythms. Or maybe was stoned and being guided by other voices. Or deranged, Sam thought. He stopped at every car, empty or not, looked in the window, waved, and moved on to the next. Bouncing and swaying at the waist all the while. Setting a pattern. Definitely a mental case.

Sam moved his hand behind his back and closed his fingers around the K-frame as Raymond approached Pink Shirt's car. Raymond looked in the passenger window, actually put his head inside, waved hello as if he were a child, and proceeded on. Several buildings past the car, he turned in and disappeared, never giving up the act.

Midday traffic was picking up, and the sidewalks were becoming busier. The increasing pedestrian traffic made Sam uncomfortable. A cool breeze tunneled its way up the street. Sam didn't know if the weather or the predicament facing him was causing his skin to tingle.

Raymond had circled around and come up behind them.

"It's a garbage dump," he said, "and definitely old Pink Shirt. Not wearing it today though. Has on a fake embroidered cowboy shirt, yokes and all that. He's positively staking out something and looks like he has been for awhile. Car's full of food wrappers, drink cups, bunch of clothes in the back seat. There's also a cardboard box in back, tape, and several plastic bottles. Angola makings."

The same thought hit all three of them at the same time. Pink Shirt had been watching Karen. The possibility she had voiced earlier was confirmed.

"I'm not sure—" Raymond began.

"Got to do it," Sam said. He reached behind to loosen the Smith and Wesson in his belt. "You two cross the street and come down the other side. I'll approach from the passenger side and squat to ask him directions. I want to be able to get below the door if he reacts."

Raymond retrieved a rubber band from his pocket and pulled his hair back tight to his head in a ponytail. "Disguise," he said and smiled.

He and Karen crossed the street and began meandering toward the end of the block. Sam started toward the car. Thirty feet away, he saw the driver look in the rearview mirror with a slight rising of the head. He moved quickly to the side of the car and squatted at the open window.

The man was watching Karen and Raymond across the street, maybe recognizing the jitterbug who had passed earlier. Sam had one hand on the door handle and the other behind his back clutching the grip of the K-frame. He cleared his throat.

Pink Shirt spun in the seat. "Wha—"

"Wondered if you could give me some directions?" Sam asked, watching the man's hands. One went to the ignition. Then the man smiled. He looked silly rather than friendly.

"Not from 'round here, man." He turned the ignition and pressed on the gas in one swift motion. Sam was still grasping the door handle. After a few steps, he lost his footing and let go, falling to the sidewalk. A car coming up the street nearly sideswiped the one parked immediately behind Sam in order to avoid a head-on collision with Pink Shirt. Sam heard the squealing brakes and rolled away. When he raised his head, the old car had moved into traffic and was passing out of sight.

He felt hands helping him up. Karen and Raymond had run across the street to him.

"Nice move, Sam. Are you hurt?" Karen asked.

"Lost a little skin, nothing else. The damned guy smiled at me," Sam said, finally on his feet and brushing himself off. Both elbows were torn out of his shirt, and he was bleeding.

He reached behind him to make sure his gun hadn't fallen out.

"What the fuck were you doing, pal?" the driver from the car which had nearly wrecked screamed.

"Asking for directions," Sam answered.

Karen and Raymond had started moving Sam in the direction of the Rover. "Talk about dumb luck," Raymond said, chuckling.

"I think we just intensified the urgency of identifying this guy," Sam countered. "And finding Pettigrew." He turned to Karen. "Why don't you go up to his office and see what you can find out. If he's hiding or running, we may have a problem. I thought he might be our best bet to get inside. Raymond and I will be in the car."

"I'm on it," she said, leaving the two men standing on the sidewalk.

"We could cruise Arabi and see if we could locate Pink Shirt's car," Raymond suggested. "It ain't hard to overlook."

"Doesn't mean we'll find him. He may look ridiculous, but he obviously knows what he's doing."

"Just a thought."

In fifteen minutes Karen was back at the car. "No luck. His receptionist said he's been out of the office two days with some kind of bug. She didn't know when he'd be back. She said he called in every day, but I think she was lying. She looked too nervous."

WAITING INFURIATED VALDRINE. Joe and Bill had begun their search for Pettigrew's car sixteen hours ago, and they had come up with nothing. There were a lot of motels, hotels, suites—all manner of lodgings—in and around the city of New Orleans, he kept telling himself. When Bill called to report their lack of progress, he sent them back out to canvass areas farther outside the city.

The woman in Biloxi still bothered him. Who and what was she? Valdrine believed strongly in knowing his enemies. Inside and out, if possible. The list of people who posed problems was getting longer, and there had to be a stopping point. Connections between people on a list of deaths would be revealing to even the most half-assed investigator.

Larkin was the main problem. He could be anywhere. Without Pettigrew, Valdrine knew nothing about the man's current appearance, nothing. Valdrine caught himself studying faces when he was leaving the office, when he was driving, when he was on the street. He speculated about whether Larkin would walk into his office, same as he had done with Pettigrew.

The ringing of the telephone was white noise against the background of his thoughts. He snatched it up on the fourth ring.

"Dey see me, yeah," René Grosjean said.

"Who? Who saw you? What do you mean?" Maybe Pettigrew had surfaced.

"De boyfrien'. Dat girl from Biloxi an' anodder guy. He come up and stick his head in my car window."

"Where were you?"

"Watchin' dat office like you say. Just walked up. I t'ink de girlfrien' across the street wit anodder man, not the boyfrien', but I t'ink dey all togedder."

"You're not telling me they were looking for you." Valdrine didn't want to think about that.

"Dey notice me anyway, yeah."

"What did he do? Did he say anything?" He fought to keep his voice calm.

"Axe for directions."

"Directions for where?"

"Don' know. Didn't wait. He fell down when I pull away. Den de girl an' de other boyfrien' run across the street to him. How I figure they all togedder."

"Did they follow you?"

"Naw. Cain' follow me, no. Where you want me now?"

"The house. Watch the house. He's got to come home sooner or later."

"Got to get somethin' to eat firs'," Grosjean said.

"Make it quick. And René—"

Grosjean cut him off. "Don' use my name." The sound was quietly threatening.

"Call me at seven AM sharp if he doesn't come home tonight. Immediately if he does. But don't leave there."

"You hear from me."

The woman, and now two men. But who in hell could they be? An idea presented itself that almost knocked him out of his chair. Larkin. One of the men might be Larkin. Sent the woman out to do the research on the property. It fit, even though he didn't want it to. But surely not. How would Larkin know about the house?

The list was growing longer, and he was becoming insecure. "Goddamn it!" he screamed. "Get these fucking people out of my life!"

CASEY AND MUSGRAVE customarily ate dinner early. Musgrave said it allowed him to digest before going to bed. His stomach was not the steel-coated organ it had once been. Too much booze, too much rich food eaten at three o'clock in the morning before passing out. Sometimes no food at all, depending upon the party and who he was with and what they were doing. It had all taken its toll, he often said. But he said it with pride. Glad he had done it, and happy he didn't have to do it again. He viewed everything he had done in life as a gift. It was all part of what had brought him to where he was, and he was liking himself more and more.

He and Casey frequently walked down to the pond after dinner to watch the sweet bugs swim in circles, never getting anywhere, and the skitter bugs making their slight indentations on the mirror surface and moving on, bream and bass breaking the surface to gobble up the intruders. They listened to the frogs sending their sundown message and watched nature paint the horizon in stripes of scarlet and pale white. After a while they went back to the house to sit on the gallery and watch the moon rise. It was a different life than Musgrave had ever led before or even imagined leading.

Sometimes they just sat and read, not talking, being close. They watched a movie once in awhile if a good one managed to make it to one of the cable channels. Not much else. They rarely went out, and that suited Musgrave fine. He had been out enough for two lifetimes. Casey never seemed to mind the sylvan lifestyle. Maybe she had been out enough, too. He never asked her for any details about her past.

Casey handed Musgrave the phone when Pettigrew called at seven-thirty. "Where are you, Jordan? Arthur's been trying to reach you. Even called me, and you know that's a rarity. Did he get you?"

"Interesting choice of words. No, he didn't get me, but I don't have time to explain it all right now. Let's say I don't want him to reach me, much less get me, and I'd appreciate it if you didn't tell him you'd heard from me."

"You have my word, and, regardless of what some people may think, that does mean something."

"I believe it does. I've had some time to think, Harold. You've always been upfront and, to my knowledge, honest in your dealings with me. That's the reason I called you. I believe I can trust you, and you may be the only person I can say that about right now."

"I appreciate that, Jordan." For all his new-found sincerity, Jordan Pettigrew was slippery, and Musgrave would not reciprocate trust based on a few kind words.

"The man you were so curious about, the one you baited me with—and I'm not upset about that; you were on target—Sam Larkin is back in New Orleans. Without going into details, he means a lot of trouble for Arthur and Thornton—and myself, if I were to allow it."

"I believe it, Jordan. I spoke with him here, today."

"There?"

"It's a long story, but I'll make it short. The name came up from that reporter, as I told you. I thought it might be important to Hunnycut, might be a wedge if I knew who he was. Then when you panicked at the sound of his name, I knew damned well it was important. So, I hired someone to find him. And he did. It was after Larkin appeared in your office. He told me about that."

"Good Lord," Pettigrew said.

"What is it, Jordan? Maybe I can help you. Would be a switch, wouldn't it?"

"I don't think I've ever really helped you, Harold, not even as much as a rookie just out of law school should have. I'm calling to tell you that I'm getting out, that I won't be available to you any longer. I don't want you to get involved."

"I don't know what you don't want me to get involved in, Jordan, but it would appear that I already am."

"You don't know what you're facing," Pettigrew said.

"I think I do. What can I do to help you?"

"Harold, I truly have underestimated you. I was going to ask you for a relatively uncomplicated favor, that you simply mail a package for me; however, now that you have made contact with Larkin, I believe this would be a better way to go. Please don't hesitate to refuse what I'm going to ask, because I don't know what the ramifications might be. I want you to be sure you know what you're doing."

"I know what I'm doing, and I don't run from responsibility. From what I've heard today, I sure as hell don't have any responsibility to Valdrine or Hunnycut. And, Jordan, I didn't have any to you either until this phone call, but I've changed my mind. Like you. Now tell me, damn it, and don't feel guilty about it."

"I have something, something no one knows I have. If Hunnycut or Valdrine knew, I'd have been dead long ago. It's more than enough to destroy them. I wasn't sure how I was going to use it, thought maybe in a tough situation with them, it would be my deliverance. Now I realize it won't be. You've told me a better way."

"I'll do whatever you want, if you'll tell me how I'm supposed to get whatever it is you won't tell me about and what I'm supposed to do with it once I get it."

"I will have a package delivered to you tomorrow evening. It may be late. I have some arrangements to make tomorrow and a letter of explanation to write. It will be safer finding someone else to deliver it than doing it myself. It can't be too much longer before they find me. Whoever brings it will have a note from me for you to sign. I want to be sure it gets there. I don't know what time it will be delivered; I haven't made any arrangements yet, but leave some lights on outside, and one of you will have to be on alert until it arrives. I don't like putting this on you, Harold."

"Hell, I'm beginnin' to enjoy it."

"I want you to get it to Larkin. Can you do that?"

"I can," Musgrave said.

"Don't open it. I know it's a cliché, but the less you know the better. And don't deliver it to Larkin; ask him to come and get it. If you can't reach him within a day or so, open it, read the letter, and send it and the rest of the material to the *Times-Picayune*. There are enough of my notes in there that someone will pick up on it."

"What about you, Jordan? What are you going to do?"

"You don't need to know that either."

"But—"

"You're a better man than I ever gave you credit for, and I apologize for underestimating you. Now that I look back, there are probably a lot of people who fit in that category."

"Can I ask you one question?" Musgrave said.

"No. Just watch for the package." Pettigrew hung up.

Casey had left him on the gallery and gone back inside. Musgrave rose and walked through the French doors, toward the living room, where he knew she would be reading. He was trying to make up his mind how much to tell her about the conversation.

"You must be relieved to hear from him," she said as he sat on the couch.

"Yes. Yes, I am."

"Is he all right?"

"He seems to be. He's taking a little trip." He had to decide what else to tell her, something that rarely required any thought.

IT HAD BEEN a long and frustrating day. First they'd lost Pink Shirt, though they had no real plan for what they would have done with him if he hadn't taken off. At least Sam could now identify him even if they didn't know his name. Aside from this unexpected encounter, little had been accomplished in the afternoon.

Putting a name on Pink Shirt was a priority, but there was no quick way of doing that, other than scanning shots at the NOPD. It was also imperative, Sam suggested, that they locate Pettigrew, but the odds on that seemed slim since whoever hired Pink Shirt to find him had obviously not been successful either. Late in the day, Sam and Karen left Raymond at his office and went back to Biloxi.

When they walked through the door into the condo, Karen went to the kitchen, unclipped her holster, and put her gun on the counter. As she turned to join Sam in the living room, she noticed a fax on the machine. She tore off the paper and went to Sam.

"A fax," she said. "First one since I've been here."

*Karen: Contact me immediately. I can tell from reading Neil's notes that we have made little progress regarding Thornton Hunnycut, other than what we already knew. There is, however, some progress being made in Washington. I would have called, but I want you to see what follows.*

*I would appreciate a report on what you and Sam are doing, since you have not seen fit to inform me.*

*I spoke with Buck Link regarding Neil's death. He thinks he may have seen the man responsible. The following is an artist's rendering made from his description of the man.*

*Again, contact me immediately.*

*Michael Regan*

They looked at the drawing. A man with a simple-minded smile looked back at them.

"It's him," Sam said. "The guy in the car. Pink Shirt."

"You're kidding me."

"Not about this. Call Regan."

Karen dialed the number. Regan picked up on the second ring.

"I was beginning to wonder if I was still in the loop. This is the most unorganized, unregulated, un-by-the-rules operation I have ever been connected with. Agents everywhere fighting their individual wars and nobody calling in. Why haven't I heard from you?"

"We were coming in tomorrow, had decided that before I got the fax. Sam recognized the drawing."

"What? He knows the guy?"

"Not by name. We saw him watching Jordan Pettigrew's office this morning, and Sam confronted him, but he took off."

"Wait a minute. Let's slow down. I need to know everything."

"We just got back from the city, and I don't have anything that won't wait until morning. We're going to compile a report. I don't want to leave anything out, and I'd rather do it in person. Let's say between ten and ten-thirty. It looks like the gang is getting antsy," Karen said.

"Should I get Buck Link over here?"

"Not yet. I want to lay out what we've got and then hear what you've got to say." She gave Sam a look.

"I'll be here."

"Compile a report?" Sam asked when Karen had put the receiver down.

"Just letting Special Agent in Charge Regan think he's in control."

After the initial excitement of seeing Pink Shirt on paper, they realized that other than giving it to the newspaper and local law enforcement agencies, either of which would expose their investigation, or looking at mug shots, which they agreed would be too time consuming, they still had no way of identifying the man. They decided to wait until morning and their meeting with Regan before moving forward. They also wanted to talk to Raymond.

In bed, Karen lay spooned against Sam's back, her left arm over him, her hand resting on his chest, the softness of her breasts pressed into his back. She was sleeping; he could tell by the pace of her breathing and the relaxed state of her muscles. They had made love twice. Sam was awake, enjoying the warmth of her skin and the resurrection of something he had thought was gone between them. He felt a slight movement, then her breath changed its rhythm and a voice whispered on the back of his neck.

"Nice report we're compiling, don't you think?"

"Some parts are pretty interesting," he replied and then felt her hand slip between his legs and grasp him.

"What was that? I didn't hear."

"I said whatever you want to hear." She relaxed her hold to let him turn over, and they made love again.

"Three times in one night. Think people down here would be shocked?"

"I don't think they'd even notice. In this part of the country, Larkin, we're amateurs."

# TWENTY-TWO

AT 8:45 RENÉ Grosjean, carrying a paper sack, entered the Place St. Charles, walked through the Galleria to the elevators, and went to the sixteenth floor. He was relieved finally to be doing something other than watching. Stakeouts were not his passion. He'd seen movies about elite assassins, million dollar paychecks, fine hotel rooms, flying from job to job, in and out and collect, and that was where he saw his future, one of his few fantasies. But he knew he was like the farm girl who dreams of being a movie star—it would never happen.

What he also knew was the secretary's routine. She entered the building at 8:15 and was in the office by 8:30. Absolutely time conscious. When he opened the office door and walked in, she looked up startled, then disdained. He thought he looked good: silver lamé shirt, black pants, black-and-white loafers, and steel gray straw hat. No matter.

"Can I help you?" she asked.

"Mr. Pettigrew," he said.

"He's not in."

Grosjean was smiling. He wanted to tell her he knew that, see her get nervous, but he didn't. "You know when he be back?"

"I really don't know. He's out of town on business, and he hasn't called in to give me his schedule this morning."

She was getting uneasy, and Grosjean was enjoying that. The bitch didn't have any idea where Pettigrew was, and she didn't lie very well, but he had to make sure. He kept smiling, knowing that unnerved her, as it did most people when the circumstances didn't fit the expression. "You t'ink he will?"

"Will what?" Her voice was getting shaky.

"Call in."

"I don't know. He should. Yes."

"Did he call in yesterday?"

She stared at him, a puzzled look on her face. "Uh, yes. Yes, he did. Now what did you want to see him about? Maybe I could recommend—"

"Where did he call from?"

"I'm not sure. He had several stops on his—"

"I don' t'ink he did." He put the paper bag on her desk.

"Listen, I'll take your phone number, and when he . . ." She was shaking uncontrollably.

His smile widened. "You know where he is? You mus'. Big lawyer leave on bidness and not tell his secretary where he's goin'? Don' sound right. You wan' tell me where he be?" He let the accent out and watched the fear on her face escalate.

"I'm going to call security," she said and reached for the phone. Grosjean grabbed her wrist with one hand and ripped the phone from its connection with the other. She began to whimper.

"Don' you scream, no." The fear in her eyes had progressed to deeper terror. Tears began to gather on her bottom lids, and her chin began to quiver. He liked that. "You know where he be or no?" He took a pair of surgical gloves from the bag and snapped them on.

"I—I don't know," she said, her voice breaking into sobs. "Please don't hurt me. I don't know where he is. I was going to call the police if he didn't . . ."

"Oh, I t'ink he all right. Jus' don' want to be foun', no. Police cain' do nothin' 'bout dat." He picked up the bag. "Let's go look in his office. You done 'at?"

"Yes. I didn't see anything that—"

He pulled her up out of the chair and pushed her into the inner office. Grosjean pointed to a chair in front of the desk. "Sit down." She did as she was told. He put the bag on the desk and took out a gun, a plastic bottle, and some tape. The secretary's eyes rolled up, and she went limp in the chair. Her legs splayed in slow motion, and her body slipped to the floor.

Grosjean searched the top of the desk, throwing papers to the floor. Nothing to indicate where Pettigrew had gone. He hadn't really expected to find anything. The desk drawers were locked, but they popped easily. Nothing. He turned back to the secretary; she was still out. He picked up the gun, the bottle, and the tape and put the items back in the bag. They had done their job.

"You lucky, you," he said. He ripped the phone cord from Pettigrew's desk phone and walked out of the office.

It was time to call his employer and find out what to do next. He was getting frustrated. He liked to finish jobs and walk away. "I ain' no detective," he said to himself as he left the building and walked toward his car. "Not me, no."

THERESA KELLY CAME out of her faint and didn't move for thirty minutes. She listened but heard no sound save her own ragged breathing. When she finally tried to get up, her stomach heaved, and she vomited on the Chambon carpet. She didn't even consider cleaning it up. She went into the bathroom and wiped her face with cold water, went to her desk, got her purse and jacket, and left the office for good.

Reaching the street, she looked both ways and began walking. Tears streamed down her face, and she could see people staring at her. Her body was shaking as if in seizure, but she could not stop it. The only thing on her mind was home. If she made it, she thought, she might never come out again. She didn't need any part of the world she had just seen.

AFTER A QUICK breakfast, Sam and Karen left Biloxi and started toward New Orleans and Raymond Gaynaud. He lived in the Bywater, a section of the city less than thirty blocks from Canal Street, between Faubourg Marigny and the Industrial Canal. Karen had never been in the downriver neighborhood and was fascinated by the architectural mixture of Creole cottages, shotgun houses, and camelbacks. The atmosphere was distinctly Creole, accented even at this hour of the morning with steam whistles and church bells.

It took a bit of searching to find the address on Burgundy, three blocks east of Desire, which Karen remarked was where she had evidently been, in Sam's opinion, for the past few nights. He reminded her of the previous night and advised her not to be greedy.

They spotted Raymond sitting on the steps of his small shotgun house. Karen was surprised, considering his dilapidated car, that the house and yard appeared neat and well kept. Some of the others in the neighborhood were not in as good repair. He stood up as he saw the Rover coming down the street, drained the cup he held, and set it on the steps.

"Early," he said as he climbed in the back seat.

"Right on time."

"I mean in the morning."

"You're still alive," Sam said with a smile.

"I guess that's a blessing."

"It was in Angola."

"I was never sure about that. So what's going on? Anything new?"

"Show him," Sam said. Karen passed the faxed drawing of Pink Shirt to the back seat.

"Holy—where did you get this?"

"Regan faxed it over this morning. Buck Link thinks it might be the guy who killed Neil," Karen said.

"He saw him?" Raymond asked.

"After the fact. He was at the scene."

"Incredible. So where are we going now?" Raymond asked.

"To see Regan," Sam said. "Do you need to stop by your office on the way?"

"No, I can do it later. I'm not exactly overrun with clients. Pink Shirt. I can't believe it."

REGAN STOOD UP behind his desk when the door opened. Karen walked in, followed by Sam and Raymond.

"I've been waiting," he said.

"I said ten, and it's ten," Karen said. "Agent Regan, this is Raymond Gaynaud. To make it brief, he's a friend of Sam's, now mine; they met in Angola, and Raymond's father is Judge Gaynaud, here in New Orleans. Raymond's a private investigator."

"That's the most succinct bio I've ever heard," Raymond said, and held out his hand.

Regan gave it a perfunctory shake. "Well, it appears that this 'covert' operation is about as open-ended as a pep rally. I'm working with two ex-cons who have no obligation to me and one irresponsible officer who has become a loose cannon. It's a comedy. And if you think I'm being funny, I'm not." He slid the drawing of René Grosjean across his desk. "Sam, Karen says you know this guy."

"No, I don't know him, but I've seen him up close. It's a good likeness, particularly the smile. Raymond saw him staking out the condo. He went inside but didn't bring anything out. Raymond followed him, but then lost him in Arabi."

"Wait a minute. What was Mr. Gaynaud doing there?"

"Looking for me," Sam said. " We'll get to that. Yesterday, as Karen told you, we spotted him watching Jordan Pettigrew's building. That's when I saw him, but he took off. End of story."

"Car? Tag number?" Regan asked Raymond.

"Old Cadillac. Not exactly difficult to pick out. The tags were mudded over."

"Nothing else?"

"I think he's a good bet for the Prather murders in Biloxi," Raymond said.

"And why would you say that?" The sarcasm was obvious in Regan's voice.

"I investigated the crime scene as a favor to my father for the Prathers' son. There wasn't really anything to see, and the report gave up nothing; however, the officer who escorted me over indicated a homemade suppressor had been used. When I looked into this guy's car on St. Charles, there were plastic bottles, rags, and tape on the back seat. All the makings."

"Which gives us nothing concrete. Why do you think he was watching Place St. Charles for Pettigrew? Maybe he was just parked there. And why were all of you there?"

"Pettigrew seems to have disappeared," Sam said, then explained Raymond's connection with Musgrave, why he had been at the condo, and the visit to Musgrave's home. "He told us that Valdrine had called asking if he knew anything about Pettigrew's whereabouts, that he sounded uptight about not being able to reach him. I would have to believe that Pettigrew told him I was back in town."

"How would he know?"

"I went to see him," Sam said. He saw anger overtake Regan. "Nothing happened. I just wanted to let him know I was back."

"Goddamn it!" Regan barked. He looked at Sam with angry disbelief. "Using yourself as bait? Don't you know anything about procedure?"

"Procedure got Neil nowhere. You don't know these people and their resources," Sam said. "They are going to be ahead of any procedure you can come up with. They're nervous. Musgrave also gave us some information on the transactions leading up to Hunnycut's ownership of the house in Gulfport, and we believe that Karen's snooping around the real estate transactions is what drew Pink Shirt to her."

"Pink Shirt?" Regan looked confused.

"It's what he was wearing the first time I saw him," Raymond said. "The guy in the drawing you faxed."

"And Colonel Mustard did it in the conservatory with a wrench. We're dealing with multiple murders, and you people act like we're on a scavenger hunt."

"You want us to quit?" Karen asked. "Neil brought me here, and he wanted Sam here. Who doesn't know what everyone is doing?"

Regan stood up, went to the window, and looked down on Canal Street. "Have you come up with anything other than this guy in the picture? A guy who may have done a lot or who may have done nothing?" he asked without turning around.

"He's done a lot," Raymond said.

Regan turned and came back to the desk. "You don't know that."

"I'd bet on it."

"You've found nothing on why you went to prison and were released, Sam?"

"I think Pettigrew, Valdrine, and Hunnycut are the only people with the answers to that, and I don't think they'll give up those answers without something much heavier hanging over their heads than my sudden reappearance, despite the fact that they were all involved."

Regan looked at Karen. "Anything specific on the real estate deals in Gulfport?"

"Just what Musgrave gave us. It was a payoff, supposedly from this Dixie Mafia guy, Sykorus. Hunnycut helped him avoid trial in Mississippi by getting him put up on a misdemeanor here. Musgrave couldn't give us a lot of details. What about Washington? They coming up with anything?"

"Quite a bit on misconduct, but that'll just amount to getting Hunnycut off the ticket, censure, maybe get him kicked out of the senate, which will all add up to nothing more than hurt pride. He'll become a consultant or lobbyist and triple his salary or become governor of Louisiana and own the state. It might narrow his options, but it won't slow him down."

"What about blanketing the city with this picture?" Karen said, gesturing toward the sketch.

"That would make him go under. It is still our objective to keep our work here and Neil's death within our own circle. That is critical," Regan said. "Link sent it to a couple of department heads he can trust and only those, but nothing so far. It's only been a day. We don't want the general law enforcement community to know about it. As you said, we don't know who might be a resource for these people."

"Why don't we see who we can eliminate?" Sam suggested.

"You start," Regan said.

"OK, here are my thoughts. Musgrave is out of it. He may know some of what's going on, but I don't think he's involved. I'm pretty sure he told us everything he knows, and I think he wants to see Hunnycut go down as badly as we do."

"Could be. Go on."

"That leaves Pettigrew, Valdrine, and Hunnycut. Hunnycut's in Washington, which doesn't mean he's not responsible for all this—I believe he is, one way or another—but someone here is the expeditor."

"Which leaves Pettigrew and Valdrine," Regan said. "Can we eliminate either of those?"

"Pettigrew," Sam said. "He's too weak. I think he did only what Hunnycut and Valdrine told him to do at my trial. And I would guess he's on the run, probably from one of them, which leaves Arthur Valdrine. It's the pecking order. He's the only one other than Hunnycut with any power."

"What about this guy?" Regan gestured toward the sketch.

"He's the mechanic," Raymond said, "and if he's a pro, even if we get him, we're not likely to get much. Not right away anyhow. Maybe if we latch on to one of the others and offer a deal."

Regan looked at Raymond. "If this is our man, he doesn't know he killed a federal agent yet," he said. "That can carry a lot of weight even with a professional. Makes two thousand volts seem more likely and can cause the vocal chords to light up."

"May I make a suggestion?" Raymond asked.

"I'll listen to anything."

"I think he probably lives in Arabi, since that's where I lost him, but if he's the man I believe he is, nobody there is going to cooperate, and looking there might spook him. He'll come back to Karen's place. I have little doubt of that. I'd like to talk to the officer in Biloxi who accompanied me to the Prather crime scene. He might know more than he let on."

"You're probably correct about the condo. Whoever's in charge is troubled by Karen's curiosity. Do you want me to send—"

"We can handle it," Sam said.

MUSGRAVE DID NOT sleep well. The call from Pettigrew had unnerved him. His bravado and judgment had been colored by his opportunity to stick it to Valdrine and Hunnycut. That was still his objective; however, foremost on his mind was Casey. He had to make sure she was not put in jeopardy.

At breakfast, he told her about the phone call. "Casey," he added, "if you don't want me to get involved, all you have to do is say so. Jordan gave me the option of just putting it in the mail. We'd be out of it."

"Harold, I trust you. I know you wouldn't do this if it were avoidable, and I'm not sure it's avoidable. Don't you think I know this could clean up a lot of things you've had hanging over your head? I also trust Raymond Gaynaud and Sam Larkin, as little as I know them. I'm a pretty good judge of character, which is why I chose you."

Musgrave smiled. "*You* chose *me*?"

"Absolutely. You don't think I had other options?"

"I'm sure you did, sweetheart."

"Anyway, you've got a federal agent involved. I'm not worried."

"So you're all right with it?"

"When is the package supposed to arrive?"

"Sometime late tonight. Jordan said he had some things to tie up today." He smiled. "I think you'd better get in touch with Rockford and put those folks on alert. We all need to be on the same page."

"Any idea what's in the package?"

"None. He did say one other thing. That I wouldn't be hearing from him again."

"You don't think . . ."

"No. Jordan's gonna be all right. I never heard such strength in the man. I just wish he'da shown it while he was representing me."

"DAT LAWYER AIN' 'round, no," René Grosjean said. "An' he ain' at his office. I gone in 'ere an' seen the woman, me."

Valdrine felt the blood pulsing through the veins in his neck. "Why in hell did you do that? Did I tell you to do that?" He felt as though he had been punched in the chest. "Of all the stup—"

"You be careful. I t'ought I ought to see was he hidin' in 'ere. 'At place is bigger dan my house. He coulda been hidin' in 'ere. You ever t'ink about dat, you? Won' nothin' in 'ere, no."

"What about the secretary?" Valdrine asked.

"She all right. Scared. She pass out while I look 'round. I din' hurt her none, no. What you wan' me to do now? Only t'ing we got lef' is dat girl in Biloxi and her boyfrien'. Dey done seen me, and dat cain' be."

"I need to know who they are. What their connection to all this is. Don't confront them yet. Keep an eye on them, and let me know what they do."

"Be hard. Dey seen my car," Grosjean said.

"Get a rental, borrow a car. I don't care how you do it, just keep them in sight."

"I'll borrow my cousin's. He like to drive mine anyway. Make everybody t'ink he's me."

Valdrine's smile was wry. So much for the cousin. "Check back in a few hours." Grosjean was beginning to make his own decisions, and that wasn't good. When the Cajun was gone, Valdrine dialed Pettigrew's office. No answer. His secretary had either gone home or to the police. His contact at NOPD eased his mind on the latter possibility.

The phone had not been its cradle for ten seconds before it rang. "I haven't heard from you," Hunnycut said.

Valdrine felt a sheen of sweat cool his arms. "Nothing to report, Thornton. Pettigrew has not reappeared. I've had his home and office watched, and nothing. I also have two people looking for his car, as I mentioned; they haven't come up with anything either. Our friend is keeping an eye on the woman in Biloxi. She has someone staying with her, and the thought occurred to me that it just might be Sam Larkin; however, without a description from Pettigrew, there's no way to know."

"Sounds like you're between a rock and a hard place, Arthur."

"Me?"

"You know what I mean."

"I will get it cleaned up. Just make certain that, when the dust clears, you remember your bargain."

"You don't trust me?"

Valdrine didn't comment. When the conversation was over, he thought how strange it was to feel in control of a United States senator, a potential future vice president, and yet so out of control with a Cajun half-wit.

FROM HIS HOUSE, Raymond called the dispatcher at the Biloxi PD and asked for Officer North. The dispatcher remembered Gaynaud and gave him the name of a bar on the strip frequented by off-duty cops.

She suggested he would probably find North there around four-fifteen; his shift ended at four.

The timing was good. Four-fifteen would allow him enough time to get to Biloxi, with a little extra to find the place. The dispatcher was true to her word. North was sitting at the bar and recognized Raymond as soon as he sat down next to him.

"Beer?" North asked.

"No. Every time I drink, I break out in handcuffs."

"Terrible disease to be saddled with," the officer said, sipping his beer.

"I can live with it," Raymond said. "Do you mind if I ask you a couple of questions?"

"You can ask."

"You ever think of anything else regarding those murders I was investigating?"

"The Prathers? Naw. Not that I can think of right now."

"I believe you said when I saw you before that you read it as a professional hit."

"I don't believe I said anything before." He turned to face Gaynaud with no humor in his expression.

"Right. I remember."

"You already know what I heard. Most everybody thinks it was a pro, but nobody knows why. I've heard a lot of theories, but you know those, too," North said, taking a drag from his cigarette and looking straight ahead.

"But what do *you* think?"

"I don't."

"I know you're not gonna say anything, but what do you think?"

"I really don't know, but I'd say if anybody did, it'd be Gustave Sykorus. He's the man around here."

"Who would he hire? Any idea?" Raymond asked.

"There's quite a few of the Dixies that might take that kind of contract, but this one? I don't know."

Raymond pulled the drawing of Pink Shirt out of his pocket, unfolded it, and laid it on the bar. "Ever seen this guy around?"

North brought the drawing up close to his face. "Almost," he said.

"What the hell does that mean?"

"The drawing's not exact. His eyes were a little wider apart, and there was a scar or something, like maybe he'd had a broken jaw or got his face cut or something. Wasn't bad, but it gave him a stupid grin like this guy."

"Got a name?"

"Prob'ly down at the station. He was drivin' through town and didn't have a visible license plate. Chickenshit bust, but when I passed him, I thought he was laughin' at me. He had so much mud caked on his plate, I couldn't tell if he even had one. Had to scrape it off with a pocket knife."

"Any idea how I might get that name?"

"You think this guy's the shooter?" He pointed at the picture.

"Maybe."

"Doesn't look smart enough to pull a trigger." North called the bartender over. "Would you hand me that phone, Chris?"

The bartender brought it to him, and North dialed. "Hello, darlin', it's John. Can you look somethin' up for me right quick?" A smile crossed North's face. "You got it."

Raymond wondered what she was going to get. If the desk officer who had directed him to the bar was the one he'd met on his first visit to Biloxi, she was attractive, and John North wasn't bad. "'Bout three weeks ago I busted a guy from Louisiana because his license pla—I know what kind of bust it was; you don't have to tell me. I need his name. Why? Because he just walked in the bar, and I want to apologize to him. Yeah, I'll hold." He held his hand over the receiver and turned to Raymond. "She's lookin' it up. You got anything to write with?"

Raymond pulled a ballpoint pen from his pocket.

"Yeah, that's it," North said. "Can you spell that for me? Okay. Thanks, darlin'. I said you got it. No, I won't forget." He pushed the drawing with the name written across the bottom toward Raymond. "That's it. I don't know how you pronounce it. Reeny Gross-gene?"

"René Grosjean." Raymond pronounced it correctly.

"If that's the hitter, why would he give me his real name? Somebody in that business has got to have more than one driver's license."

"Maybe he wasn't planning on getting stopped and wasn't prepared."

"Pros are always prepared."

"Sometimes up front is the best way to avoid problems. As dumb as they are to do what they do, they aren't dumb overall, and they do know how we work."

North nodded in agreement and raised his eyebrows.

"You run him and see what else he's got?"

"No. I was embarrassed enough. It wasn't a major criminal offense."

"I appreciate this," Raymond said, as he got up to leave.

"Appreciate what? I didn't say anything." He raised his voice. "But I do think your theory about catchin' shrimp is dead wrong," he said loudly to Gaynaud's back.

Raymond was laughing as he left the bar.

# TWENTY-THREE

SHORTLY AFTER MIDNIGHT, having completed a long letter to include in the package for Musgrave, Pettigrew gazed out the window of his motel room. Given the few cars in the lot, he couldn't imagine how the place stayed in business; maybe a fourth of the rooms were occupied. He remained at the window for a few moments, watching the cars, but didn't see any movement. Satisfied that he saw nothing unusual, he stepped outside his room and took in the fresh air.

He carried a large package wrapped in two of the white plastic dirty-clothes bags provided by the motel. The wrapping was held together with the glued flaps of envelopes supplied with the room. It wasn't pretty or terribly secure, but it was all he had. He proceeded to the stairs and went down to ground level at the rear of the building, through the back entrance, and toward the desk.

No one was in the lobby except the clerk. Pettigrew reflected that being the night clerk in a cheap motel with little traffic and only an occasional hot-sheet room had to be one of the most solitary jobs in the world.

The clerk looked up from a crossword puzzle. "Can I help you?"

"I hope so. I need a package delivered." Pettigrew fought to resist continually looking back at the entrance.

"UPS comes about ten in the morning. We don't get FedEx unless I call them. Do you have a preference?"

"I can't wait for that. I need this delivered tonight. As soon as possible, in fact. I know it sounds strange, but it's critical. The destination is in the area. Mandeville."

"Well, I don't know what I can do. Call a cab maybe." The clerk was beginning to eye him suspiciously. A package delivery at night was strange. Not a little, a lot.

"I'd rather know the person delivering it. It's worth five hundred dollars to me, and it's not far."

"Sounds like drugs." The clerk looked at him straight on. "I'm not getting involved with anything like that."

"No. I can assure you there is nothing illegal involved," Pettigrew said, wondering if that were an oxymoron. "If I were in the city, I would call a courier service, but I'd never get one out here at night."

"I don't know . . ."

"Let me explain. I'm an attorney." He pulled one of his cards out and showed it to the clerk. "Before you ask, I am registered under the name Daniels because of the case I'm working on. I know it sounds a bit clandestine, but due to the nature of what I'm doing for my client, we thought it wise that our competitors didn't know I was in the area."

The clerk looked at him skeptically.

"My client is a construction company bidding on a multimillion dollar project to maintain bridges in the area. I'm out here visiting sites. It's highly competitive. The sealed bids have to be delivered to the highway department's attorney by seven AM or we're out of the running. My client won't be disturbed by receiving a package at this hour. I also need to have the courier get a receipt signed and delivered back to me."

"If it's so important, why don't you deliver it yourself?"

"As I told you, I'm not supposed to be in the area."

The clerk was silent, thinking about the five hundred dollars, Pettigrew was sure. Probably more than two weeks' salary. Or maybe he was just wondering where this nut case came from. "It has to be someone you know personally and can trust," Pettigrew added, hoping it would push him over the edge.

"Maybe my wife could do it," he said hesitantly.

"This sort of stuff goes on all the time in business, everyone trying to get an edge. I just want to make sure they have time to review it before tomorrow's meeting. If it will put your mind at ease, I'll give you my car keys. You can hold them until your wife returns. That way, if everything is not as I say, you know where to find me." He took out his wallet and laid two one hundred dollar bills and a fifty on the desk. "Half now and half when I get the receipt."

"And the car keys," the clerk said.

Pettigrew retrieved them from his pocket and laid them next to the bills.

"Let me call Susan and see if she'll do it." The clerk sat at the manager's desk and made the call. Pettigrew could tell by the young man's body language that he was having to do some convincing, but then he relaxed, obviously winning out. Five hundred dollars had to be like winning the lottery.

When the clerk came back to the counter, he picked up the keys and the bills. "That the package? Looks weird. It could use some tape. I don't want to be blamed if it comes unwrapped."

"Thank you," Pettigrew said as the young man sealed the edges of the package with scotch tape. "Here are the directions." He handed the clerk a sheet torn from the motel's note pad. "And here is the receipt I need signed and the time delivered written on it. I have to stress the importance of this getting delivered safely. Direct from here to the address I've given you. Please ask your wife not to stop anywhere on the way. It's my job if it's not delivered promptly," he added, hoping the clerk could relate to that.

"Don't worry, it'll get there. I'm taking it myself. My wife works weekends here, so she's going to cover for me."

"Perfect. Please return the receipt and keys to my room as soon as you get back. I won't be asleep. I would also appreciate your not telling the recipient where I am. I'd like to get some rest and don't want to have to answer any questions before morning."

"I'll take care of it."

Pettigrew watched the man take the package, place it under the desk, and turn back to his puzzle. If only he knew what he had just become part of.

MUSGRAVE WATCHED THROUGH the glass panels that bordered the front door as the delivery man's car rolled slowly back down the long, curved driveway and disappeared into the night. When the taillights faded in the distance, he took the package into the den. He and Casey had been watching Katherine Hepburn and Spencer Tracy in *Adam's Rib* while they waited. Casey had suggested that they do this more often since it seemed the good movies came on only in the middle of the night.

"What did I miss?" he asked, sitting down on the couch as though a package that, according to Pettigrew, could blow the lid off Louisiana politics and destroy the state's major Washington connection were an everyday occurrence.

"Nothing you haven't seen before. We've seen this three times, and you probably more than that. B.C."

"Before Casey." He smiled at her. "I'm not sure I care to remember anything before Casey."

She looked at the package. It was bigger than she had expected. "Who delivered it?" she asked.

"Some young man. Wouldn't say where he came from." Musgrave laid the package beside him on the couch.

"Aren't you curious?"

"As hell, but Jordan was adamant that I not open it. For our own safety, he said, though I don't have a notion what that means. You'll have to try our detective again in the morning and let him know we need to see Larkin out here as soon as he can get here."

"Why don't I call him now and leave a message? He might even be in. He doesn't seem the type to keep regular hours."

When Raymond's answering machine picked up and Casey heard the message, she laughed. It changed every time she called, a testament to his lack of clientele.

"Whaddaya want?" the deep, rough, mob voice said. Then, "But seriously, folks, you've reached the office of Raymond Gaynaud. You know what I do, or you wouldn't have called. Zelda and I are occupied with something that can't be interrupted right now, but leave your name and number, and I'll call you back. *When* is a matter for conjecture, but if you're lucky . . ."

"Raymond, this is Casey. I would appreciate your calling as soon as you get this message." She paused. "Say hi to Zelda for me."

"Zelda? Who's that?" Harold asked.

"It's from Mickey Spillane. You'd have to hear Raymond's answering machine. The man's a brilliant whacko, but I think he's happy."

"Something to be said for that." Musgrave took her hand and pulled her onto his lap. "I love you," he said.

"Me, too," she answered, and kissed him.

AT 2:15 AM, THE clerk knocked on Pettigrew's door and handed him the keys and the receipt. Musgrave had signed it. In return, Pettigrew handed the clerk the money he had laid on the dresser. It was done. He turned the deadbolt, slipped the security chain into its slot, and lay down on the bed. Maybe it was a sense of redemption, or perhaps just exhaustion, but he felt relaxed for the first time in days. In a couple of hours he would leave this room, and Louisiana, for the last time.

IT WAS GETTING late, but Raymond couldn't wait. He knew he was operating on the cusp of possibilities, not probabilities, but at least he had something. If Grosjean was Pink Shirt's real name, the investigation had just taken a giant leap forward. If not, they were back at square one. There was also the tag number, which North had given him with the name, but that had likely been changed several times since the car had been stopped in Biloxi.

There were no lights on in the condo when he pulled into the parking lot, but that did not stop him. He had done some good detective work, and, by God, he was going to bask in the glory. At least until they proved the information he had garnered from North was useless.

KAREN THOUGHT SHE'D heard something, but she had been in such a deep sleep, she couldn't put together what it was. The second ring of the doorbell brought her fully awake, and she sat up. Sam turned toward her.

"What the hell was that?" he asked, his eyes still closed.

"The doorbell."

"Who would . . ."

"I don't know," she said, and reached over to the night table and picked up the Ruger. "But I intend to find out."

"We'll both find out." Sam got out of bed. The bell rang again. "Impatient," he said, "but I doubt anyone intending to do us harm would ring the bell to announce his arrival."

"Whatever, he's in for a surprise. I might just shoot him for waking me up."

"Let's go." Leaving the lights off, Sam felt his way into the living room and then to the small foyer. He stayed against the wall and moved to the door. Karen had crossed to the opposite side of the room and stood in the opening to the kitchen, her weapon directed at the front door. The bell rang yet again.

Sam eased up to the front window and peered through the curtain. There stood Raymond. Sam opened the door and met the grinning face of his friend.

"Hey," Raymond said.

"Hey? In the middle of the night, 'Hey'?"

"Got some news." Raymond stepped inside the room and saw Karen holding her gun. "I'm glad it's not bad news," he said, and laughed.

"Do you know what time it is?" Karen asked.

"No, but I knew you'd want to hear what I've got to tell you."

They moved into the living room and sat down. "Okay," Sam said. "You got us up, so talk."

"I've got a name. Pink Shirt has a name." He had their attention. "René Grosjean, and he's from Louisiana. He was traffic-stopped in Biloxi shortly before the Prather murders. The cop who accompanied me at the Prather house made the stop and recognized the drawing right away." Raymond sat back on the couch, a look of supreme triumph on his face. "We need to get it to Regan or somebody who can confirm it."

"I'll call Buck first thing in the morning," Karen said. "I don't want this to get to Regan before we talk to him. He might overreact."

"You headed back to the city?"

"I guess," Raymond answered.

"Stay here. It's late. We have a guestroom."

"You don't have to ask twice. It's been a busy day."

"STILL NO ANSWER," Casey said, sitting at the kitchen's large island counter.

"You were right; boy dudn't seem to keep regular hours," Musgrave answered. He, too, was sitting at the counter, the *Times-Picayune* spread out in front of him. Casey could read his restlessness. Morning coffee and the paper were usually taken on the gallery, but apprehension about the package and not being able to get in touch with Gaynaud had changed their routine. "Nothin' in the paper that I can see might relate to Jordan, so I guess he didn't commit suicide."

"Did you really consider that?"

"Only because you brought it up last night. All this cloak-and-dagger stuff. I just wish to hell I knew what was goin' on. I hate to be caught in a situation where I have to wait on somebody that might or might not come through."

"Raymond will come through, and Sam Larkin will, too," Casey said.

"You like him?"

"If I didn't have you, I'd probably like both of them. But I have you, and that's all I need."

"I wish I could always say the right thing." He chuckled. "I would like to find out what this is I'm holdin' and then get it out of my hands."

"I agree." The whole situation was getting beyond anything she wanted either of them to be involved in. She seldom let Harold see her anxiety because she knew it troubled him.

"I'll give him 'til three o'clock," he said.

"And what then?"

"Open it, I guess, and go from there."

"I'm not sure that's wise," she said.

"I'm not either."

KAREN AWOKE EARLY and slipped out of bed, trying not to disturb Sam. She glanced back at him and wondered how he could sleep so soundly amidst all that was circling around them. She went to the kitchen, put the coffee on, tried Buck's number without success, and walked out to the deck. Standing at the railing, she looked across Highway 90 to the Gulf beyond.

It had been days since the revelation of Neil's death, and she had been successful in putting her grief on hold. She wasn't sure whether that was a virtue or a fault. She was certain it wasn't normal, yet she had convinced herself that she had to do it until this case, this table, was cleared. She had allowed herself only moments of sadness, which she had managed to mask from everyone else. She found it terrible to live without the relief of expressing her anguish, but it was the path she had chosen for the present, and she knew Neil would understand.

The sun had broken the horizon and cast golden highlights across the surface of the water. A line of pelicans glided along the shore. The crisp winter morning would soon fade into the warmth of the day. She was enjoying the solitude when she felt Sam's arms come around her waist.

"Good morning," he whispered in her ear.

"Good morning to you." She put her hands on his, pulling them tightly against her stomach. They stood silently. She knew he was seeing and feeling exactly what she had just experienced.

"I guess we'd better get ready to go see Buck," she said after a moment. "I called his direct line before I came out here, but he's not in yet. If he doesn't answer before we leave, I'll try again when we get into the city."

"You broke the spell," he said. "You'll have to pay for that."

"I can't wait." She was smiling.

"I guess I'd better get the maniac up." Sam went back through the open door to awaken Raymond.

THEY FOLLOWED RAYMOND into the city and to his office. He was to drop off his car and pick up his gun—a precaution Sam had suggested now that René Grosjean, if that was his name, could probably identify all three of them. If he was the man they were looking for, he would have no qualms about killing any time, any place.

Parking was difficult on Dumaine Street, but Raymond found a place less than a block from his office. After getting the car in its space, he walked back to the Rover.

"Right back," he said through the window. "Circle the block and pick me up." Sam watched in his rearview mirror until he saw Raymond enter a doorway between two stores. There was already a car honking behind him.

Upstairs, Raymond went to his worn desk and opened the bottom drawer. The gun was wrapped in an old, oil-soaked pillowcase. It was a 9mm Walther, given to him by one of his clients. His father had cleared him for a permit, despite his record. He took out a holster, attached it to the back of his belt, checked the clip in the gun, and was ready to go back out the door when he noticed the light flashing on his answering machine.

He punched the PLAY button, heard the machine rewind. Three new messages. It gave the time of the first at 11:30 PM, then he heard Casey Landrieu's voice. "Raymond, this is Casey. I would appreciate your calling as soon as you get this message. It's important." A pause. "Say hi to Zelda for me."

Second message. 7:46 AM. "Casey again, Raymond. It's after seven-thirty in the morning. Please tell Zelda to let you answer your messages. This can't wait."

Third message. 9:55 AM. "Raymond, we have something for your friend. Please call. We're waiting to hear from you." He heard a note of desperation in her voice.

He dialed Musgrave's number.

"Casey? It's Raymond. I'm sorry. I didn't get back to the office yesterday. What's going on?"

"We have a package. I'm not sure I should say any more. Actually, I can't. I'd like you and your friend to get out here right away."

"My friend?"

She didn't say anything.

It finally hit him. "Oh, my friend. On our way. We'll be there within the hour. You okay?"

"We're all right. We'll be waiting," she said.

He had one more thing to do before he rejoined Sam and Karen. He took his wallet out of his back pocket, removed a small piece of paper, and dialed the number that was written on it.

"Hello?"

"Good mornin', *cher*," he said, putting on a Cajun accent.

"You ain't gone fool nobody, you," she said and chuckled. "Whoever this is, you've watched *The Big Easy* too many times. *Cher*?"

"It's Raymond Gaynaud, Celine. I thought you were supposed to be gone."

"Don't tell Sam," she said, not sounding particularly happy.

"Something wrong?"

"Is that a joke? Suddenly having your life interrupted? Being asked to leave your home or else keep a shotgun loaded? Sounds like a great way to live to me. When is this all going to be over, Raymond?"

"I wish I could say. Soon, I hope. We're making progress. But I'd feel a lot better if—"

"No. I won't leave." Her voice sharpened. "What about Sam? Is he okay?"

"You know Sam; he doesn't let much show, but I think he's mad as hell."

"He doesn't get mad often."

"Most people wouldn't recognize it. I do. I've seen him mad."

"Bad news on the bayou," she said. "For somebody."

"I just wanted to make sure you're okay."

"Why didn't Sam call?" she asked, amusement in her voice.

"He trusts you." Raymond laughed.

"Knew I wouldn't leave, huh? But he didn't want to know for sure, or he'd have had to come out here and sit. Closer to the truth?"

"Probably."

"I'm okay, Raymond. Shotgun's loaded, and I've got a deputy checking on me several times a day. Told him I had a boyfriend I couldn't get rid of. Now I'm worried about getting rid of the deputy when this is over. Keep me posted. You're a friend, Raymond, but you ain' no Cajun, no."

"Got it."

He took the stairs down two at a time. The Rover had just turned onto Dumaine and was heading toward him when he came out the door.

"What took you so long? Couldn't find your weapon? Helluva private eye," Sam said with a smile.

"Change of plans," he said when he was in the car. "We're going to Mandeville." Sam and Karen both turned to look at him.

"What's wrong?" Sam asked, tension rising in his voice.

"Hey, that's as close to panic as I've ever heard in your voice, my man." He was leaning forward, resting his forearms on the back of their seats. "I had a message, three actually, from Casey. She wouldn't be specific, but she said she had a package for you."

"A package?"

"That's what she said. She wants us out there right away. She started calling last night. Go. I told her we were on our way."

AT NINE-THIRTY, REGAN began his daily telephone list. It was a ritual bred of order, procedure, and organization. First on the list was Karen Chaney, and, as usual, he came up dry. Not once since he had been in New Orleans had she answered her phone. He was beginning to think of her as a renegade agent. Working with her was like being in an automobile with no steering wheel.

The second call was to Buck Link, but he didn't answer either. The final call he was certain of. When Troy Urban, the agent who had replaced him as the Washington liaison, answered, Regan got right to the point. "Looks like our boys down here might be getting a little nervous, Troy." Urban was a real agent who followed the rules, knew the pecking order, and abided by it. Talking to him after being stonewalled by the others was a relief.

"How so?"

"Larkin came out of the dark and let them know he's here. It shook them up. One of the primaries has disappeared, and we have mounting evidence the same guy that hit Dougherty did the Prather murders in Biloxi."

"How so?"

"You're a pretty good agent for a man with a two-word vocabulary. We got another visual ID on the drawing. He was seen staking out the condo in Biloxi, probably due to Chaney's research, which possibly connects the Prathers. No name yet, but we'll get one."

"Have you still managed to keep Neil's identity under wraps?"

"So far," Regan said. "Any static on that up there?"

"I'm not sure who's aware and who isn't. I keep waiting for it to come up, but nobody's said anything. You know how paranoid everyone in this office is. If they know and think they're supposed to know, they think they're special and don't want to share it for fear of losing it. And if they know and think they're not supposed to know, they won't let anyone know."

"What's happening with Hunnycut and Cole? Getting close to anything?"

"Hell, we're close to everything, just not quite there yet. He's still watching his ass on the phone calls; we're not picking up a lot of information. We're working on getting the pay phones bugged, but you know how that goes. He uses a different one each time, but all at the station."

"What about Cole's meeting in Fredericksburg?" Regan asked.

"We identified the guy; he's from that Government Guard organization. After him, she met with Clemmings. Didn't look happy when she left, but only he and she know why. These people are so used to being under scrutiny that, if they're even half smart, they've learned how to hide."

"That's why they make the big bucks. Do you think Hunnycut has any idea who's really pushing for a congressional investigation?"

"I said they knew how to hide, not who to hide from. I don't think he has a clue. Both he and Cole are banking on Clemmings, as far as we know. I'd wager they've got enough arrogance between them to consider a world war a minor inconvenience."

"Good. Keep me informed. James won't wait forever."

"Let me know if anything pops."

"Will do."

In Regan's opinion, Hunnycut's political career was a done deal, but it was conspiracy to commit murder Regan wanted him for.

# TWENTY-FOUR

SAM TOOK THE interstate to the Lake Pontchartrain Causeway. The twenty-four-mile crossing over the flat water seemed to stretch into forever. The sky washed from blue to transparent gray with a few low clouds creeping in from the west, one of those days when it could go either way. The conversation in the Rover was all conjecture, and all between Raymond and Karen. Sam said nothing. They wondered what kind of package Casey meant. They considered the possibility of a setup, but Raymond was confident that Casey would have found a way to let him know if she and Harold were under duress.

It took less than an hour for them to reach Mandeville and another fifteen or twenty minutes to arrive at the entrance to Musgrave's house. The massive lawn, the white columns supporting the gallery, and the live oaks, hung with Spanish moss that danced in the moving air, created an atmosphere of an older, quieter era. There were no cars in the driveway loop that fronted the house. Without saying anything, they checked their weapons before getting out of the car.

Casey answered the door, and three sets of eyes searched her face. "I'm glad you're here," she said. "It's been a long night. Come on back." She led them into the den. Shelves of books lined two of the walls, and the others were hung with oil paintings and prints depicting Civil War skirmishes that had taken place in the area.

Musgrave got up from his easy chair. A large package, crudely wrapped in white plastic, rested on the coffee table in front of the couch. He gestured toward the package. "Glad y'all are finally here. I don't think it's a bomb, or it would have gone off by now." He laughed. "Sit down. Sit down."

Karen and Raymond sat on the couch; Sam remained standing. Casey came in from the kitchen with a tray laden with coffee cups, a cream pitcher and sugar bowl, and a large carafe. She set it on a server that sat against a side wall.

"Who's it from?" asked Sam.

"It's from Jordan," Musgrave said.

"Pettigrew was here?" Sam asked.

"No. Had it delivered. He called and told me it would be coming. Said he didn't want to take a chance on bringing it himself, in case they were watching me, but I haven't seen anyone. Wouldn't tell me where he was. I got the feeling he also called to say goodbye. He said you were back in town, and I told him you'd been here. Wouldn't have, but you had to hear his voice. I swear I heard a change in the man. He was talkin' to me with respect I have never heard from him before. Anyway, he said he had something that would destroy Hunnycut and Valdrine, and he would, with my permission, send it over. He asked me to put it in your hands."

Sam looked at the package and then at Musgrave. "Why now?" he asked.

Musgrave got up and poured himself a cup of coffee. He looked at Karen and Raymond. "Y'all ought to have some of this. Comes from the Café Du Monde. Chicory coffee." He took a long sip, making a show of enjoying himself. "I think Jordan's tired of being Valdrine and Hunnycut's everyday punch. Sounded like he had suddenly found himself, or something in himself, some purpose in life other than himself. If you knew Jordan Pettigrew like I do, you'd know that ain't, pardon my grammar, the man I been seein' for thirty years. I did wonder from time to time if there wudn't a man in there somewhere. Thinkin' about it, I suppose we had a kind of respect for each other; we just never let it show." He looked at Sam. "Now, will you open that damned thing, and let's see what's inside?"

Sam picked up the package and was surprised at its heft. He sat it on the floor at his feet. The plastic came off easily. There were three items inside: two large, overstuffed accordion files and a letter addressed to Sam. He opened the letter—it was handwritten, several pages long. At a prompt from Musgrave, he began reading aloud.

*To: Sam Larkin*

*From: Jordan Pettigrew*

*To say I was shocked when you walked into my office two days ago would be an understatement. I was dumbfounded. Although it has only been a short time since then as measured in minutes and hours, it has provided a lifetime of reflection. I am grateful that you chose me. Maybe it was because you thought I was the weakest, and, if so, you were correct. I use the past tense because I don't believe you will think me weak after you have read this letter and examined the files.*

*I know that none of this, no matter what it accomplishes, gives you anything back. What was taken from you cannot be returned. It does, however, give something back to me that I lost a long time ago: my self-respect.*

*I want to establish that I am not innocent in this conspiracy, but I never considered committing murder. These documents consist of the record of your trial (the only one, as far as I know and believe to be true, in existence) and copies of notes I took of conversations with Arthur Valdrine and Thornton Hunnycut. I was charged by Valdrine, working on behalf of Hunnycut, to make sure that no remnants of the trial remained. It was not an easy task, but money, blackmail, and favors can accomplish most anything when wielded by someone like Hunnycut. No one wants to incur his ire.*

*The question in my mind throughout this whole orchestration was why? And why Sam Larkin? It took a while for me to find out. You were just a convenience. Gustave Sykorus, whom you probably never heard of, was listed on the indictment with you, his name added after your preliminary hearing. The contraband that you were charged with was his.*

*Sykorus wanted to avoid the heavy hit himself, so you were made the fall guy. He was convicted on a much lesser charge and given six months by Hunnycut. The reason was simple: Sykorus had already been indicted in Mississippi on a charge that would have put him in prison for the rest of his life. He was desperate to miss his Mississippi trial date and use the time to buy his acquittal there. Incarceration in Louisiana provided a solid excuse.*

*Hunnycut put it all together, and Sykorus paid him with a house in Gulfport. Masley Prather, an attorney in Biloxi, arranged it. He was in financial and political trouble over there and came to me recently for help. He actually made a veiled threat, which worried me. I made the mistake of telling Valdrine, who passed it on to Hunnycut. I would give my life not to have done that. Like me, Prather had been seduced into becoming a pawn.*

*Eleven years ago, Parker Hamill, an attorney who worked for me, had a stroke of conscience. He had handled your divorce and given your wife a modest payoff. Neither Hunnycut nor Valdrine believed you would survive Angola and in fact attempted to see that you didn't. Obviously, they underestimated you. When Parker found out about the attempt, he panicked. He wanted no part of murder.*

*He convinced Valdrine and Hunnycut that you would not sit still forever and that, in time, someone would take up your case, which would be a disaster for all of us. The options were another attempt on your life or freedom and money. Parker came up with the process for release, the payoff, and the conditions for acceptance, and I—not out of honor, but fear—backed him up, and the deal was made. How Hunnycut engineered the payoff and where he came up with the money, I have no idea. You may have been a "consultant" on a government project for all I know.*

*It all appeared to have worked well until Parker had another stroke of conscience and talked to Valdrine about it. That threat was eliminated with Parker's "suicide." I never knew the details, but I have no doubts as to what really happened.*

*Sadly, things have escalated with Hunnycut's political ambitions. The possibility of his being second in command of this country seems ludicrous to me, but then I have apparently been naïve about much that has gone on. I will add that my association with Harold Musgrave, his business associations with Hunnycut, and my contacting him under these circumstances in no way suggest that he had any part in or knowledge of these events. As his attorney, I cannot discuss Harold's business or legal affairs. Whatever may arise in that regard will have to be handled by someone else. I do not, however, believe he has done anything with criminal intent.*

*I believe the transcript, the notes, and this letter should provide you with adequate documentation for any path you choose to pursue. I apologize for not being available to back up any of this in person, but I don't think it will be necessary.*

*This is not, for the record, a suicide note. I have never and will never consider that. Conversely, I believe I may have just begun to live.*

*I also apologize to you and to Celine and all others to whose pain I may have, knowingly or unknowingly, contributed. I am certainly not without guilt.*

*I wish you well and ask you to be very careful.*

*Jordan Pettigrew, Esq.*

"I guess that about settles the hash in those boys' fryin' pans," Musgrave said. Casey put her hand on his knee.

"Maybe," Sam said, "but it's all got to be corroborated, and I'm not sure how we're going to do that with Pettigrew out of the picture. It'll take time, and we don't have much of that."

"But you have a record of the trial," Casey said.

"I'm sure it's a copy, and the letter could be shot down as a phony or as written under duress. I don't know; I'm not a lawyer. It's like looking through the window at a candy store: it's all there, but you can't get to it without breaking the window, and that requires some risk. I don't have a lot of faith in the system, where these guys are concerned."

"Got any ideas?" Karen asked.

"None I'd bet my life on," Sam said.

"What about Pink Shirt?" Raymond asked.

"Pink Shirt?" Musgrave asked.

Karen picked up the folder she had brought in and removed the sketch of Grosjean. "Have you ever seen this guy?" she asked.

Musgrave took the drawing and looked at it. "Looks like a damned idiot," he said. "Who is he?"

"We believe he's a professional killer," Karen said. "He may have killed the Prathers and some others. And he may be the one who set up Parker Hamill's suicide. He's not to be taken lightly, despite his looks."

"I'd remember that one if I'd ever seen him," Musgrave said. He laughed. "He wears pink shirts? That's his trademark?"

"Among other things," Raymond said. "He's a real fashion plate."

Sam kneeled down and looked through the files. He removed several pages of Pettigrew's notes and the first ten pages of the transcript and handed them to Casey. "Would you make two copies of these for me?"

"Of course." She took them to the office.

Raymond looked at Sam. "Can you let us in on what you have in mind? I can see something going on in there."

"I'm working on it. This might not be all we need, but it should work as good bait."

"You gonna let us know what's goin' on?" Musgrave asked.

"Of course. I want you to let me know if you get any calls from Valdrine or Hunnycut. Or Pettigrew, of course. And be careful of anyone you don't know coming to your house. I think it's pretty clear that these guys don't have any conscience."

"I'd love for them to send somebody out here. He'd be in a world of shit."

"Don't get cocky," Sam said harshly. "If someone shows up, call the police."

"Lotta good they'll do," Musgrave said.

"If you have any trouble," Karen said, "call Commander Link at state police headquarters. Use my name. They'll find him."

"I'll do that, if I have time," he said.

Sam didn't like the look on the man's face. Given the chance, Musgrave would try to handle whatever happened himself.

"Harold," Sam said, "there is one other thing. No one is to know about what Pettigrew gave us. No one."

"You have my word."

Casey came back into the room with the copies. Sam put the originals back in the accordion file and the copies in the folder with the drawing of Grosjean. He picked up the files and the letter, thanked them for what they had done, reiterated his warning, and the three of them left.

BILL CALLED IN at three-thirty in the afternoon.

"We found his car. It's in a motel parking lot over in Hammond, but he's not there. Checked out, paid in cash, and left before daylight. He'd been there a coupla days."

"Did you check out the room?" Arthur Valdrine asked.

"We went through it, but by the time we found the car, the maid had already been in. I caught her and checked out her trash bag, but didn't find anything."

"Damn it!"

"I'd say he's long gone. Don't know what else to tell you."

"Can you—"

"We got a shift comin' up at four. Tomorrow maybe we can do something."

"Give me a call when you get off. I don't care what time it is. I may have something else I want you to check out."

"We'll do it."

Pettigrew's behavior was baffling. He had always been a team player. The team was his security blanket. He couldn't operate on his own for five minutes. If he tried to, it would be a disaster.

The next puzzle to work on was finding Larkin. He picked up the phone and dialed information.

"What city and state, please."

"I'm not really sure. Let's try Thibodaux. Here in Louisiana."

"Listing?"

"Celine Larkin, or maybe Celine Aguillard. I'm not sure which name she might be listed under."

"I have a Boudreaux Aguillard in Thibodaux."

"Could I get the address as well as the number?"

"Certainly, sir."

She gave him both, and he dialed.

A woman answered. "Hello?"

"Is Boudreaux in?"

"No," Celine said.

"Are you his daughter?"

"Who is this?" she asked.

"Just an old army buddy."

"He was never in the army." The phone was slammed down.

MARLENE COLE BEGAN to see years of work adding up to nothing. Some token jail time might also be a possibility. She could accept all that—she had learned early you did not sit on the track if you were afraid of the train. She had enough money out of the government's reach to live comfortably for the rest of her life, and the prospect of actual jail time was slim. What pushed her to act was Thornton

Hunnycut. No one hit her without retribution. Once that line was crossed, it was likely to happen again and again. She wouldn't let it go.

Her appointment with Senator Harrison James was for 3:45. At 3:15 she walked into his outer office, power-dressed: navy blue suit with a buttoned v-neck jacket, no blouse (offering a suggestion of cleavage), an above-the-knee skirt, navy blue stockings, and high-heeled pumps. It was all accented with a rope of lustrous cream-colored pearls and matching stud earrings.

He was offering a quarter hour of his time. She never worried about preset time limits; once she was in his office, she would stay as long as she wanted. No one had ever thrown her out. James had been reluctant to meet with her, but after she dropped a few subtle reminders of her power, he had agreed. And she'd gotten the impression his reluctance was feigned. The senator was essentially a good man, but she knew of a few tarnishes on his bright and shiny image; her investigator had done a good job.

Five minutes after her arrival, she and the senator were eye to eye across his desk.

"May I call you Marlene?" James asked.

He wasn't handsome. Thornton or Clemmings either one would help his ticket. "I would prefer it," she said.

"Good. Now, what can I help you with?" An offer before being asked. Interesting, she thought.

"May I cut right to it without any politically correct bullshit?" she asked, her eyes locked on his. He appreciated strong women, she knew. Would walk over people if allowed.

He smiled and looked down at the top of his desk, playing with a paperclip. Then he looked up. "I don't like bullshit," he said, still smiling. "It's the one natural resource we have too much of here in Washington. I assume you're here about Hunnycut."

"Not only him; I'm concerned about myself as well."

"In what way?"

"Senator Clemmings is pushing the Government Guard to promote an investigation of some—in his mind—breaches in the ethics between Senator Hunnycut and myself, as well as some other matters."

"Yes, I am aware of that."

"I don't think the fact that it's politically motivated is in doubt."

"I agree."

Very nice, she thought. No excuses or defenses. "Before I go any further, I'd like to know your take on all of this."

James waited for a moment, glanced down at his desk, looked at the paperclip and then put it down before he resumed eye contact. "I'm trying to determine my own position in talking to you about this."

"I can tell you—with no way to guarantee it to your satisfaction, of course—that I will keep this meeting and anything you say confidential. From this point on, you have to trust me or not say anything else."

"*Trust* is a word seldom used in this city."

"Not trusting in it is a basic rule," Marlene said.

James smiled. "As you know, I have to come up with a shortlist of potential running mates before the convention. I will tell you from the start, and I am trusting your promise of confidence, that Senator Clemmings will not be on that list. Now—and let me stress this, if that should become public—I will not make any attempt to neutralize the investigation."

"Why are you telling me this, Senator?"

"Please, call me Harrison. I'm putting myself out on a limb, but I—"

"You'll do that every time you walk out the door or open your mouth as president," she flashed her smile at him. It was the first time since she had entered his office, and it hit its mark.

He smiled back. "Good point. I know what you've accomplished. I know you've woven yourself into the fabric of the system. And I know you have made fewer enemies than friends and have made a lot of money at the same time. That's a phenomenon in itself."

"Thank you."

"You could be a tremendous asset to my administration, should I be fortunate enough to have one. Not in a staff position, but as a liaison between myself, lobbyists, and business in general. In other words, I guess you could say that I would rather have you as an accomplice than as an enemy."

"If I am discredited, I couldn't be very effective at either. I'm not interested in a staff position. I would, however, like to not have to worry about this investigation."

"I don't think that's a problem," James said, with a smile at the corners of his mouth. "Since I'm the one pushing for it, rather than Senator Clemmings, I think I can determine what direction it takes."

His words blew her strategy out of the water. "You?"

"It is simply a method of eliminating people without making personal enemies. Senator Clemmings thinks he's driving the charge by the Government Guard, but they petitioned him at my request."

"He's a shill."

"Exactly."

"And Thornton?" She was trying to think one step ahead.

"I don't know how to say this gently. He is a victim of political necessity. The South is important, but he doesn't need to be on the ticket to deliver it to me. The people of the South know he's being considered, and if he is then discredited and dropped, they will respect the fact that he was considered. He won't blame me; he'll blame the senate or the Government Guard, and he'll continue to support me. And, the South will always believe a native son over a bunch of Washington politicians. They'll support his endorsement of me, regardless of what is being said about him."

"He was never a serious possibility?" she asked.

"No."

Marlene's expression was bittersweet. "And I thought I was tough."

"Probably more than I, but you're not running for president. It's not the way I like to play the game, but in the thick of it, you find things in yourself you didn't know were there. I'm trusting you not to disclose any of this to Hunnycut. I can get him off with a censure, or they may ask for his resignation. No more than that. If he drops his support for me, I will assume you have told him what I said, and I will make sure that he goes to prison. Possibly you as well." She saw steel in his eyes. "I hope you can handle it. You will have to be a very good actress until after the convention."

"What is politics but theater? Comedy and tragedy."

"No sitcoms?"

"Isn't that what this city is?"

James stood up and came around his desk. Marlene stood and put out her hand. He took it in both of his, and she put her left hand over his. "This will be very good for you," he said.

"I hope it will be good for you, too."

His eyes followed her out of his office.

SAM HAD GONE for a run; it was his tranquilizer. Karen poured Jack Daniels Black over the ice in her glass. It had been an eventful twenty-four hours. Having Sam back, the drawing of Pink Shirt, Pettigrew's package. It all seemed to be coming together, a cornucopia of good things. She was tired, but it was a good tired. She was relaxed, too, and that was an unfamiliar feeling of late.

She sat on the couch, legs up, facing the front door. Waiting for Sam. She would join him in the shower when he returned.

In a moment, Karen heard the sliding glass doors behind her opening. *Why was he coming in that way?*

"You don' make no moves, you."

She knew who it was without looking. Where was her gun? She had unclipped it in the bedroom when they got home. Must have left it there. Sam had checked the parking lot for Pink Shirt's car when they pulled in and then gone straight for his running clothes. How could she warn him? The man stepped into her line of vision, pointing a .22 caliber pistol at her.

"You kinda pretty thing," he said. "Not too pretty, but pretty 'nough."

Karen said nothing. The sliding door should have been locked. Unprofessional. Careless. "You've made a mistake," she said, having no idea where she would go with that line, no idea how Grosjean might take it.

"I don' make no mistake, me. You don' wan' me to kill you, you tell me somethin'."

"Columbus discovered America in fourteen ninety-two."

The statement puzzled Grosjean for a moment, then he swung his free hand and caught her hard on the side of the head. It knocked her to the floor. "You mout' gone get you killed. You wan' dat? Killed?"

"I don't think I have a choice," she said. Can't get to the gun; can't warn Sam.

"Prob'ly not, but you need to tell me why you here."

"I live here."

"Not long. I don' see no pictures on the tables, no brodders and sisters, no momma and daddy. You don' live here, no. You here lookin' for some'tin'. What and who for, what I need to know."

"I just moved here. I plan to live here permanently. Work. Buy a house."

"Oh, yeah? Wha' you work at, you?"

Interesting question, she thought. Tell him? Not a good idea. Have to stall, wait for Sam.

"I'm a dancer." She had no idea where that had come from.

His eyes got wider. "You dance?" He looked like he was going to laugh. That damned simple smile.

She put on an insulted look. "Yeah. Out on the Strip. You find that amusing? You're pissing me off."

"You don' look like no dancer, no."

*Keep him going*. She was sitting on the floor, her back against the couch. "You want to tell me why? My legs not long enough? Tits not big enough? Why don't I look like no dancer, *no*." She saw anger come into his eyes, as cold an anger as she had ever seen.

"Don' make no fun of me, you. Why you here? Goin' down checkin' on houses?"

"Wait a minute," she said. "You said I don't look like a dancer. Why?"

"You might do lap dancin'," he said, and smiled.

Karen looked at the clock on the stove; Sam had been gone over thirty minutes. She prayed he was getting close. One chance. The move had to be quick. Be near, Sam. She was wearing a sweatshirt, no bra. In one fast motion, she stood up and pulled the sweatshirt over her head. Grosjean was taken by surprise, couldn't take his eyes off her. She screamed as loud as she ever had. "Goddamn it! Aren't these tits good enough? Is that why I don't look like no dancer?" Still screaming, she put her hands beneath her breasts and pushed them up. "Look at these. Not good enough?"

"Stop," he yelled. "You crazy." Grosjean aimed a blow at her jaw, but she managed to turn and catch it on her shoulder. She went to the floor again, knocking over a chair in the process. She pulled herself to her feet, fighting dizziness and disorientation. When she was up, he slapped her again, hard, on the right side of her face, and she fell across the coffee table.

"Now you're in real trouble," she said as she struggled to turn over.

"You don' know 'bout no trouble, you," he said and kicked her in the ribs. It wasn't a solid blow, but it was enough to explode the air from her lungs. She was going to die at the hands of a smiling Cajun simpleton. She sucked in as much air as she could but couldn't get it into her lungs. Fighting the pain in her chest, she screamed as loud as she could.

Grosjean hit her again and then kicked her in the back. "I tol' you don' scream, no. You gone die." He kicked at her again, but missed his mark.

If she stayed down, Pink Shirt would kill her. The pain was making her eyes water, and she feared she might pass out. She held up her hand in surrender, willing herself to stay conscious, visualizing the picture she presented—naked from the waist up, her face already beginning to bruise, awkwardly working to regain her feet so a Cajun psychopath could blow her head off.

Using the coffee table for leverage, she was almost up on her knees when the table slid out from under her and she went back down. She repeated the effort, using the arm of the couch and managed to get upright. She placed herself between the intruder and the front door, praying Sam had heard her scream and would come around to the Gulf side to see what was going on before bursting in. If he didn't, they were both dead; it was as simple as that.

Her prayers were answered when, out of the corner of her eye, she caught a movement on the deck.

Pink Shirt was smiling. "You pretty strong, you, but you ain' no dancer, no."

Karen was fighting for balance, could feel torrents of consciousness trying to maintain equilibrium in her brain. "No?" she asked. Not loud—she didn't want to get hit any more. She had to stay on her feet until Sam came in. The thought that the movement on the deck might be Pink Shirt's accomplice also passed through her mind. "You ain't seen nothing yet. You want to see the real thing?"

Her voice was giving out, but she had to hold his attention. She forced a pained smile and began to unbuckle her belt. Then she saw Sam begin to ease the sliding door open. Pink Shirt had made a mistake—he had left it open about two inches. Her belt was unbuckled, and she was easing the zipper down. Slowly.

"Wait 'til you see this, and then tell me I ain't no dancer."

Sam came through the door. Grosjean reacted, but too slowly. He swung the pistol around, catching Sam on the side of the head. It was a hard blow, but Sam didn't go down. He grabbed Grosjean's arm with one hand and reached for his throat with the other.

Grosjean anticipated the move and swung at Sam's wrist, knocking it away. Karen started for the bedroom, but Sam and Grosjean were in the way. Sam couldn't duck fast enough and took a hit to the middle of his chest. His grip on Grosjean's pistol hand loosened, and the Cajun jerked it away. He took a roundhouse swing at Sam with the pistol and caught him on his ear.

Sam was going down when Karen started her attack. She head-butted Grosjean in the middle of his back. He fired, but he was off balance, and the shot went wild. Karen hit the floor and rolled, trying to catch his knees with her feet, but missed. Grosjean kicked her on the side of the head, and purple and white shapes burst in front of her eyes. She knew she was only semiconscious, but she had to do something. She just couldn't put together what.

Looking toward Sam, she saw him trying to get to his knees. Grosjean's attention had been drawn to Sam as well. He brought the pistol down on the back of Sam's neck and flattened him. It was time to act or die. She tried to speak, but her throat was dry, and nothing came out. It was over.

Grosjean turned back to Karen. There was nothing she could do. Her body had gone into neutral. He turned back to Sam and laid a heavy kick into his side. The force of the blow caused an expulsion of air.

"Dat not be your las' breath, but it be close," Grosjean said. "I ain' gone. I be back. You see, yeah."

Karen was still waiting for the sound of the pistol when she looked up and saw the Cajun go through the sliders, leap the railing, and disappear. She crawled toward Sam. He was stunned but not out.

"He's gone," she said.

Sam's eyes fluttered. "We've got to . . ."

"He's gone. We'd never catch him."

"This could become an unhealthy habit."

"Losing your touch?" she asked, kneeling next to him.

"Your breasts distracted me."

She looked down. Her sweatshirt was still on the floor.

"Pretty good thinking, officer," he said. He pulled himself to his feet and staggered to the couch.

"May be the birth of a new career for me. I'm surprised he got you," she said.

He looked at her critically. "I'd just run four miles."

"Then you should be on an adrenaline high," she said, retrieving her sweatshirt.

"How did he get in?"

"Same way you did. He was in before I could react."

"Probably saved your life." He saw her wince as she put her shirt on. "I think we need to get you to the ER. He got you pretty good."

She eased down next to him on the couch. "I'm okay, just woozy. He didn't get a solid hit." She ran her hands down her sides and grimaced at the pain.

"Ribs?" Sam asked.

"Nothing moving around," she said as she felt each one with her fingers. "Probably just bruised. If they're broken, there's nothing they can do anyway; you can't put a cast on ribs."

"I still think—"

"You want to get arrested for girlfriend abuse? This would be pretty hard to explain," she said.

"So much for the fearless crime fighters, huh? What did he want?"

"Wanted to know what I was looking for, who I was working for. I told him I was moving here, but he didn't buy it. Wanted to know what kind of work I did, and I told him I was a dancer out on the Strip."

"And he made you undress?"

"He didn't believe me."

"And you had to prove it to him." He was trying to grin, but the pain kept it from playing.

"I thought it would distract him."

"Seems to have worked. Think that technique might work for me?"

"I don't imagine you'll find yourself in this kind of circumstance once we're finished here. Should we call Regan or Buck? Put out the word on him?" she asked.

"Not much they could do. He wasn't driving his car. I checked the parking lot when we got home, and then going and coming, and checked the surrounding area on my run. I'd know his car; he was in something else." He reached over to touch her face, and she flinched.

"He slapped me around a little bit before he beat me up."

"You get smart with him?"

"A little," she said.

"Your mouth's going to get you killed."

"That's pretty much what he said. I hope not. It's got to be a better asset than my body. At least it got a reaction from Pink Shirt."

"So would you have done it?" he asked.

"What?"

"Taken 'em off. Shown him the real thing?"

"Absodamlutely, as your friend Skeeter Crewes would say. Anything to keep that boy's attention until the cavalry arrived."

Sam laughed and winced. "You are tough; I'll give you that."

"Don't ever doubt it, Larkin. Let's take a shower and check out the damage. You don't look so good yourself."

# TWENTY-FIVE

IT TOOK SEVERAL moments for Karen to hear the telephone. She and Sam were beyond exhaustion. Most of the blows Grosjean had landed on them were not in areas vulnerable to cuts, but they would have severe bruises. After a shared hot shower, they had each taken four aspirin—Sam's recommended dosage—and gone to bed. Karen stared at the clock and saw that it was just before dawn. "Hello?" she asked groggily.

"Karen?"

"I'm not sure. Who is this?" she asked.

"Raymond. You don't sound like yourself. Anything happen?"

"Funny you should ask. We had a visit from Pink Shirt last night."

"Are you all right?"

"Not perfect, but not disabled. It was our own stupidity. He broke in while Sam was running. Pretty scary. We'll tell you about it. We survived," she said, "but I don't think I was supposed to."

"You want me out there?"

"No. Why the call so early?"

"I'm too charged up to sleep. Want to know the plan for the day."

"I'm not sure yet. You at home?"

"Yeah."

"Stay there. Sam'll call you in an hour."

"I'll be here."

Sam was lying on his back, his breathing even. She was pleased he hadn't awakened. His hair was evenly splayed on the pillow. The son of a bitch was beautiful even when he was sleeping and beaten up. He wouldn't make a movie star, there was too much living in his face, but he was surely charismatic.

She leaned over and began lightly kissing his chest. He didn't move. She moved down to his stomach and felt his muscles give a slight reaction, as if a chill had washed across his bare skin. When she took him in her mouth, he moaned softly but didn't stir, didn't say anything. Her magic worked. She straddled him and guided him inside her, leaning forward, moving her hips slowly, careful not to put pressure on her damaged ribs.

It didn't take long; all the muscles in the lower half of her body began to contract. She sat up and increased her momentum, not fast or greedy—the aches in her body wouldn't allow that—rhythmic, moving toward her peak. She felt Sam release inside her, and she lost control. Everything went loose. He opened his eyes.

"Good morning," he whispered.

"Good morning." She rested her head on his chest.

"Helluva way to wake up."

"I could just set the alarm clock or maybe scream in your ear."

"I like it this way better," he said and squeezed her to him. "Creates less anxiety."

"You were sleeping so soundly, you didn't even hear the telephone."

"Who was it?"

"Raymond."

"And where am I supposed to call him?"

Karen sat up. "You bastard. You were awake. You let me do all the work. And you look like hell, by the way. You should be grateful."

"Thanks for the compliment. I didn't know it was work." She threw a pillow at him as she got out of bed. She also realized how sore she was, how badly her face hurt.

CELINE WAS EATING breakfast when she heard the knock at the front door. Through the lace-curtained windows she could see two men standing on the porch. She turned, went back into the kitchen, and retrieved the loaded shotgun. She held it against the wall on the left side of the door, having practiced getting it to her shoulder from that position at the first sign of suspicion.

"Yes?" she said, standing behind the screen, the wooden door only partly open.

"Ms. Aguillard?" the man asked.

"Yes."

"I was wondering if we might talk to you for a minute."

"What about? I don't need any insurance or magazines."

"Well, to be truthful, we're trying to locate your ex-husband and thought that maybe—"

"He due some money or something?"

"No, nothin' like that," he said. "Could we come in?"

"No. Right here is fine. I don't know where he is. Actually, I wasn't even sure he was still alive. You telling me he is?" Celine asked.

"I'd really rather you let us in, and then we can tell you what this is all about."

"Can't imagine anything honest that can't be said out on the porch. Nobody here to hear." Her hand closed around the barrel of the gun. She saw his hand reach for the screen door handle.

"I think we need to be inside," he said and yanked the door hard enough to rip the latch out of the wooden frame. By the time he swung it open, he was looking down the barrel of her 12-gauge.

"It's a quail gun. Spreads pretty good. Has number twos in it. Not much good for quail, but it'll play hell with a man."

He stopped in his tracks. "You'd shoot us?" He looked ready to laugh.

"The safety's off, and you just broke my screen door. You want to play the lottery? I can call a deputy and have you stopped and arrested before you get through Thibodaux. Or you can tell me why you're out here harassing me."

The men had stepped back to the edge of the porch by the time she was finished speaking, then turned and walked quickly toward their car, which was parked at an angle that made the license tag hard to see.

"Fuck!" she heard one of the men say as they were getting in.

As they drove out, she got the tag number and repeated it to herself on her way back to the kitchen.

She called the number Sam had given her. He answered the phone on the second ring.

"Sam, two men were just here asking about you. When I wouldn't tell them anything, one pulled the screen door so hard it pulled the latch out of the wood. He stopped when he saw the shotgun and they left. Wouldn't tell me who sent them."

"Celine, I think you should—"

"They were driving a Chevrolet Caprice, license plate JPM-six-nine-one. Louisiana," she said.

"How did I know you wouldn't leave?"

"Couldn't. I'm fine. Kinda fun actually. Don't worry, and don't come out here. Please. I mean that. You okay?"

"Yeah, I—"

"Hello to Raymond for me," she said, and hung up the phone.

"CELINE?" KAREN ASKED. She was standing at the counter, already dressed.

"Couple of guys came out to her house asking about me. One of them tried to force his way in, but she ran them off with a shotgun. She got their tag number. I'm sure it's stolen, but let's get it to Buck anyway."

"You need to go out there?"

"She asked me not to. Besides, if I did, I'm afraid I'd get shot. Celine always was a better shot than I was."

Karen smiled. "Sounds like Valdrine, or whoever, is pulling out all the stops," she said.

"It also tells us he's got more than Grosjean working for him."

"I liked Pink Shirt better than Grosjean," she said.

"Call Buck. And I also want to get ten pages of the trial transcript in front of Valdrine's eyes."

"How would you get to him?" Karen asked.

"I'm thinking about that. And we need to talk to Regan and find out what's happening in Washington. We need to know if there's a time frame when that's going to come falling down."

"Do you want me to call him, too?"

"I think he's one of those people who's more honest face to face," Sam said.

"You don't trust him, do you?"

Sam looked at her. "The temptation's too great. Solving another agent's murder, bringing down a vice presidential candidate and the state commissioner of administration, not to mention solving the Prather murders and possibly Parker Hamill's, is a lot to resist. Might put him in line for the director's job." Sam stood up. "Call Raymond and tell him we'll pick him up in an hour and half. I need to get dressed. And don't forget Buck."

"Yes, sir," she said, making sure the sarcasm didn't go unnoticed.

Sam stopped and turned around. "I'm sorry. Please?" he said.

"Better. Go get dressed."

IT WAS DIFFICULT to think of the downfall of someone with whom she had worked for years, had shared good times and weathered a few downs with, made love with, and whom she had listened to and encouraged. It could be depressing if she let it, but all Marlene had to do was remember the slap of flesh on flesh, the blow to her face, and she had no trouble accepting it.

It was also difficult now to be in his presence, knowing that his life was going to be shattered, and keep that knowledge hidden. Worse was keeping up the pretense and seeing money, influence, and time being spent on a well she knew was dry. Her life, in spite of Harrison James's pledge to protect her, was about to change. Her comfort zone would be gone, and she would have to construct another—no easy task.

She experienced something nearly foreign to her as she lay next to the sleeping Thornton Hunnycut, watching the night sky lighten through the windows. A shadow of guilt. She had to remind herself: she had not undermined him, had not caused what was going to happen. He had designed his own problems with ambition and arrogance; they would bring him down. No one she knew would feel sorry for him, and, most likely, no one would have any sympathy for Marlene Cole. But she could live with that; sympathy didn't pay any dividends.

"Trouble sleeping?" His voice startled her.

"Good morning, darling." She turned on her side to look at him.

"What's the matter?" he asked.

"Nothing. Just woke up, and my mind was on warp speed, thinking about some of the things we've done together."

"Anything we haven't that you want to?"

"My imagination is not that creative," she said. "And I have to get up and get going. Busy day ahead." She kissed him on the forehead and got out of bed.

"I can always run for governor, you know."

She froze, wondering if she had talked in her sleep. "Why would you say that?" She was in the bathroom, out of his sight and glad of it. She stood stock still. Listening.

"I don't trust James. And then this committee stuff. Maybe I'm getting tired of Washington."

"Have you heard something you haven't told me?" she asked.

"No. I haven't heard anything."

"Then I wouldn't start worrying."

He didn't respond, and she began washing her face. She wasn't prepared to vie for an academy award. She would have to orchestrate her schedule so their time together would be limited.

"Have *you*?" he asked.

"Have I what?"

"Heard anything."

"I would have told you," she answered.

"I hope so."

BUCK LINK WAS driving into the city when Karen's call was patched through to him.

"Good morning, Buck. Got any news for me?" she asked.

"Nothing yet. I'd like to widen the distribution of that drawing. As you know, the longer it takes, the colder it gets, but I don't want to step on the government's toes."

"You may not need to do that. I've got a name. René Grosjean. He had a traffic stop in Biloxi shortly before the Prather murders." Silence. "You there?"

"Yes. I'm just looking for a spot to pull over. I want to get all this down." Karen waited. "Okay, give it to me again."

Karen told him about Raymond's discovery and then Grosjean's attack.

"Are you and Sam okay?"

"We're fine. I'll tell you the details later. I also have a tag number for you to run down."

"Grosjean's?"

"No. Two guys went after Sam's former wife." She couldn't say *ex*; it made divorced women sound like ciphers. "The woman must be pretty strong," Karen said. "Ran them off with a shotgun. She got the tag number as they were leaving. They told her they were looking for Sam." She read out the number to him. "We've got something else, too, Buck, but I want to tell you in person. It's strong."

"Bluebird at eleven?"

"Better make it noon," she said. "We're getting ready to come in now and pick up Raymond, but we're moving a little slow."

"Once this starts, it will gather momentum. Work on something for months, you're nowhere, and then it's all over in twenty-four hours."

"Don't think this'll happen that fast."

"You never know. That traffic stop? They all get hit when they least expect it."

"As I learned in cop school," she said, "we usually catch 'em by accident."

"Most of the time. I'll bring Grosjean's jacket with me if he has one."

Sam walked into the kitchen just as Karen was hanging up the phone. He was wearing jeans, a white shirt with the cuffs rolled up two folds, and polished black boots she had never seen before.

"Don't tell me, cowboy," she said, eyeing the boots, "you're going to Valdrine's office."

"Maybe. Haven't made up my mind yet. I might let Raymond do it."

"I could do it."

"Phony lap dancer delivers devastating document to angry administrator?"

"Bastard."

"You talk to Buck?"

"We're meeting him at the Bluebird at noon."

"Was he shocked, thrilled, and elated?" Sam asked.

"Pleased, I guess. You know Buck. Stoic. Like you sometimes, though you do seem pretty chipper this morning."

He crossed to her and put his arms around her. "I was scared for you last night," he said, eyeing the bruises and swelling on her face. "Did you see Grosjean's eyes? I mean really see them?"

"Yep. Nothing there. He could put his fork down and slice your throat while he was eating."

"And then chew on a piece of bacon. I was scared for you."

"Thank you."

"Ready?"

"Ready."

He picked up a windbreaker to hide his gun, took the folder with Pettigrew's letter and the copied transcript pages, and they left for the city.

"FUCKIN' WOMAN PULLED a shotgun on us," Bill said.

"You couldn't handle that?" Valdrine asked.

"I'll do work for you, but I ain't gonna get killed for you."

"Nobody else was there?"

"How the fuck should I know? I started to open the screen door, and she came up with a gun. She got the drop on us. Like she was fuckin' waiting. And I have no doubt she would have blown us off the porch. Even told me it was a bird gun, modified with a good spread and loaded with number twos. Any woman that knows that ain't worth fuckin' with. Not in my book."

"No other cars there?"

"A home-painted yellow pickup truck with weeds growin' up around the tires, which were flat, and some Jap car musta been hers. Nothin' else."

"Okay. Just be available. I may need you later. Four o'clock shift?"

"As always," Bill said. "What about the money?"

"You can pick it up where we agreed after one o'clock."

Valdrine was getting worried. Grosjean hadn't checked in, and calls to Hunnycut got his receptionist, who didn't know when he'd be in. He dialed Musgrave's number, thinking the call would be a waste of time, but it was an avenue that needed tending.

"Arthur. Pretty amazing. Two calls in one week. Hear anything from Jordan yet?" Musgrave asked brightly.

"Your energy at this hour is refreshing, Harold."

"Well, you know, haven't got started yet. Won't be long before it'll be five o'clock. What can I do for you?"

"I guess you've already answered what I had to ask. If you'd heard from Jordan."

"As a matter of fact, he did call."

Valdrine had to work to keep his voice steady. "Really? Can you fill me in?" he asked.

"Wudn't much. Just called to let me know he wouldn't be around to help me anymore. Advised me to get another attorney."

"Did he say where he was?"

"That he did not confide," Musgrave answered. "I did get the feeling though, that—for whatever reason—he was heading for parts unknown. What's caused all this, Arthur? Got any idea?"

"No, I haven't. He's told you more than he's told me."

"Sorry I can't be of more help."

"Well, at least we know he's alive," Valdrine said.

"Did you have some idea he might not be?"

"Not really, but you never know what people are going to do. Look at Parker Hamill. Who would have guessed that?"

"I'm not sure even Hamill would have guessed that."

Valdrine heard amusement in Musgrave's voice. "You're not subscribing to that old idea that he was murdered are you?"

"As you said, you never can tell what people are gonna do."

"Well, I think that theory was pretty well disproved. Anyway, no need to get into that right now. If you hear from Jordan again, will you call me? I'm concerned, that's all."

"I'm sure you are."

Valdrine didn't miss the sarcasm in Musgrave's voice. "Son of a bitch," he whispered, as he hung up. He couldn't let Pettigrew get out of reach. His car was at that motel. Bill and Joe could check the cabs and shuttle services to the airport. The time frame was pretty clear. His secretary could call the airlines and say it was urgent that he reach Jordan; the airline would tell someone from his office whether Pettigrew had booked a flight. He doubted the man could have acquired a decent false ID already.

That left Larkin and the woman. Grosjean should have checked in. He tried Hunnycut again and got the same response, and no answer at Marlene Cole's place. There was nothing more he could do at the moment. His hands were shaking. He took a bottle of pills from his desk drawer, removed one, and swallowed it with a glass of water. Valium. He hated to use the damned things. A weak man's crutch.

He looked down at the few papers on his desk. He had neglected his office for days, but his staff had taken up the slack. He surrounded himself with competent people, and very little actual work ever reached his desk.

IT WAS 9:00 AM, uncommonly early for a strategy meeting. Most such meetings on Capital Hill took place in the late afternoon or at night, so the day's gossip could be sifted and digested. Harrison James sat in his office with his political advisor, press secretary, attorney, and campaign manager. The conversation centered on Senators Hunnycut and Clemmings.

"It's time to clear the table, Harrison," the political advisor said. "The convention is not as far away as it seems. You've got a lock on the nomination, barring disaster, and you're going to have to name a running mate as soon as it's sealed. Hell, we need for the voters to have a strong idea who it will be even before the convention. A lot of losers have dilly-dallied on that and wound up losing support and the election when the electorate wasn't impressed with the candidate's choice."

"Any suggestions?" the campaign manager asked.

"Well, we've already pretty much decided we don't want Clemmings or Hunnycut. Clemmings we don't need—"

"He *is* from California," James interjected.

"None of your competitors could carry California even with him. If he's offended, so be it. We'll give him a post in environment or something. Hunnycut will be taken care of by the committee hearing and still support us in the South, as you said. By the way, have you decided when to break that?"

"What do you think?" the attorney asked.

"Has he prospected most of his supporters for the campaign already?" the political advisor asked.

"I think most," the campaign manager said.

"Checks in and cleared?" James asked.

"Probably ninety-five percent. All the big ones. We get those in as soon as they're pledged. Don't want buyer's remorse setting in."

"The sooner the better," James said, thinking of Marlene Cole and knowing that, with enough time, she might be able to kill the committee and force him to name Hunnycut. Unlikely, but possible. He thought other things about her, as well. The campaign manager and the political advisor looked at each other.

"No reason we can't plant the seeds today," the press secretary said. "Can you get someone on the ethics committee to say that an investigation is being strongly considered and drop a few hints as to what's involved? Very general."

"No problem. They've been talking about the damned thing for weeks," the campaign manager answered.

"Get that to me by noon, and I can have Walter Cronkite talking about it by six-thirty."

"I'd like to do that without mentioning Cole at this point," James said. Everyone looked at him.

"But she's the main point of the committee's—"

"Focus on the money," James said. "Illegal use of campaign funds, gifts, improper influence peddling. No Cole."

"I'll do the best I can," the press secretary said. "When do you want it to hit the papers full force?"

"Day after tomorrow, but check with me first. There could be some last minute reason to hold off."

"The governor of Illinois?" the political advisor suggested. "He's a strong man, and it's a critical state." He looked at each member of the group. They all seemed to agree without saying anything. He looked at James, who shrugged.

"As good as any," James said. "I don't see anyone else with more power and less ambition. He speaks well."

The attorney asked, "What about Abbot? He's closest behind you in the polls. Wouldn't the public expect—"

"He won't accept," James said.

"You've asked him already?"

"No." With an abrupt gesture, James ended the meeting.

"WHAT HAPPENED TO your face?" was the first thing Buck asked when Karen, Raymond, and Sam walked into the Bluebird Café.

"Grosjean," she said. "I'm okay."

"You don't look it." He turned to Sam. "Neither do you."

The restaurant was crowded, but after a brief wait they were seated in the back. Buck looked at the three of them and smiled. "In spite of the physical wear and tear, you three look like that cat whose stomach is full of canary," he said.

"Not quite," Sam replied, "but we're getting there. Did you come up with anything on Grosjean?"

Link pushed a sheet of paper across the table. "This is it. Not much. We thought it was a pro. It would seem we thought correct. Most of these guys don't get to this level if they're carrying a big jacket. Couple of arrests as a juvenile, questioned in one killing in Algiers, but nothing stuck. Did a few months in Mississippi for receiving stolen property. That's all. I'm concerned that his confrontation with you might send him underground."

"Or he may just come after us again. He still doesn't know who we are or what we're doing," Sam said.

"Possibility, but I doubt it. Might farm it out."

"What about that tag number we gave you?" Karen asked.

"Nothing. Tag reported stolen two weeks ago. No vehicle report. Car probably belongs to one of the guys who went out there, and he changes tags for this kind of work. Have they shown up again?"

"Celine would have called," Sam said.

"Well, what's this other news? The strong stuff Karen was telling me about?"

Sam put Pettigrew's letter in front of Link. "This was delivered to Harold Musgrave with instructions to get it to me, along with a transcript of my trial. It's from Pettigrew. According to him, it's the only documentation that exists. His letter indicts himself, Hunnycut, and Valdrine for collusion in getting me convicted. It also explains Hunnycut's Gulfport house. It was a deal between Hunnycut and a Dixie Mafia guy named Gustave Sykorus."

"I'm aware of Sykorus," Link said. "Some people call him the Gulf Coast Godfather."

"Pettigrew also accuses Valdrine and Hunnycut of direct involvement in the Prather murders and Hamill's suicide. I don't think he was aware of Dougherty. He was probably kept in the dark about some things. He might have had some suspicions, but I don't think he wanted to know everything. I guess, finally, he couldn't deny it."

"Have to be pretty naïve," Link said. "I can't buy that. Give me a minute here." He picked up the letter and began to read. When he finished, he gave it back to Sam, a bitter expression on his face. "They're worse than Grosjean," he said. "I take it from the letter that Pettigrew has skipped."

"He called Musgrave to tell him he wouldn't be around to represent him any longer and that he would have a package delivered," Sam said.

"Buck," Karen said, "I'm not sure how much we should tell Regan. I don't quite trust him, and Neil warned me about trusting people outside the operation. But I can't keep him in the dark about everything."

"You're a real loose cannon, in fed speak."

"Been called that, but so was Neil in his own way, and he raised me in the agency. There's a few of us around, but nobody talks about us much. They just give us the dirty, offbeat work."

"Regan's a hard one to figure," Link said.

"This all began as a federal investigation of a politician," Karen said. "We didn't know we were going to come up with all this."

"That's my point. You all are the road team; we're playing at home. I'd like to have more time. A day or two."

"That's reasonable," Sam said.

"Any idea what you want to do with this?" Link asked, gesturing toward the letter.

"We don't have any corroboration. We'd be on pretty thin ice taking any legal action or contacting the press, and investigating all of this could take months. Without Pettigrew, live and in person, we're nowhere. What I'd like to do is lay it in front of Arthur Valdrine's eyes and see what happens."

"What would that accomplish other than putting him on guard? I think Grosjean's the key, and even when we find him, he's not going to be easy."

"That brings us back to Regan," Karen said.

"You going to see him now?"

"Planned to," she said.

"My suggestion? Let him read this. Don't give him Grosjean. Let me handle that for the time being. Tell him what you told me, that none of this has any backup, and that I need a couple of days. Most important, keep these in your hands. Don't let him make copies."

"How are we supposed to do that?" Karen asked.

"You'll have to figure that one out. Want to eat?"

"Pecan waffle?" Sam asked.

"They're hard to beat." Link raised his hand and caught the server's eye.

# TWENTY-SIX

RENÉ GROSJEAN WAS driving his cousin's car through Slidell when he saw them. Flashing blue lights. He had not been speeding, hadn't ignored any stop signs or red lights, yet here they were, out of nowhere, pulling up to the back bumper of his car.

From the condo in Biloxi, he had gone directly to a motel down on the Strip to get off the road. He didn't think the woman or her boyfriend would call the cops. They were doing something they didn't want anyone to know about, but he always played the percentages, even waited until the morning rush hour was over to avoid traffic stops. Why take a risk? He was glad now that he had dumped the gun.

He looked in the side mirror as the officer approached. A local. Grosjean took his wallet from his back pocket and removed his license. He had no idea if his cousin had a registration in the car or not, but he wasn't about to reach for the glove compartment. That might get him killed. He lowered the window and waited.

"Good afternoon, sir. Could I see your license and registration, please?"

"I got my license," he handed it out the window, "but dis ain' my car. Is my cousin's, an' I don' know where he keep the registration. I can look in the glove box."

"That won't be necessary. Sir, please step out of the car."

Grosjean opened the car door and stepped out. Another police cruiser had arrived, and the officer was walking toward them. He saw another car, lights flashing, coming fast from the opposite direction.

"Did I do some'tin' wrong? I didn' see no red lights or stop signs, no."

"Put your hands on the top of the car and spread your legs." One officer patted him down while the other watched, his hand on his weapon. The third police car pulled up.

The officer studied his driver's license. "Why are you driving your cousin's car, Mr. Grosjean?" he asked.

"He let me use it 'cause mine broke down."

"What's your cousin's name?"

"Tommy Algeron."

"Where does Mr. Algeron live?"

"Algiers Point," Grosjean said.

"Is he at home?"

"I don' know. He not much dere, no."

"Do you have his phone number?"

"No."

"Where is your car, Mr. Grosjean?"

"At my house."

"The address on this driver's license?"

"Yes, sir."

"Please turn around. Hands together." Grosjean obeyed the man. "We're going to have to take you in and see if we can straighten this out. This car was identified leaving the scene of a home invasion out here last week. That's the reason you were stopped. If you weren't involved, you have nothing to worry about. We'll have the car towed in while we try to reach your cousin. You're not being arrested, Mr. Grosjean."

"Seem like I am."

"The cuffs are for our safety. We just need to identify and locate the owner of this vehicle. If you know where we can find him, that will speed things up. When that happens, if you've done nothing wrong, you will be released. Do you understand that?"

Grosjean nodded. He would surely give up his cousin if it came to that. Bastard. Lending him a car the cops were looking for.

The officer guided him into the back seat, putting a hand on his head to keep him from injuring himself. He was sitting behind steel wire that separated him from the driver.

"Dumb son of a bitch," Grosjean said under his breath when he was seated.

The officer's head immediately came down to his level. "What did you say?"

He would love an excuse, Grosjean thought. "Nuttin'."

"I heard you say something. You called me a dumb son of a bitch."

"No. My cousin. Lettin' me borrow a car 'at's in trouble."

"You sure it wasn't me you were talking about?"

"Yes, sir."

"Better not have been." The steel in the officer's voice left no doubt.

"Yes, sir."

"Good." He closed the door, spent a moment speaking to the other officer, then came back and got in behind the wheel. "Your car is tagged," he said to Grosjean. "The tow truck will be here shortly."

"Yes, sir."

"WHAT THE HELL happened to you two?" Regan asked when Karen and Sam walked through the door.

"Should I say we fell down the steps?" Karen asked.

"Wouldn't work. Tell me."

Karen went through the details of Grosjean's attack, referring to him only as Pink Shirt.

The exasperation on Regan's face didn't seem to indicate concern for Sam or her. "Working with the two—no, three—of you, is like trying to get cooperation from a local police department," Regan said. "You don't trust me, and I don't trust you. You're letting me know everything after the fact, which wasn't the deal."

Sam said, "We have something you need to see." He removed Pettigrew's letter and the transcript from the package and pushed them across the table to Regan. He watched the agent's face as he read in silence, unable to contain or disguise his astonishment. "We've got a lot of information, most of which I believe is true, but without Pettigrew we don't have one piece of real evidence. Even the trial transcript would be difficult to verify. That's why I need to confront Valdrine. Get him to react."

"I can't let you do that. You don't make decisions. That's my job. And if I hear that you've done anything like what you suggested, I'll find a charge to drop on you."

"Thanks," Sam said.

Regan reached for the papers on the desk. Sam snatched them away.

"What are you doing?"

"These are mine. I think, in my own interest, I need to hold on to them."

Regan smiled. "Obstruction," he said.

"Hardly. Who knows they exist besides us?"

Regan looked at Karen, who stared back, impassive. "You people are nuts! Agent Chaney, are you looking to get fired?"

Sam spoke after a tense moment. "Look, the transcript isn't enough. I'm not sure it would be accepted as valid. And if it were, it might get Valdrine disbarred, maybe lose him his position, but that's all. And who knows what Hunnycut might be able to engineer? He might be able to drop it all on Valdrine and Pettigrew and walk away without damage."

"I think that would be impossible," Regan said.

"Most people would say making a trial and prison term disappear would be impossible, but they did it. Who are Louisiana's greatest heroes? Jean Lafitte and Huey Long. In that crowd, Hunnycut's still a minor player. We need a little time. Let's see if Link comes up with something."

"I don't know about this."

"Valdrine wants Pettigrew out of the picture but doesn't know he already is. He's still nervous, and he sure as hell doesn't know what we know. Having to look for Pettigrew will allow him less time to focus on us. Give me forty-eight hours. If we don't have something popping by then, we'll play your game."

"Think it will happen that fast?"

"Somebody's got to make a move. Us or them. They've got forty-eight hours if you agree."

"Forty-eight, and I get all the papers."

"Copies," Sam said. "Until you need the originals."

"What's going on in Washington?" Karen asked. "A time frame. We need to know that."

"Right now everything's predicated on this committee investigation. I don't think anyone knows where that's going. It's in wait-and-see mode as far as we know. In Washington, everybody lets everyone else put themselves in jeopardy first."

"You can't push it?" she asked.

"Congress is a closed shop. We seldom have any idea about what they're doing until we read it in the paper."

"What does Link think about all this?" Regan gestured to the papers on his desk. "I'm sure you talked to him before you came here."

"He agrees with you," Karen said. "He doesn't think Sam should confront Valdrine."

Regan nodded. "What about Pink Shirt? I assume there's nothing new on him except that he can beat up an agent and a civilian and walk away untouched."

"Buck doesn't have anything yet. Has the picture out to his guys and a couple of sheriffs he trusts. He's worried the guy will go underground. He's going to call you today."

"Do you know what's really under my skin?" Regan asked Karen.

"No," she said.

"I don't have anything to do. I'm an information center. If there's no progress in forty-eight hours, I want what you have here, and I'm going after Valdrine myself. Do you understand that?"

"We'll keep you posted," Sam said.

"I'll be watching the clock."

"GET WHAT YOU wanted?" she asked when they were outside.

"Exactly," he answered. He looked at Karen and saw pain on her face. It was there every time she moved. "Ribs?"

"I'll be all right." Hoping what she said was true. She wasn't concerned about the ribs or her face. Grosjean's kick had hit her square in a kidney, and she had begun passing blood. Two days, she promised herself, and then the doctor.

MARLENE COLE WOULD be out with a client for the afternoon and evening. Some labor group, she had said, but Hunnycut couldn't remember which one. And then she would come to him tomorrow or the next day asking for his help, but now was not exactly the right time for him to be exercising power. After James's announcement, in or out, he'd do whatever he could do for her that was prudent, but she was going to have to learn the meaning of the word *no*, and that would not be an easy lesson. As intelligent as she was, her priorities were fucked up.

Hunnycut was glad she was out. He needed some quiet time, and her house was the perfect place. He was tired of thinking about Valdrine, Pettigrew, and Larkin. Clearing up the work on his desk had taken longer than he had expected, so it was a little later than usual by the time he arrived and settled in.

He fixed himself a drink, went into the den, and turned the TV on. A political commentator and his guest, a congressional insider, were talking about what moves were being made on Capital Hill with the conventions looming. There was a discussion about a few pending bills and how they would affect specific congressmen's likelihood of reelection. Then a question from the show's host caught Hunnycut's attention.

"I know this is early, but word on the Hill is that Senator Harrison James is narrowing down his running mate possibilities even as we speak. Possibly even naming someone within a week or two. Isn't that pretty risky?"

"It is early. The senator hasn't been nominated yet."

"I know, but taking that as a consideration, what do you think? Have you even heard that as a possibility?"

"I've heard some things. The most interesting is that the Senate Ethics Committee will proceed with an investigation of Senator Hunnycut of Louisiana, whose name, as we all know, has been seriously mentioned as Senator James's choice."

Hunnycut couldn't breathe. Marlene had said it was taken care of, that she had the wedge. It would never happen, she said; Clemmings would back down. "Fuck!" he yelled, then stood up and threw his glass across the room.

But couldn't it just be hearsay? Capital Hill scuttlebutt? Which was usually wrong. Listen to what they're saying, he thought. He knew the insider as a man who liked to hear himself talk and considered himself at the peak of Washington's political wisdom. He picked it back up in midsentence.

". . . Cole also brought into it?"

"I'm sure if the investigation does occur—and it certainly looks as though it will—she will be called, but from what I've heard, it's more about the senator's misuse of campaign funds, inappropriate acceptance of gifts, and influence peddling. Of course, I don't know any of this to be true. Let me state that unequivocally," he said with a smile.

"I would think that some of those things would involve Ms. Cole."

"It's possible." It sounded to Hunnycut as though the pundit were protecting Marlene. His anger escalated again.

"Do you see this as eliminating Senator Hunnycut from the ticket? Innocent or guilty?" the interviewer asked, his soft voice taking the edge off a loaded question.

"I don't think there's any doubt. Even if they started the hearings tonight, they would run well beyond the convention, and Senator James wouldn't carry that kind of baggage for a minute."

"Senator Clemmings?"

"Not on my list of choices."

"Anyone you think could be a front-runner?"

"I think the governor of Illinois might be the best possibility, but that's only my opinion." Again, the acerbic smile.

Hunnycut stared at the screen. Maybe it was just gossip, but he felt his dream fading. He knew he should call his attorney and tell him what he had just heard, but he didn't have the heart. And Valdrine. He wondered if James had ever seriously considered him. If he ever found out that it was all a scam, he would finish James. Even as a sitting president.

GROSJEAN WAS ASLEEP in his holding cell when a cop came to take him to an interrogation room. He'd refused the opportunity to make a phone call, saving it in case things got sticky. He wasn't fully awake when he sat down. The cop who had brought him in was sitting at the table.

"You find my cousin?" he asked in a sleepy voice.

"You're pretty relaxed, René, sleepin' while the sun's still shinin'. You musta been in jail before," the cop said.

Stupid, Grosjean thought. "You know I have. Coupla little t'ings. I know you look it up. Dat's all."

"Yes, I did. Receiving stolen property. You know, home invasion kinda goes together with that, wouldn't you say?"

"I don' know, but I ain' done no home invasion, me."

"Well, we got you. We got the car. We can't find your cousin, and your car's not at the address you gave us."

"I don' know 'bout dat."

"Puts you in kind of a bind. You must know something. What kind of car do you drive?"

"Cadillac, but I 'spect you already know dat."

"Must be doing okay," the officer said.

"It old. Nineteen seventy."

"What color?" He never could understand why the police always asked questions they already knew the answers to.

"Blue."

"You know your tag number, René?"

"Not 'less I'm lookin' at it."

"Registration in your car, or do you carry it?"

"In the car. S'pose you cain' find my cousin? He mighta fix my car and took off. I t'ink it was jus' a dead batt'ry."

"Would he do that? Just take your car and leave?"

"Prob'ly. If he in trouble he might."

"Did you tell him when you'd have his car back?"

"No. Said I'd call," Grosjean said.

"You said you didn't have his number." The officer gave him a hard look.

"I got it at home."

"Anybody there we can call?"

"No."

"And you don't know your tag number. Got an insurance card in your wallet?"

"You got my wallet, but I ain' got no insurance, me."

The officer shook his head. "Well, all we can do is put out a bulletin on your car and hope we find it and your cousin. Otherwise, we're gonna have to start looking at you as a suspect in that home invasion. I'll get a description of your car out to all our patrols, NOPD, and the state police and see if we can't find it."

"You find him, you put him in the cell wit' me."

"I'm not sure I'd be smart to do that, René."

Walking back to the cell, Grosjean was looking forward to going back to sleep. "You gon' wake me for dinner?" he asked.

"We'll wake you. Don't want you to starve." Grosjean did not like the sound of the cell doors slamming shut.

"WHAT NOW?" KAREN asked.

"Wait, I guess. Got any other ideas? You're the professional law enforcement officer."

"How far is Thibodaux?" Karen looked straight ahead. They had dropped Raymond off at his office and were headed out of town. Sam didn't respond. "I'd like to see her, Sam."

"Why?"

"It's important to me. I like to know what I'm up against. Hard to visualize someone you've never seen."

Sam smiled. "I would have thought you were more confident than that."

"I'm a woman. You forget that, me being a law enforcement professional and all? Plus, she's a player in this, like it or not, and I need to know the players."

"And?"

"And I'm trying to put a lot together here." The words began to cascade, and she didn't try to stop herself. "You come down. I screw things up. You leave and come back on the same day, but you're different. You don't want to touch me. You sleep in the guestroom. Then after you go off to see your former wife, you return to my bedroom with a different personality, and we make love. I ask you why, and you say it's because of me. Why? I don't know, any more than I know where I am or what I'm doing with you. I'm not sure I even want you, but if I decide I do, I'd like to know what I have to live up to."

"Thibodaux's an hour and a half at most," he said.

"I need to see your past. You saw Neil, and I didn't hold anything back. And what you haven't seen or heard about from my past, you will if you want to."

"Okay," he said, and drove west.

SAM DROVE PAST the house without saying anything. Celine's car was parked beside the yellow pickup truck.

"You nervous?" Karen asked. He had been quiet for a long time.

"She might shoot us. She's got a shotgun."

"Well then, maybe this isn't such a good idea."

"Probably isn't, but we're here."

"Then why didn't you stop at the house?" He braked and looked at her. "I saw you looking as we passed. The one with the yellow pickup truck?"

"Wanted to give you a chance to change your mind."

"If you don't want to—"

"It's your deal. Let's do it." He turned the car around. When he pulled into the driveway, he honked the horn. Then he got out and came around the car to open her door.

"I'm not getting out."

"What do you mean, you're not getting out?"

"I just wanted to see her."

"You said you wanted to *meet* her," he said.

"No, I didn't."

Sam shrugged and started walking toward the porch.

Celine opened the door and stepped out as he came up the steps. "Just in the neighborhood?" she asked, her teeth brilliant against her tan complexion.

"Actually, no. I drove from the city to see how you're doing. Any more trouble?"

"Long way to drive to ask a question. None I can't handle. That deputy is a bit over-protective."

"Can you blame him?"

"What about you? You look like you've been through a threshing machine."

Sam told her about Grosjean, what was going on, and what he expected to happen. Celine looked toward the Rover.

Karen was watching. She had expected Celine to be attractive, but the woman was unbelievably beautiful. And she and Sam were talking as if no time or space or trouble had passed between them.

"Did you remember anything else about the two guys who came out here?" Sam asked. Celine continued to look at his car.

"There's nothing to remember really. They were average and not very brave."

"If they had been, they'd have been dead."

"Or severely injured," Celine said. "Anything on the tag number?"

"Stolen."

"I figured." She turned to him with a smile. "Who are you hiding in the car, Sam?"

"A DEA agent."

"You're kidding."

"Karen Chaney. The one I told you I helped in Carolina. The one who got me down here to work on Hunnycut."

"You going to introduce me?"

"I'd love to."

"This was really stupid," Karen hissed between gritted teeth as Sam and Celine walked toward the car. No way was she getting out. Rude or not. Sam opened the door.

"Karen, I'd like you to meet Celine Aguillard," Sam said. Karen got out of the car. Celine was taller by two inches. "Celine, this is Karen Chaney. DEA. She's working with me on Hunnycut."

Celine put out her hand, and Karen took it.

"I'm pleased to meet you. Sam's told me a lot about you," Karen said.

"There's not a lot to tell, but if he has, I appreciate his efforts. He told me about your visitor. Are you sure you're all right?"

"I'm fine. Just a little roughed up. Part of the job."

"So you and Sam have known each other for awhile?"

Karen could see that Celine was enjoying every minute of this, but only in an amused way. How could you not like the woman? "Not really. A couple of months working in South Carolina and now a little while here," Karen said.

"That's probably enough. You gonna let her catch you, Sam?"

Karen was surprised to see Sam's face redden.

"I don't think she's exactly chasing me, Celine."

"I'm not sure you'd know," Celine said. She reached into her jeans and came out with a trinket. Sam looked at it and smiled. It was the tab off a beer can bent around a copper penny. She handed it to Karen.

"What's this?" Karen asked.

"A Cajun money clip. For luck. It's good to meet you, Karen. Take care of him. He's all we've got." She turned to go back in the house. "Back at you, Sam. Karen."

Karen was in her seat by the time Sam got in the car. "Shit!" she said when he was seated.

"What?"

"You didn't tell me she was *that* beautiful." She paused. "*And* nice."

"You never asked."

"What was I supposed to ask? *How beautiful is your former wife*?"

"What was I supposed to say when we were driving over here? *I can't wait for you to meet my beautiful, nice former wife*?"

"Damn, Sam, she is. I don't know how you could . . ."

"We talked about that, and we agreed it was better not to try to recapture the past."

"That's noble," Karen said, not sure she believed him.

"She'll always be dear to me, but it would be impossible to reconstruct. We've both changed."

"I guess I understand that."

"What time is it?" he asked.

Karen looked at her watch. "Four-twenty. Why?"

"Just wondered. I've got a couple of phone calls to make, and then we can get something to eat."

"Phone calls?"

"Check in with Raymond, you know."

She looked at him skeptically. "I'm not sure I do, or that I believe you, but I won't ask."

"Good," he said.

SAM MADE HIS calls from a gas station in Thibodaux. They were brief and to the point. Raymond took his instructions without question, and Sam never heard Valdrine's voice after the initial hello.

Sam and Karen had dinner at Ralph and Kacoo's on Toulouse. It was close to where he planned to be later. They shared a platter of fried crawfish tails, then split a piece of satin pie, a mousse-like concoction of peanut butter with a thick layer of chocolate.

During dessert Sam told her what he planned to do.

ARTHUR VALDRINE WAS suspicious, but nothing else had worked. The voice on the telephone had said only, "If you want to find out about Jordan Pettigrew, I will meet you in Jackson Square at eight o'clock. Sit on a bench directly across from St. Louis Cathedral. You can wait ten minutes. Five before and five after. If I don't show, it's because you've brought somebody or the police show up. This is not a shakedown, and you won't be harmed. It's the only time I will contact you. Don't ask why I'm doing this. Just consider it your lucky day." Then the caller hung up.

Valdrine's first thought was to take Grosjean with him, but the man hadn't returned any of his messages. Bill and Joe would be on shift and could probably swing by, but if the guy got spooked, he was out of luck.

Pettigrew had become more than a loose end; he was a threat. Valdrine had to go alone.

Jackson Square. Eight o'clock. Five minutes before and five after. He would be early. He considered taking a gun, but it would be useless in his hands and probably get him killed besides. He would follow orders. He couldn't remember the last time he had done that.

IT WAS 7:40. The lights along the Riverwalk and on Jackson Square prolonged the day. Street vendors and performers from mimes to fire-eaters were packing up after a day's work. Some persisted, mostly artists, their watercolors and charcoal scenes still on display until the dinner hour was over and the parade of tourists had dwindled.

Sam was sitting on a bench at the south end of the block. Karen was lingering on the corner of Madison and Chartres, watching for any backup Valdrine might bring with him. Sam didn't doubt that Valdrine would show up. His only concern was that the administrator might be dumb enough to try and slip someone in with him.

Valdrine turned onto St. Peter Street from Decatur and proceeded up the square. He passed within two feet of Sam and went to a bench directly across from the cathedral. He looked around before he sat down.

Sam watched as he stood up, sat back down, looked from side to side, got up, walked across the square to the cathedral entrance, turned, looked back at the bench, went back across the square, and sat down again. He checked his watch. Sam could tell he was taking deep breaths, trying to relax. It was 7:59, and there had been no alert from Karen.

At 8:00 Sam began walking toward Valdrine, all of his senses on alert. At one point, the administrator looked in his direction but took no notice. He jumped when Sam sat down next to him. Sam said nothing and began looking at the papers he carried, as though he were casually reflecting on some business of the day. Valdrine was very uncomfortable, and Sam was enjoying every second of it.

"Uh, if you don't mind, I was waiting for someone to meet me here," Valdrine said.

The arrogance of the man who had put Sam away was gone. For the moment anyway. In a different setting and under the proper conditions, Sam thought, Valdrine would kill him without compunction.

"I do mind," Sam said. "I think these benches are public." Valdrine clearly didn't know what to do. Sam let him suffer for a few moments. "Do you often tell people where they can and cannot sit?"

"No, I just . . . I told them I would be sitting directly across from the cathedral."

"You are sitting across from the cathedral," Sam said.

"Yes, but it might look . . ."

"And do you know the person you're supposed to meet?"

"No, I don't, and I don't think that's any of your business." Valdrine reached in his pocket.

Sam tensed.

"Look, would it be worth ten dollars for you to let me have this bench?"

Sam could not believe it. Or, maybe he could. "You know me, Arthur." Valdrine's mouth opened, but he didn't say anything. "You just aren't remembering. Sam Larkin." Valdrine's face lost its color. There was nothing of the man Sam remembered from the courtroom.

"I—"

"You're not going to be hurt; I told you that."

Valdrine managed to gain some control, "You said you had information about Jordan Pettigrew. I thought—"

"You thought wrong, and I lied. I only know he's gone and you're looking for him. What I do have for you is a partial copy of the transcript of the trial you and Pettigrew and Hunnycut concocted to send me to Angola. I am in possession of the entire transcript." He handed the sheets to Valdrine.

Valdrine glanced down at the sheets, recognized the format, and paused. He smiled. "You have no proof these are genuine. Anyone could have—"

"But anyone didn't, and just bringing it to the public's eye would ruin you and the senator. I also have notes of your telephone conversations with Pettigrew regarding this trial, Thornton Hunnycut, and a number of other things."

Valdrine's smile had gone sickly. "And what do they say? And what would you do with them? Pettigrew sure as hell wouldn't back them up. You don't think he'd take a chance on going to jail, do you?" His voice was gaining strength. "You've got nothing. You know where Pettigrew is? Maybe his body? Maybe you killed him. I heard you were capable of that. You were not supposed to come back to Louisiana—" Valdrine stopped abruptly.

"I'm not wired," Sam said. "Go on."

Valdrine looked uncertain, then dropped the volume level of his voice. "You must've liked Angola. Killing people." A sneer had replaced the smile.

"I'm not as prone to that as you are, and I can promise you that unless you've found Pettigrew, he's alive and well."

"What do you mean unless I've found him? I'm worried about—"

"I'm sure you are. Probably even more than you were about Parker Hamill."

"Parker took his own life," Valdrine said.

"Of course he did, but not by his own hand. By being involved with you. Prather? I'm sure you were worried about him. But you've made another mistake. A bigger one than sending me to prison in the first place."

"What are you talking about? You're crazy."

Sam lowered the boom he had been planning all day. "There was a reporter. Harry Landers. Do you remember him?"

"I didn't have anything to say to him."

Sam stared off into the distance. "He was killed and his body burned in Jefferson Parish. Took his teeth out, so he couldn't be identified. I'm sure you read about it in the paper."

"I don't know anything about that, just that he called me."

"He was not a reporter, Arthur. He was a federal agent, working down here, and I think you probably know exactly what happened to him."

Valdrine looked as though he were going to collapse.

"Have a good evening, Arthur. And I wouldn't try to run—you'll never make it."

Sam got up and walked north to Chartres. He joined Karen, and they walked to the car.

"Well?" Karen asked.

"He's a hard man to shake. I was surprised. I told him about Dougherty."

"And?"

"He knows he's in over his head," Sam said.

"What do we do now? I'm afraid to ask, but I think I ought to know." They were at the car.

"Go home."

"What about Valdrine?"

"He'll go home, too. Where else would he go at this time of night? I don't think he's a party animal, and he's not feeling well. Retreat to the nest, I imagine."

"And?"

"Raymond's following him. He'll stay on him until he does something."

Karen shook her head and climbed into the Rover. "I can't wait for this day to end," she said.

Sam looked at her and grinned. “Fun, idn’t it?” he said, doing a fair Harold Musgrave imitation.

# TWENTY-SEVEN

WHEN MARLENE COLE walked through the front door of her townhouse a little after nine o'clock, Thornton was staring at her from the couch. Drunk.

"Thornton?" she said, then dodged the glass he hurled at her.

"You lied to me, Marlene," she heard above the shattering glass. "You fucking lied to me. You could handle it. Everything's under control. Clemmings will back down. You should have seen the news tonight. You could have gotten some *real* insider information."

He was screaming. Out of control. A new Thornton Hunnycut was standing in front of her. Close. A street fighter she had not seen before. She could see the struggle in his face as he fought the urge to hit her—or worse—and it would come to that if she didn't stand her ground.

"Stop it!" she yelled. "You need me, goddamn it!"

"I need you? Why? You just screwed me. Remember your little homily? The difference between fucking and screwing is that you have to have my permission to fuck me? Remember that? I did not give you permission to talk to Clemmings. I did not give you permission to lie to me. I told you he wouldn't back down, and you said you had him by the balls. I guess you lost your grip."

"It wasn't Clemmings," she said, but he didn't hear her.

"It's over, lady. The ticket won't have Thornton Hunnycut on it." He pushed his face into hers. "And I lay that right at your feet. People are dead who have done less to me than you have done."

She thought he was going to have a stroke; his face was the deep purple of red garden beets. The words shook her.

"Hell, you can testify against me at the hearing to get yourself off. Probably put me in jail. You think you're safe? Don't bet on it. You'll never have any influence in this neighborhood again. You'll be shunned like a fucking Amish adulterer!"

"It wasn't Clemmings!" she shrieked when he took a breath. It stopped him. She said firmly, "It was James!"

He looked at her, confusion registering on his face. "What? What do you mean, James?"

"It was Harrison James."

"What are you talking about?" Disorientation was subduing his anger.

"The investigation was never pushed by Clemmings. James did it. He wants the South, but he never wanted you." She had broken her agreement with Harrison James, but it was too late to stop. She would take up damage control later.

"How do you know that?"

"He told me. I met with him. I wanted to know if he could stop the hearings. He believes if they happen, the worst possible outcome would be your going back to Louisiana and still supporting him."

"That bastard! Why does he think I'd do that? He's humiliated me. I feel like a third grader who pissed his pants during class. I'll bury that son of a bitch."

"Thornton, I told him I wouldn't tell you." She walked past him to the bar, put ice in two glasses, poured scotch into them, and turned back to him.

He took a glass from her hand and drank. "Why would you do that, Marlene?" His voice was calm. Too calm.

"To save you," she answered.

"Save me?" Louder. "How the fuck was that going to save me?"

"He can control the direction of the inquiry; he started it. He'll orchestrate it so no charges can be brought. He wants you back in Louisiana, not in prison. You've often said being governor would be better than being vice president. The glass is half full, Thornton."

"And you? Is he going to protect you, too?"

"Yes," she said.

"Marlene, I don't know what you have in mind, but don't ever expect anything from me again. If I can ever hurt you, I will. And if you or Harrison James try to screw me any further, you have no idea how swift my sword will fall upon you both." He grabbed his coat off the chair and walked out the door.

Marlene Cole was left standing in the center of the room, and she wasn't sure in which direction to take the first step.

BUCK LINK GOT the message just before midnight. He'd been asleep, but the information woke him more effectively than a cold shower. The Slidell Police Department had issued a BOLO, Be On the Lookout, on a 1977 blue Cadillac belonging to René Grosjean. One of Link's officers had learned they were holding Grosjean. Link did not want him charged in Slidell; there was too much else on Grosjean's plate, and a penny ante charge would muddle things immeasurably. It might even give the man an alibi. Within twenty minutes Link was dressed, and forty minutes later he was standing at the duty officer's desk in Slidell.

"This guy is one cool dude," the duty officer told Link.

"Has he talked to anyone? Lawyer? Phone call?"

"No, sir. Just me and the officer who brought him in. Seems quite content to be in jail."

"I'd like to see him," Link said. "The state police have an interest in him as well."

"Let me get the officer-in-charge. I'm sure it's no problem."

After a brief conversation, the officer-in-charge led him back to an interrogation room. Within minutes, Grosjean was brought in. Seeing a suspect he had been seeking, up close and personal for the first time, always stimulated two emotions in Link: gratification and disappointment. Regardless of the heinous crime he had committed, the perp never looked dangerous in handcuffs or an interrogation room. Grosjean just stared at him. Link noted the imbecilic smile that had haunted him since the day he first laid eyes on him.

"You find my car?" Grosjean asked.

"No, we didn't find your car. I'm here to talk to you about something else."

"Wha' dat be?"

"Well, several things, René. Why don't we start with this home invasion the officer out front was telling me about?"

"I ain' done it, me. I tol' 'em. Dat was my cousin's car dey stop me for. I ain' done no home invasions."

The man is totally relaxed, Link thought. "Maybe not that one, but what about the one in Biloxi?"

"Mi'ssippi? I ain' never done no home invasion over 'ere neidder. You ain' from Mi'ssippi."

"That's correct, but you did do a home invasion over there. And a break-in. We have witnesses. Do you want to tell me about it, or do you want me to tell you about it?"

Grosjean was silent. His face didn't change.

"Okay, I'll tell you about it," Link said. "A few days ago you broke into a condominium in Biloxi. You were seen going in and coming out. Last night you went back to the same place, walked through the door with a gun in your hand, and attacked a woman and the man who came to her aid. You beat them both up pretty good. Do you want to deny that? Tell me some lies?"

"You gon' arres' me for dat?" Grosjean asked.

"Probably, but there are still a few other things. By the way, I got a search warrant for your house. My people are there now."

"Why you wan' do dat? I ain' got nothin' 'ere."

"I guess we'll see. Why'd you go after that woman in Biloxi? You going to rape her?"

Grosjean reacted quickly. "I don' do dat stuff."

"Then why?" Link could see Grosjean's mind working, making decisions. The man knew he was in trouble; he was just trying to decide how much. Once they started thinking, they always screwed up.

"I pick her up at a bar. I didn' come t'rough no doors, no. She say she a dancer down on the Strip. I was willin' to pay her, but she want to rob me. Pull a knife out de kitchen. I didn' have no gun. He come in an' start beatin' on me. I took off. He was bigger dan me."

"That's a pretty different story than they tell."

"All I can tell you is the trut'."

"I don't believe that. You talk about real estate while you were trying to do whatever you were trying to do?" Link asked. Nothing was more entertaining than questioning a suspect when you had all the answers.

"Real 'state?" Grosjean looked at him with disdain. "I went dere to have a lady. Real 'state? Lady did say she was gon' move dere. Dat's all I know."

"Did you ask what else she was doing in Biloxi other than dancing?"

"I tol' you I went dere to—"

"What do you know about the Prather murders?"

"I don' know nothin' 'bout no murders, me. I don' know no Prathers."

Link noticed a slight quiver in Grosjean's left eye. "You were stopped in Biloxi just a day or so before the murders, René. You asked that dancer what she was doing there. Do you want to know what she was doing there? She was investigating the murders of Masley Prather and his wife. He was involved in some shady real estate deals, and somebody saw her doing research and called you to pay her a visit. Isn't that the way it went?"

"I don' know—"

Link stood up. "You don't know anything, I know. But somebody does, because they sent you over there, and I want to find out who that is."

Grosjean shifted around in his seat. "I need to go to de bat'room, me," he said.

"Not now. You know what, René? That dancer is a federal agent. They're probably going to be here next. I don't know how much you know about the feds, but assaulting a federal agent is commensurate with murder." He figured Grosjean would think *commensurate* meant something worse than it did.

"I t'ink I want to see my lawyer."

"If that's the way you want to play it. Let me ask you one more thing, René. Have you ever seen me before?"

Grosjean looked at him, squinting. "I don' t'ink so."

"Jefferson Parish. State Route 3257. Burned-out car with a body in the back?"

"I want to see my lawyer and go to de bat'room."

As small as he is, Link thought, he just got smaller. Link asked the officer-in-charge to keep him personally apprised of Grosjean's status and not to release him under any circumstances, since the possibility of federal charges was hanging over his head. He was wary about leaving Grosjean there, but there was nothing else he could do.

Only momentous events ever truly excited Link, and they were few: his first wedding (which had later proved not worth the effort); getting out of the Marines after two tours in Viet Nam; catching a serial killer who had murdered nine women and had four police departments, the state police, and feds running around in circles for three years. Now this. Cooperation and coordination, not areas he trusted a lot of law enforcement agencies to respect, would be a problem.

Grosjean was the key. Link did not want to play his whole hand at once. Regan might accuse him of interference, but that bothered him not at all. Regan, Karen, and Larkin had been scatter-shooting and coming up with nothing. Now he had something tangible, but the question remained how to use it.

It was 3:00 AM when he called Karen Chaney.

"Buck? What time is it?"

"Early. What time does Regan get to his office in the morning?" He heard a yawn.

"I really don't know him that well, but if he's like Neil, by eight always, usually seven. What's going on?"

"I would appreciate you and Sam being there at seven."

"What's wrong?"

"We may have gotten a break in the case. Seven o'clock."

"We'll be there."

ARTHUR VALDRINE DIDN'T go home after Larkin left him. He drove aimlessly. Several times he was forced to pull the car to the side of the road because he was shaking so badly he couldn't steer and breathing was becoming difficult. He wondered if he was having a heart attack and thought that might not be a bad thing. When he could drive no longer, he went home. How much time had passed, he couldn't guess.

Valdrine didn't notice the old Crown Victoria that followed him and parked across the street from his house. Once inside, he closed and locked the door, fell back against it, closed his eyes, and tried to lose himself in the darkness. Larkin's words still echoed in his ears. Hamill. Prather. A federal agent. The man had it all.

He walked to the bar in his den and poured two inches of scotch into a glass. He drank half of it in one swallow, poured more, and then sat at his desk. He opened the top drawer and took out a gun. A .38-caliber Saturday night special he had been given by a client back in the early days of his practice. It was loaded; it always was, though he had never fired it. He laid it on the blotter and looked at it.

The scotch was settling him. He went to the bar, refilled his glass, and sat down in a Chippendale wing chair. The trial transcript was a copy, easily discredited. There was no original; he had watched Pettigrew shred that. The letter and notes were worthless without Jordan to back them up.

Perhaps the situation was as not as bad as he had thought. Larkin had caught him by surprise, but there was really nothing to link him to any of it except Grosjean, and Bill and Joe could handle that. If they didn't, and he went down, they would go to prison. Cops did not do well in Angola.

He was beginning to see some small amount of light, a ray of hope. He would survive. After awhile it would all be forgotten, just another scandal to be discussed at cocktail parties. For some New Orleans social celebrities, scandal was the only attention they ever received.

Hunnycut was not a real threat. Let the man become vice president. Valdrine would disassociate himself. He would never be attorney general, but he would survive. The ray was becoming brighter. Larkin had nothing, and, down the road, he would pay. He wouldn't mind doing it himself.

The telephone rang. He went to the desk, put the gun back in the drawer, sat down, and picked up the receiver. "Hello?"

"I need a lawyer, me," the familiar voice said.

Valdrine hung up without saying a word. His stomach began to heave, followed by severe cramps in his stomach and colon. The bile rose in his throat. He would never make it to the bathroom, and he didn't try.

THORNTON HUNNYCUT SAT behind his desk, facing his attorneys. He had assembled them at 6:00 AM. If the hearing was on, he wanted to be ahead of the game or, if possible, avoid it altogether. The vice presidency was no longer possible. He had started building a plan for the Louisiana governorship. It would depend on the investigation. A simple censure or even a dismissal would not kill his chances.

"You've got to find out what they've got. Where they're going," the senior attorney said. "According to Cole, James controls the direction the investigation would take."

"That's what she said, but he said that to her. I have no idea what she might have offered him. In any case, we can't depend on her for support," Hunnycut said.

"I think you're wrong about that. You could put her in jail."

"Are tax returns going to be a problem?" another attorney asked.

"No," the senior attorney said. "They go after spending records, campaign funds misuse, and influence the senator's exerted on Cole's behalf. Can you think of anything else we are dealing with here, Thornton?"

"Marlene's salary for one."

"How much and what for?"

"Eighteen thousand a month as a fundraiser."

"What else?"

"Probably a hundred and fifty, two hundred thousand this year for travel and sundries. Maybe a hundred thousand on food, but I would think a lot of this is irrelevant. A lot of politicians spend a hundred thousand dollars to raise a hundred and fifty. It's the cost of doing business."

"Not in the public's eyes, and not when they want to get you. What are the chances of your dealing with James directly?"

"Throw myself at his mercy?"

"That could solve your problem. Offer to admit to lesser charges to the committee, none that would put you in jail. Accept a censure, offer to resign, and give him support in the South. You're out. It's over. And you run for governor."

"I don't know there's any way in hell he'd accept that. Maybe he couldn't if the wheels are already in motion," Hunnycut said.

"Thornton," said the senior attorney, "I've been doing this for thirty years. I have seen things you could not conceive. I've defended politicians against almost every charge on the books. The two things I have learned are that every politician I have ever met should be jailed for something, and that every political and personal decision is made in the best interests of the decision-maker's career. I don't think you are in serious trouble. Harrison James has already put himself in a catch-22. He needs to get rid of you, but he needs your support. You can likely give him the South, or maybe not. But, without question, you can sure as hell take away a good portion of it. He's not going to let that happen.

Let me approach him. Work this thing out. Get a time frame." The attorney stood, rapped his knuckles on the table. "Third lesson I've learned about Washington politics: everything is possible."

BY THE TIME Sam and Karen reached the city, rain was sweeping across the streets, and rivers were moving swiftly in the gutters. Lightning flashed, thunder broke the silence, and breakers smashed into the seawalls that protected the city.

They were wet and chilled when they walked through the door of Regan's office at ten of seven. Buck Link and Regan were waiting for them. Sam had not heard from Raymond. He assumed Valdrine had gone home and Raymond was still baby-sitting him. As soon as they were finished here, he and Karen would head out to the Garden District to relieve him.

Both he and Karen were tired, and Karen was still in obvious pain, though she had said nothing. There had been little rest between Buck's call and their leaving Biloxi; with the weather beginning to come in, Sam had pushed Karen to leave early. The strain was showing in her eyes.

"You okay?" Regan asked Karen.

"Getting there. Yesterday wasn't too bad, but I'm a little more stiff and sore this morning. Third day's supposed to be the worst. I've got a few new bruises showing up, and the face still requires a little extra makeup, but I'm okay. Now, Buck, tell us why we made the drive from Biloxi in this minor hurricane."

"I wanted all of you together," Link said.

"What the hell is going on?" Regan asked. His patience was not thin—it was nonexistent. And Sam didn't doubt for a moment that Regan would consider whatever Link had to say a trespass.

"The Slidell police have René Grosjean in custody, but he has not been charged with anything yet." He related the circumstances of the man's being stopped and held. "But we have some problems."

"What kind of problems?" Regan asked.

"He probably didn't do what they brought him in for. Consequently, they won't be able to hold him very long, and if they do charge him, it might protect him from our case."

"I'll get a warrant issued and go pick him up."

"You don't have anything," Buck said. "If you bring him in now and can't prove the charges, he's gone. If we're right, he's working for two of the most powerful people in the state. We're not dealing with a common street criminal here; I don't care how he talks."

"How would you know—"

"Because I talked to him."

"You talked to him? Why didn't you call me?" Regan was clearly angry.

"I wanted to make dead certain he was the man we're looking for. I had to see that face with my own eyes. Second, I wanted to find out exactly what the Slidell police have and how they intend to pursue it. Other than him driving his cousin's car, they don't have anything. As far as they're concerned, we can probably have him if we have anything, or he can demand to be released."

"You said there was a problem. So far I haven't heard one. I'll get a warrant, go to Slidell—"

"You can't bulldoze your way through this. We've got the Prathers in Mississippi, maybe Hamill here in Orleans Parish, and Dougherty in Jefferson. You've got two parish police departments, another state, and the federal government involved."

"We take precedence," Regan said.

Karen and Sam watched the skirmish with no doubt which of the two men would prevail.

"Only in your eyes. Do you realize how many jurisdictions will be fighting over this guy once they find out what a prize he is? They're not going to just let you step in and take it away. I can see this guy slipping through the cracks. I know how these things work down here. There are few rules, and everybody wants the biggest piece of the pie."

"What about the interview?" Sam asked, trying to sideline the dispute.

"He's tough. And confident, though I do believe I rattled his cage a little. He's careful. Without that traffic stop, we might never have found this guy."

"You tape it?" Regan asked.

"No. I was unofficial. I was never there, and it never happened. I'm on the pad for a few favors though. There wouldn't have been anything we could use in any case."

"Anything else you want to tell me you did?"

"We searched his house."

"And?" Sam asked.

"Nothing conclusive. Couple of pieces of foam rubber, duct tape, plastic bottles. All multipurpose items. We did find some .22-caliber bullets, but no guns or anything that could link directly to our investigation. I said he's careful."

"What rattled his cage?" Sam asked.

"I told him about the Prathers, that he was in Biloxi about the time of the murders. And I mentioned Hamill. Neither one fazed him. I didn't mention Dougherty; however, I did tell him Karen was a federal agent and that he would have a hard time beating that assault charge. He took a little notice of that. By the way, looked like you got in a few licks on the man, Sam. He had a few bruises."

"Not nearly enough."

"Why would you tell him about Karen? I can't—" Regan began.

"I thought it might get him to move toward opening up, and I believe knowing what she is might keep him from going after her again if he gets out."

"He won't get out," Regan said.

"Don't be too sure. I've seen more bizarre things happen. Remember where you are."

"I think we're traveling the yellow brick road here," Sam said.

"You want to explain that?" Regan asked.

"You'll never break him. Even with a federal agent's murder hanging over his head. He's got ten or twenty years before he has to worry about the needle, and he probably never planned on living that long anyway."

"I don't believe anyone—"

"You're wrong. I lived with these guys. They sacrifice years for a short time in 'the life,' and most of them enjoy the odds. They're very pragmatic when it comes to living or dying, and a lot of them can do either with a smile on their face."

Regan gave him a disgusted look. "You know, you think because you were in prison, you're the only one of us who really understands—"

"I am," Sam said with authority. There was silence. He softened his voice. "Let me tell you what I believe."

"Go ahead," Link said. Regan shot him a look, festering, as Sam began.

"Grosjean's been around long enough to know there's little chance of copping a plea on a federal agent's murder. When he learns that's what Landers was, he'll know his only hope is friends in high places who can keep stalling it. He knows he has Valdrine in his pocket, and he's going to protect him as his only chance. Without him, he'll last ten years; with him he might die of old age."

"Sam's right," Link said.

"Goddamn it!" Regan said. "I'm tired of experts."

"Michael, we're all working toward the same goal here," Karen said. "We don't have anything conclusive other than his breaking into my condo and taking a few swings at me. We're treading water. At least let's hear what he has to say."

"Valdrine is the weak link," Sam said.

"You're sure of that?" Regan asked, not disguising his sarcasm. "I thought he was the driving force in all this, that he was the strong one. Now you're telling me that the commissioner of administration of the state, a man who engineered four murders, is going to roll over? You're insane, pal."

"I don't give a damn whether you like me or not, or whether you approve of what I'm doing, but Valdrine's the keystone. Pull him out, and it all comes tumbling down. He's weakening. I know. I talked to him."

Both Regan and Link stared at him. Regan got up and walked back to the windows.

"I also told him about Dougherty."

Regan turned around and started for him, livid, but Link got between them.

"Who in God's name do you think you are?" Regan yelled. "We lost an agent, and you take it upon yourself to ignore everything we've discussed, make the murder of a federal agent public, and give the perpetrator an opportunity to run?"

"He won't run. But you know what I'm tired of hearing? Federal. Murder is murder. I may not be working with you, but I am working alongside you. Keep that in mind."

"You're only concerned with what you believe are your own little personal injustices. I should have you put in custody."

"Your agency invited me down here."

"And I'm sorry as hell it did. Neil Dougherty was insane." Everyone in the room stared at him.

"And you're getting nowhere." Sam's voice was intense. "You lost one agent, and if I hadn't walked through that condo door in Biloxi, you'd have lost another. Put that down as a definite. Valdrine won't run; Raymond's watching him."

"What was Valdrine's reaction?" Link asked.

Sam told the story, leaving out no details, and then went on. "We've got Grosjean, who is a dead end without something to move him forward. He's only the mechanic. Valdrine and Hunnycut are the killers. They engineered it all. I would lay most of it on Valdrine, according to Pettigrew's letter, but you can bet he didn't do anything Hunnycut didn't either incite or approve. He was complicit."

"But without Pettigrew—" Regan started.

"It's all been a game to Valdrine," Sam said. "Not real. His hands are clean in the physical sense. I doubt he's seen a body. In his mind, he's removed, insulated. He's never been in any trouble that shuffling a few papers and money couldn't solve."

"I think you're wrong," Regan said. "These guys don't worry, no matter what. They think they're above the law, and Valdrine's no different now."

"He's never faced multiple murder charges."

"Do you have any suggestions how we might get to Arthur Valdrine?" Buck asked.

"I think I can do that, but it would be tricky. I can talk to him again. Wear a wire."

"A wire is inadmissible evidence."

"Hearing Valdrine might push Grosjean over the line," Link said, then looked at Sam. "Or you could testify."

"Hearsay," Regan stated.

"Suppose that, in addition to the wire, you witnessed it," Buck said, addressing Regan. "That you heard whatever it is he might say. I believe that would be more than admissible."

"You're assuming he's going to say something," Karen said.

"I have a feeling he will. The problem will be getting Regan in there."

"I said it would be complicated," Sam said.

"When do you want to—"

"Now. He's already shaky. Do we have anything we can use on him from Washington?"

"Hunnycut's out of the running. Word on the Hill is that it's the governor of Illinois. The Senate Ethics Committee is going after Hunnycut, and probably Cole, full force. It's supposedly beyond the rumor point now."

"We can't let him escape," Sam said.

"I'd say that's up to you."

# TWENTY-EIGHT

RAYMOND WAS TIRED, but still in position across from Arthur Valdrine's home. Link, Karen, and Regan were parked one property down from Valdrine's house, manning the receiver for Sam's wire. Regan had picked up federal warrants for Arthur Valdrine, Thornton Hunnycut, and René Grosjean. Link had state warrants in case of jurisdictional problems.

The plan was simple: turn Valdrine, or get enough incriminating information on the wire to open Grosjean. The prospects were shaky because they had no idea what to expect. The first hurdle was getting Sam into the house.

Sam went up the sidewalk and stepped onto the porch. There was no answer to the first ring of the bell, but he did hear movement inside. A few moments after the second ring, the door opened slightly. Arthur Valdrine looked out. His face was ashen, his clothes soiled. A harsh odor emanated from him. "Yes?" Valdrine croaked. He was drunk.

Sam wedged his foot in the door.

"Wait a minute, who are . . ." He stared into Sam's face. "You." He tried to push the door closed, but Sam used his shoulder to open the door wider. "Get out of here," Valdrine said, struggling, losing his balance and stumbling backwards.

"We have to talk." Sam pushed his way inside the foyer. The stench was awful.

"I don't have to do—all that stuff you showed me last night is worthless." Valdrine turned and walked deeper into the house, occasionally putting a hand to the wall for support. Sam followed him into an office just off the den. Valdrine sat down behind his desk. No lights were on, and the blinds were down. Sam pulled a saber chair out from a corner and set it directly in front of the desk.

"I have nothing to say to you," Valdrine said, holding his shoulders back. A half-full bottle of scotch, two empties, and a glass sat on his desk. Everything else—telephone, rolodex, papers—had been swept to the floor. He tried to be casual about filling his glass, but his hands were shaking so badly that it took both of them to steady the bottle.

"We have René Grosjean," Sam said.

"I have no idea who that is." Valdrine gazed at the ceiling as he took a drink.

"The state police checked with the Slidell police, and they said he called you here last night. He was highly agitated when you hung up on him."

Valdrine remained silent.

"He might get out, Arthur. They don't have a lot to hold him on. That would concern me if I were you."

Valdrine took another drink, struggling to swallow it. "I don't know the man," he said, his lips not moving in sync with the sound, his words muffled.

"Let me read you something." Sam took Pettigrew's letter from his pocket. "This is from Jordan Pettigrew. I think you ought to hear it word for word." Sam began reading, watching Valdrine's face. When he finished reading, he put the letter on the desk. "Any answers to that?"

"Even if it's true, you don't have any corrorror . . ." Valdrine could not get the word out.

"Corroboration? You don't know that. You don't know that I am not in contact with Pettigrew. Just because you couldn't find him doesn't mean I didn't."

There was a growing sadness in Valdrine's eyes.

"I also have Grosjean, and I witnessed him beating up a female federal agent. That will not go easy for him, nor will the Prathers,

Parker Hamill, and federal agent Neil Dougherty. You may have a shot at saving your life, but you're the only one who can do it."

"And spend the rest of my life in prison bent over a shower room sink?" He was becoming more coherent, forcing himself. "You know I wouldn't survive in there."

"There are ways, Arthur. I can help, especially with the feds. You're a lawyer; you know how it works. You didn't kill anyone. We don't even know that you solicited it." Sam was banking on Valdrine's condition to override the inconsistencies in his argument.

"Of course you do." The statement caught Sam by surprise. "Who else could have done it?" The statement sounded proud.

"According to Pettigrew's letter, Thornton Hunnycut had a lot to do with it."

"Well, old Jordan's smarter than I gave him credit for. He always thought I was on his side, but I wasn't." Valdrine took another drink, and his voice deteriorated again. "Do you know what Thornton promised me if he became vice president? Attorney General of the United States."

"How could he promise that?"

"Don't ever underestimate Thornton Hunnycut. That's a bad mistake. All I had to do was cover his tracks, clean up the messes he left behind. People always do that for Thornton." He changed tracks, rambling. "I apologize for the condition of my house; I was sick."

The information was coming, but Sam was concerned Regan might not be receiving it. Even if he did, its validity, considering Valdrine's condition, might be questioned. Sam was not sure this would be a slam dunk. "He asked you to do these things?"

"Clean up."

"The Prathers? I can't see anything there to clean up, as you say."

"Prather was getting greedy, hard to handle. Tried to pressure Thornton. You don't do that."

"What about Hamill?"

"You were the cause of that."

"Me?"

"Hamill got a stroke of conscience, like Pettigrew said. Would have been better if he'd had a real stroke."

Sam wondered why Valdrine was suddenly opening up. It worried him.

"Hamill was going to go to the feds, but made a compromise on your getting out." He looked up at Sam. "I wasn't for it. Thornton covered all the legal tracks. How in God's name, I don't know, but that's Thornton. Hamill was a liability."

"You know Hunnycut will let you and Grosjean take the fall, don't you?"

"Grosjean just does what he's told, although I do think he enjoys it a little more than he should." Valdrine poured himself another drink. He seemed to be sobering up in spite of what he was consuming, seemed to be actually enjoying himself. Sam wondered if the confession was soul-purging, but he couldn't imagine Valdrine concerning himself with his soul. The man had managed to skirt the one thing Sam needed most.

"Where did you come up with Grosjean?" Sam asked.

"I didn't. Never liked the man."

"Who did?"

"Thornton. Had him in court one day and let him off. I don't remember the details, but Grosjean was grateful. Gave him a call the day after and told him if there was ever anything he could do, he'd be glad to repay his debt. And he did. Thornton put him on retainer, like a lawyer." Valdrine smiled. "Not everybody believed Hamill committed suicide, but enough did."

Sam was silent.

"You don't think any of this is going to do you any good, do you? Me telling you about Thornton and me?"

"Maybe. I can testify to what you've told me, and there's the letter." Sam lowered his eyes. When he raised them, he was looking at a .38 pointed directly toward him. "You think that's a way out? Killing me?"

"Hell, I don't know, but it would give me a great deal of satisfaction. You took everything away from me."

Sam's brain was racing. He couldn't get to his gun, and Valdrine had the desk as a barrier. There was no way to reach him. One move, and Valdrine could shoot him where he sat.

"You've haunted all of us for a long time, Sam Larkin. God, how I hate your name. I wanted you dead in prison, and when they let you out, I wanted . . ."

"But you didn't."

"Parker fucking Hamill. But all that can be taken care of now." He released the safety.

"It won't help."

"I know." Just like that, he gave up. His shoulders sagged, and he leaned forward and extended his arm to give the gun to Sam. But then— "Aw, hell." He pulled back, and, before Sam could react, put the pistol in his mouth and pulled the trigger.

A warm spray hit Sam in the face. The stench in the room was supplanted by the odor of cordite. Plaster, painted with blood and bits of Valdrine's head, fell from the ceiling. The impact had sent Valdrine's chair over backward, and he lay there, dust falling into his open eyes.

The front and back doors crashed open. Once inside, Karen, Buck, Raymond, and Regan stood in a semicircle around Sam and stared at what had moments before been Arthur Valdrine.

Regan turned to Sam. "You okay?"

"Not really," Sam replied.

"There's blood on your face and shirt."

Sam was unaware. "Yes."

"Buck," Regan said. "I want this place secured. Not a lot of cop cars. Unmarked vehicles if you can get them. Call in whoever you need and can trust. I don't want this getting to anyone else who doesn't absolutely have to know. No media. I don't want Hunnycut warned."

"Done," Buck said, and went to the phone.

"How did we do with the wire?"

"We got everything," Karen said.

Sam looked at her. Karen was unshaken, all business when she wanted to be.

Regan continued. "Raymond, take Sam to your place, and get him cleaned up. Karen and I are going to see Grosjean with the tape. If we get anything, anything at all, I'm on my way to Washington. Buck, you'll hear from me in two hours."

"I didn't want it to happen this way," Sam said. "He caught me by surprise."

"Can't save people from themselves, Larkin," Regan said.

"Sounds like something I told Karen once. Good luck with Grosjean. Be as unemotional as he is. It's all about appearance with these guys. Cool scares the hell out of them. They're used to people being afraid of them," Sam said.

"We'll do the best we can."

Sam looked for condescension and saw little. He looked back at the remains of Valdrine lying on the floor. Every violent act he was a part of cost him a little bit of himself. He felt no sorrow for the man, but he would have to deal with himself in days to come.

"WE WERE JUST about to start processing him out when you called," the Slidell duty officer told Regan. "Found his cousin early this morning, so we didn't have anything to hold him on, even though we were told y'all were interested."

Regan handed him the warrant for Grosjean. "Hold him until we can have him transferred, probably later today."

"No problem there. 'Bout all he does is sleep and eat. I'll take you back to interrogation and have him brought in."

While they were waiting, Regan got out his tape recorder and put it on the table. Karen was carrying another with the tape of Sam and Valdrine.

Regan turned to Karen. "What do you think?"

"I have no idea. Sam did a good job."

"I know he did."

"I appreciated your concern at Valdrine's."

"I wouldn't want anything to happen to him." He smiled. "Might need him in court."

When Grosjean was brought into the room, he stopped and stared at Karen. "Wha' she doin' here?" he asked, not taking his eyes off of her.

"She's a federal agent. I think you've met," Regan said.

Grosjean sat down without responding.

"I'm going to tape this interview, René." He turned on the recorder, dated and timed it, and gave the preliminaries. Then he Mirandized him. "Do you understand what I've just said?" he asked.

"Yeah."

"Do you wish to have an attorney present?"

"Not yet. I can ask you to turn dat t'ing off anytime I want, right?"

"That's correct. René, I am placing you under arrest for the murder of federal agent Neil Dougherty, also known as Harry Landers."

Grosjean's eyes flickered.

"There are also warrants from the State of Louisiana for the murder of Parker Hamill and from Mississippi for the murders of Masley and Mary Francis Prather. Do you have anything to say to these charges?"

"Dey wrong."

"Before I ask you any questions, Agent Chaney has something she would like you to hear."

Grosjean looked unconcerned. Karen put her recorder on the table and pressed the PLAY button. Valdrine's voice came through loud and clear. They watched Grosjean as he listened impassively. When it was finished, Karen turned it off. Grosjean still wore his idiotlike smile.

"Anything to say now?" Regan asked.

"I don' know."

"You want a lawyer?"

The man laughed. "Dat was pretty much him. Him and dat Pettigrew."

"I don't know what I can do for you, René. I want to make that clear, but there is a possibility of your getting something from the prosecutors in each case if they know you're cooperative. Possibility. No promises. I think it's a life-and-death decision, to be blunt."

Grosjean looked at the floor for a moment, then focused on Regan. "Wha' you wan'? Sound like you got everyt'ing, you." Grosjean was pragmatic, as Sam had said he would be. A professional.

"Not everything."

"If I tell you, you gone help me?"

"I said I couldn't give you anything. That'll be between your lawyer and the prosecutors, but I will tell them you were cooperative." Regan knew what Grosjean was considering: he had ten years of appeals before a capital sentence could be carried out, and the death penalty itself was a day-to-day proposition. If he got life, he wouldn't be in isolation. It was the best possibility at the moment. No lawyer could beat all the charges. And last, what difference did it really make? None that he could see.

"I'm cooperatin' now," Grosjean said.

"If you'll tell us what we want to know." There was one sentence he needed from René Grosjean's mouth, and the only way he knew to get it was to ask. "René, if I think you're lying to me, I will not tell the prosecutors that you helped us. Do you understand that?"

"Yeah. Wha' you wan' to know, you?"

"Who hired you?"

Grosjean directed his smile toward Karen. It made her skin crawl. He turned back to Regan. "My lawyer, Mr. Valdrine call me. It was for Judge Hunnycut. I owed him."

"Senator Hunnycut?"

"Yeah. Whatever."

SENATOR THORNTON HUNNYCUT was in his office, waiting for a call from his senior attorney, who was meeting with Harrison James. They had decided upon the strategy that his legal staff had recommended, with one added incentive: a guarantee of two million dollars in legal campaign contributions to James. It sounded like a good deal to him. He couldn't understand what was taking so long.

The meeting had begun at two o'clock. It was now after six. James's answer would determine his next step. He would not go to jail; if necessary, he would leave the country, though he considered that only a remote possibility. He had tried to call Scottie and warn her not to talk to any reporters, but she was not in Baton Rouge, and the housekeeper didn't know when she would return. That was troublesome.

When his intercom buzzed, he looked at his watch. 6:20. "Senator Hunnycut, there are three gentlemen out here to see you."

"It's after office hours. Who are they?" Hunnycut then heard his assistant protesting, and the door of his office opened.

"What the hell are you doing? You don't just walk into my office without being—"

"Senator Hunnycut, I am Agent Michael Regan of the DEA Special Task Force, currently working under the direction of the FBI. This is Agent Troy Urban, and this is James Blackmon of the New Orleans, Louisiana, district attorney's office." Regan handed papers to Hunnycut. "These are warrants for your arrest, sir, charging you with solicitation of the murder of federal agent Neil Dougherty and solicitation of the murder of Parker Hamill in Louisiana. There are also warrants charging you with the same crime being issued by the state of Mississippi for the murders of Masley and Mary Francis Prather."

Hunnycut looked at Regan and laughed. "You're out of your fucking mind. What is this, some kind of joke? You're walking in here and telling me that you're arresting me for paying to have someone killed? Get serious."

The man's act was almost good enough to buy, Regan thought. "Sir, these are the first warrants. As I said, there will be others."

Hunnycut smiled again. He moved into the agent's face. "Listen, fuckhead, I don't know who you are. I haven't seen any identification. You—"

Three shield cases were pulled out.

Hunnycut waved a hand of dismissal at them. "Do you want to tell me how you bureaucratic MPs managed to come up with this nonsense? Proof? Witnesses?"

"We have René Grosjean in custody. He named you."

"I never heard of the man."

"We can prove you have. We also have Arthur Valdrine's admission that he was working on your behalf."

"That's the son of a bitch behind all this, isn't it? He's the bastard you should be after. Disappointed he's not going to be AG."

"He's dead, Senator."

Hunnycut's bravado faltered. "Arthur? How?" A genuine look of shock transformed Hunnycut's face.

"By his own hand after he confessed his complicity. There are witnesses to that confession."

Hunnycut collected himself and straightened his shoulders. "Hearsay."

"We also have written testimony from Jordan Pettigrew and a copy of the transcript of the trial of Samuel T. Larkin."

"Who's he? A con making a deal?" Hunnycut said.

"He's a witness to Arthur Valdrine's testimony. And to his own trial. Senator, you have the right to remain silent. Anything you say . . ." Regan went through the Miranda process. "Do you understand these rights as they have been read to you?"

The senator gave him a confused look.

"Sir, do you . . ."

"Yes, I understand them. I have some calls to make," he said.

"You can make one call when the booking process is complete. We have arranged for you to be held temporarily here in DC until you can be transferred. Sir, you are under arrest. Please put your hands behind your back and turn around."

Hunnycut turned in a daze, and Regan closed the handcuffs on his wrists. A wry grin crossed the agent's lips ever so briefly.

Thornton Hunnycut said nothing as he was led out of his office. His assistant was nowhere to be seen.

IT WAS 10:00 PM in Mandeville, Louisiana. Harold Musgrave and Casey Landrieu were sitting in bed watching the late news, something they did most nights. Harold liked getting a head start on the next day's news. It was also a soft time for them, feeling the warmth of each other with quiet conversation. The rule was no business talk, nothing of great consequence. They both came to attention when local anchorman Jim O'Brian began with the top story.

"Louisiana was dealt a double blow today with the death of one of its highest officials, Commissioner of Administration Arthur Valdrine, whose death was ruled a suicide, and the arrest in Washington of Senator Thornton Hunnycut on charges of solicitation of murder." He shook his head and turned to his partner, Louise Capps, who looked grim.

"That's right, Jim. Commissioner Arthur Valdrine was in his Garden District home when he apparently took his own life. According to police, he was being questioned in connection with the same case that involves Senator Hunnycut. Police would not discuss further details, but do say that their investigation of the case is ongoing." She turned back to O'Brian.

"The same applies to Senator Hunnycut, Louise. The only information we have is that the charges against Hunnycut involve a murder-for-hire scheme. He was taken into custody at his office in Washington and is presently being held in a District facility. A bitter fall for a man who, only days ago, was being considered for the second highest office in the land. We will, of course be following this story as it develops. In other news—"

Musgrave hit the remote and Jim and Louise faded into blackness. He looked at Casey. "Well, I'll be damned," he said. "Hard to believe Arthur had the guts to do it."

"I never knew the man, but it's sad."

"Sad?"

"Sad when anyone does that, puts himself in such a desperate position that death is the only solution."

"Don't waste your tears on them, darlin'. Arthur didn't find a solution; he escaped. They brought it on themselves."

"But they were your business associates, your friends," Casey said.

"Honey, Arthur Valdrine and Thornton Hunnycut were nobody's friends. Not even each other's. I'd bet that before he did what he did, Arthur was throwin' all the blame he could come up with at Thornton, and I'm sure Thornton will say it was Arthur who did whatever they're accusing him of and that he knew nothing about it."

"I guess I'm just not used to people like that."

"You don't know many politicians. Remember, most of them start out as lawyers."

"What does this do to Laurel Grove?"

"It will be investigated, found wanting, and either be brought up to standard or closed down. Thornton made all of the decisions, and I can document that and my disagreements with those decisions. I'm in the clear. I guess Jordan and I turned out to be the survivors in all this. Who would have guessed?" He looked at Casey. "Things may get a little rough financially, but, as I have always said, any problem that can be solved with money ain't a problem."

Casey leaned over and kissed him.

KAREN WAS FEELING better, at least physically. The soreness was diminishing, the swelling in her face shrinking, though the bruises still remained, and she hadn't passed any blood in twenty-four hours. She had never mentioned that to Sam. To her way of thinking, that meant she was all right, no big problems. She stood inside the glass doors, watching Sam on the deck and wondering where that wandering mind of his was traveling.

Rain, not much more than a mist, was falling silently. Occasionally enough would collect on the roof for a few drops to fall from the eaves. The Gulf was largely lost in fog. Looking in the direction of the water, Sam's eyes found a lone tree that had been planted in the landscaping just beyond the deck; it was dying. He saw a tree of pearls, leaf-bare branches holding small droplets of rainwater that sustained themselves until they gained too much volume and fell to the ground. They shimmered with brilliance even in the fading light.

Karen came through the doors and sat in the rocker next to his. It was forty-eight hours since Valdrine had shot himself and Grosjean had confessed. Both Regan and Buck were keeping them apprised of events as they took place.

They had read the headline articles regarding Valdrine and Hunnycut and the secondary item about Grosjean. Their names were not in the articles, and Link and Regan were only mentioned briefly. The agent had kept his promise to Sam so far.

One obstacle had been removed, but another stood between them. It was over, their reason for being here. "Did Regan say what will happen to Hunnycut?"

"It's too early to know, but life is the least he can get. I don't know whether they'll go for death or not. Solicitation can carry that. If they do, he'll probably die of natural or unnatural causes before they get a chance to execute him. His life is going to be no bowl of cherries; there's no doubt about that."

"Living without power will be worse than death to that man. I wonder what will happen to Marlene Cole."

"They'll go after her. Whether they can convict her or not will largely depend on Hunnycut's testimony. He could protect her," Karen said.

"He won't. There's no profit in it. Regan have anything else to say? About what happens from here on out?"

"Just that it's likely to be a long, drawn-out process."

"I don't want to come back here to testify."

"I don't think that will be necessary. I doubt he would want to bring you into it. At most you'd have to give a deposition, and you could do that in Carolina. They've got Grosjean. He's really all they need. Your trial will come into it somewhere along the line, I'm sure, but that's minor compared to the other charges."

"Minor." Sam shook his head in resignation.

Karen put her hand over his on the arm of the chair. "I wasn't suggesting . . ."

"I know."

"What about Raymond? Think he'll stay in touch?"

"I don't know. I told him to come east sometime, but I doubt that he will. We shared a painful time together." Sam smiled. "He asked my permission to call Celine."

Karen looked at him, laughter in her eyes. "He asked your permission?"

"I think he's taken with her, as they say."

"Would she like that?"

"I think she might. She's mentioned him several times."

"Would you like that?"

"They're good people."

Karen looked out at the Gulf, trying to see beyond it, beyond this situation and this time. She was aware that Sam knew no more what to say next than she. He was going back to South Carolina, and she was stuck in Louisiana until the investigation was completed. There was still work to be done.

"There's no easy way, is there?" she finally asked.

"I can't stay here," Sam said.

"I know, and I can't leave just yet." Tears began to form in her eyes. She dabbed at them with the sleeve of her sweatshirt. "This is getting ridiculous," she said. "I think I'm allergic to you, Sam Larkin. You make my eyes water."

They went inside.

In bed, they made love, each trying to memorize the details and nuances of the moment. It would be awhile before they were able to explore each other through touch again. It was slow, and their bodies gave in to the rush that enveloped them.

"Will you come to Carolina?" Sam asked.

Karen tried to see behind his eyes, know what was there. She felt the solidity of him on top of her, closed her arms and legs tightly around him, and tried to fuse them into one.

"We can't write each other off, Karen. You know that."

"I know, but we're having a lot of trouble writing each other on," she said before her eyes closed.

"Yes."

SAM DIDN'T LEAVE a note as she had done in Carolina, and he didn't leave her asleep when he left. He kissed her awake, and they had coffee one last time on the deck, looking out to sea. The weather had turned, and there was a promise of summer like a brief reflection in the air. They said little. It was not a time for promises or dates. And then he was gone. He was going home, which lightened his spirit.

# EPILOGUE

SAM STOOD IN the bow of his boat, gazing at the stretch of water in front of him. He was casting for shrimp. He enjoyed pausing between casts to take in the things he had missed during his time on the Mississippi coast and the atmospheric streets of New Orleans. The day was bright, but the air was cool as the lowcountry continued moving toward spring.

There were few shrimp to be found in the shallows at this time of year. The waters of the lowcountry in general, and particularly those throughout the Covington area and surrounding counties, were subject to the largest tidal fluctuations anywhere on the East Coast, south of Maine. As the water temperature went down, so did the shrimp, to deep holes where there was warmth. Sam was stationed over one such hole that he had found several years before. With a weighted cast net, he was confident he would pull in more than enough for what he needed. The rest would go in the freezer. He always knew where to find the shrimp.

He put the rim of the net between his teeth, twisted his body, elongating his arms as he unwound and hurled the net and watching it form a large umbrella shape before flattening out and floating down to the water's surface. He let it sink and then waited until it had time to settle. Even in this place, doing what he was doing, he found it difficult not to think about all that had happened, to wonder what lay ahead.

He had been surprised when he returned from Mississippi to discover that all his questions had not been answered. His own personal floor had not been swept clean. Arthur Valdrine was dead, and he felt no pity for the man. The New Orleans DA was going to seek the death penalty for Thornton Hunnycut, but that was lip service, he was sure. The DA would be seeking publicity and probably votes for some future election. Hunnycut would not die by lethal injection, but there was little doubt he would end his years in prison. Sam guessed there weren't many years left in that life under any circumstances.

René Grosjean would have more years to work the system, but a smart betting man would not pick him to win. It was probably how he had always expected his life to end. And Sam figured he would probably still be wearing that idiot smile when the end came.

Jordan Pettigrew was gone. It was assumed he had cut his losses and left the country. Some thought to Costa Rica, others to Mexico or Europe, just another expatriate seeking anonymity. Even Marlene Cole was under indictment and was expected to spend some time in federal custody, but, according to Karen, the government had not been able to track down all of the money she was rumored to have made. Officials hoped that before it was all over, Thornton Hunnycut would shed some light on that. Sam could only imagine the deal-making taking place. From all he had heard of Marlene Cole, she would survive.

They had all drawn their own maps and decided on the routes they should take, but none of them would reach the destinations they had set out for. Sam was still traveling his road. Some days the destination was clear—on others it faded from sight. He'd found an emptiness when he returned to the house on Fiddler's End, but it wasn't in the lowcountry or in the house. It was in himself. All of the space within him that had been taken up by the anger, resentment, and self-pity he had never acknowledged was now a void. Losing it meant losing part of himself, at least the self he had been. Now the challenge was to fill that void with other things. Better things.

He pulled the net in and found a dozen large, wriggling shrimp, struggling to free themselves. He emptied the net over a bucket and went through the casting process again. As the net sank into the water, a flight of pelicans floated overhead and dissolved into gull-winged pen-and-ink lines as they passed into the distance. Again he pulled the net in and found it had been a productive cast.

He thought of Raymond and wondered what he would think of this life. He had called once and sworn he would come east, but the city boy doesn't often go to the country. There was another element that made his coming unlikely: Celine. Sam had experienced mixed emotions when Raymond told him that they were seeing each other rather frequently and had quickly changed the subject to Musgrave and Casey. They were doing well, had come out of everything better than anyone, but then maybe that was the way they had gone in.

He had been shrimping for more than an hour, taking his time between casts. He knelt down in the boat, looked in the bucket, and judged his catch. He released those that appeared smaller than twenty-count and estimated that more than twelve pounds remained. He took care of the net, secured his other items, and started the engine. The run to his dock would take thirty minutes.

It was a good day. He removed the silver ponytail ring and let his hair blow free in the wind as the boat sliced through the water. The sun was on the downside of high. Maybe four o'clock. He wondered where Karen was. Probably somewhere in Florida or Georgia.

He wondered what she was thinking. What she was seeing through the windshield of her car.

She was due at Fiddler's End by dinnertime.

# ACKNOWLEDGMENTS

First and foremost, I would like to acknowledge my publishers, Carolyn and Al Newman, who have vested their faith and trust in my work.

Also, the gang at River City Publishing: Jim Gilbert, my editor; Gail Waller, assistant editor; Lissa Monroe, art director; April Jones, publicist; William Hicks, Mr. Do-It-All; Kimberly Palmer, who keeps track of the dough; and Travis Jones, who sends out the books. Thanks to you all.

Special kudos to Joe Dennis, a sidekick, an inspiration, a devil's advocate, and an encourager in the most difficult of times, who stood by me through thin (thick ain't happened yet). You have never been anything but honest about the words, been angry for me when I was not, and always there to listen. I love you, man.

To Archer Lee Smith, who was the prime mover at the inception of the book and put up road signs as to the directions it would take.

To David Stern and Bill Taub for their expertise, unerring advice, drams of hope, belief, and faith in the project.

To "Mellowicious" Marshall Chapman, whose music transported me from the toils and isolation of authorship when it was needed.

To my readers and friends and supporters. You all know where you fit in. Nancy Dennis, Dee Hayden, Thomas Thomas (yes, that's correct),

Barbara Deeb, James 'Buck' Hundley, Susan McKenna, Florrie Kichler. Investigator Matt Averill of the Beaufort County Sheriff's Department, for his technical expertise with which I took some liberties. Joe Formichella, whose opinion about the words I respect as much as anyone's. And to Chuck Larkins, an inspiration from the outset of this trilogy.

And, the guiding lights: Pat Conroy, Les Standiford, Tom Robbins, and Bernard Martin.

Finally, to give credit to all those who kept me going and on track would require more pages than the story. I hope you recognize who you are and take full credit for your contributions.